# TIME
# CRIME

# TIME CRIME

## CARNEGIE OLSON

Humble Hogs Press, Ann Arbor

© Carnegie Olson, 2020

First Edition, Third State
ISBN-13: 978-1-7342832-0-4 (eBook)
ISBN-13: 978-1-7342832-1-1 (paperback)
ISBN-13: 978-1-7342832-4-2 ("cloth" hardcover)
ISBN-13: 978-1-7342832-8-0 (case laminate)
ISBN-13: 978-1-7342832-9-7 (audiobook)

Moleman & Mothman illustrations: © Kevin Ewing
Cover & book design: Robin Vuchnich - mycustombookcover.com
Editing: Veronica Marian – marianeditorial.com
Print edition typeface is Garamond

Cited works under copyright are reproduced by written permission.

To Angie

*For an unconventional life.*

To Kevin

*Because there is no mythology without an image.*

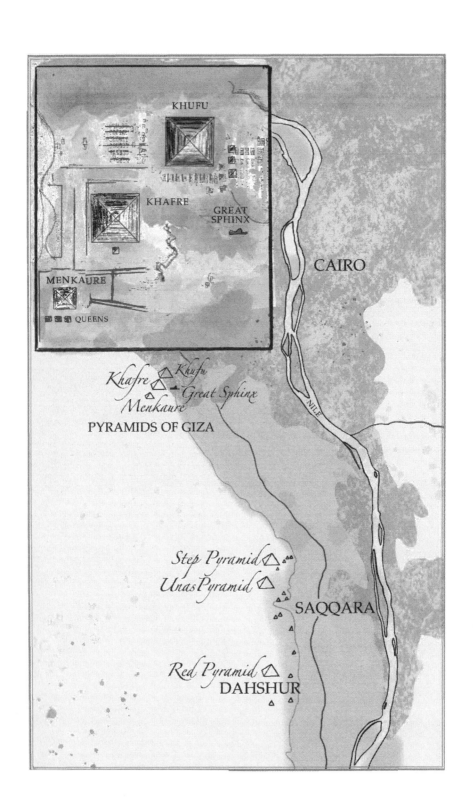

KHUFU

KHAFRE

GREAT
SPHINX

MENKAURE

QUEENS

CAIRO

NILE

*Khufu*
*Khafre* *Great Sphinx*
*Menkaure*
PYRAMIDS OF GIZA

*Step Pyramid*
*Unas Pyramid*
SAQQARA

*Red Pyramid*
DAHSHUR

# Contents

*For the essence of time is flux, dissolution of the momentarily existent; and the essence of life is time.*[a]


—*Joseph Campbell*

# CHAPTER 1

# SOMETHING OLD & SOMETHING NEW

**THE TRANSPONDER PULSED AND PULSED** and Mr. Z. couldn't think. "Ahem," he said, peering over his spectacles at the expressionless faces of his students. He jammed his finger into his vest pocket and disabled the device. A priority one summons by the feel of it.

A floorboard creaked. Someone muffled a cough. The old, half-empty auditorium waited, poised like an ancient sailing vessel in want of a trade wind.

He cleared his throat again and the students began shifting in their seats. All except Vixy. She reclined in her chair with her legs crossed and her hands folded carefully in her lap, gazing impassively beyond the tall windows of the classroom, as remote and unperturbed as the Sphinx.

He scratched his temple and strode to his desk, sifted amongst his books and papers and one by one shoved the lot of them into his case. He swiped at his reader and diminished the lecture projection. "I dare say none of you will mind starting the holiday early?"

"There's no assignment?"

Mr. Z. squinted into his case. "Yes. Well, I suppose there is."

2 • TIME CRIME

There was a collective groan and the students who were clamoring towards the door piled into each other, turning to listen.

He yanked out a thin volume and wagged it at them. *The King and the Corpse.*

"We already read it."

Mr. Z. reached for his coat. "Right. But, we've yet to *write* anything about it. So, twenty pages? Double-spaced."

A murmur of disappointment. "What do we write about?"

"If you have to ask after eight weeks then I can't help you. Nothing glib, that's all."

"Glib, Sir?"

"Glib. You know. Superficial. The opposite of profound." He waved the book at the door. "Off with you. Enjoy the break."

"Well, we might have...."

When they'd gone he stood relishing the whispering quiet of the old room, contemplating the branches of the venerable oak outside, its last leathery leaves fluttering against the windows and whisking themselves into tattered windrows on the crisscrossed footpaths below. A vision overtook him – himself as a young student trundling across a similar courtyard; the crisp air and long shadows of late autumn; dry leaves skittering across a path. His sense of earnestness and passion and troubling... what? A consuming anxiousness. Or was it merely longing? He tried to recall something of that pained, naive, ambitious, desperately impatient self. All he managed were some lines from Conrad:

> I remember I preferred the soldier to the philosopher at the time; a preference which life has only confirmed. One was a man, and the other was either more – or less. However, they are both dead... and youth, strength, genius, thoughts, achievements, simple hearts – all dies.... No matter.[b]

He frowned, frustrated, as usual, by the penetrating irony of the words – he both cherished and despised such sentiment - and reached for the transponder, letting it tumble onto the desk. "Shit." The device's indicator flashed like a fiery ruby. A priority one summons but at *red level*. He'd be required to attend a debriefing in person at the T.E.[1] He ground his teeth. How often had his commitments as a time detective and an adjunct professor clashed, complicating his scholarship and making his writing impossible? He cleared the notification and stuffed the device into his pocket. So much for the idea of a quiet holiday spent catching up with his books and his manuscripts. He pulled his trench coat on, shoved his case under his arm, and turned to flee the room.

Vixy leaned against the doorway with her hip jutting out, the rakish angularity of her bag outlined against her shoulder - she did not go in for anything as pedestrian as a backpack. She cupped her slender, manicured fingers round the cigarette she was lighting, its coarse ash a contrast to her fair skin and the taut vitality of her features. "Shit," she said, and teased a bit of tobacco from the tip of her tongue. She pursed her lips and aimed a plume of smoke in Mr. Z.'s direction. "What's so shitty?"

"We've somewhere to *be*, Miss Velure." He brushed past her, guiding her out the door with a firm hand upon her elbow.

Vixy huffed and stopped short, glaring at him marching down the hallway in the direction of the stairwell. She fumed at the quaint "squeak, squeak, squeak" of his sneakers, at the manner in which everything about him seemed to contradict itself - his impossible lack of fashion sense, his maddening indifference and impeachable, ridiculous resolve.

"And!" he hollered over his shoulder, "we've discussed my displeasure with your smoking inside this building too many times before!" Whereupon he disappeared down the stairwell with a flourish of his voluminous coattails.

"Damn these bullshit transponders, Z," she growled. She flicked away the cigarette, grinding it into the floor with the tip of her boot, burying her hands in her pockets. What in hell was it about him that made her so crazy?

The entire university, meanwhile, seemed to have emptied itself of humanity, its grand old architecture – the broad marble floors, hewn granite

---

[1] Tetrahectatricontakaidigon Enclave. See Glossary.

corridors and vaulted ceilings; the ornate lintels and heavy wooden doors, deeply carved, expressing… she didn't know what. Her own insignificance? Her absurdity and silly self-absorption? "Oh, Vixy," her mother would say, "you've got your father's stubborn pride. And those high-strung emotions? They're from me, Lord help you." She felt herself flush and envisioned her parents at home, dad in his workshop with sawdust dusting the tops of his shoes, wood shavings clinging to his shirt, the smell of cedar and the red gash on his thumb where he'd cut himself sharpening the adze. Mom in her garden, kneeling close to the earth, tugging on the greens, talking to the beets and carrots and onions, coaxing them from the soil. Vixy's heart ached and she sighed. She set her jaw, shouldered her bag and strode towards the stairwell.

When she finally caught up with him across the street from the clock tower in front of the Four Winds Bar, Mr. Z. acted as if he'd been holding the door of his air cruiser ajar for an intolerable century.

"No drink?" she said, dodging the traffic and climbing in.

"Molemen."

He'd mouthed the words at her and she scowled, watching him pause to peer at the passenger side mirror and buff it with his coat sleeve before hustling round the front of the vehicle, pulling the door open and clambering in beside her.

"What about them?"

Mr. Z. raised an eyebrow at her. "Pardon?"

She frowned. "Molemen. Isn't that what you said?"

"Right. Yes." Mr. Z. buckled his five-point harness, stabbed his finger at the ignition switch and the motor rumbled to life.

"Their entire race vanished when their sun went nova three thousand years ago."

"Almost correct," said Mr. Z. "That is to say, that's the textbook history. But we both know the Molemen were, or should I say *are*, the most accomplished and remarkably successful engineers in the cosmos." He squinted into the rearview and tightened his grip on the gear shift. "Hence, their ability to manufacture the means of their own salvation."

"Their own salvation?" Vixy hurried to stow her bag behind the seat and buckle her harness. "What have they been doing all this time, while the rest of us have considered them extinct? With all due respect, Z, you and your off-the-wall anthropology – if you ever found anyone to agree with your maverick theories...."

"Then I ought to be capable of publishing something, is that what you mean?" He tapped his finger impatiently on the steering wheel, eyes focused on the traffic, glancing back and forth between his mirrors. "Well, you'd be right about that."

"Right about what?" Vixy rolled her eyes. "Don't tell me your article got rejected." She eyed the gaps in the traffic, determined to anticipate their take-off.

Mr. Z. furrowed his brow and Vixy braced herself, cinching her harness as he pounced on the accelerator, the cruiser lurching up heavily, struggling to gain altitude, the motor revving.

She winced when they nearly clipped the vehicle beside them and again when they almost took the rear bumper off the one in front. Somebody honked but Mr. Z. merely redoubled his concentration, cranked the wheel and double-clutched, downshifting, the motor gasping, the cruiser shuddering precariously as if about to drop out of the sky. He twisted the choke lever, blipped the throttle then stomped on it, the engine finally roaring to life like a horse responding to the whip, the vehicle accelerating in a powerful surge, thrusting them against their seatbacks, the skyway opening up before them.

"Whew," mumbled Vixy. She unbuckled her harness and resettled herself. "That was... interesting. Life without a transmission synchronizer - I don't know how you put up with it."

Mr. Z. leaned back, gripping the steering wheel comfortably with both hands, eyes bright, his attention on the skyway ahead, a hint of a smile on his lips.

Vixy shook her head at him and peered down at the teeming, congested ground-cars struggling against each other like frustrated turtles. Then she glanced back, the little town vanishing behind the low hills, the sun disappearing into a skein of purple-pink clouds at the horizon and the dark farmland opening up beneath them. She strained to find the clock tower, somehow anxious for a last glimpse of it, the symbol, such as it was, of her adopted home. Gone. She turned and flopped into her seat, sighing into the oncoming darkness.

Mr. Z. set the air-cruiser at sub-Mach and settled the machine into his preferred altitude: twelve-hundred feet; a considerably slower and therefore rarely used slice of the vehicular band width – the portion of the so-called sky highway that had long since fallen out of favor with anyone younger than, say, his grandparents. The traffic rushed past overhead and crawled along dutifully below, bumper to bumper.

Vixy slouched in her seat. "The old road?" she said; "do we have to putter along like this all the way to New York?"

Mr. Z. thrummed his fingers on the steering wheel and looked ahead. "You know, Vixy, you're developing into a crack anthropologist. Despite your idiosyncrasies."

Vixy huffed at him.

"A talent for initiative, like yours for example, is well and good. But a time detective understands the value of patience. And meticulous observation. And the difference between something that's merely old and something that's considered..."

"Vintage." Vixy rolled her eyes. "I swear it's your favorite word. God, Z, you're like a character in an old movie or something. Or whatever they're called."

Mr. Z. murmured something.

"What?"

"I said *films*. Moving pictures."

"Whatever." Vixy peered out. "There's the moon, already. It always seems funny when you see the moon and the sky's still blue."

"Bluish," said Mr. Z. He endured a twinge of anxiety, the sense of foreboding and poignant temporality that nevertheless assailed him whenever he began a long trip, especially when night was coming on. "It'll be dark soon enough."

"The cities will be pretty," said Vixy, tucking her legs beneath her on the seat and leaning against the door panel. "I always like how they look from the air at night."

Mr. Z. smiled to himself in the darkening cockpit. It occurred to him that he enjoyed driving but merely suffered traveling – it made him feel fraught, at least in the beginning. And then just prior to an arrival, too, an unsettling mixture of anxiety and anticipation. Traveling with someone helped. Meanwhile, if he had to travel, he preferred it this way, in real time, at a pace and proximity to the Earth that invited contemplation, even meditation.

He glanced at Vixy, listened to her snoring softly – already asleep! How he envied her knack for dropping off so quickly, so completely, into what seemed to him such a profound restfulness. In spite of everything. In spite of their red-level summons and his dubious intuitions about a Moleman resurgence. Innocence in the face of the ominous somehow amplified the impression of both. So be it. He gripped the wheel, listened to the low thrum of the motor and focused on the road ahead.

"I need a cigarette," said Vixy, yawning as she talked. Her voice was hoarse from sleep. She squirmed in her seat, struggling to stretch her legs, leaning forward to peer into the vanity mirror, her eyes thrust open, looking askance at herself - first one side then the other - smoothing her makeup with her fingertip, picking at her lipstick with her fingernail. She flipped the mirror back into place and sat back in a huff, frowning at the dashboard, the gear shift and seemingly everything else in the cockpit. "When are you going to get rid of this antique and get a proper vehicle, something *modern*?"

Mr. Z. feigned indifference and pressed the control pad on his steering console. Strains of music poured luxuriously from his beloved audiophile system, a retrofit that had cost him nearly a month's salary.

"And what's with you and David Bowie? – you may as well listen to aboriginal chants, it's so twentieth century."

Mr. Z. shifted in his seat. "Twenty-*first* century. And it's not David Bowie. It's King Crimson." He increased the volume a little.

"Whatever. It sounds like a funeral. I have to pee."

"Welcome to the Fuel Stop," said Mr. Z. He braked and downshifted, allowing the cruiser to descend to ground level, rolling up the driveway entrance and easing the machine into the parking lot, gliding to rest beside one of the twenty-odd fuel kiosks. "Beckoning travelers by way of shamelessly garish vintage neon for over two-hundred years." He glanced sideways at Vixy.

"I happen to like neon signs. And it gets your attention, doesn't it?" She shoved her door open and swung her legs out. "If I quit criticizing your music maybe you'll quit criticizing my favorite rest stop. I mean, clean bathrooms matter to a woman. And you and your parking spaces...." She stood facing him outside the vehicle, tugging shamelessly at her short skirt and jacket and glancing at her reflection in the cruiser's window. "What's wrong with parking beside the building like everyone else?" She delivered an accusatory glance and turned away. "And don't tell me the walk will do me good, either."

Mr. Z. got out and stretched. Grumpy. But he understood - there were passenger types and Vixy wasn't. Neither was he. Meanwhile, why risk a door ding? And public restrooms? – men preferred well-maintained facilities as much as any woman. Speaking of which... he locked the cruiser and made for the facilities.

He emerged mildly reinvigorated, keen to get going, but Vixy might be a while. He sauntered towards the far corner of the parking lot, outside the intensity of the neon and performed his deep knee bends. Then he planted his foot and extended his other leg behind him, reaching his arms straight up, his chin pointed at the sky, eyes closed. He inhaled deeply.

"Sun salutation?" said Vixy. "In public?" She shook her head. She set a paper cup on the hood of the cruiser. "Here's your coffee."

Mr. Z. plucked it from the hood and frowned at the reflection in the polish.

Vixy lit her cigarette. "No, I didn't get any coffee on your precious paint job." She rummaged through her bag until she'd found her compact and stared into it, teasing at her hair. "The lighting in that damn bathroom is horrible."

"Not your favorite?"

She acknowledged the barb with a sideways glance. "Hey, there's clean and then there's properly lit. If you used make-up you'd have some sympathy." She shoved her compact into her bag. "Anyway, what makes you think this summons has anything to do with the Molemen?"

"Mere speculation," said Mr. Z., slurping from his cup. "Combined with intuition. I had a dream about them last night."

Vixy raised her eyebrow at him. "We're going to the T.E. because you had a dream?"

Mr. Z. pitched the rest of his coffee aside and tossed his cup into the trash. He corralled Vixy towards the cruiser and opened her door. "All will be revealed when we get where we're going."

They buckled themselves in and Mr. Z. eased the cruiser out of the parking lot, throttling hard into the skyway entrance ramp, gaining altitude until they were once again at speed.

"Well?" said Vixy.

"Well, what?"

"God, Z. Your dream. About Molemen of all things." She punched at the buttons of the music system, cutting the songs off one after the other before they'd barely begun.

"It's more than a dream," he said, shifting into overdrive. He tapped a control, silencing the music.

Vixy scowled, fidgeting. "God, I'm bored." She glanced at the trip meter on the dash. "Two hours till New York?" She sat staring out the windshield for a time, until she felt her impudence or whatever it was melting away and she sat staring at Mr. Z. across the darkness of the cockpit. "What's going on? Why aren't you telling me anything?"

They sped along, the faint whisper of the wind passing over the cruiser the only sound. They were still traversing the vast expanses of farmland and forest that separated them from the encroaching metropolises of the East.

"It all started before you were even recruited into the TDC.[2] Years ago. The Captain and I were in the midst of what we assumed was a routine investigation – a spike in second or third sub-quadrant ghosting variances that the CRP[3] wanted us to investigate. They'd been doing routine GID[4] scans and they had unresolved data – what they considered fishy looking gaps in the continuity spectrum. Anyway, the CRP apparently managed to get a budget allocation to commission us for a short-term investigation and right off the bat we found, or should I say I found, what I was convinced were worm-hole casings in the GTA."[5]

"Worm-hole casings?" Vixy frowned. "But worm-hole technology eliminated casing residues eons ago."

"Right. Along with superluminal wakes. Which we also discovered. At least in my opinion. It was a deep dive into the data but for whatever reason people get impatient for results and then don't see any value in acknowledging the patterns."

"That's because they don't see any patterns. Or any connections between them if they did. The kinds of observations you make, Z, they're pretty theoretical. I mean, arguable. Or something. I don't know. People like facts."

---

2  Time Detective Contingent. See Glossary.
3  Consequence Research Project. See Glossary.
4  Ghost Impression Database. See Glossary.
5  Galactic Transparency Alliance. See Glossary.

"Well, the facts are, as I always say -"

"The facts are after the fact, I know, I know."

Mr. Z. raised his finger as if to make a point.

"Don't say it. The facts are after the fact of the intuition, yeah, yeah. I get it. I agree with you. Most of the time. Anyway, let me guess, you had a bunch of intuitions regarding worm-hole casings and superluminal wakes and since intuitions aren't evidence, they aren't facts -"

"That's right, I'd made some conclusions that we ought to, if nothing else, reopen some of the Moleman archives and try to match up some of the obvious leads. But the funding was drying up and, as usual, everyone wanted to believe it was just spurious, remnant data – noise in the database which, as you know, is a notorious... how do you say? -" Mr. Z. struggled for the word.

"Pain," said Vixy. "Yeah, when I was assigned my first round of GID sanitation screens I thought I'd lose my mind."

"Right. Tedious doesn't quite describe that type of work. But assigning that stuff to cadets is a way of weeding out the personalities who -"

"Are only in it for the glamor?"

"Or lose patience with the subtleties, yes." He looked sideways at her. "I have to say at one point I was convinced you yourself were better suited to criminal justice work. Where all the facts are."

Vixy affected an imperious posture. "Well, I *was* about ready to apply to GIA[6] Enforcement early on. As a matter of fact."

"I know."

Vixy looked incredulous. "What do you mean? I didn't tell anyone I was looking -"

"You're not the first TDC recruit to convince themselves the grass is greener over at the GIA."

"Well," said Vixy, "everybody says they pay better and there's more fieldwork and less, I don't know." She shrugged and stared out her window.

"Scholarship," said Mr. Z. "And intellectual rigor. Yes, as a GIA cop you ramble around the cosmos on a big expense account and make arrests."

---

[6]  Galactic Intelligence Administration. See Glossary.

"And get bonuses."

Mr. Z. smiled broadly. "Yes, bonuses. For making arrests. And whether the case holds up in court depends on how well the TDC did building the evidence. Meanwhile, the Captain and I have a couple friends over at the GIA and we like to keep tabs on how many TDC recruits make a play for a job there." He watched her out of the corner of his eye – he'd learned that for all her headstrong bluster he had to be careful how far he took their repartee. He waited.

"So, you and the Captain blocked my application?

"No, heavens no. The TDC isn't interested in anyone who isn't interested in the TDC. It never works out to hold anyone back, you ought to know that. No, we were okay with letting you go."

Vixy looked puzzled. "What do you mean? That the GIA wasn't...?" She trailed off.

"Wasn't interested?" Mr. Z.'s tone was matter-of-fact. "That's right." He hummed quietly as he drove, again, waiting for silence to have its effect. Then he changed his tone. "Look here, Vixy. When I say it's all about observations and seeing the patterns and that the intuitions precede the facts, well, it applies to my impressions of you. And your abilities."

Vixy remained quiet, pricking her ears a bit.

"That's right, your abilities. Your talents. Which I'm keen to turn into strengths. Someday."

"Someday?"

"That's right. Meanwhile, we share a perspective on the past as it relates to the future."

"How so?"

"You'll just have to trust me on that."

"Trust you."

Mr. Z. shrugged.

"So," said Vixy, vaguely appeased; "when you say you had some obvious leads about the Molemen and worm-hole casings and superluminal wakes and all that, I take it that's where everyone left it. Besides you, of course."

Mr. Z. winked at her.

"Well, then?"

"Well what?"

"God, Z., you're impossible. What about the Molemen?"

"All in due time. Let's get to the T.E. and see what comes of this summons."

It was almost midnight when the interchange came into view - a knotted, densely trafficked surface-road and air-highway complex that shunted travelers north, south, east and west at multiple altitudes. High-speed express lanes soared overhead, ground-car roadbeds intertwined below and between, at the level Mr. Z. and Vixy were fast approaching, lay a maddening crisscross of exit and entrance ramps, business loops, toll roads, construction barricades and a forest of signage intended to describe it all.

"I hate this," said Vixy; "give me a jet lane any day."

A trip-alert flashed across the cruiser's display.

"Eastbound skyway detour? But I don't see any detour. Do you?"

"Incredible," grumbled Mr. Z., scanning the signage. "No." He checked his mirrors.

Vixy sat stiffly in her seat, teasing her hair and staring ahead.

"One of your anxiety attacks?" said Mr. Z. "Do you want to drive? I can pull over before we -"

"No, I'm fine. I mean, yes. Anxiety. But it's not a bad one. I'm okay." She gripped the armrest.

"There's the detour," said Mr. Z. "But look at that back up." He braked hard, looked wildly at his mirrors and hauled on the steering wheel.

"Holy shit!" said Vixy, bracing herself, "what are you doing?"

They careened headlong onto a local exit. "Getting off the road."

They plummeted into the shadowy underbelly of the interchange's superstructure, Mr. Z. wrestling with the controls and the cruiser's balky descent while seemingly obsessed with the rearview.

"What's the matter?" said Vixy, glancing back.

Mr. Z. shook his head. "Nothing." Then, under his breath, "Just checking a hunch."

Vixy had become too fixated on the scenery, such as it was, to hear. They plunged past billboard-sized murals of graffiti, fantastic riots of unrestrained imagery rendered grotesque in the planetary glow of the arc lamps.

"Mythology in the raw," murmured Mr. Z.

"What?" said Vixy. She sat clutching the armrests. "I'm not opening my eyes."

"Not getting any better? The anxiety, I mean?"

They descended sharply and Mr. Z. tapped at his controls, the clunk of the deploying road gear snapping Vixy to attention. She tightened her harness and looked out, incredulous. "The street looks deserted."

Mr. Z. was engrossed in his landing procedures. "Touching down."

The cruiser's wheels chirped sharply against the pavement, Mr. Z. killed the thrusters, engaged the ground drive and downshifted, the vehicle rolling along quietly for half a block until he stopped across from a decrepit-looking fuel station. Litter choked the gutters and a dismal streetlamp flickered above them.

Vixy grimaced. "Pleasantly urban. What in hell are we doing here?"

Mr. Z. ducked to peer into the rearview then twisted round to look out the back.

Vixy attempted to follow his gaze. "What is it? Is someone following us or something? You're making me crazy."

Mr. Z. clucked his tongue, still keen on the mirror. "It's nothing." He shoved his door open and climbed out.

"Not here, Z, are you kidding?" Vixy's eyes were wide. "Tell me we're not getting out in the middle of this ghetto." She waited impertinently, forcing Mr. Z. to open her door.

"C'mon. Let's get something to eat."

Vixy affected an exasperated sigh and made a drama of swinging her legs out and hoisting herself onto the street. She stood tightening her collar and looking warily about her, shivering a little and yawning nervously. "Jesus, it stinks out here. Worse than Manhattan. Where is this, New Jersey? C'mon, Z, shouldn't we be getting to the T.E.?"

"This way," said Mr. Z. "I'm starving." He gestured across the street.

Vixy glared at the vacant coin laundromat and the decrepit hair and nail shop beside it.

"Come on, Vixy, aren't you hungry? We'll get something to eat. It'll help your anxiety."

"Where? At the laundromat?"

Mr. Z. smiled. "The restaurant's around the corner."

"China Sea Diner," said Vixy, nonplussed. She scowled at the faded, dimly lit sign and the roast fowl – ducks by the look of them – dangling side-by-side behind the steamy window glass of the diminutive restaurant storefront, their skins puffed and taut, gleaming like caramel-colored balloons. "I don't eat Americanized Chinese, you know that."

"You ought to know real ducks when you see them. This is authentic *Cantonese* cooking. Hmm," he said, beaming as he inhaled. "Smell that? Offal, chicken feet, duck's tongue, snakes and snails."

Vixy tucked her chin into her collar. "Anything to get off the street."

The door burst open just as Mr. Z. reached for it and a slew of patrons spilled past, buoyed by a heady aroma of steamed fish, fryer oil and roasted sesame.

"Follow me," said Mr. Z.

They barreled into a fray of bustling patrons, white-shirted waitstaff and diners crammed elbow-to-elbow over their meals. Vixy clutched her bag, shuffling close behind him. She bumped into his backside when he stopped short, craning his neck, peering about for an open table. Customers closed in behind her, waitstaff shoved past, the clatter of tableware and yammering voices was at a din and she clutched at Mr. Z.'s arm.

He grasped at her hand and shouted over his shoulder. "This way!"

They practically tumbled into a tiny empty table in the back and flopped into their chairs.

"Sanctuary." Mr. Z.'s face was bright.

Vixy, flushed, took an exhilarated breath, clutching at the table edge as if to a life raft. "This is crazy! Where the hell did all these people come from?"

Mr. Z. leaned forward and grinned accommodatingly. "It *is* crazy. And it's always like this, if you can believe it." He offered her a menu. "I can recommend the steamed frog legs on lotus leaf or perhaps deep-fried goose wrapped in tofu skin."

Vixy snatched at the menu and buried herself in it.

A flush-face waiter in a dingy white t-shirt elbowed up to them and nodded. "Long time no see, Mr. Z."

"Hello, Soo."

They lifted their elbows to avoid the wadded dishtowel Soo swiped across the tabletop. He eyed Vixy and addressed Mr. Z. "What she eat?"

Vixy thrust her menu at Soo. "Lobster with ginger and scallions. And *baijiu*, warm - *To Mei Chiew*[7] if you have it."

Soo raised his eyebrows, seemingly surprised, and scribbled into his notepad. He glanced sideways at Mr. Z. "The usual?"

Mr. Z. nodded.

"Deep fry pigeon," said Soo. He nodded – a perfunctory bow of sorts, apparently - and made off in the direction of the kitchen.

"I'll be back," said Mr. Z.

Vixy watched him work his way towards the front window of the restaurant. He wiped a bit of steam from the glass with the edge of his hand and peered out, looking this way and that before ducking back through the tables and chairs. He'd barely finished wedging himself into his seat when Soo appeared as if from nowhere brandishing a pair of shot glasses and a small ceramic carafe.

"Drinks on house," he said, and disappeared into the crowd.

---

7  *To Mei Chiew* is a Cantonese liquor produced in Xiaolan Town near Zhongshan in Guangdong. It is made from rice wine, with added *to mei* flowers and crystal sugar syrup.

Mr. Z. poured the spirits. Vixy raised her glass in the proper two-handed manner, one hand beneath the cup: "*Gan bei*!" she said, and they toasted, grimacing at the liquor's fragrant bite.

Mr. Z. smacked his lips. "You know, I'm not sure women drink *Baijiu* in China."

Vixy shrugged. "I did."

Soo arrived with their meals and promptly departed, leaving them to regard Vixy's formidable-looking lobster, its black eyes staring, its antennae dangling off the edge of her plate as if it had just crawled from the sea. Mr. Z.'s glossy, denuded pigeons, meanwhile, lay with their necks bent backwards and their beaks thrust skyward like chicks, begging.

"Heads," said Vixy. She took up her chopsticks and tore at the lobster. "Do you eat them?"

Mr. Z. grasped the beak of one of the birds between his fingertips, used his chopsticks to clamp the thing's neck and twisted. He set the caramel colored skull on the edge of his plate. "No. I love this dish but crunching into their craniums?" He shrugged and dug into the breast meat. "I'd need a few more *Baijiu*." He gestured at Vixy's lobster head with his chopsticks. "How is it?"

Vixy chewed heartily and nodded.

When they'd finished, Soo appeared as if on cue, pouncing upon the empty plates and slapping their check on the table. "Enjoy?" he said.

"We hated it," said Mr. Z.

"Terrible food," said Soo, frowning. "Always bad."

Mr. Z. counted out several bills and Soo snatched them up. When he made to turn away, Mr. Z. grasped his arm and nodded towards the kitchen.

Soo glanced behind him and then side to side as if the room had become suddenly suspicious. "Back door?"

Mr. Z. got up and gestured at Vixy to do the same.

She flashed a quizzical look at him and snatched her bag from the back of her chair, following on Mr. Z.'s heels as they pushed through the crowd and into the kitchen, diving between a phalanx of cooks, knives flashing, pots clanging, stove fires belching and steam billowing.

"*Bèihòu! Bèihòu!*"[8] shouted Soo, clearing the way. He shoved the back door open and stood with his back to them, filling the doorway, craning his head this way and that, peering back and forth into the alley, the perspiration glistening on his fleshy neck. Then he turned, waved them past and they burst into the bracing chill and moonlit silence of the alley.

The two men nodded at each other and Soo pulled the door shut with a decisive "thump."

"What the hell is going on?" Vixy demanded.

"Sshh." Mr. Z. pressed his finger to his lips and crouched behind a dumpster, motioning for her to do the same. He peered around it into the street.

Vixy recoiled at the grime. "Jeezus," she hissed.

"Stay down," he whispered. "There's somebody in the cruiser."

Vixy's heart stopped. She crouched lower, pressing her back against the metal container. "What?" She reached into her bag for her plasma pistol, her heart pounding so hard it seemed anyone could hear it. "But it's cloaked, isn't it?"

Mr. Z. nodded, watching.

Get your shit together, she told herself. She shut her eyes, took a deep breath and turned to peer over Mr. Z.'s shoulder. Nothing. Only the dimly lit street, the filthy curb and the dilapidated fuel station beyond. "I don't see anything."

"There," whispered Mr. Z., pointing at where the cruiser ought to be. They heard a clicking and a tell-tale mechanical "clunk" – the sound of the cruiser's door being opened. A hulking, dark shape appeared at the curb.

---

8 "Behind! Behind!"

"Holy shit," hissed Vixy.

Just then a crowd piled out of the diner, laughing and gesticulating and teetering from drink. When they ambled into the street Vixy almost failed to see the shape appear to gather itself and leap away soundlessly in the direction of the fuel station.

Mr. Z. stood up. He shoved his hands in his pockets, hunched his shoulders and began shuffling towards the cruiser.

"What are you doing!" Vixy clutched at her pistol, disabling the safety.

"It's fine," he said, gesturing for her to catch up. "It's gone."

"What's gone?" She shoved her pistol into her bag, flexing her hand and wincing at the pain - she'd never gripped anything so hard in her life - and hurried across the street, eyeing the scene warily. "God, Z," she hissed, I'm back there with my pistol in my hand and you're sauntering into the street." She stood hugging her elbows. "What *was* it? And what are we doing standing here like this? How do you know we're not being watched?"

Mr. Z. reached into his pocket, disabled the cloak and the cruiser materialized exactly where they'd left it. "You don't have to whisper. It's gone, I'm telling you." He promptly flopped onto the pavement, reaching beneath the cruiser.

"How do you know they won't be back?" Vixy took a step back, peering askance into the vehicle's windows. "For shit's sake what are you doing?"

Mr. Z.'s muffled voice came from underneath the cruiser. "I'm just looking at something." He got up. "It's a telescoping mirror." He stretched the slender device to its length as if to demonstrate, then collapsed it and clamped it on his belt. He regarded her as if for the first time. "Are you alright? You look a little –"

"You're freaking me out, Z. Are you looking for a car bomb or something? Christ."

"Your teeth are chattering. Here -" he made to take off his trench coat and hand it to her but she waved it away. "It's just your nerves, Vixy - I'm sorry to have upset you like that – pulling your gun and everything." He put his arm around her and reached for the passenger side door. "Take some deep breaths, it happens to everyone the first time or two. Somehow it's different than training, isn't it?"

Vixy nodded.

"You'll get used to it. C'mon, get in."

Vixy resisted.

"It's alright. Really."

She ducked in, slammed the door and double-checked the lock.

"Whomever or whatever it was won't be back," said Mr. Z., flopping into his seat. "But don't touch anything." He ran his fingers delicately underneath the dashboard, up and down the steering column, under the seats and between the seat cushions and the armrest, finally reaching across Vixy's lap to inspect the door panel. "I'm just checking for a tracer."

Vixy scowled. "Whomever or whatever? What the hell do you mean?"

"Ack!" He sat up, frustrated. "We'll be here all night with me looking for the damn thing." He reached for the ignition switch and Vixy grabbed his arm.

"What are you doing, trying to blow us sky high? I mean for shit's sake why in hell don't we just take a cab to the enclave?" Vixy looked suspiciously round the cockpit.

"I'm sorry, Vixy. I should've explained some things – a lot of things - but I've been struggling to make sense of it myself. And I'd just as soon let things play out a bit more before speculating. Meanwhile, I'm convinced that if anyone or anything wanted to kill us we'd already be dead."

"Dead?" Vixy stared blankly at him. "No, I think you owe me all the speculation you can manage. And how long have you -"

"Since the Fuel Stop."

She blinked at him. "The Fuel Stop." She shook her head. "I didn't notice anything out of the ordinary. What are you talking about?"

"Buckle up," he said, "let's get to New York." He stabbed at the ignition and revved the motor.

Vixy growled and hurried to buckle her harness, clutching at the armrests as Mr. Z. floored the throttle. They rose vertically, the vehicle rotating disconcertingly as they accelerated upwards, Mr. Z. checking his mirrors and his gauges until once again the congested traffic of the interchange loomed above them. He retracted the mechanicals, shifted gears, and the cruiser lurched forward, speeding past the congestion of the eastbound skyway detour, heading straight for a barrage of air-traffic barricades and warning flashers.

"The emergency skyway? But that's tracked by the State Police. It's against summons protocol to -"

Mr. Z., tapped at the dashboard controls. "We've got to make up some time." The cruiser's authorization halo glowed brightly on the tracking display, the barricades flashed from red to green and the hard barriers fell away as they sped into the tunnel-like atmosphere of the emergency skyway. "We'll bail out at Weehawken."

The New Jersey shoreline dropped away at Weehawken Park and they dipped low over the dark waters of the Hudson then quickly up again to confront the towering, glittering architecture of the ancient city. Manhattan. Mr. Z. throttled down and merged the cruiser into a line of eastbound traffic snaking its way at skyscraper level across the midtown section of the city. Clearing FDR Drive, they plummeted over the eastern edge of the island towards the water and banked northward, accelerating hard up the East River, the cruiser hurtling beneath the Queensboro Bridge and rocketing up the West Channel. He downshifted round the apex of Hallets Point, burying the throttle as they thundered beneath the Triborough Bridge then coasted, the engine silent, through Hell Gate. He braked hard, flaps up, downshifting along Shore Boulevard, gliding into the dimness of Astoria Park at treetop level, the soft lights of the sprawling neighborhood beyond winking at them. Mr. Z. slowed the cruiser to a crawl, virtually brushing the tops of the leafless trees as he inched forward.

Vixy loosened her harness, watching Mr. Z. adjust the down-view mirrors and glance at the landing display. "If you weren't such a nostalgia freak you'd trade this junker in for something with decent flight aptitude and proper instrumentation and then you wouldn't have to endure such a wrestling match."

"Unnecessary paraphernalia." Mr. Z. struggled at the controls and the cruiser shuddered angrily. He redoubled his focus, his voice tense. "But we've had this conversation. And you can't tell me you weren't impressed with the way she handles over the river."

Vixy rolled her eyes at him, peering at the mirrors herself. They drifted over an opening in the trees. "There's your mark," she said, "you're plenty clear on my side." Mr. Z. eased the machine downward, a flurry of dust and leaves billowing out from beneath the cruiser's belly as the landing retros fired, the chassis pitching and shuddering as if reluctant to come to rest.

"Touching down."

Vixy peered round at the crumbling walls and the seemingly incongruous expanse of concrete. "A bunch of rubble. Are you sure this used to be a park or something?"

Mr. Z. shifted into park and extinguished the landing lights, leaving the motor running. "More than a park. It was the Astoria Pool. Huge. Open to the public. Yes. A protected site until, I don't know, a few decades ago – this whole area, lots of ancient history. Until it fell off the heritage acquisition list and was due to be demolished for another high rise. If it weren't for the T.E. purchasing it..." he trailed off.

The red filigree of an identification web enveloped the cruiser, the laser-light flickering over the contours of the sheet metal and projecting a distorted geometry into the dimensions of the cockpit, the intricate pattern of light stretching across their extremities, fluttering over their laps and chests and faces before crawling over the seat cushions, door panels, ceiling, floor and dash.

A voice croaked from the telecom: "Z and V, long time no see!"

"Hi, Bull!" said Vixy.

"How was the trip?"

"Z should've let *me* drive - he almost clipped a tug under the Queensboro."

"That true, Z?" Bull's brusque, consonant heavy, Bronx-style accent blared from the cockpit speakers.

Mr. Z. scowled and adjusted the volume.

"I bet he's giving you the stink eye for that, V. Hey Z, you really think the girl could handle the old war chariot? I saw you rocking and rolling up there, you know what I mean. You had your hands full, my friend."

Mr. Z spoke carefully into the console of the steering wheel: "I am reminded, Bull, of the youthful hubris of our friend Phaëthon who insisted upon driving his father's chariot."

"Phay who?"

"Phaëthon was an ambitious young man who'd convinced himself he could drive the sun chariot across the sky like his father, but when he tried he lost control of the horses -"

"And he fell out of the sky to his death," said Vixy, rolling her eyes.

"Hmm...," said Bull. "I don't know Z, you and your mythographicals or whatever. Something tells me Vixy might do a little better than that."

"Mythology, Bull."

"Mythology, Z, that's right, good stuff. Even though I can't ever make any sense of it. Pull her into Gate One and we'll get you processed."

"Hold on, Bull," said Mr. Z. "I must apologize, but we've come bearing gifts, so to say."

"Z thinks we're booby-trapped, Bull," said Vixy.

"Hmm," said Bull. "The scan was clean as a whistle. But sit tight. Don't get out, don't touch anything and leave it running. I'm sending the boys out now."

Momentarily, from the vicinity of the deep end of the pool roared two armored hover-scooters, their blast-blades lowered and their blue-white search lamps flooding the pool area.

Mr. Z. and Vixy shielded their eyes at the glare. A moment later various mechanical knocks, taps and vibrations seemed to emanate from everywhere under the vehicle. Then all at once the door locks unlocked themselves, the hood and trunk lids popped open and the motor turned itself off. There was an odor of electricity, a low vibration, more strange noises - hums, rumbles, clicking sounds, electronic "beeps" and then suddenly the vehicle doors flew open of their own accord, the search lights dimmed and they found themselves staring into the face of a dashing, blonde-haired young man in a coffee-colored business suit, long hound-stooth coat and leather gloves.

"Good evening," he said, peering in at them. "I'm Herman Neutic, your attaché and special escort. This is quite a vehicle, sir, I must say. A Series One Panther, isn't it? Original. Not a reproduction."

Mr. Z. nodded. "Indeed, thank you."

"I understand you've been a frequent visitor to the T.E. over many years, sir. I'm very glad to meet you. Welcome back." He brought his attention to Vixy. "Likewise, Cadet Velure, welcome to the T.E." He stepped back, his eyes attentive and bright. "If you'll follow me, I'll escort you to your rooms while Security completes the disposal procedure." He offered Vixy his arm.

Vixy waited. Something about this man's courtesy and self-possession, his incongruously resonant voice – he seemed so young – made her hesitate. She found herself staring at length into his vivid blue eyes and it wasn't until she felt her cheeks flush that she managed to grab his arm.

He helped her out and stood regarding her mildly, adjusting the lustrous yellow knot of his tie with one hand and smoothing his immaculately parted hair with the other.

It was the first time she'd ever encountered anyone besides Mr. Z. who behaved in so gentlemanly a manner. She wasn't certain she liked it. She glanced at Neutic's shoes. Who wears oxfords? She shivered, her breath visible, and suddenly the cold, the exhausting drive and the lateness of the evening – everything about her trip – seemed to overtake her.

Neutic seemed to register her fatigue, eyeing her discreetly, tempering his tone. "This way." He shed his coat and draped it over Vixy's shoulders.

She was too tired and chilled to be anything but glad for it.

❋

Neutic led them away from the cruiser and Mr. Z. followed behind wordlessly, his hands shoved into the pockets of his trench coat, his arms stiffened against the cold and his chin buried against his chest. Vixy fell in beside him as if drawn to their shared fatigue.

They stopped in front of a featureless concrete wall and waited.

Vixy stomped her feet against the cold.

"A little closer, Miss Velure," said Neutic, gesturing towards the wall. "The bio-scan is a little touchy since the last calibration." A green light flashed and a non-descript, windowless door materialized. It slid open and Neutic ushered them into a small vestibule.

"Brrr," said Vixy, rubbing her hands together. "Finally some heat."

They passed into a much larger lobby, a gleaming, armored elevator door on one side and ahead an impenetrable-looking, armor-fiber-reinforcement (AFR) style portal. To the right, a personnel door of the same AFR material, save for the large porthole window at eye level which provided a "fish-eye" view of the interior of the security office.

Vixy stood on her tiptoes to peer inside. Bull could be seen floating half in, half out of the water tank which ran the length of his security office, now and again gently twitching his legs so that he darted almost effortlessly back and forth in the water while at the same time reaching his webby amphibian fingertips towards various knobs, dials, levers and switches. A large conference table occupied the middle of the room behind Bull's work-tank and a bank of video screens filled the opposite wall - a uniformed technician stood before them, variously tapping at a keyboard, swiping the screen's touchpads or placing his finger against his ear and speaking soundlessly into his headset.

Vixy pressed her face to the thick glass - armor reinforced crystal - and rapped on it, her knuckles barely resonating. Bull nevertheless interrupted himself to peer out, an enormous amphibian grin stretched across his face. He winked a huge gelatinous eye at her and reached for the intercom.

"You look tired, girl," said Bull. "No explosives in the cruiser, folks, but we found something else. Something, well, let's just say that forensics might be awhile with it. You'll have a copy of the report as soon as I do. But it probably won't be till morning. Get some rest, the both of you. Noots, you take good care of these friends of mine, you hear?"

Neutic gestured towards the elevator. "This way, folks."

The three of them stood shoulder-to-shoulder as the elevator descended and Mr. Z.'s own fatigue compelled him to focus on the part of Neutic's cuff that protruded past the sleeve of his suit jacket. "Turnback style."[9]

"Yessir."

"Calfskin," he said. "Oxfords."

Neutic wiggled his feet inside his shoes and nodded, restraining a mild grin.

Deeply creased top leathers, thought Mr. Z. Toying with observations, however pedestrian, always helped keep him alert, helped restore his dulled intellect. Edges of the soles abraded. But buffed and polished. New laces. The suit jacket: fine wool, well-tailored but not new; the sleeves at the elbows a bit shiny, lacking the texture of the surrounding fabric, the kind of wear brought on by several seasons of regular use. But no snags, no loose threads, seams tight. Shirt collar bright, crisply pressed, perhaps some starch. The canary-yellow tie with white pin dots. Windsor knot, well executed. Nice gloss to the silk, perhaps a recent purchase.

The elevator continued its descent and in the closeness of the cabin, Mr. Z could examine the various scents. His own pipe tobacco. A hint of Vixy's cigarettes mingled with her sandalwood and lavender perfume. Menthol, a wisp of citrus and a grassy but clean base note of something he couldn't place at first. Neutic's aftershave. "Green vetiver."[10] The words hung in the air.

---

[9]  This style of cuff was first made by the Jermyn Street tailor Turnbull & Asser and then popularized by Sean Connery in the first James Bond film, *Dr. No.* The so-called turn-back cuff combines the elegance of a French cuff with the ease of buttons.

[10]  *Chrysopogon zizanioides,* commonly known as vetiver, is a perennial bunchgrass native to India, and mainly cultivated for the fragrant essential oil distilled from its roots. Vetiver is most closely related to Sorghum but shares many morphological characteristics with other fragrant grasses, such as lemongrass, citronella, and palmarosa.

Neutic shifted his weight from one foot to the other, shrugged slightly beneath his suit jacket as if suddenly ill at ease and opened his mouth as if to respond but Vixy spoke up.

"Green what?"

"Vetiver," said Mr. Z. "An essential oil."

Neutic put his hand to his mouth and cleared his throat quietly. "Common in aftershave, Miss Velure."

"Not too common, Mr. Neutic," said Mr. Z. "Not these days."

Vixy eyed Neutic and squirmed, handing him his coat and adjusting her skirt further down her thighs.

The elevator decelerated and Neutic, his coat folded neatly over his arm, returned his attention to the display. "Sub-Floor 42."

The elevator doors slid apart and they padded down the carpeted hallway. The spare accommodations within this area of the T.E., typical of that granted to field operations personnel, resembled a cross between a modest hotel and a college dormitory; not as Spartan as a military barracks but undeniably utilitarian; the subterranean rooms themselves void of frills besides carpeting and private baths.

"Keyed to your bio-scan," said Neutic. He turned the handle and held the door ajar. "Goodnight, Miss Velure."

Vixy hardly heard him. "Thank you, Mister..." she trailed off, pressed her fingers against her forehead and yawned, stepping into the room. "I'm sorry...."

"Neutic, ma'am. Herman Neutic. At your service. Good night." The door closed and he brought his attention to Mr. Z.

Mr. Z.'s expression was vaguely apologetic. "She's tired. Usually quite sturdy on the road - excellent endurance for a cadet but our trip had its, well, issues."

"I understand, sir," said Neutic. They stopped in front of Mr. Z.'s room. "The debriefing is scheduled for 8:00AM."

"Wake-up call? We'll need it, I think."

"Yessir. Also, your console is set to alert you with any updates. Our conference room tomorrow is at the far end of the hall. If there's nothing else...?"

"Nothing, thank you, Mr. Neutic. Goodnight."

# CHAPTER 2

# BLACK TIME

**THEY ENTERED THE EMPTY CONFERENCE ROOM** and Vixy made directly for the coffee pot. "Thank god," she mumbled. She peered listlessly over the rim of her cup at the modest breakfast buffet.

Mr. Z. busied himself with a small, earthenware pot and a tin of loose tea. "That tray of salmon over there, did you see it?"

"Cold smoked. Nice color." She shuffled towards the conference table and flopped into the first chair she came to.

Mr. Z. poured his tea and inhaled the aroma. He layered cream cheese and salmon onto a bagel and sunk his teeth into it, speaking with his mouth full, "Cold smoked, you're right."

"Nothing like my dad's." Vixy gulped at her coffee and leaned forward, scowling at Mr. Z.'s food.

"Try it, see what you think," said Mr. Z..

She got up and ambled to the buffet. "It's Pacific."

"You can tell by looking at it?"

She placed a piece on her tongue, sucked on it indifferently and swallowed. She poured more coffee before flopping into her seat again. She shrugged at Mr. Z. "Not bad. Makes me miss my dad's."

"Good morning." Neutic stood in the doorway. He wore a close-fitting navy cardigan that buttoned to a high V neck and trim dark slacks. His tie was wine-red against his collared white shirt. He seemed exactly as well put together as he did the previous night.

"Good morning, Neutic," said Mr. Z., smiling. "May I call you Neutic?"

"Yessir." He took a seat near the door and began tapping perfunctorily into the control panel embedded in the tabletop. "About the salmon," he said, glancing almost imperceptibly at Vixy. "It may not measure up, I apologize. You'd think living in New York I could tell lox from Nova and gravlax but when I go to a deli I just stick to the pastrami on rye."

Vixy began toying with her transponder.

"I like pastrami," said Mr. Z. "But I don't know any good delis in Queens this close to the river."

"There's one in Brooklyn that I like."

"You live there?"

"Yessir."

"But you're originally from Queens, I can tell by your accent." He shoved the last of his bagel into his mouth. "How is it you came to be an attaché?"

"I am from Queens, yessir. I was hired six months ago. I'd been an analyst with Galactic Intelligence off-planet. I crossed paths with a T.E. envoy from the Time Guard division who convinced me my interest in CTA[11] might be better served here, especially given the new initiatives undertaken between the TDC and the T.E."

"That's our funding increase in action," said Mr. Z. "And you've been working with Captain Chase, then?"

"Yessir. Reporting to him, actually. Under a temporary contract between the T.E. and the TDC. Technical administrative support."

---

[11] Cosmic Time Architecture. See Glossary.

"Excellent." Mr. Z. slurped his tea. "How do you find it so far, working for the Captain?"

"I like it." Neutic's tone seemed genuine.

"You've probably already discovered that the TDC tends to suffer under the weight of its own bureaucracies. Administrative red tape and all that. Like any institution. But the organization has strong bones. Even if its joints are a little stiff."

"Bureaucracies and red tape," said Vixy, talking over the rim of her cup; "that's an understatement."

Mr. Z. smiled wryly. He noticed that Neutic's eyes seemed to sparkle whenever Vixy spoke. He leaned back in his chair and watched the two of them as he finished his tea.

Neutic seemed intent upon filling the silence. "No, sir. I mean, yessir. That is, I think it's been a good fit, as far as it goes. At least on my end. Though I'm sure I could be picking things up more quickly." He returned self-consciously to his typing.

They heard a door slam somewhere down the hall, then voices. In another moment a stocky, white-shirted man with a thick neck, short cropped hair and an eye patch burst into the room. Virtually on his heels was a uniformed T.E. security officer.

"Any coffee left?" He tossed an overstuffed manila folder on the table and strode to the buffet, rolling up his sleeves as if preparing for a confrontation with the carafes. "Good morning." His back was to them as he poured a cup. He tilted his head towards the Lieutenant. "This is Lieutenant Grace of T.E. Security in charge of counter-terrorism."

The Lieutenant had remained standing, ramrod straight, projecting an air of self-possessed, military decorum. She was middle-aged, slender, her femininity enhanced by the plainness of her uniform and professional reserve. She was in immaculate military dress – skirt, blouse and jacket, her shoulder festooned with ribbon badges – the relaxed coif of her short hair the only counterpoint to her air of military precision.

The Captain's most striking feature besides his thick-boned, broad-shouldered bulk was his black eye patch, a startling rarity – routine transplants had been available for a millennium. He wore starched khakis and his crisp dress shirt hung open at the collar. Otherwise, he appeared mildly exasperated, as if everything around him were somehow lacking. He commandeered a seat at the middle of the table.

"The Lieutenant has been reviewing your arrival," said the Captain. "Forensics is having problems with the disposal." He flopped open his file folder and puffed his cheeks at his coffee cup. The rims of his eye were reddened, his chin displayed a pronounced stubble and he presented the sallow complexion of someone who hadn't slept. "Let's get to it, Lieutenant."

The Lieutenant seated herself, smoothing her skirt with one hand and logging into the audio-visual control panel with the other. A hologram materialized over the center of the tabletop. She tapped at her screen and the image began rotating.

Mr. Z., Vixy and Neutic leaned forward to inspect it.

"We discovered these during the sanitization of the cruiser," said the Lieutenant.

"Our cruiser?" said Vixy. She shot a baffled glance at Mr. Z. "Where?"

"The glove compartment, ma'am."

"Of course." Her tone was ironic. "Because that's the last place we would've looked for anything ourselves."

"They were categorized among your personal sundries and, as such, of no consequence from a security standpoint – it's simply routine that we impound and temporarily quarantine all items within a vehicle as part of a suspected security risk. However, the items cleared the BIS, indicating no evidence of biological contact. That is to say, no one has touched them, at least as far as our analysis can determine. Which of course begs the question as to how they found their way into the vehicle's glove compartment."

Vixy frowned. "Biss?"

"Biological Inheritance Scan," said the Lieutenant.

There was a pause and the Captain, otherwise preoccupied with his papers, looked up. "It's a new technology," he said. "Currently in beta-testing. The T.E. was selected for the trial. It's impressive engineering wouldn't you say, Lieutenant?"

The Lieutenant barely nodded.

Vixy folded her arms. "What about an origin analysis?"

"An OA was initiated, ma'am," said the Lieutenant, "via protocol, which ran continuously until zero eight-hundred hours."

"But an OA only takes a few minutes."

"Correct, ma'am," said the Lieutenant. "Most analyses indeed are completed within minutes, very often within seconds. In fact, within the two years T.E. Security has been utilizing this version of OA, we have completed over five thousand such analyses, all results falling within the standard parameters. These items, however, stand as the exception. They were ultimately rejected as so-called Black Time Objects by the machine, the first and only such designation our unit has produced and despite the scientific interest such an object provokes, the security risk mandates their destruction." The Lieutenant glanced at her display. "That is to say, following the quarantine period which expires this afternoon."

Mr. Z. tapped his finger quietly on the tabletop, his eyes still fixed upon the hologram.

"We've read the report of your encounter," said the Captain; "I appreciate you getting that to me last night, Z. You both saw something – someone or something; a shadow of some sort. You say it may have infiltrated the vehicle." The Captain ran his finger down one of his pieces of paperwork. "In Hoboken?" He focused upon Mr. Z. "Across the street from that Asian joint you like, I assume?"

"The China Sea Diner, Yessir," said Vixy. "And we're certain it entered the vehicle because we heard it messing with the door lock."

"We've got to assume, then," said the Captain, "that these, whatever they are –" he gestured at the hologram.

"Coins," said Mr. Z.

Neutic glanced back and forth between the Captain and Mr. Z. "Coins, sir?"

"Chinese coins look just like that," said Vixy. "Square holes and every-thing. They were typically crammed onto a square-shaped rod to be filed after casting and afterwards the hole allowed them to be strung together in long strings of, say, a thousand at a time." She pulled herself closer to the table and squinted at the image. "These are strung together, too."

"It looks like silk," said Mr. Z. "And the silk is likewise untraceable by the BIS?"

"That's correct, sir," said the Lieutenant.

"What's the metallurgy?" said Mr. Z.

"Bronze, I bet," said Vixy.

"So-called alpha bronze," said the Lieutenant. She tapped at her control console. "Eighty-five percent copper, five percent tin. Common in ancient coinage, certain types of springs and turbine blades, etcetera."

"What about impurities?" said the Captain.

The Lieutenant double-checked her display and shook her head. "Our metallurgists classified this particular alloy, including the trace impurities, as too ubiquitous for a definitive identification. Alloys of this type are found virtually galaxy wide. On Earth, from approximately thirty-five BC onwards and elsewhere..." – she leaned closer to her display – "considerably earlier – another several millennia."

"Well, that's *something* of a useful boundary," said Mr. Z. "And the minting technology itself? Is it likewise generic?"

"Generic enough, sir, to preclude any further effort at analysis. These happen to be stamped, machine struck. Versus cast or laser cut. Stamped is by far the most common method, apparently. According to our consultants a comprehensive origin and identification study would require weeks, perhaps months, to complete. Otherwise, the official determination from a security standpoint is that these are indeed coins, or imitations of coins, of Oriental design, just as Miss Velure described."

"Loose change." The Captain rubbed his face again. "Somehow un-traceable." The rotating image seemed to irritate him.

"They're not just coins," said Vixy. "They're oracle coins. First of all, there are three of them. And that design – those patterned marks – are imprinted on only one side."

"Oracle coins?" said the Captain, squirming in his seat. His voice was weary and he ran his finger inside the collar of his shirt as if he wanted to crawl out of it.

"As opposed to yarrow stalks," said Mr. Z. "Vixy's right. It makes me think we ought to get a copy of the text in front of us."

"What text?" asked the Captain.

"The *I Ching*, sir," said Neutic. He'd been tapping at his keyboard.

Mr. Z. raised his eyebrow, regarding Neutic afresh. "Indeed."

"Why can't they simply be old-fashioned, Chinese style coins?" Exasperation was mounting in the Captain's tone.

"They're Black Time coins, Captain," said the Lieutenant. Her matter-of-fact response cast a silence over the room, interrupted only by the click-clack of Neutic's persistent typing.

"Is there a preferred translation?" asked Neutic. No one responded and he looked up, his fingers hovering above his keyboard. "Mr. Z.?"

"Yes, as a matter of fact, there is. The Carey Baynes translation. Baynes with a 'y.' From Richard Wilhelm's German rendering. Published by Bollingen Foundation in the nineteen fifties or sixties, I think. Still regarded as definitive."

"First edition in two volumes published nineteen fifty," said Neutic, tapping. "Second edition in one volume published nineteen sixty-one."

Mr. Z. shut his eyes and scratched at his temple. "Second edition is the one I'm familiar with. There's an appendix, if I'm not mistaken – it explains how to cast an oracle using coins."

"'On Consulting the Oracle,'" said Neutic.

"That's it," said Mr. Z. "Can you read it, please?"

Neutic appeared tentative, as if he'd suddenly become self-conscious.

"Go ahead, Neutic," said Vixy. Her voice was uncharacteristically encouraging.

Neutic cleared his throat and spoke up. "'In addition to the method of the yarrow-stalk oracle, there is in use a shorter method employing coins:'" He projected the text and continued.

Old Chinese bronze coins with a hole in the middle and an inscription on one side are used. Three coins are taken up and thrown down together, and each throw gives a line. The inscribed side counts as yin, with the value of two, and the reverse side counts as yang, with the value three. From this the character of the line is derived. If all three coins are yang, the line is a nine; if all three are yin, it is a six. Two yin and one yang yield a seven, and two yang and one yin yield an eight. In looking up the hexagrams in the *Book of Changes*, one proceeds as with the yarrow-stalk oracle.[c]

A silence ensued and the Captain frowned. "None of this oracle business begins to explain anything about how or why the coins were planted in your vehicle."

Mr. Z. smacked his forehead. "By God, I've been a fool!" He looked round the room at them as if suddenly in possession of a revelation. "I'm sorry, Captain. I've not been making any of the connections. Answer me this. Anyone. What's the off-world culture that most closely resembles that of the so-called Far East here on Earth? In its pre-industrial incarnation?"

They stared at him.

"C'mon – the most esoteric, most occult humanoids in the cosmos?"

Neutic spoke up. "In anthropological terms, sir, or, I don't know... mythological?"

"When it comes to Mr. Z.," said Vixy, "that's a loaded question. He means both." She addressed Mr. Z. succinctly. "The Mothmen."

Mr. Z. and the Captain exchanged a queer glance.

"Jesus, Z." The Captain straightened his sheaf of papers, stuffed them into his folder and slammed it shut. "Mothmen of all things. We know they exist and that's it. The rest is conjecture. Their Confucian bent and all that." He counted off on his fingers: "No communication, no record of diplomacy, nothing but nothing." He eyed Mr. Z. from beneath his brow. "There hasn't been a successful penetration of their isolation veil since, we don't know when."

The Captain shrugged. "My point is, we're speculating. And even if we *could* make some kind of legitimate connection it's going to take more resources, including time, than we've got. The clock is ticking on these coins, folks. And hashing over a hundred-thousand-year-old legend about an off-world Oriental mystery culture isn't getting us any closer to resolving how or why so-called Black Time Objects ended up in the glove compartment of Mr. Z.'s cruiser."

The room fell quiet.

"What little it says here," said Neutic, addressing nobody in particular, "is that the Mothmen eschew technology."

"And there's no mystery in that," said the Captain. "Luddites. Technophobes. It's a type, that's all. The Mothmen couldn't have transported anyone or anything to Earth if they wanted to, except on a magic carpet – they've never possessed nor even been known to pursue acquisition of HDT[12] technology. If they had, we'd know about it, we'd have HDT impressions, we all know that."

The hint of a wry grin crept across Mr. Z.'s face.

Here it comes, thought Vixy; he's got some scandalous scholarly factoid; a bomb he's going to drop.

"HDT impressions, indeed," said Mr. Z. "Are we absolutely certain that all such impressions are untraceable?"

"As a matter of fact, sir," said the Lieutenant. She swiped at her display. "The GID – the Ghost Impression Database; there's been word of a recent anomaly, something about...." She shook her head. "I'm sorry, I don't have the memorandum in front of me."

There was a flurry of keystrokes. "Hold on, Lieutenant," said Neutic, "I've got it." He struck the entry key with authority. "Yes. Within the

---

12 Hyper-Dimensional Travel. See Glossary.

last forty-eight hours an anomaly was submitted by the Consequence Research Project."

"Status?" said the Lieutenant.

"Unresolved.'"

"Who performed the analysis?" said the Captain.

"Clearance Required. That's all it says."

"The Time Guard," said the Captain, his voice condescending.

"Sir?" said Neutic.

"The Time Guard are the ones who performed the analysis. I know because they assigned the TDC the investigation. Which led to the summons you both received. Which had nothing, of course, to do with these coins. So, on the one hand we've got an HDT anomaly that the Time Detective Contingent has been asked to investigate – a possible time crime in the form of a Ghost Impression database anomaly. And on the other, a mysterious set of oracle coins, or whatever these are. Meanwhile, I'm not convinced there's a connection. Assuming – just assuming – Mr. Z., that you're correct about the physical possibility of a Mothman infiltrating your vehicle, why in hell would they bother? We need a motive. And why you, Z? Why your cruiser? Why now? Why Hoboken?"

"Why exactly, Captain," said Mr. Z. He appeared unruffled. "The Mothmen exist some two-hundred-thousand light years from Earth. Let's say they've projected an initiate – that shadow creature we encountered breaking into the cruiser. Then they've necessarily utilized time-space projection to get him here. Which means they've more or less suspended their antipathy regarding high technology and have challenged their own cultural mandates – they've risked engaging in something – namely, HDT, which is fundamentally contrary to their beliefs. How to do that and still remain culturally stable? Well, as history tells us, you appeal to the symbols of your mythology just as you're attempting to subvert them. In other words, you transform the meaning of the symbol to fit the new mythology or, in the worst case, the new ideology."

"And the strategy?" said the Captain.

"It may be simply that the Mothmen have used oracle coins – appropriately symbolic, sacred coins – to somehow establish a strategic technological link to our world – a tangible, physical connection, like a place marker or foci of some type. We know that HDT coordinate targeting experiments have legitimized the effect."

"But to what end?" said the Captain. "What's the motive? They're homing in upon the T.E. for what reason? Terrorism? It's not as if a handful of so-called oracle coins are going to, I don't know –"

"Blow it up?" said Vixy. She shrugged when everyone stopped to look at her. "Well, how is that any crazier than anything else about all this?"

"Excuse me, Captain," said the Lieutenant, "but the hold time on the coins expires in fifteen minutes. I'm afraid I have to authorize –"

"What about extenuating circumstances?" said Vixy. "Our work here must have some priority, doesn't it?"

"Yes, ma'am. Hence, the amount of time we've been allotted for this meeting. And I would indeed prefer to continue to work to resolve the provenance of these objects, to generate a proper origin analysis. But with all due respect, the protocol is strict."

"The Lieutenant is right, Vixy," said the Captain, "it's not up to anyone here. And we don't need the coins themselves to continue the investigation. At least as far as I'm concerned. Go ahead, Lieutenant. Burn them." He gathered his files and stood up.

"Wait," said Mr. Z. "Is there anything preventing us from inspecting the coins in person?"

"Do you mean inside the Quarantine Cell, sir?" said the Lieutenant.
"Yes."

"We'd require a waiver," said the Lieutenant.

"Which the Captain can authorize, if I'm not mistaken," said Mr. Z.

God, Z. thought Vixy. She watched the monitor closely. "Black Time Objects," she murmured, "do you know what you're doing?"

"What's that?" mumbled the Captain.

The Captain seemed absorbed in his transponder and Vixy didn't repeat herself. She abandoned the monitor and pressed her face close to the observation portal. The coins rested on an isolation pedestal; their earthy, commonplace appearance conflicting with the high-technology of the luminous, blue-green light of the security web that flickered over them. She recalled a similar filigree crawling across her lap when they'd arrived at the T.E. The memory made her skin crawl. Mr. Z. suddenly entered the frame. What could possibly go wrong? She took a deep breath and held it.

Each of them – Vixy, the Captain and Neutic – craned their necks to stare into the window of the quarantine cell. The Lieutenant, meanwhile, stood back, peering at the monitor, her finger pressed against her headset.

Mr. Z.'s voice crackled across the intercom. "Is it possible to handle them?"

"At your own risk," said the Lieutenant. "What do you intend?"

"To cast an oracle."

The Lieutenant raised her eyebrow. "I repeat, sir, whatever action you take will be at your own risk."

Vixy endured a rush of anxiety and tapped at the intercom. "Mr. Z.", she said. She ignored the mild panic evident in her voice. "Maybe it's best to let them be...."

Mr. Z. glanced, unseeing, towards the one-way armored mirror glass and affected an ironic smile, his voice mechanical and distant through the intercom. "I think it's important to exert our influence, Vixy, such as it is. Do you understand me?"

*But you told me the Mothmen were assassins.* She wanted to say it to him, wanted to scream it at him but she couldn't do anything but turn away. They're just coins, she told herself – they're just goddamn coins.

The Captain stepped back and stood beside the Lieutenant, frowning at the observation monitor. Neutic stood beside Vixy, peering into the cell.

Mr. Z. addressed the coins. "Shall we, Lieutenant?"

"Yessir," said the Lieutenant. The security web vanished. "Go ahead."

Mr. Z. snipped the thread that bound the coins together, cupped his hands around them and shook once, twice, three times and cast them unceremoniously onto the quarantine pedestal. He made a note on a slip of paper and repeated the procedure another five times.

Vixy had turned to look. "He's building a hexagram."

They watched Mr. Z. stack the coins together, arrange the silk beside them on the pedestal then turn and leave the room. The security web re-illuminated, the bulkhead locks disengaged and Mr. Z. emerged from the cell.

"Well?" said Vixy.

Mr. Z. addressed the Lieutenant. "Thank you, Lieutenant."

The Lieutenant nodded, speaking into her headset. "Ten seconds to burn."

There was a flash and the coins vanished. They stood staring for a moment at the empty pedestal.

"Well," said the Captain, frowning at his transponder. "I'm late for a meeting. Lieutenant, thank you. Meanwhile, Z, Vixy – we've got that CRP anomaly to look into. Neutic, set up a debriefing – I'll be free in a couple of hours." He turned and hurried off.

"Vixy," said Mr. Z. He seemed at ease, as if he'd dismissed the entire event as incidental. "I think we can still make the Wilhelm lecture." He checked his transponder. "If I can remember how to get to the theater from here."

"Follow me," said Neutic.

# CHAPTER 3

# THEFT OF PERSEPHONE

**THEY PASSED BETWEEN THE ARTFUL COLUMNS** of an impressive portico and stopped short. Vixy gasped and clutched at Mr. Z.'s arm.

"It's like being on the edge of a cliff." She hesitated.

"Follow me," said Mr. Z. He took her hand and stepped down, raising his voice over the din of the audience. "You'll be fine."

The seating area plunged towards the empty stage and Vixy forced herself to look away, focusing on the audience crammed shoulder-to-shoulder.

She managed to negotiate the first steps, reminding herself to breathe. The seats, she discovered, were nothing more than stone benches, unadorned but for a thin pad of velvety, red upholstery. "It's supposed to be like, what, ancient Greece?"

Mr. Z. was busy scrutinizing the aisles. "Greco-Roman, actually."

Vixy still clung to Mr. Z.'s arm. "How many people does this place hold? A thousand?"

"Eleven-hundred, perhaps twelve-hundred, I can't recall exactly. Hmm. We may have to sit apart, if we're to sit down at all."

"God, I passed up a cigarette for this? It's impossible, we'll never find a -"

"There!" Mr. Z. gestured towards an enormous bear of a man several rows down. He'd turned towards them with his arm in the air, apparently motioning for them to sit.

They shuffled past the protruding kneecaps and toes and squeezed themselves into their seats.

"It's never been this crowded," said the man. "You'd think they'd anticipate this kind of response and book a proper auditorium. A *cavea*? It's ridiculous."

Vixy leaned close and whispered into Mr. Z.'s ear. "*Cavea?*"

Mr. Z. smiled. "Latin for 'enclosure.' In Roman times it referred to this tiered style of theater seating." He gestured at the stage. "The backdrop, or *scaenae frons*, is actually quite famous. Above are scenes – so-called metopes - depicting the feats of Hercules. Within the middle and bottom level you see niches containing sculptures, many of which are said to be modeled after the people who funded the work — junior members are portrayed as Roman soldiers of antiquity, senior members as senators and so forth. It was sculpted by Francesco Maffei."

"The arch in the center," said Vixy, frowning; "what's that behind it? It looks... I don't know – there's something weird about it; that can't be a real street, can it? Behind the stage?"

Mr. Z. appeared bemused. "That's a false perspective. Designed by Vincenzo Scamozzi. It's an art technique known as *trompe-l'œil* intended to provide the illusion of long street views. The set recedes only a few meters. The central archway is known as the *porta regia*. You see the six smaller arches on either side?"

"Yes." Vixy squinted at the stage.

"They each contain their own scenes – all intended to reproduce the streets of Thebes."

Vixy looked sideways at him.

"Greece," said Mr. Z, "not Egypt."

"That's crazy," said Vixy. She sat back and looked around with renewed interest at the ornate strangeness of the auditorium - its architectural intricacy seemed almost obsessive but when she examined the details

- the faces of the carvings, their postures, clothing and the objects some of them held, she enjoyed a sense of being transported into their world. The *porta regia* fascinated her and she stared deeply into it, surrendering to the illusion, drawn into the street as if it were indeed ancient and real, as if the stone under foot were newly laid and the buildings were filled with people. She could almost imagine the voices of the audience - their indecipherable murmuring – as those of the people of Thebes instead, going about their lives in full bloom behind the stage. "What's this place called?"

"*Teatro Olympico*," said Mr. Z. "The Olympic Theater."

"Where was it? I mean, where was it originally?"

"Vicenza, Italy. The original architect, Andrea Palladio, died before it was completed in 1585."

"It's amazing," said Vixy. "But this can't be the original. I mean, I've heard of buildings being dismantled and reassembled elsewhere -"

"It's fake," grumbled their acquaintance. He'd had his nose buried in the theater program throughout Mr. Z's exposition. "It's nothing but an elaborate reproduction. Constructed, God knows, by the T.E. at some outlandish tax-payer expense."

"Actually," said Mr. Z., "the funds came from numerous private individuals – wealthy patrons of the arts, scholars and intellectuals – in many ways akin to the Olympic Academy of 1580 that commissioned the original construction. So that this reconstruction is all we have left, sadly enough, of the original."

The man held his program even closer to his face and feigned interest at the pages. "Humph!" he said. "Patrons, indeed."

Vixy and Mr. Z. grinned discreetly at each other.

The lights dimmed and the audience hushed. A spotlight illuminated the lectern and a youngish, conservatively dressed woman in a light-gray, knee-length skirt, low shoes and pale pink blouse strode towards it. She tucked a strand of her shoulder-length hair behind her ear. She appeared earnest and self-effacing, a little knock-kneed, her narrow shoulders drawn close.

"Hello everyone. Welcome to our continuing lecture series, *The Mythology of Time*. My name is Leila Morrison and I'm the director of the program."

She'd be pretty, thought Vixy, if I did her hair and put her in slacks. Pink works, but her blouse is too blousy.

"Our guest today hails from the University of Groningen in the Netherlands and she is currently Visiting Professor of Comparativism at the University of Chicago. Her many published works have enjoyed critical acclaim and unprecedented influence within academia and to an ever larger extent, popular culture as well. Her lineage includes, of course, the twentieth century father and son sinologists and *I Ching* scholars Richard and Hellmut Wilhelm. Without further ado, then, I present Professor Hannah Wilhelm."

The auditorium filled with sturdy applause and a middle-aged woman of elegant bearing made her way across the stage, hindered slightly by the necessity of a cane, pausing to wave it at somebody she apparently recognized, her face beaming with recognition. She wore a shawl-length fringed cardigan, taupe-colored, a black turtleneck with a generous, draping collar and dark slacks that flared at the bottom over a pair of glossy clogs. She came to her place at the lectern, her face open and un-self-conscious; her dark hair flowing back from her face in dense waves. She fingered a striking, oversized choker necklace, silvery, and encrusted with emerald green stones that shimmered under the lights. The effect was of a self-possessed, somewhat imperious woman of exuberant intelligence, worldly sophistication and sincere presence.

"Thank you," she said, nodding graciously. She rested her cane against the lectern and the applause diminished. She donned a pair of reading glasses. "Thank you very much, indeed. It's been longer than I care to remember since I've enjoyed a visit to the T.E." She glanced behind her at Miss Morrison who nodded encouragingly. "In any case, I'm thrilled to be here, absolutely thrilled to discuss the mythology of time, a topic so dear to me, so perpetually relevant. It was in the year 1933, in fact, that a man named Gerardus van der Leeuw described time as a riddle; the riddle of the beginning. 'There can be no true beginning,' he suggested; 'for something has always gone before.'"[d] She grasped the lectern with both hands and addressed her notes. "'In the beginning,' he suggests, 'lies the whole past.'"

> The beginning *is* the past. Yet we say that we begin something, that we make a new beginning. And we call the long list of such beginnings, time. We live in time. We live out of the fact that we always begin anew: on awakening in the morning, at the beginning of the year, with every task we undertake, with each move from one place to another. And we do not understand this magic of the new beginning, this eternal transition from past to today, from today to past. The mysterious divide between yesterday and tomorrow, the intangible now, in which and through which we have our existence, is incomprehensible to us.[e]

She looked up. The quality of her voice and the learned ease of it seemed to have mesmerized the audience. *"Time as the riddle of the beginning. Incomprehensible to us.* At least when we're not busy taking it all entirely for granted." She smiled and an image appeared overhead.

"Consider Kali, the remarkable Hindu goddess so terrifying and beguiling. To this day worshipped by millions. Kali of the blue-black flesh and the flailing tongue; wielding a blade and a bloody, severed head; bestowing life and death at once, the embodiment of the active principle, of time itself. Black time. Why is she black or blue-black? Because she is the mother-void from which everything arises and into which everything returns.[f] Here, in this famous image by Ravi Varma, she straddles Siva, her consort; Siva the destroyer and the great ascetic, pale as a corpse; his lingam in the form of a cobra beneath her, his body prone, present yet removed, vital yet meditative. Together, they symbolize life as we know it – our experience of the ever-changing phenomenal world coupled inextricably with eternity, our sense of the play of opposites, of life and death, creation and destruction, time and timelessness."

Vixy yawned. She's got charisma, I'll give her that. And she's attractive enough for her age. Well preserved, as mom would say.

She glanced at Mr. Z. He appeared rapt, intensely focused on the Professor in the manner she'd come to know, the manner that precluded any interruption. Did he find the Professor attractive?

She watched him watching her. He sat with one leg crossed over the other despite the cramped seating, his absurd high-topped sneakers on display, his shoulders accentuated by the way he leaned on his hands. The bones in his face were strong without being heavy, his flesh lean where her father's, for example, was full. The line of his jaw, his expressive eyes and his tousled hair she found dashing. The pale scar on the bridge of his nose endearing. She'd dated a boy once with a similar mark and he'd told her it was because he'd broken his nose. He's thoughtful and sensitive and wise and kind. *Mostly* kind, anyway. When he's not being mean and indifferent. And self-absorbed. He's only alone because no woman understands him; nobody understands the intensity of his passions, the way his mind works. If it weren't for his ridiculous sneakers and that ever-present trench coat he might be irresistible. It occurred to her that he might be the most fascinating man she'd ever met.

Meanwhile, she'd been watching him fend off her silly, fawning female classmates all semester. Likewise, the T.E. cadets that seemed so bitchy and jealous when they'd learned she'd drawn him as a mentor. None of them would've understood him anyway. Not like she did.

The boys? From what she could tell they seemed impressed by his subversive enthusiasm and wit. It made all the other mentors seem stuffy and difficult.

Sometimes when he looked at her she could imagine, well.... Why was it, then, that half the time she wanted to scratch his eyes out?

"Hmph." It was their bruin-like acquaintance, dozing, making noises in his sleep - the man's eyes were closed peacefully, his chin on his chest, his hand open upon his knee and his crumpled program on the floor at his feet. She had a mind to elbow him in the ribs. If he starts snoring for Christ's sake, I'll....

✦

"What, then, is Time?" said the Professor. She waited, scanning the audience as if inviting a response. "'If no one asks of me, I know; if I wish to explain to him who asks, I know not.' It's a famous enough expression. Who can tell me who said it?"

"*Saint Augustine...*" whispered Mr. Z.

There was a pause before a few hands went up. "Saint Augustine!" exclaimed someone close to the stage. "From the *Confessions!*"

"Thank you," said the Professor. "It's an oft quoted line. But rarely do we encounter the full context of it. Which has to do with the Saint, who died at the age of seventy-five in CE 430 in the ancient Roman city of Hippo Regius in Algeria, describing or otherwise confessing, ostensibly to his God, the nature of his conversion. *Confessions* is still widely regarded, by the way, as the first Occidental autobiography ever written." She adjusted her spectacles and read aloud.

> At no time, therefore, hadst Thou not made anything, because Thou hadst made time itself. And no times are co-eternal with Thee, because Thou remainest for ever; but should these continue, they would not be times. For what is time? Who can readily and briefly explain it? Who even in thought can comprehend it, so as to utter a word about it? But what in speaking do we refer to more familiarly and knowingly than time? And certainly we understand when we speak of it; we understand also when we hear it spoken of by another. What, then, is time? If no one asks me, I know; if I wish to explain to him who asks, I know not. Yet I say boldly, that I know that if nothing passed away, there would not be past time; and if nothing were coming, there would not be future time; and if nothing were, there would not be present time. Those two times, then, past and future, how are they, when now is not the past and the future is not yet? But the present, should it always be present, and never pass into time past, verily

it should not be time, but eternity. If, therefore, time present, in order to be time at all, comes into existence only because it passes into time past, how can we say that that is in existence whose cause of being is that it shall not be? How can we say truly that time is only because it tends not to be?[g]

Ugh, thought Vixy, she's quoting obscure texts at length. As if anyone could figure out what she's talking about. She endured a twinge of guilt at her own impatience and glanced at Mr. Z. She knew better than to question his tastes. Not that she'd ever admit it to him. *Confessions*. Exactly. She took a deep breath and returned her attention to the stage.

The Professor brought her water glass to her lips. "Excuse me," she said, and paused before drinking. The audience waited. And waited. The Professor remained wordless and unnaturally still, staring as if transfixed. The water glass slipped from her hand and the audience gasped.

Vixy flinched when it shattered. She watched the Professor shut her eyes, the woman's expression pained. Vixy felt welded to her seat. The Professor fumbled for her cane with one hand and grasped at the lectern with the other.

"*Tat tvam asi...*," she said, laboring over the words, her voice hoarse.

An anxious murmur arose and the Professor swooned.

She'll fall, thought Vixy.

The audience stirred en masse and several persons, Miss Morrison among them, rushed from off stage, reaching out.

At the sight of Professor Wilhelm's difficulty, Mr. Z.'s guts twisted and he felt compelled to stand. He looked round, a vague sense of menace distorting his perspective, as if he'd slipped into a threatening dream. A man in an aisle seat suddenly stood up and just as suddenly crumpled, slumping onto the steps in a motionless heap. There came a gasp from the stage and Mr. Z., astonished, watched the Professor collapse into Miss Morrison's arms.

It was then, when the Professor fell, that the otherwise tense cohesion of the audience seemed to unravel. Some shouted, others close to the stage tried to scramble onto it, most looked wildly about, frozen in their seats or standing aghast.

A woman screamed - a keening wail - and Mr. Z. instinctively reached under his coat for his pistol, catching sight of a man high up in the aisle behind them lurching down the steps as if blind drunk, waving a Mauser-style plasma rifle. Mr. Z. elbowed his way through the audience towards the gunman, shoving people aside – "Let me through!"

The man opened fire, people screamed, cowering from the spray of bullets and Mr. Z. leapt, slamming into the gunman, the collision sending them sprawling. Stunned, gasping, the wind knocked out of him, Mr. Z. watched the rifle rattle down the aisle steps. He tried to get up and couldn't - he couldn't breathe - the pain in his chest was excruciating and he felt paralyzed, his arms and legs flailing ridiculously. Nonetheless he willed himself to move, to crawl towards the gunman who was now scrambling down the steps towards his weapon, one arm dangling uselessly. Mr. Z. dragged himself forward, gasping soundlessly, unable to regain his wind, getting nowhere, as if trapped within the clutches of a nightmare.

The audience fell away as the man regained his gun, scattering in a wild panic, all except a single brave soul near the aisle who rushed forward only to be cut down when the gunman turned and fired indiscriminately, felling several more who collapsed as they ran, bullet-bursts shattering plaster from the ornate walls beyond.

Mr. Z., his lungs on fire, straining desperately, willing himself to move, clambered to his feet just as the gunman turned upon him. Mr. Z. aimed his pistol and fired.

The gunman fell and Mr. Z. swooned, his arm ablaze, the room spinning. Then silence, no pain, he saw himself from above, sprawled

motionless upon the theater steps, the surrounding chaos reeling, everything receding... darkening....

Vixy, meanwhile, had watched the murderous scene unfold; saw the man
rise from his seat and collapse into the aisle – blood pouring from his nose
and mouth - she saw the commotion on stage when Professor Wilhelm
collapsed and she watched Mr. Z.'s spectacular leap at the oncoming gunman, watched them crash against each other and career down the aisle;
saw the gunfire, saw them fall.

"Z!" she cried, and thrust her way through the crowd, leaping down
the benches after him, people diving away from her, terrified.

"Look!" someone yelled, and Vixy whirled to see another gunman
– another one! - descending the steps of the *cavea* towards the stage. She
whirled again, something was happening on stage - a bristling knot of people struggling against each other near the lectern. No, they were struggling
against one man who was thrashing violently, kicking and flailing at the
others like a madman.

The Professor! Vixy found herself scrambling headlong down the
*cavea,* bounding down the steps, leaping across the benches, jumping over
cowering bodies and anyone adept enough to avoid her. She struggled
towards the stage, felt her energy surge when she saw the blade, saw the
man slashing and kicking and tearing at people; saw him advance towards
the Professor lying in Miss Morrison's arms, the knife held aloft, flashing.
Miss Morrison raised her arm against it, screaming; the knife came down,
the scream cut short.

When the knife raised again over the Professor's body, Vixy was upon
him, striking at his arm and tearing at his face so that he wailed, the weapon
skittering across the stage.

The attacker swung wildly, Vixy slashed at his eyes and kicked at his
groin. He stood his ground, deflecting her blows until she drove her heel
into his knee, the joint snapping like a tree branch. He crumpled, screaming,

writhing, clutching at his leg. When he didn't get up, she looked wildly about her and it was then that she saw the chaos - the entire *cavea* it seemed was a roiling mass struggling towards the exits, pinned against the walls, or cowering for protection amongst the benches.

A guard rushed towards the attacker Vixy had felled, pointing a gun at him, screaming into the man's face, "Freeze! Goddammit don't move!"

Vixy flinched at the sound of gunfire and ricochets behind her – bullets ringing against metal - armored panels had thrust themselves up from the floor at the edge of the stage, shielding the podium. A guard - 'T.E. Security' emblazoned in fluorescent letters across his jacket - leaned hard into the gap between the barricades as if between the crenellated merlons of a castle under siege, aiming his weapon - yet another armed assailant was careening down the steps! Bullets rang against the ramparts, the security guard fired once, twice, the terrorist collapsed to his knees and hurled something at the stage.

There was a blinding flash and Vixy buried her face in the crook of her arm, choking at the stinging, obfuscating fumes. There was a rumble from above and she looked up, half blinded by the smoke - a gun turret dropped into position, rotated, and fired, seemingly into the crowd. "Z! My god, Mr. Z.!"

"Get down!" She whirled - a security guard was aiming his pistol at her. "Get down!" he shouted.

Before she could even move there was gunshot, she watched the guard clutch at his chest and fall back and suddenly there was an arm around her neck, wrenching at her throat, lifting her off her feet. She kicked, flailing behind her, unable to breathe, then a blazing whiteness and nothing....

# CHAPTER 4

# THE GREAT DIVIDE (CLOSING RANKS)

"**YESSIR. SIX TERRORISTS. FIVE DEAD.** The sixth escaped, copy that. Yessir. We're en route. I'm with him now."

The voice was familiar, but Mr. Z. couldn't place it. Moreover, it was obscured by a persistent mechanical whining –was it in his head? He opened his eyes and struggled to focus. A low ceiling. I'm lying on my back. Narrow bed. Left arm. Numb. No, it aches. Bandaged. Shoulder, too. "Where am I?" he mumbled. He tried to turn his head and gasped at the pain. My God, my neck.

"Stay still, Mr. Z." A stocky, middle aged woman dressed in nurse's whites stood over him.

"Vixy...," he said. "Where...?"

"You've been injured sir, and you're to remain quiet." The nurse turned toward the countertop an arm's length away. She spoke with her back to him: "I'm Nurse Quick. Mr. Neutic and I are taking care of you on this flight."

"Flight?" Mindful of his neck, he examined his surroundings - the tiny room was crammed with equipment. He recognized Neutic standing in the doorway.

"He's awake, Mr. Neutic," said Nurse Quick. "But he's not quite himself yet, are you Mr. Z.?" She grasped his wrist, peered intently at his face then glanced at the equipment; tapping buttons, swiping at displays.

"Good morning, sir."

"Morning?"

"Yessir, Mr. Z.," said the Nurse. "It's nine thirty in the morning. His vitals are acceptable, Mr. Neutic, given the effects of the sedation."

"And his arm?"

"Hairline fracture of the humerus. Trauma to the trochlea, capitellum and glenohumeral joint."

Neutic looked flummoxed.

"His elbow and shoulder joints, sir. Besides the impact wound, a plasma bullet typically inflicts significant trauma – mostly swelling - to the surrounding connective tissue. Depending on the range and caliber of the firearm, of course." She turned to address Mr. Z. and touched him on the shoulder and elbow. "Hence, the discomfort you're feeling here and here."

"And my neck?" mumbled Mr. Z.

Nurse Quick nodded. "Your neck, your back, your ribs. It's not unusual for plasma round victims to suffer discomfort throughout their bodies, from head to toe, so to say. It all depends upon your particular physiology and body chemistry, your level of conditioning, etcetera. Trauma like this affects the entire body."

"Lucky me."

"You *are* fortunate, sir," said Nurse Quick.

"Fortunate?" said Neutic. He stepped into the room and put his hand on the edge of Mr. Z.'s bed.

"Indeed," said Nurse Quick. "Fortunate that your arm is still attached to your body. If it weren't for that unusual trench coat of yours - it's some kind of textile armor, isn't it?" She glanced back and forth between the two men. "But it's none of my business, certainly."

Mr. Z. groaned and put his hand to his head. "This grogginess...." He looked to Neutic. "What happened? Where are we going? All I remember is -" he shut his eyes and grimaced, speaking slowly. "I remember the Professor was lecturing. Some crazy gunman. Where's Vixy? And what happened to Professor Wilhelm?" He squirmed under the covers.

"There now, sir," said the nurse, her hand on his shoulder; "you mustn't exert yourself."

Mr. Z. sighed fitfully and the nurse propped him up with pillows.

"He's to remain still and rest, Mr. Neutic. To minimize the risk of complications."

"Certainly," said Neutic. "But I need a few moments in private with him, please."

Nurse Quick collected herself, straightened Mr. Z.'s blanket, fluffed his pillows and stepped out of the room, closing the door behind her.

"We're en route to Moscia, sir, to Eranos and the rooms at Casa Gabriella.[13] The Professor is doing well, she's weak but expected to recover fully."

"Is she on this plane?"

"No, sir. I actually don't know *where* she is – she's sequestered under the auspices and security protocol of the IMC. Until we get the all clear not even the TDC is privy to her whereabouts."

"Why Eranos?"

"TDC leadership recommended an off-world safe zone but Captain Chase argued for Eranos. He said you'd do better there. We arrive at Lugano Airport in three hours. Meanwhile, I should let you rest."

"No," said Mr. Z. "I want to know what happened."

Neutic looked resigned, tugged Nurse Quick's chair to Mr. Z's bedside and sat down. "Well, sir, the terrorist who shot you, the one you killed,

13 The Eranos conferences, an intellectual discussion group (*eranos,* a word of Greek origin meaning "shared feast") established by Olga Froebe-Kapteyn at her home on the shore of Lake Maggiore, near Ascona, Switzerland is dedicated to the scholarship of psychology, religion, philosophy, mythology, natural sciences and spirituality and has met annually in Switzerland since 1933. The lectures are archived as the *Eranos-Jahrbucher* and selections translated into English have been published in *Papers from the Eranos Yearbooks.*

was identified, if you can believe this, as one of four T.E. cadets – three young men and a young woman - all of whom apparently had Professor Wilhelm as their target. T.E. security gunned down two on the steps of the *cavea*. The other cadet, well, I'll get to that one. The attacker whom Miss Velure injured on the stage - a male of indeterminant race - was not a cadet but otherwise remains unidentified. According to descriptions, he was older, perhaps thirty, and he seemed to possess some level of hand-to-hand combat skills. The sixth terrorist escaped."

"Escaped?"

"Possibly via an HDT event but it hasn't been verified." Neutic squinted at his device. "Male. Plain clothes. Dark hair and olive skin. That's all we have from the witnesses." He shrugged. "Nothing shows up on video. Apparently there was a lot of smoke. Meanwhile, the T.E. is in terrorist suppression mode and the cell containing the Olympic Theater is locked down – they've intentionally collapsed its space-time signature and crime scene forensics is at work as we speak. We'll have access to their findings in real time the moment they begin transmitting. Otherwise, per the T.E.'s anti-terrorism resilience protocol, as you know, all four-hundred-thirty-two components of the facility are to remain operational as a show of force."

"What about concurrent attacks?"

"Nothing yet, sir. Galactic anti-terror scans are coming up negative - no unusual activity of any kind anywhere. The event might be isolated to the Olympic."

"There were others hurt." said Mr. Z.

"Yessir. Miss Morrison, the theater director, suffered a fractured skull and severe lacerations - she was stabbed by her assailant. She remains in critical condition; comatose, in fact. If not for Miss Morrison and Miss Velure, well, together they probably saved the Professor's life. A guard, part of T.E. security, was killed as part of the melee on stage. An audience member died of his wounds – that was the man who attempted to help you against the terrorist in the *cavea*. Do you remember that?"

"Yes. An automatic weapon."

Neutic nodded. "Twelve members of the audience suffered plasma-round wounds – their injuries range from serious to critical. Another twenty-eight members of the audience suffered minor injuries – cuts and scrapes, sprains, smoke inhalation, a broken ankle I think. Other than that, given the firepower possessed by the assailants and the number of rounds – we're lucky it wasn't a massacre."

Mr. Z. grimaced.

"I'll get the nurse, sir."

"No." Mr. Z. shook his head slowly, his voice weary. "No Nurse. The Professor. Has she given a statement?"

Neutic tapped his transponder and projected a virtual doc between them, gesturing at it. "From what she was able to communicate after she regained consciousness, she endured some sort of psionic attack which she somehow managed to deflect, or *re*flect, as she termed it. Which brings me to that first cadet, the one who was sitting in the audience. He was unarmed and died of a massive brain hemorrhage. Witnesses confirmed that his collapse coincided with that of the Professor's, but there's nothing else to connect the two events. Besides the idea that the Professor is apparently a documented psychokinetic adept of the first order - whatever that is. So that she may have killed this man in self-defense. That's the theory, at least. Killed him, somehow, with the power of her mind." Neutic looked dubious. "I don't claim to understand any of it." He pointed at something in the virtual doc. "Right here. I can't pronounce it - it's what the Professor was heard to utter before she collapsed."

"'*Tat tvam asi*'," said Mr. Z. "Sanskrit. It means *thou art that*. A phrase from the Chandogya Upanishad. Ancient Indian wisdom texts. Eighth century BCE or so."

Neutic frowned. "Sorry, sir, I have to admit I'm at a loss."

Mr. Z. spoke slowly as if for emphasis. "*You yourself are that which you seek to know.*" He sighed at the effort. "The Professor may have reflected the energy back at the attacker in a kind of automatic, psychokinetic retaliation. Which is fascinating. But go on Neutic, tell me the rest."

Neutic dismissed the virtual doc and rubbed his forehead. "I don't have anything else, sir. Just that one of the terrorists, the one Miss Velure crippled – she shattered the guy's knee and practically tore his eye out before T.E. security got to him – he managed to swallow a suicide capsule - cyanide of all things – before he could be interrogated."

"Where is Vixy, Neutic?" Mr. Z. looked hard at him. "And don't try to avoid the question. It's not like I'm going to get more rest by you not telling me."

Neutic forced a sigh. "We think she's alive."

Mr. Z. clenched his jaw, reached over and yanked the window shade up, shutting his eyes against the stabbing pain as if he deserved the punishment. When it subsided, he opened his eyes and stared at the blue sky and the steely expanse of ocean. "They've kidnapped her. They've taken her, haven't they?"

Neutic waited. "We don't know. There's no trace of her, sir. Or the man that witnesses said had her in a choke hold. She apparently collapsed and he was hauling her offstage when they said they both somehow disappeared. But no HDT ghosting. No transport residue. And no ransom or claim of responsibility. Not yet, anyway. Nothing. It doesn't make any sense."

"The coins," said Mr. Z. "There has to be...." He trailed off and tried to sit up. "This is my fault, Neutic. My fault. I never should've – oh, the poor girl!"

Neutic reached out to restrain him. "Sir."

"We've got to turn this plane around, Neutic. We've got to get back to the T.E. We need to help her."

He flailed weakly and tried to get up, then collapsed stiffly, nearly tumbling from the bed.

Neutic struggled with him. "Nurse!"

Nurse Quick rushed in and snatched a syringe from the pocket of her blouse, jamming it against Mr. Z.'s neck. Mr. Z.'s body relaxed, his head lolling as the two of them gathered him back into bed.

"His bandages look good," said Nurse Quick, looking him over keenly. She tapped at a control panel, peered at a display and smoothed her blouse. "He'll sleep now; perhaps until we land."

Neutic had been standing at the end of the bed, out of the way. He bent to peer out Mr. Z.'s window. The ocean was blue-gray, cruel looking, abutting the whitish haze of the horizon. "Part of me wishes we never had to land this plane," he murmured.

"He needs rest, sir, that's all," said Nurse Quick. "And no excitement. He needs to rest and be still and he'll make a full recovery. He's going to be okay."

Neutic nodded. "I know." He sounded tired. He regarded Mr. Z. from the doorway for a moment then turned to make his way the short distance into the main cabin, slumping into his seat. Who in hell do I think I am getting involved in all this? He took up the dossiers he'd been provided on Mr. Z. and Vixy, flipping aimlessly through the documents he'd already memorized – the meager data he'd been authorized to view. What in hell compelled me to want to come to Moscia, to help look after a man I hardly know? What makes me think I'm cut out for any of this?

*Don't think so much, Herman. Especially about outcomes and things you can't control. You'll think yourself right into a corner.* Hettie's voice. She was right. She knew him too well. Better than anyone. Better than he knew himself, it seemed. Since her murder he'd felt trapped. Paralyzed. By what? Rage. That's what the counselor had called it. But what did anyone know about it? Not even his parents could understand what it was like to lose your twin sister. He'd find whoever killed her. And then what? He sighed and rubbed his face. And now Vixy was kidnapped. What if she were tortured? Killed? Stop thinking so much, dammit. Stop speculating. Do your job. That's what the Captain would tell him. Assume Miss Velure is alive. Perform your job accordingly. Apply your energies to outsmarting, out-maneuvering, out-strategizing and otherwise out-doing the captors. A fraught drowsiness overtook him, welled up like a tide within him. He'd help Mr. Z. run the terrorists down if it was the last thing he ever did.

# CHAPTER 5

# LOST IN TIME

**THE BOAR RAISED ITS ENORMOUS HEAD,** its red-rimmed eyes wild, and thrashed its legs as if desperate to escape the roiling sea. It gnashed its teeth at the brackish, foaming waves surging across its back and sounded – a horrible, rasping roar. Vixy clutched at its spiny fur and lowered her head against the outcry and the stinging spray. I can't hold on, she thought. I'll drown.

In the distance loomed a foreboding black crag - an immense, jagged mountain of bare rock thrust against the glowering heavens, ragged storm clouds scraping its peak, the sea crashing against sheer cliffs. The storm was a fury - winds whipping, waves tossing higher as if churned by the crag itself. The boar foundered, Vixy choked and gasped at the engulfing water; she lost her hold and felt herself hauled into the depths....

She awoke to a view of a dusky plaster wall and a beam of sunlight angling onto the bare dirt floor. Otherwise, the small room was dim and dank.

"*Bon jour*, Charles." It was a man's voice, muffled and distant as if from another room.

"Yah, yah," said another man.

The sunlight made her eyes ache and she looked away. She felt awful. Nauseous. Achy. Her head pounding.

"Where in the hell...?" she moaned.

"Shush, child. You were dreaming."

A woman stood over her, her face obscured by an ornamented black veil - the nose cord glimmering; the fabric bedecked with tiny, silvery discs. Her skin was olive, her dark-lined eyes luminous, her hair black and coarse. She wore a loose, lavender-colored scarf and a deep-blue-colored robe that seemed antiquated, the fabric a course muslin. She smelled of frankincense, musky oil and sweat.

"Where am I?"

Two large clay urns rested on a rough-hewn wooden table in the corner of the room. The woman went to one, tipping its contents into a small cup. Vixy raised herself onto her elbow to watch. The woman's palms, fingertips and the soles of her feet were stained reddish-brown. I know this, thought Vixy. I've studied this. Henna.

"Drink," said the woman.

Vixy hesitated.

"It is clean water. Drink."

The woman dabbed at Vixy's forehead with a damp cloth and she relented, the water cool down her throat and tasting of minerals, as if from a well.

"You're Egyptian."

"Be still." The woman seemed anxious but her voice was breathy and soothing.

Vixy lay back, the throbbing in her head having eased a bit. "Who are you? Please. Where am I?" When she made to repeat herself, the woman pressed her fingers lightly over Vixy's mouth and shook her head, the trinkets sewn into her veil trembling. The woman rose and stepped towards the door, pausing in the threshold to glance back, her hand poised uneasily on the doorframe.

"Dammit, what is this?" Vixy forced herself to sit up. "What's going on? Where is Mr. Z.?" She sat clutching at the edge of the cot, listening hard at the murmuring somewhere beyond the doorway.

A man's voice boomed forth. "It's your own doing! You and your idiot henchmen!"

More murmuring and again, the voice. "I wanted nothing to do with the Olympic! Or your damn worthless cult! And now look! A human shield? A hostage? What of it now? What's done is done - at least I'm intelligent enough to make use of it! She's valuable if I say she is! And I'll lower my voice when I damn well please!"

The shouting was getting closer and Vixy fought the urge to flee. She watched the woman vanish from the doorway and struggled to her feet, swooning a bit. A rotund man in dusty shirtsleeves filled the doorway, his shiny face twisted into a scowl. In one of his fat fists he clutched a pipe, in the other a crumpled sheaf of paper.

He bellowed over his shoulder without looking. "Amu!"

He looked Vixy up and down, shoved the end of his pipe into his mouth and chomped on it, puffing impatiently, filling the small space with an acrid, barnyard brume. He yanked the pipe from his mouth and shouted again, "Amu!" He stepped into the room belly first, his breathing loud and labored, his chest heaving as if he had bellows for lungs. The sheen of perspiration made his face and neck appear obscenely fleshy, the dark tangle of his loosely knotted tie askew across his chest as if an afterthought. He stood with his shirt clinging to him and coughed into his elbow. "Stupid bitch."

His suit pants were dark, the cuffs dusty and his shoe tops scuffed. Otherwise, everything about his manner of dress seemed oddly anachronistic, as if he had gone to great trouble to affect an image, albeit a rumpled one, of nineteenth century Europe.

Another man, a shabby khaki blazer draped over his shoulder, slipped through the doorway and sauntered across the room, slouching against the far wall with an impatient air, affecting a detailed examination of his fingernails. He was boney and thin, but somehow heavy jointed and sinewy. Also starkly pale, hook-nosed with pink-pupillary eyes, a sloping neck and a prominent Adam's apple. He resembled a cross between a long-legged bird and a reptile instead of a man.

"*Bon jour*, Miss Velure." His voice was both incongruously sonorous, arising as it did from such a gangly frame, and despicably arch. "Welcome to exotic Cairo." He dug into his pants pocket for a cigarette case, flicked it open, shoved a cigarette into the corner of his mouth and offered the case to Vixy, his cigarette dangling as he spoke. "Charles, my fine fat fellow, is there a reason you can't spare us the crass stench of your shitty tobacco?"

Cairo? Vixy's mind raced. She tried to focus on piecing together what had happened. The T.E. Yes. The lecture. The Professor had dropped her glass and collapsed. Mr. Z. and the gunman. I was fighting. The chaos on stage. The arm around my throat. She grasped absently at her neck.

"Please, my dear woman," said the thin man, wagging the cigarette case at her; "I assure you they're at least palatable. And I'm sure you could use one."

"Shut up, Laron," said the fat man.

Laron looked pained, gestured with the case again and Vixy reached out. He obliged her and struck a match.

She leaned towards the flame, her eyes darting between both men. The woman with the veil appeared just outside the doorway. "I want to know what in hell is going on."

Charles examined his pocket watch and coughed indifferently into his handkerchief. "The year is 1881. You are in Cairo, Egypt. And we are your captors."

Vixy felt the blood drain from her face and she swooned.

The woman with the veil rushed into the room and grabbed Vixy's arm. "Sit."

"No." Vixy steadied herself, waving her away.

"I see you're still feeling poorly, Miss Velure," said Charles.

It struck her that she was without her handbag and she instinctively glanced about.

"Oh, and we have both your pistol and your transponder," said Charles. He stuffed his watch into his pants pocket and coughed again. His tone was cruelly singsong. "There is no escape. Nowhere for you to go. You are beholden to us. The sooner you accept -"

"You're lying," said Vixy. "Who in hell are you?"

Laron rubbed his face as if pained by the exchange and slid towards the door.

Charles barked at him. "Laron!"

Laron affected a limp-handed salute and nevertheless left the room.

Charles shouted after him. "You have a caravan to organize before morning! It will be your own neck this time if you fail to assuage the leadership! Do you hear me?"

"Amu!" said Charles, redirecting his irritation at the woman. He scratched his belly then attempted to relight his pipe, puffing at it and talking at the same time. "Drum up proper clothing for her. Something to get us to the Plateau without looking like a spectacle. Do you hear, woman?"

Amu nodded.

"Plateau?" said Vixy.

Charles shook his head at her and puffed. "Your fretting will avail you nothing, Miss Velure. You are trapped here as surely as the day is long. As such, you go where we go. To the Giza Plateau, to the planet mars, should I so choose. Meanwhile, I am Charles Bruggs of Vienna. I am a scholar, archaeologist, curator and expert in Egyptian antiquities, employed under Mr. Flinders Petrie – I am director of his excavations within the Western Cemetery." He puffed his pipe, which had once again gone out, coughed and checked his watch.

Vixy glared at him.

Bruggs chuckled. "That's right, my dear. You are, as they say in America, getting the picture?"

Vixy made to smoke but her hand was shaking. For Christ's sake keep it together, she thought. What would Mr. Z. do? All she could think was that she hated this asshole. "What picture is that?" she snapped. "That you kidnap college students? This is absurd. What do you want with me?" She was loathe to reveal anything about her connection to the TDC. But the damn transponder - what would they make of it? She stepped to the window and peered out. The view was of a shabby stone wall, a sliver of blue sky and a narrow, cobbled street. There was a whiff of manure. And dust. Dust everywhere. If this is really Cairo, she thought, and 1881 at that, then God help me. Where are you, Mr. Z.? What's happened to us? To me? To everyone?

"By the way," said Bruggs. "We might just as well have killed you to save us the trouble. And we may yet, Miss Velure, should you prove too burdensome." He waddled towards the door, his voice cold and flat. "You will accompany us to the Giza Plateau. You may be of some use. Regardless, we have no need to restrain you. To bother to imprison you. Where would you go and what would you do, after all? You must stay with us and do what we tell you. No one knows where you are. No one knows *when* you are." He huffed at her. "Run away, attempt to escape and you will escape into nothing. You are lost to everyone and everything, Miss Velure. Lost in time."

# CHAPTER 6

# An Instrument
# of Power

**THE PLANE CLEARED THE MOUNTAINS** and dropped. Mr. Z.'s stomach lurched and he winced, clutching at the bed rail as the plane pitched and rolled - the approach to the Lugano airstrip, he knew, was severe and technically challenging; an angle of descent more than twice the worldwide standard. Vixy would love this, he thought, but only if she were the pilot.

He'd only just caught his breath when the plane touched down with a jolt, braking hard into the short runway. He groaned, relieved beyond words for the smoothness of tarmac and their gentle taxiing towards the hanger.

Nurse Quick hurried into the room, breathless. "Lord, what a landing! How did you do, Mr. Z.?" She unbuckled his lap belt and inspected him with her usual scrupulousness, checking his bandages, peering into his face and monitoring the displays. "I swear that pilot of ours is a madman - I was praying like a sinner!"

"If you don't mind me asking, Nurse Quick, how did you come to be assigned to this flight?"

"I volunteered." She was busy unfolding a wheelchair she'd hauled from under the bed. "Frankly, sir, I'm not much for travel, but it pays better than anything on the ground."

Mr. Z. frowned at the wheelchair.

"Doctor's orders, Mr. Z."

Neutic appeared in the doorway. "Doctor's orders for what?"

"This chair, Mr. Neutic - you're just in time to help me get him into this thing."

Mr. Z. scrambled into the taxi, relieved to be free of the wheelchair. He felt out of sorts and strangely fragile; a shadow of himself. It didn't help being carted around like an invalid, pampered and coddled while Vixy languished somewhere, lost and alone. Neutic piled into the back seat next to him and slammed the door.

"It's forty-five minutes to Eranos, sir. Is that correct, Nick?"

"Yessir." Nick put the car in gear and they pulled away, turning gingerly onto a service road.

Mr. Z. watched the airport control tower disappear behind the shoulder of the mountain behind them and felt a pang of nostalgia. Or was it foreboding? It was awful, this queer state of unhealth he was in – he couldn't trust his own reactions to anything. "Two years," he murmured.

"Two years, sir?" said Neutic. He noticed Nick glancing back at them in the rearview.

"Two years this past summer," said Nick. "Since Mr. Z. was here last."

"You're right," said Mr. Z. "I'm sorry, Nick - how have you been?"

"Not at all, sir, you're not yourself, that's all. I've been fine, just fine. Good to see you."

"Speaking of which, sir," said Neutic, "there's a medical technician on call. Near enough to Eranos, I suppose. In Ascona, I think?" He glanced at the map screen.

Mr. Z. nodded.

"You'll have everything you need."

"What I need is to get some work done." He immediately regretted the sharpness of his tone. "Don't mind me, Neutic. I'm sure you've already discovered what a lousy patient I am."

Neutic's device chirped and he tapped at it. "They've identified the attackers." He handed the device to Mr. Z.

"These are photos of T.E. cadets."

"Yessir. Four of the six terrorists were identified as employees of the T.E. Not imposters as we'd assumed. All of them first-year cadets, as it happens."

Mr. Z. frowned at the images.

"Each cadet had been assigned to a separate T.E. training cell," Neutic continued. "Preliminary investigations haven't identified any connection between them, workplace or otherwise. Anyway, conspiracy in that regard has been ruled out. If they were being organized and directed by anyone, it's a mystery at this point. They had disparate backgrounds, obviously no questionable histories or affiliations or they wouldn't have been accepted into the program. And the background checks have all been re-verified as legitimate. Also, the results of the autopsies were negative in terms of biochemical or physiological anomalies – no drugs, no biotronic or physiotronic implants."

Mr. Z. handed Neutic his device.

"There's more," said Neutic. "Much of the attack was captured on video, at least until the feed was scrambled, and preliminary analysis notes the clumsiness of the attackers' movements - their stiff, almost mechanical affectations." Neutic scratched his forehead. "Captain Chase has speculated the cadets were under some kind of hypnosis or mind control; perhaps a psionic influence."

"You sound skeptical," said Mr. Z. "That's usually the Captain's job." He managed a weak grin. "That he even volunteered such an idea goes to show perhaps how desperate we are."

Neutic looked thoughtful. "Skeptical. I suppose I am." He looked ahead, out the windshield. "I just don't have any sense of... what do you call it, psi-work? Psionics?"

"Psionics, that's right. It amounts to the discipline of applying engineering principles – practical science – to the study of the paranormal. It's not an ancient field, but it's certainly old. Twentieth century is when the idea originated. But even with all the advancements, all the documented results, it's not like it's ever been required reading for any engineering students or scientists." He shrugged. "But I can tell you, it's worth looking into, not least of all from the Captain's perspective. There's a fine database at Eranos, in fact – some exclusive research. Anyway, we can't rule anything out."

Neutic nodded.

Mr. Z. regarded him intently. He was familiar with gratuitous responses when he discussed psi, but there was something convincing about the way Neutic listened; the way his skepticism seemed to fuel rather than diminish his interest in things. "So, let's think through this from the beginning. Multiple terrorists. Perhaps under psi influence. Regardless, the nature of the attack implies organization, a centralized motivation, perhaps a mastermind. What about terrorism itself? Terrorist are distinguished by their ideology – nationalist, fundamentalist, what have you - which in turn determines their choice of targets. They justify their violence by blaming it upon their enemies, as if the victims brought it upon themselves."

"Well," said Neutic, "the attack seemed aimed at the Professor. And she describes herself as an apolitical scholar."

"Sometimes the targets are symbols," suggested Mr. Z. "Which of course begs the question as to what the Professor symbolizes. And to whom? Symbols, after all, like ideologies, can be culturally dependent."

Neutic tapped his device. "Officially her dossier reads like someone with no time for anything but writing, teaching and lecturing. She endorses no ideology, at least publicly. She sells quite a few books but she's not in the news. No evidence of activism, no polemical slant to her views.

She's described as... let's see -" he scanned the text. "Here it is. Somebody from Stanford University described her as" – he affected a declarative tone – 'intolerant of intolerance.' Could she be a symbol of that?"

"Tolerance? Hmm. Well, certainly an uncompromising affirmation of tolerance has throughout history inspired no end of its opposite."

"Right," replied Neutic. "I mean, there's always some crackpot or charismatic cult leader - some psychopath who manages to corral a group of malcontents, or create one around a skewed vision of reality, isn't there? And militarize them?"

Mr. Z. nodded. "Indeed, Neutic, one can never rule out zealotry. But let's focus on the facts. We have the theme of the lecture series at the Olympic: *The Mythology of Time*. Some twenty or so presentations, intentionally cross-disciplinary, with speakers from academia but also business, politics, science and the arts. It's akin to the kind of thing that takes place here at Eranos, in fact. Anyway, why the Professor? Up until now none of the presenters have incited even a hint of violent opposition – no demonstrations, no special interest groups; no protestors trying to block whomever from doing their thing."

"Let alone an assassination attempt," said Neutic. "If that's what it was."

"Oh, I think that it was. Yes, indeed. Was it clumsy and ultimately a failure? If it was a failure then it was barely one. What if it was in fact a demonstration of cutting-edge sophistication? Let's face it, the Professor is alive, thank heaven, but by a hair's breadth. And we're sitting here at a loss to explain the technology or anything else about it."

"Sophistication?" said Neutic. "It sounded as if it were more like chaos to me, at least from the description."

"I understand. But chaos, if nothing else, happens to be one of the goals of terrorism – to utilize chaos to generate fear. Fear in the moment and fear of the future - of what might be coming next. But I think you'd agree that penetrating T.E. security defenses, to say nothing of possibly infiltrating the minds and bodies of T.E. cadets, indicates a deep sophistication, a deeply ordered chaos, if you will."

"The Professor's topic," said Neutic. "'The Mythology of Time.'" He shook his head. "Maybe that was irrelevant? I mean, it's scholarly. I don't know, I'm just having trouble with the symbolism, with the motive, with what these terrorists intended by targeting the Professor."

"No, you're good to pick at that, at the Professor's topic. It's a fact and we have to assume it has value, that it matters. Look here, Neutic. In antiquity, time was perhaps the only subject that couldn't be politicized because it couldn't be manipulated. It was egalitarian. What about now? Since the advent of hyper-dimensional travel, time has become an instrument of power."

"But these cadets-in-training, if they were somehow brainwashed or under some exterior influence of some type – psi or what have you; if they were merely pawns, then -?"

"Then, who was controlling them, exactly. The coins, Neutic." Mr. Z. clenched his fist. "I can't help thinking they've something to do with this."

"And therefore the Mothmen are involved?"

"I know it sounds crazy." Mr. Z. shrugged. "It sounds crazy to me, too. There are holes in my argument. But that's only because...." He shook his head as if to dismiss the idea.

"The Mothmen," said Neutic. "I tried reading up on them, which wasn't easy. You're right about them being mysterious and occult – there's virtually nothing about them in any of the databases. But I managed to dig something up; something I should've mentioned at the debriefing."

"Why didn't you?"

"I guess I was waiting for you to do it." Neutic seemed reluctant to continue, staring at his hands for a moment before looking Mr. Z. square in the face. "They're rumored to be assassins. In fact, not just rumored. But you know this."

"I do."

Neutic sat stiffly, tapping his foot on the floorboard, his jaw set.

"But there's something else, isn't there? Out with it, Neutic. What else did you read?"

"Your name, sir. But you know that too, I suppose."

Mr. Z. nodded.

"And that there was some investigation, some controversy involving... I can't say for certain." Neutic sat back and looked out the window at the passing landscape. "Just because you read something somewhere, as they say, it doesn't mean...." He trailed off.

"Yes, Neutic. Me and the Mothmen. There's a backstory, for what it's worth. You probably found the report itself still sealed. But there was an investigation. And a controversy, of sorts. None of which matters to me." He regarded Neutic patiently for a time. "The Mothmen, I'm convinced, are indeed assassins. Or *have* been. No matter what you may have read to the contrary."

Neutic seemed to brighten, as if Mr. Z. having been forthcoming meant the world to him.

"I have my reasons, Neutic. But all of this is just between you and me, for now, okay?"

Neutic nodded. "It's not unreasonable, then, to assume a psionic attack could've been initiated from anywhere, correct? Including from the Mothmen realm? And the motive would have something to do with Time."

Mr. Z. slapped his thigh. "Exactly. And what if those coins were a test? - an adept testing his skills, proving himself, even performing a rite of passage from adolescence to adulthood, from initiate to master? A herald. Who's to say? We're dealing in conundrums, unfortunately. The coins were an occult, hidden thing, for example, weren't they? Whereas the attack on the Professor was flagrant. And it's significant that there's been no claim of responsibility."

"And then there's Miss Velure's abduction."

Mr. Z. looked rueful. "It goes without saying that Vixy's kidnapping doesn't make a damn bit of sense – even her being a cadet-in-training - none of it fits with the logic of the event. Unless she was just in the wrong place at the wrong time. Which I swear, Neutic, would be the greatest tragedy of all."

They sat in silence for a time, looking absently out the windows.

When Mr. Z. spoke up, he sounded weary. "Nevertheless, if the coins and the attack turn out to be unrelated events I'll eat my hat, as they say. You know, Neutic, if there's anything I've learned about crime, to say nothing of time crimes, it's that the perpetrators often don't consider it so. They don't consider their actions to be a crime, that is. *Mens rea* - guilty mind – they don't possess it. Just as often they've convinced themselves they're righting wrongs rather than committing them."

Neutic's tone was wry. "Righteousness."

Mr. Z. shrugged. "Wars have been waged."

"What about Miss Velure, sir? If she were just in the wrong place at the wrong time, I don't know; it seems to me the terrorists, if all they needed was a shield or a hostage to escape, they could've grabbed anyone on that stage."

The taxi slowed, winding its way around a tight curve. When the road straightened, the hills had fallen away to reveal a grand vista with Lake Maggiore shimmering in the foreground, nestled like a sapphire amidst the lush green of the sloping alpine uplands, the trees seemingly poised to tip themselves into the water's edge. Beyond, majestic in the distant haze, lay the indomitable Alps. A gate loomed ahead and the taxi slowed.

"I assume we've got a debriefing scheduled with the Captain?" said Mr. Z.

"Seven AM."

"We also need to speak with Professor Wilhelm independently of the T.E.'s investigation, Neutic; see if you can convince the Captain to grant us access to her if only via telecom. And it goes without saying that we need to remain vigilant regarding any attempt at communication by the terrorists, unorthodox or otherwise."

"Unorthodox?"

"To your earlier point: if the terrorists didn't already know the value of Vixy – if they don't know exactly who -- or for that matter what – she is, they're nevertheless bound to assume, simply by her presence at the Professor's lecture that she's a significant capture. If they *do* know that she's a TD cadet, then by unorthodox communication I mean whomever we're dealing with may try to step up their game and present clues – lures – to test Vixy's value regarding the larger fish they may indeed be attempting to catch."

The vehicle came to a stop before a clutch of formidable impact pylons beyond which was an equally substantial steel gate secured with crash cables. It was an incongruous interruption to the otherwise bucolic surroundings and they waited impatiently for the inevitable security laser-web to pass over the vehicle and scan the interior. Finally, an androgynous voice - synthetic speech - crackled over the telecom of the taxi: "Welcome to Eranos, gentlemen. Please proceed. Enjoy your stay."

# CHAPTER 7

# SHARED FEAST

**MR. Z. OPENED HIS EYES** and blinked at the brilliance of the afternoon sun dancing on the lake. A temperate breeze sifted through the trees and brushed his face. Birds twittered. The serenity was like a drug. He was drifting off again when a knock at the door disturbed him. *Maybe I dreamed it.* More knocking. He filled his lungs, straining against the stiffness in his arm and shoulder. He stretched and struggled to his feet, shuffled towards the door. Again the knocking. "I'm coming!" The security scan indicator was green and he tapped the display, peering at the image of a fresh-faced valet bearing an earthenware crock on a tray. "I didn't order room service."

"No, sir. I'm sorry to disturb you. Lunch is served in the dining room. Your meeting begins there in one hour." He offered the tray. "Meanwhile, a hot washcloth."

Mr. Z. opened the door and stepped aside, gesturing for the young man to enter.

The valet swept in, set the crock down, slipped the tray under his arm and turned to leave.

"Pardon me," said Mr. Z, "but you look familiar."

"Yessir. I'm Nick II." He grinned.

"That's it. Nick's son. Nick the driver."

"Yep. I mean, yessir." He nodded awkwardly, appearing suddenly self-conscious.

"Indeed," said Mr. Z. "Let me see, you must be thirteen or so by now?"

"Fourteen this past Wednesday, sir."

Mr. Z. nodded. "Well you've grown quite a bit since we've last seen each other. Do you remember me?"

"Yessir, I think so. That is, I remember you drove an old ground car. You showed photos to me and my dad."

"That's right. Boring old photos of a boring old car."

Nick smiled, shaking his head. "No, sir, not boring. I like old things."

"Ancient things, too? There's no shortage of them here, is there? Including some of the people, am I right?"

Nick seemed eager, his eyes wide, then immediately doubtful, as if perhaps he misunderstood. When he answered he seemed to have remembered he was a valet again, straightening his shoulders and speaking with an adult severity. "I'm interested mostly in anything to do with dragons right now."

Mr. Z. responded with all seriousness. "That's a fine thing to study. Powerful imagery, indeed. You probably know there are dragons of the Orient and dragons of the Occident – East and West, as they say. Do you have a preference?"

"Oh, I prefer the Orient. Or sometimes the Occi -" Nick stammered a bit. "Well, sometimes I prefer... both, really. As long as the story is good."

"You know one of my favorite stories about a dragon is that of old King Beowulf. Have you heard that one?"

Nick shook his head.

"Let me see." He turned to peck at the data console. "Where's Neutic when you need him?" he mumbled. "Here!" He read aloud in a theatrical tone, all the while eyeing Nick's response.

First the monster's breath, fuming hot, broke forth; the earth resounded; and the warrior, strong of heart, swung up his battle-shield for what was destined. The dragon coiled and came: at first slowly moving, then hastening, until, smitten by the sword, he cast forth a deadly fire and the blade gave up its strength. Again the two became engaged.

And it was then that a young shield-warrior, Wiglaf, perceiving his lord hard laboring, moving into the slaughter-reek, bore his helmet to his lord's side. But his shield immediately melted, and the spoiler of people, with bitter fangs, took Beowulf's whole throat, whose blood gushed forth in waves. Wiglaf struck the dragon's neck; his sword sank in, the fire failed: the old king drew from his burnie a dagger, and those two together cut the worm in two.[h]

Mr. Z. stopped as abruptly as he had begun, savoring the ring of the action perhaps as much as the boy.

Nick, for his part, seemed rapt. He stood blinking at Mr. Z, his cheeks flushed.

"I see you're listed here in the Eranos directory." Mr. Z. swiped and tapped at the display. "I'm sending you that story, Nick, the whole thing. You read it and let me know what you think." He glanced at his crock. "Meanwhile, it's time I took advantage of that hot towel and got myself downstairs to lunch."

"Yessir." Nick seemed a little beside himself, as if he didn't know whether to stay or go.

Mr. Z. gestured towards the door. "There you go, then, Nick, thank you. When I see you next, remember, you'll tell me what you think of old King Beowulf and Wiglaf and the dragon."

❁

The steaming towel was a pleasure – Mr. Z. stood over the sink and held it to his face, inhaling the moist, citrusy, cleansing heat. Refreshed, he changed from his bathrobe into a pair of khakis and struggled to get his bandaged arm into a collared white dress shirt before he realized he couldn't button it. He rummaged through his dresser drawers and discovered he'd been provided with several loose-fitting, stretchy pullovers. He guided the shirtsleeve over his bandaged arm, shoved his good arm through the other sleeve and managed to scramble his way into the rest of it, irritated by the effort. He stood in front of the full-length mirror. "It'll have to do." When he realized he couldn't don his vest coat and therefore had no place for his pipe, he lost all patience. "Damn it all!" He crammed his pipe and tobacco pouch into his pants pockets and hurried out the door.

The cafeteria, such as it was, rather resembled a comfortably proportioned dining room in a fine restaurant. Except he was the only one in it. A low fire crackled in the fireplace as if to ward of the chill from the surrounding woods. Mr. Z. made his way to the far side of the room, peering beyond the large, glass paneled doors that opened onto the terrace. The sun shone in the trees, the blue sky was bright, there was another fine view of the lake and there, exactly where it had always been, was the famous Eranos "round table" where score upon score of renowned scholars had sat elbow to elbow to over the centuries, chewing over their ideas along with their lunch and perhaps a few drinks.

"Good afternoon, Mr. Z."

Neutic, entered the room in a pair of trim tweed trousers, shirt and necktie and close-fitting blue cashmere cardigan. His shoes were short-topped boots, so-called Chelsea style.

"Likewise, Neutic." He took a seat at a table in the center of the room and gestured for Neutic to do the same. "I must say, you're a man with a legitimate talent for wardrobe."

"Thank you. A fine room isn't it, sir? And this tableware...." He held up a fork, examining the pattern on the handle. "It's as if everything in this place is bestowed with runes or symbology. This looks *rune-ish*, at least to me." He shrugged.

"Celtic, I'd say," said Mr. Z. "And it certainly isn't every day that one enjoys flatware of British sterling silver." He turned over his own fork. "See here? The *lion passant*."

"Passant?"

"A hallmark indicating sterling silver at ninety-five percent or so." He was peering intently at the fork. "Yes. A '*lion passant*' is a lion walking in profile, with the right forepaw raised. This happens to be a *lion passant guardant*, a lion walking but guarding; with its face towards us. Otherwise known as a 'Lion of England.'"

Neutic smiled, amused. "I never would've guessed."

"Hallmarks and heraldry are interesting in their own right. It's all fascinating symbology. But I apologize, Neutic – it's the surroundings; all the fantastic imagery and antiquities. I get carried away."

Neutic looked around. "It never occurred to me we'd be the only ones eating. It seems like we're the only ones in the whole place."

"It's the off-season. When the *Tagungen* aren't in session it can be very quiet."

The kitchen doors swung open and a stalwart, matronly woman swept towards them bearing a heavy a platter.

"Good afternoon, gentlemen," she said, a little breathlessly. She set two steaming casseroles between them and stepped back, dabbing her chin absently with the back of her wrist. Her face was flushed. She smiled, her eyebrows high and expressive, her cheeks full, smile lines accentuating her piercing blue eyes. She smoothed her apron round her ample hips. "Älplermagronen and stewed apples. These are Swiss dishes. Älplermagronen is a gratin with russet potatoes, macaroni, cheese, cream and onions." She surveyed the table and a grave frown flashed across her face, her hand fluttering like a bird wing as she spoke. "*Mamma mia!* The wine!"

"No, we're fine," said Mr. Z.

She dismissed him with a wave. "A Pinot Grigio, dry, with beautiful minerality. Perfect."

"That sounds excellent," said Mr. Z., "but we've a meeting immediately following lunch."

"Small glasses," she declared, and turned to hurry towards the kitchen.

They'd tucked into their meals, mouths full, when she returned with the wine and a pitcher of ice water. She seemed pleased to watch them enjoy the food. "I am Rosa De Cosmos, by the way. My husband and my son - Nick and Nick II - we all work here."

Mr. Z. washed down his food down with a sip of wine and nodded. "Nick II has grown up a lot since the last time I was here. Handsome fellows. I ought to have noticed the family resemblance. And the accent."

Rosa smiled proudly and rubbed her hands together. "*Gratzi*. Yes, I've only been the cook here since last year but Nick and Nick – I call them that – they told me you've visited Eranos before." She waved her hands impatiently. "But I'm talking too much – enjoy!" She hurried back to the kitchen.

"Nice food," said Neutic. "Nice lady."

Mr. Z. smiled and sipped his wine.

"And these wine glasses," said Neutic. "I need to get some of these. I've broken every stemmed glass I've ever owned."

"Bistro style," said Mr. Z., nodding as he chewed. He dabbed his mouth with his napkin and scooped more food onto his plate, offering to refill Neutic's. "More?"

Neutic nodded.

"It's fantastic, isn't it," Mr. Z. remarked, glancing about. "How this place manages to capture the finer things in both a high and low manner, you might say?" He gestured at a broadfaced wooden mask mounted over the fireplace, its reddened lips pursed into a near perfect circle, its deep-set, widened eyes staring dramatically, the colors rubbed away from its nose, high cheeks and chin, exposing a rich patina.

"He looks as if he's either singing or blowing smoke," said Neutic.

Mr. Z. glanced over his shoulder at the piece. "It's a she, actually. Tsonoqua, the giantess. Kwakwaka'wakw culture. Northwest Coast Indian."

"Hmm." Neutic frowned at it as he chewed.

Mr. Z. held up a forkful of potatoes. "But you sound like Vixy." He spoke with his mouth full. "I swear she said the same thing when she saw it. Androgyny, after all, and for that matter the concepts of third and fourth gender, are well represented in many mythologies – it's a *very* interesting subject." He washed his food down with a sip of wine. "Anyway, Vixy, who as you may know from her file, is part Haida. I think it may have been the first class of mine she'd taken – two years ago, now? I don't recall. I know it was before we'd begun considering her for the TDC. And I remember she was showing an interest in Northwest Coast indigenous culture. I showed a picture of this mask in class one day, without any context - I like to study student's intuitive responses to mythological imagery. Vixy instantly recognized it as Northwest Coast. She didn't know it was Kwakwaka'wakw specifically, of course, but she impressed me nonetheless. She's got an eye for things. And, of course, her father is a carver."

"What kind of wood is it?"

"Cedar. Indigenous to the region."

"So, is she singing, sir, or blowing smoke, or what?" Neutic tipped his head at the mask.

"Tsonoqua? She's calling. She roams the forest calling 'Ho..., Ho...'" – he mimicked the mask's expression – "searching for children to carry away in the basket on her back."

Neutic took a bite of food. "That's pretty eerie."

"Yes, well, children, of course, love that kind of thing – ghosts and spooks and all that. But you just said it, 'eerie.' What's eerie about it?" He finished his wine, all the while eyeing Neutic. "I mean – and I like to ask this of anyone having a significant experience from an image - what's your sense of it? What does the idea of Tsonoqua skulking through the forest, calling her call, do to you?"

Neutic squirmed a bit and smiled faintly. "I don't know."

"That's okay. You've just encountered an affecting image, no more and no less. My suggestion for just such an experience as you're having – I have it too, believe me – is to allow it to work on you. That's all." He pushed his plate away, tried to fold his napkin with one hand, abandoned the idea with a frown and tossed it onto the table. "What we're discussing is a major component of what I study. I call it the psychology of mythology. It's the experience of the affecting image. It's primal. I tell you, Neutic, I come here, surrounded by all this mythological substance and I'm inspired to finish all the manuscripts I've started and begin the ones I ought to begin. The scholarly resources...." He trailed off, shaking his head, gesturing at the whole of the room.

Rosa appeared, smiling at their empty plates. "You enjoyed it?" She cleared the table.

"*Si, grazie mille,*" replied Mr. Z. "Delicious."

"On the quiet days, during off season like this, when there are no big conferences scheduled, I can serve, as you might say, the bistro style. When there are many guests we sometimes cater the meals from Ascona. But it is, if I may say so, not as good - not from the *heart*."

"Will you be cooking dinner?" asked Mr. Z.

"No. Just bread - my own bread, mind you. With nice butter, cheese, salami and fruit. It saves on the preparation and the cleaning, you know. And your meetings, they so often run late, well past dinner time, into the night."

Captain Chase's voice crackled from Neutic's transponder as if on cue. "Neutic, do you copy?"

"Yessir."

"What about Mr. Z.?"

"Yessir, I'm here."

Rosa discreetly finished clearing the table and returned to the kitchen.

"All right, then," the Captain continued. "Let me remind everyone that this communication is being encrypted under seventh-generation Perfect Forward Secrecy technology which requires random toggling of the transponder signal. So we might have to endure some temporary disconnects. Meanwhile, Mr. Z., I trust you're recovering?"

"Yessir, much improved, thank you. How are the Professor and Miss Morrison?"

"The Professor is likewise doing well. She's on the line with us, in fact. Miss Morrison, however, remains in critical condition."

A pause ensued as the events at the Olympic flooded back. Neutic tapped his device and holographic images of Captain Chase and Professor Wilhelm appeared, hovering above the tabletop.

"Miss Morrison, that dear woman," said the Professor. "It's terrible. I'm told she helped saved my life. I'm sorry, gentlemen, good afternoon to you both. Mr. Z., is it? And Mr. Neutic?"

The two men nodded.

"It all sounds horrible from what the Captain has told me. People killed and injured. I understand that you, yourself, Mr. Z., encountered a terrorist firsthand. That you put yourself in harm's way and that you were quite seriously injured."

"Not at all, Professor, I was very fortunate."

"The Captain informs me also that one of your cadets, a young woman has been kidnapped – presumed kidnapped - by this faction, or terrorist group, or whomever they are. It's simply awful. And I'm ashamed to say I don't understand any of it."

"You're no worse off than we are, Professor," said the Captain. "Which is why I'm glad you've agreed to be here, to participate in this debriefing, because frankly, we need all the help we can get." He appeared to be concentrating on something off camera. "I'm looking at the live feed. The report identifies only standard issue plasma shell casings. The Olympic Theater was turned inside out – every scrap of physical evidence was analyzed, including DNA residue. HDT ghosting analysis somehow failed, however – something about an obfuscation concussion event, it says here - I don't know what that means except that we're not looking at anything useful. No worthwhile evidence. These terrorists – the kidnappers – they've not only eluded us but as incredible as it sounds, they have left virtually no trace. Moreover, according to this latest report the cadets – the ones that functioned as terrorists in the attack - appeared to have key access to the T.E. armory. That's incredible on its own. Let's see, what else...?" He continued scanning his documents.

"Captain," said Mr. Z., "has anything been made of the terrorist's odd affectations? The cadet terrorists, that is? According to Neutic they all seemed strangely uncoordinated, as if they were intoxicated or drugged." He winked at Neutic expectantly. "You suggested they were perhaps under some sort of hypnosis or mind control?"

"Yes. And that's only because of what the Professor had told me – she's the expert. What's it called, psionics? The neurological research supporting the idea notwithstanding, it sounds to me like something out of a corny sci-fi novel. With all due respect, Professor."

"Skepticism comes with the territory, as they say, Captain. I don't take offense."

"Nevertheless," said Mr. Z., "it sounds to me that we've little or nothing else to go on."

"There are still no claims of responsibility, Captain?" asked Neutic.

"None. No ransom on behalf of Vixy; no communication of any sort regarding a motivation for the attempt on the Professor's life."

"What about the IMC, Captain?" said Mr. Z.

"What about them?"

"They're self-policed," Mr. Z. continued, "and the attack on the Professor is ostensibly an attack against one of their own. Are they undertaking an independent investigation?"

"Well," said the Captain, "there's an issue, let's put it that way. A political issue, in so many words. The PMC has enormous resources, as all of you know; including a military peacekeeping component. What they don't have is experience in investigating time crime. Nevertheless, they've a keen interest in the investigation. As such, they've placed a liaison at our disposal – his name is Mircea Ganesh and I expect we'll be tapping his expertise soon enough. Meanwhile, I'm happy to take advantage of the Professor's help this afternoon. At least as long as she feels up to it."

"I'll do my best, Captain, thank you."

"Now," said the Captain, "let me begin by stating that background checks on the Professor's associates - students, colleagues, publishers, critics – anyone with a professional connection to her, past and present, have come up clean. That allows us to put all our resources into the terrorist angle."

"Professor," said Mr. Z., "psionics, as you know, is a very broad term. It includes, correct me if I'm wrong, everything from telepathy and telekinesis to so-called extended mind and active externalism, and so on. What leads you to believe this attack had a psionic component?"

"Excuse me, sir," said Neutic, "I'm sorry. Actually, I apologize to everyone here. I'm not familiar with extended cognition nor active external-ism and, I must admit, I'm not even clear on the definition of psionics or psychokinesis or telekinesis. You're talking about parapsychology, telepathy, things like that?"

Mr. Z. made to respond but the Professor interceded. "Indeed, Mr. Neutic. Thank you for your candor; it provides me an opportunity to make certain we are all working from a similar understanding. In short, psion-ics – all of its so-called psi-studies subfields aside for the moment because each justifies perhaps a life's work - is concerned with the idea of physical systems being influenced through a distance by mental activity. Scientific justification for this idea hinges on, in my opinion, the fact that matter and energy are interchangeable. Assuming thought is a form of energy, then, logically, it follows that matter and thought are likewise interchangeable."

"I might only add," said Mr. Z., "that the etymology of the term speaks exactly to the Professor's point, combining as it does the ideas of *psi* – psy-che, and *onics* – as in 'electronics' but more aptly interpreted as *machine*. So that psionics can also be interpreted as *engineering applied to the mind*."

"Very apt, Mr. Z.," said the Professor, "very apt, indeed." She adjusted her spectacles and peered carefully at Mr. Z. as if taking his measure. "And, as I enjoy pointing out to some of my stuffier academic colleagues it was the early science fiction writers, of all people, who coined that phrase."

"Engineering applied to the mind, you mean?"

"Yes, Captain."

He scratched his head. "Well, that brings me to the assault itself, Professor. We've only been told second hand, by the medical personnel, that you've been struggling to recall anything about it. Is that still the case?"

"Yes, Captain, I'm sorry to admit that it is. I was anticipating that your report, your description of the events, would jog my memory; that I'd be capable of adding something significant to this discussion, but..., well, I don't know."

"Pardon me, Professor," said Mr. Z., "and please, I'm not intending to be difficult, nor particularly skeptical - psychic trauma, of course, as you well know, tends to impact short-term and long-term memory. I'm merely compelled by the urgency of our predicament – that of our missing cadet - to press the issue. Are you certain you've no sense of anything significant, any sense of foreshadowing, perhaps, or imagery or sounds – a scrap of something, something fleeting, even before you entered the building or perhaps soon after you awoke? You regained consciousness in the ambulance on the way to the hospital, correct?"

"That's what I'm told. But I must say, I don't quite recall anything until, I don't know, perhaps later, in the clinic."

"Don't strain yourself, Professor," said the Captain; "you're under no obligation to -"

"No, no, it's quite alright. I'd rather try to put my mind to the test a little. Hmm." She closed her eyes. "Yes. When I was coming to in the ambulance. There *was* something." She opened her eyes and reached for a stylus, scribbling something into her communication console.

They all peered at the image but it was Mr. Z. who seemed taken aback. "Why... why, that's a -"

"Hexagram," said the Professor. "I don't know why it's only now coming to me."

"Do you recall which one?" said Mr. Z.

"I'm sorry," said the Professor. "It's often assumed, since I'm related to Richard and Hellmut Wilhelm, that I'm equally adept in all things *I Ching*, so to say. Alas, I'd have to reference the text like anyone else. And I'm as skeptical of oracles as anyone, by the way. I dare say, I've never once been compelled to cast one."

"Would you mind if we tried to bring this up, to identify it here?" He glanced at Neutic who was already typing. "I'm sure Neutic could fairly quickly...."

"Certainly," said the Professor. "Absolutely."

"Neutic," said Mr. Z., "the Wilhelm-Baynes translation -"

"Bollingen Series," said Neutic, "I remember."

"Well done." He sat back, watching Neutic work. "And no doubt a hardcopy of it exists here within the Eranos library."

"A first edition, in fact," said the Professor. "Inscribed by Richard Wilhelm himself – a gift of our family estate."

Neutic tapped his device. "Hexagram forty. *Deliverance.* I won't try to pronounce the, what is it, Chinese?"

"Romanized Chinese," said the Professor. "*Hsieh.*" The Professor enunciated the word precisely. "But that's astonishing...."

"How so, Professor?" said the Captain.

"Well, it's been longer than I'd like to admit since I spent time with these things, with hexagrams and the text of the *I Ching*, but I recall that Hellmut Wilhelm delivered a lecture at Eranos of all places and it was published as part of a compilation. Anyway, in the transcript he mentions this same hexagram; something about a remark in the - what is it? – the so-called Great Treatise, or something or other. Something to do with so-called *timely action*, I think. Mr. Neutic?"

Neutic tapped the entry key with authority. "*Man and Time: Papers from the Eranos Yearbooks.* That's the title of the collection. Edited by Joseph Campbell. The Hellmut piece is entitled, 'The Concept of Time in the Book of Changes.' Yes, the hexagram is discussed here." Neutic projected an image of the page and the Professor immediately began reading a section aloud:

The text runs: "The prince shoots at a hawk on a high wall. He kills it. Everything serves to further." On this archetype of the supreme and ultimate deliverance the Great Treatise remarks: "The superior man contains the means in his own person. He bides his time and then acts." Here the superior man must await the exact time in which alone the act of deliverance can be effected. "Too early" or "too late" will deflect the arrow from its target.[i]

There was a pause.

"Well," said Mr. Z.; "That's certainly, how should I say -?"

"Spooky," said Neutic. He flushed. "Sorry."

"No," said the Professor. "It *is* spooky. And ironic."

"I was going to say prophetic," said Mr. Z.

"But it's just like horoscopes or Ouija boards, isn't it?" said the Captain. "They're only spooky because they *seem* prophetic. Until we recognize that any perceived insight into our own lives is really a generality, a commonsense type of wisdom that applies to anyone, anywhere, at any time."

"Indeed," said Mr. Z. "But the image, the symbology, if you will, of a hawk is quite specific, isn't it? Professor, does the hawk mean anything to you?"

She shook her head.

"What about this?" volunteered Neutic. He'd been typing again, peering at his display. "Here is another Hellmut Wilhelm reference, *I Ching* related, where he speaks to this business of the hawk." He projected the text:

In China the hawk is not considered a noble bird. It is an inferior creature, which draws its strength from the flesh and blood of other birds. Here an inferior person, having reached a high position, is the real obstacle, and his removal by the hand of one who is dedicated leads the deliverance to the goal.[j]

No one seemed prepared to comment and Mr. Z. rose stiffly from his chair. He stood grasping his injured elbow. "It's a tricky thing, I think, to attempt to tease apart a metaphor – one risks blunting its impact by way of attempting to literalize or concretize it. To say nothing of trying to apply it to the Professor's vision of the hexagram. And visions are tricky, too. What's the source of the Professor's vision, of the image? Memory or fantasy? In this case, we have to assume it's her memory. We can argue that she's making it up and get nowhere. Likewise, we can argue that memory is unreliable and get nowhere. Or, we can assume her vision has value as a legitimate experience and acknowledge the connections that seem apt, that seem to be clues, and go from there. Memories, visions, even dreams – I would say they so often seem spurious only when we don't understand the context. In the context of the attack at the Olympic, then, the image of the hexagram that arose in the Professor's consciousness is a clue. And clues are something left behind either intentionally or unintentionally. The coins in my cruiser were clues. Symbols, too, but they were more or less intended to be found. But this hexagram of the Professor's? Unintentional."

"How so, Z?" The Captain frowned. "How can you be sure? If we're playing around with the idea of mind control and psionics, well, why couldn't the image of the hexagram have been planted in the Professor's mind. To mislead her? To mislead us?"

"Forgive me, Professor, but you were not expected to survive the attack, that's clear enough. Let alone retain knowledge of this 'hexagramatic' key, this clue, of sorts. Whomever is responsible for this attempt on your life simply underestimated your own psionic abilities and psychological resilience."

"Deliverance, then," said Neutic. "The metaphor of the hawk - of the Professor *as* the hawk. What does it mean? What kind of clue is it?"

"Well, that the hawk in China is considered ignoble runs exactly counter to our Western interpretation. It's not an idea that the Professor, being a westerner, would naturally possess. Am I right, Professor?"

"Indeed."

"So, on top of the fact that the Professor, as I said, was not intended to survive the attack, we have an image that could not have been intended to survive either. Neither the Professor nor anyone else without an intuitive understanding of the Chinese context - barring the type of research you just accomplished, Neutic - could have been expected to properly interpret the metaphor."

"Then what was the purpose of the image?" said the Captain. "If not to communicate an Oriental metaphor to the Professor, then what? Maybe I missed something, but I'm still back at Neutic's question when he asked what kind of clue it is."

"I think, Captain," said the Professor, "that when you said 'Oriental,' you may have just revealed something of the answer. Which is to say, it reminds us that just because we believe the *I Ching* and its hexagrams are of Chinese origin, doesn't mean other Oriental-style cultures don't adhere to it or haven't in some way appropriated it or even developed aspects of it independently. This in itself constitutes an interesting idea within comparative mythology – all the arguments surrounding cultural diffusion versus independent innovation, syncretism, acculturation, convergence, etcetera. Moreover, who's to say the so-called wisdom tradition expressed within the *I Ching* – its Confucian and Daoist aspects – is not only antecedent to the text but antecedent to the Chinese culture itself?"

"Antecedent, indeed," said Mr. Z. "And perhaps off-world."

"Like the Mothmen, sir?"

"That's right, Neutic. Exactly."

The Captain frowned and rubbed his head.

Mr. Z. watched him. "And when the Captain mentioned communication, I think he revealed the other essential aspect of this clue. That perhaps hexagram forty constitutes an internal communiqué between Mothmen elders, such as they may be, or with a Mothman initiate. In metaphorical or symbolic terms. So that the hexagram may constitute a galvanizing, inspiring, motivating symbol behind whatever it is that's transpiring. Again, and I realize the Professor isn't privy to our conversation about the Mothmen at the T.E., what if they're suffering some kind of exceptional duress, some kind of cultural fatigue or perceived decline that would inspire them to reach out?"

"You mean *lash* out, don't you?"

"Yessir – certainly the violence at the Olympic speaks for itself. But to my point, a perceived decline, it could be argued, is a perceived threat. What if Mothmen mythology has become schizoid? History shows us how often this happens, how a troubled or disintegrating culture tends to look to the past, romanticizing itself in terms of a golden age and projecting or attributing the destruction of that paradisal period onto one's perceived enemies – blaming them, as it were. The future, in this sense, becomes the past. The future *is* the past. And symbols are all important. I'm suggesting that if the Professor is not herself a threat, then what she represents, what she symbolizes, may be. In a word, the Professor is indeed the hawk. And she intercepted, in spite of herself, a hexagram, a communication, a clue and a symbol of a Mothman initiative."

"Mothmen." said the Captain. "Z, we've yet to address the outstanding fact that for a Mothman initiate to have managed to arrive on Earth it would've required an HDT event. And we've no evidence for that. These connections you're trying to make - if it's evidence then it's circumstantial at best. What does the Professor symbolize that would motivate anyone, the Mothmen or whomever, to make an attempt on her life?"

"Well," said Mr. Z., "I think the connection, part of it at least, is another hexagram. You recall that I examined the coins inside the quarantine cell. Well, I cast an oracle of my own." Mr. Z. withdrew a slip of paper from his pocket and held it before the group. "This is the hexagram I generated."

He glanced at Neutic who was already typing. "Hexagram twenty-six – The Taming Power of the Great."

"*Ta Ch'u*," said the Professor.

Mr. Z. had begun pacing around the room, chewing on the mouthpiece of his empty pipe. "Hmm." He stopped short and aimed his pipe at Neutic. "Neutic, unless I'm utterly out of my depth, there's a reference to this exact hexagram in Hellmut Wilhelm's Eranos paper, the very same paper we just referenced. The Taming Power of the Great – is it there?"

"Yessir."

We have mentioned a number of cases in which time was basic to or formative of the situation of the hexagram as a whole or played a part in one of its stages. In all these situations time is one element among many. But among the sixty-four hexagrams there is one which, according to the "Miscellaneous Notes on the Hexagrams," rests entirely on time. This is hexagram 26, *Ta Ch'u*, The Taming Power of the Great:

The archetypal situation from which this sign starts is the taming of the domestic animals, the ox and the pig – that is, the herd animal and the animal of the lower individualism, which wallows in its own muck. Untamed, both animals signify a danger to life and limb; tamed, they are extremely useful and indispensable aids in the building of material civilization. The ox draws the plow and pulls the loads, the pig fertilizes the fields and serves for food.

The danger presented by these animals running around untamed is clearly expressed in the first three strong lines of the sign. Awareness of the danger (fear) is so great as to encourage "armed defense." However, despite all their masculine power it is not given to any of the three yang-lines to exorcise the danger and tame the animals. They find it advantageous to stand aside, they even fall into situations of helplessness (the axletrees are taken from the wagon) or prefer to seek an escape. It is the two yin-lines in the fourth and fifth place that accomplish the task of taming. The way in which they do this varies. To take his wildness from the bull is relatively easy. In this situation one acts even before the wildness appears. A headboard attached to the young bull keeps his horns from growing dangerously. With the boar a stronger kind of intervention is necessary. Gelding deprives the boar of his savagery (that is, his nature is changed). Both operations are wholly successful solely because of their timeliness, and thus make room for nine at the top, the way of heaven, the time when again "truth works in the great."[k]

Mr. Z. had been pacing around the room but at the conclusion of Neutic's recitation, when the room fell silent except for the quiet crackling of the hearth fire, a profound exhaustion seemed to overtake him and he returned heavily to his seat, shifting his injured arm gingerly in his sling.

The Captain rubbed his eyes. "Setting aside hawks, oxen and pigs, the symbolism of which is lost on me, all I'm picking up on is the idea of timing. That the Professor, because of her status as an influential scholar interested in the study of time or maybe just that her distant relatives studied the *I Ching*, is regarded as somehow ignoble. And that she's a threat of a magnitude that demands her assassination. But that the timing failed – the Professor survived the psionic attack and then survived the back-up plan with the plasma rifles and the knife and all that. The hawk was not killed. Because somebody or a group of somebodies screwed up the timing. And you're convinced that it's the Mothmen who are screwing up the timing because whomever it is has an affinity for communicating in hexagrams, in arcane *I Ching* wisdom. Do I have it about right?" He flashed an ironic glance at everyone. "It's all very interesting in what – an academic sense? I'm no academic. Perhaps there's something to all this intertwined, mysterious, I don't know, mystical chicanery or espionage or whatever it is on behalf of the Mothmen or whomever. Perhaps it connects to those bronze coins in Mr. Z.'s glovebox. I mean, I see the Oriental factoids or data pointing to a culture like that of the Mothmen. I get that there may be something to that logic. But for the life of me I don't know how to proceed with this stuff. Mothmen. If they or whomever plan to try again against the Professor, to improve their goddamn timing and get the job done, then what steps do we take to protect her short of keeping her in perpetual quarantine?"

"And Miss Velure, too," said Neutic flatly. "What steps do we take?"

Silence.

"That's right, Neutic," said the Captain. "It's about the Professor and Vixy, both. To say nothing of the games – terrorist games - that are apparently being played with the T.E. and their security forces." The Captain breathed a heavy sigh, regarding all of them in turn. "Look. We're all working hard at this. We all want to get to the bottom of it. I'm just wondering now how deep and wide this predicament goes. Mr. Z., you're my best detective. But in your condition I don't expect you to be at your best. Least of all capable of behaving as a soothteller. I'm looking at you slumped there in your chair with that arm of yours and it's clear you need rest. You and the Professor both need rest. I don't know. I'm afraid we may need some additional help to come at this from a different angle. A more practical one."

"Soothsayers, Captain," said the Professor.

"Pardon?"

"'Soothsayers,' not 'soothtellers,' is the word you were intending. And soothsayers, along with prophets and clairvoyants and oracles, are indeed seers - those capable, seemingly, of being prescient; of seeing into the future."

"I'm not trying to be intentionally obscure, Captain. Your implication is apt. I'm just reminding myself that any new idea, if it possesses any amount of insight, endures a certain species, so to say, of silence. I swear I've never published anything, for example, that hasn't encountered it. What I'm saying is that I find Mr. Z.'s intuitions about the Mothmen compelling. Hence, I'm compelled to remain involved with your investigation. I can't admit to needing a rest - it seems that's all I've been doing since the attack and at a certain point rest itself becomes a burden. But I can admit to needing time; time to acquaint myself with Mr. Z.'s themes, with his... syncretic ideas, such as they are."

"Fair enough, Professor. I'm not here to turn away help. Consider yourself unofficially deputized. We'll try this again the day after tomorrow, same time, twelve-hundred thirty hours. Your takeaway, Professor, if I can be so bold, is to familiarize yourself a little with the nature of the Time Detective Contingent – our capabilities and our limits, if you will, so that you can perhaps get an intuition as to where to best apply your, well, your own intuition. I'll forward you some information on the TDC that you're not going to find in the media or the databases. Also, it occurs to me that you ought to know something more about Vixy – I'll forward her bio in whatever detail our human resources folks will allow. Otherwise, we'll end this session here. Does anyone have any questions? No? Mr. Z. and Neutic, stay on frequency – I've some further business with both of you. Otherwise, Professor, thank you, I'm scrambling your feed in five, four, three, two, one...."

The image of the Professor flickered and disappeared.

"Gentlemen," began the Captain. "Frankly, despite the worthwhile speculation, I don't see a way forward at the moment; towards identifying Vixy's kidnappers, that is, and how they may or may not be connected to the attack on the Professor. There's too much noise. As much as I'm averse to making our case in any way public and as skeptical as I am regarding any connection to the Mothmen, I'm compelled to enlist the assistance of the T.E.'s Diplomacy Division to initiate a formal inquiry into their goings on. The Mothmen, that is. If the T.E., the PMC and the TDC working together can't manage to find a way to establish formal communication with them, to crack their obfuscation veil, then I don't know what. But we've got to take some practical, on the ground action. Any questions? Mr. Z., be advised that you are still under official quarantine at Eranos until you're deemed medically fit. No breaking cover. I've assigned Neutic as your attaché indefinitely. Meanwhile, I expect you to recuperate until our next debriefing. I repeat: neither of you are to break cover. You are tourist scholars, if anybody asks, doing research at Eranos and that's all you're doing. Goddammit, don't make me regret that I cloistered you at Eranos despite its less-than-top-flight security status. Anyway, anything else from either of you?"

"No, sir," said Mr. Z.

"Okay," said the Captain, "signing off in five, four, three, two, one...."

*"If the form of heaven is contemplated, the changes of time can be discovered. If the forms of men are contemplated, one can shape the world."*[1]

# CHAPTER 8

# MASTERS OF REALITY

**"WHERE AND WHEN IS FIVE?"**

Cog bristled at the General's impatience but stifled himself, retreating into the straightforwardness of the facts. "Encamped beside the Red Pyramid. Month two. Day two. Year 1881 in the Gregorian calendar."

"Did you say the Red Pyramid?"

The General glared at him and Cog felt his brow dampen.

"That's in Dahshur. His coordinate was Giza." The General seemed to swell with accumulated impatience. "Giza is preeminent. What happened?" He gestured fitfully at the stereographic projection model hovering over his desk.

Here it comes, thought Cog, and waited.

"Dammit, Cog!" The General thwacked his hand on the desktop. "Mind the Meridians!" He thwacked again. "Pay attention to the parallels!" Another thwack. "Heed the hyper-meridians! M.P.H." – thwack, thwack, thwack as he annunciated each letter. "It's a mantra any moleman learns before he's old enough to hold a knife and fork! And it's a mantra because it's a mandate! Explain to me how it's suddenly become optional!"

Cog blinked, his cheeks flushed and his guts churned. "Sir. Five reports damage to his equipment suffered within the R40 worm hole – a three-sphere warp has been detected and we're still engineering a reconcili-ation. Meanwhile, the parallax forced him to emerge at Dahshur."

The General squeezed his eyes shut and spread his gauntleted hands flat upon the surface of his desk, inhaling deeply as if to steady himself. He opened his eyes and spoke with his teeth clenched. "This mission will be the death of me, Cog. Isn't it enough that we've been shackled with this so-called alliance with the Mothmen? Must we also contribute our own technical lapses?" He shoved himself away from his desk and stood up. "Confirm for me, at least, that Logistics has patched the glyph in the hypersphere – I don't care how much activity we've undertaken with King Snefru - operations personnel should have anticipated the risk of coordi-nate bleed in that region of space-time and its impact on this mission. The finger is going to get pointed right where it belongs this time, Cog, mark my words – we've too much at stake."

"It's fixed, sir. And at least we've got Five on the ground."
"Yes, Cog." The General looked askance at him. "Five has arrived. Indeed. Things could be worse. Much worse." He grasped his temple. "Meanwhile, please tell me his signal is reliable?"

"Yessir." Cog glanced at his display. "He's been transmitting effective-ly since nineteen-hundred hours."

"Equipment status? – any more requisitions will be an embarrass-ment, you know that."

"He's made the necessary repairs."
"Well enough, then. Such resourcefulness will be required from all of us in this phase." The General began packing his briefcase. "What else before I'm off to the debriefing?"

"Regarding SnoGlobeCon, sir," said Cog; "well, the word is out that the assassination attempt on Professor Wilhelm was indeed just that – an *attempt*. That she's still alive is not doing anything for public relations, so to say. And now we've indications that the Time Guard has initiated an investigation."

The General appeared nonplussed and made for the door, his briefcase tucked under his arm, pausing to adjust his tie. He addressed Cog without looking at him. "The so-called Time Guard. And they've probably enlisted the pesky Time Detective Contingent. They can all be bothersome enough in their ultimately insignificant way, but we're the *engineers* in this universe, Cog. We're the masters of reality and that error we made on behalf of the Z individual -"

"*Mister* Z.," interrupted Cog.

The General rolled his eyes, his tone mocking. "*Mister Z.* An earthling of all things making inroads into our operations. In spite of himself, if you ask me. Nevertheless, we're not going to allow such an oversight regarding espionage again, are we Cog? We've re-engineered that possibility out of statistical relevance, have we not? I'm asking you, Cog - have we not?"

"Without a doubt, sir. Absolutely." He was careful to sound matter of fact. "One more thing, sir," Cog continued, consulting his notes and following the General into the hallway. "The Bruggs caravan appears to be on schedule for Giza, but Five's transmission indicated something about a hostage they've apparently burdened themselves with. Perhaps it's fallout from the bungling at the Olympic Theater."

"Insignificant details, Cog. We're interested in Bruggs's artifacts, not the messes he makes for himself." He marched down the hallway a few paces then turned to level his gaze at Cog. "In other words, Bruggs's problems are not *our* problems. If he fails to perform, you know what to do."

Latitude: twenty-nine point eight, zero, two, four, one, zero, zero. Longitude: thirty-one point two, one, two, three, zero, zero, zero. Dahshur, Egypt, planet Earth. Sunday, November ninth, 1881, Gregorian calendar. Sunrise: zero, six-twenty ante meridiem. Sunrise heading: one-hundred nine degrees east southeast. Fifteen degrees Celsius. Weather: fair.

The data helped keep his mind off the pain. That, and watching the sun finally begin to illuminate the desert. The training simulations hadn't quite done justice to the alien bleakness of this place. And the novelty of last night's quarter moon had worn off almost immediately – such a pale, ghostly little satellite - its penetrating silvery light a torment to try to sleep by. *I thought I'd like this place.* Five brushed sand from his face, brushed it from his arms, found himself brushing it from the front of his uniform and sighed, realizing he was practically covered in the stuff. Better get used to it.

The sun, by contrast to the pitiful moon, was large even by galactic standards - a yellow dwarf, a G-type main-sequence star in Earth parlance. Nonetheless, ugly. Ostentatious. But at least it provided an abiding, not entirely un-attractive radiation spectrum.

He bit his lip, concentrating on guiding the needle into his flesh and out the other side of the wound, wincing as he tightened the last suture. *Damned if I'm going to get much use out of this hand for a while.* The gash was messy, ragged, but should heal if he kept it clean. *I made it here regardless,* he told himself. *Alive.* He'd been lucky, almost puncturing his event horizon, and if he hadn't passed out he may have indeed overcorrect-ed and eliminated himself, vanishing into elsewhere. It wouldn't have been the first time a scout made that mistake and was killed.

"Man up, son. Let's get to work," he said aloud, affecting his father's uncomplicated tone. The words pained him. Dad would've done better in the wormhole. Despite the parallax glitch he'd have made it work - he would've at least emerged at Giza like he was supposed to.

He dug through his pack for an FSR[14] and was glad to discover his book, *The Hero with a Thousand Faces*, for which he'd perhaps foolishly risked just about everything. He'd had to surrender a day's ration because of the weight and then bribe the D.T.[15] to look the other way – it had end-ed up costing him more than a day's wages to smuggle the thing through pre-transport inspection. But he was glad to have it. He held the book in

---

[14]  Common military parlance for "First Strike Ration;" a high-calorie, reduced-weight version of the so-called MRE: "Meal, Ready-to-Eat."

[15]  Departure Technician: the individual who inspects and clears the belongings of each departing and returning 4-sphere traveling moleman.

both hands, staring at the cover as if he were drawing strength from it. He flopped it open to where he'd slipped the old screen-print of his father on expedition and began reading:

> The boon was bestowed. In a cavern chamber, deep within the womb of the mountain, King Muchukunda retired to sleep, and there slumbered through the revolving eons. Individuals, peoples, civilizations, world ages, came into being out of the void and dropped back into it again, while the old king, in his state of subconscious bliss, endured.[m]

He chomped into his energy matrix and brushed the stray crumbs from the book's pages. Reading it – he could open it to any page - never failed to restore him. Moreover, that this book was written here, on this planet, filled him with a sense of destiny; of having arrived, somehow, or returned, he didn't know what, exactly. To be sure, his mission was officially altruistic; engineered to reengineer the cosmos for the benefit of everyone; every race within the cosmos would benefit despite their backwards ways. But that's not what had kept him going through all the agonizing training, all the months of tedious preparation. He hefted his book. It was more than a book. So it wasn't that strange when he found himself talking to it. "*We made it.*"

"We're not a chosen people, Five," his father had told him; "We're beyond the mythologies and the beings who propagate them merely because we've worked hard. Turn your talents into strengths through deliberate practice and you can attain the truth, that's all. And the truth is nothing but the facts. We've earned our authority as the superior race, son. But remember, superior talent bears the burden of superior effort. The so-called Way? Well, any moleman engineer worth his salt knows it's all about the Will. *Make* the way. *Create* it. *Engineer* it. The Will is the way."

The familiar anxiety assailed him – his pained sense of both soaring and sinking. I love those words. I love my father. Why, then, do I have an intuition of something else, something other? Why aren't I welded to the same sense of heritage and vocation as my father? Why do I read banned books? Why do I contemplate off-planet ideas and try to write about them? In secret? He grabbed a handful of earth and tossed it aside, wiped his hand clean on his thigh and plucked the image of his father from between the pages of his book, staring at it like he'd done countless times before.

"Your father is the best there is at what he does," his mother would tell him; "but that's not to say there aren't other things to do in life that matter." Despite her wholesome intentions he always felt patronized, somehow demoralized, whenever she told him that, seeing as it was usually following one of his failures – after he'd bungled another engineering exam, for instance; or botched some field test or some project or other. His father made being a Moleman engineer seem not merely easy and exciting but heroic. *There he is.* The image showed his father in his prime, famously working the pyramid field of Giza soon after its completion. *He was the same age then as I am now.* The success of the mission had transformed his father into a household name, bestowed promotions and fame upon him and had likewise transformed their lives – they'd become well-off as a family. Influential, some said. "Your father is a legend." He'd heard it so often growing up that for a long time he'd disregarded its meaning. But now he found himself aspiring to the same.

He forced himself to breathe deeply, doing his best to ignore the odd, arid taint to the atmosphere – somehow he'd never considered that Earth would smell any different than Mega City One. Meanwhile, the pale light of dawn had finally given way to the immensity of the sunrise. He felt the heat penetrating his flesh, the warm breeze on his face and the ground beneath him, struck by the sense of having finally arrived upon his adventure. "You were right, dad," he whispered. He closed his book and stowed it. Checked his stitches. He'd staunched the bleeding. "There really is nothing like hyper-dimensional travel to make a moleman feel alive."

He hadn't gotten to his feet when the chime of his transponder startled him – he'd forgotten to mute the damn alert. The words scrolled across the display: "Status? Do you copy?" He fumbled to key in his data - his hand throbbing. DEPLOYING: GIZA. 40KM. UPDATE @ 16:00. He gulped down the rest of his ration, slurped his energy gel, stowed the debris and slipped his bad hand gingerly into his glove. He hefted his pack and crawled from his hovel, careful to backfill the depression. He brushed himself off, tightened the straps of his pack, doubled checked his coordinates and moved out in cloak mode, his trek lenses dimming as he stepped away from the pyramid and into the full sun of the vast, featureless desert.

# CHAPTER 9

# ZIZO & AMU

**"WHY DO WE LIVE IN CAIRO?"** said the boy. He tugged at Amu's robe.

"Zizo, I'm busy; you can see I'm making dinner; why can't you play with your toys?"

"*Why*, Amu? Why can't I live in Big Ben with papa?"

"Your father lives in *London*, Zizo, not Big Ben. You know what Big Ben is. Big Ben is a big clock in a very tall tower; like the towers here in Cairo."

The boy stomped his feet, petulant.

"You don't want to live here? With your mother and me? Cairo is where you were born; it's your home. You don't like it?" Amu patted her hands on a towel, turned away from her preparations and looked down. Zizo was still clutching her robes. "Dinner is almost finished. If you promise to be quiet and behave I'll tell you a story. And you can have a *fatereeh*. Do you promise to listen?" She lifted the boy onto a chair and handed him his pastry, his eyes wide as she spooned a glistening dollop of honey over his treat. She turned to her work. "I'll tell you the story of how the city of Cairo came to be." She periodically glanced at him over her shoulder.

Zizo squirmed in his chair and wagged his head back and forth, chomping, his mouth and fingers covered in honey and bits of pastry.

"Once upon a time, a long time ago, before Cairo came to be, there was a great and terrible famine in Egypt. Do you know what a famine is, Zizo?"

Zizo spoke with his mouth full. "No!"

"When there's no food for anyone to eat. No *fatereeh*, no *dukkha*, no bread. That is a famine. People are hungry all the time. Can you imagine that?"

"I feel hungry all the time." The boy affected a devilish grin.

Amu ignored him. "As I was saying, there was a great and terrible famine. People were starving and terribly unhappy. Then a sickness came. Many, many people died. No one knew what to do and everyone was afraid. Then a man came from the desert, a famous general. He rode a white horse. He was in charge of thousands of soldiers who followed behind him; some marching, some riding horses like him, some even riding chariots."

"Why?" said Zizo. He sat smacking his lips.

"Because," said Amu. "They just came. To find new lands. That's what generals and their armies do. They came from the Western Desert far beyond the pyramids." She paused to take his plate away and wipe his face and fingers. "The general's name was Jawhar and when he saw how everyone was hungry and sick and suffering and unhappy – how they were dying - he decided to help them. He ordered a new city to be built where the people were living – a new, rich city to replace the poor one that was there. He promised they would have plenty of food and no sickness and everyone would be happy again. He decided to make the city in the shape of a square and to make each side two kilometers long. The general and his men marked out the distance with long ropes stretched taut."

"What's a kilometer?"

"A very great distance for little boys. You'll have to be much older than you are now to walk two kilometers on your own."

Zizo shrugged. "I can walk all the way to the market."

"That's fine. Meanwhile, you'll learn about kilometers in school. It's a long way for people to walk but not long for a general on a horse. Or chariots. And neither for thousands of soldiers, who are used to marching great distances. Now, listen to what happened.

"The general asked the astrologers, who were also starving and sick and unhappy, to look at the night sky – to look at the stars and the planets for an omen to tell him when it would be best to start building the city. The time has to be right according to the stars and the planets to begin digging the foundations for a new city, Zizo. The astrologers did as they were told – they waited for the night and looked hard at the sky. And, as always, the stars and the planets provided an omen and told them what to do. They ran to inform the General and his men. Now everybody knew when to start the work. But to make sure nobody made a mistake; to make sure nobody started too early or too late, the General made sure bells were hung on the ropes. He would shake the ropes and ring the bells when the time had come to start building the city."

Zizo's attention was flagging and with a great flourish, Amu spread her arms wide apart, wiggling her hands and making her eyes wide. "And then something *strange* happened...." She continued in the most grave and mysterious voice she could muster: "After the bells were hung, along came a raven – an enormous, black raven." She flapped her arms and cawed and the boy giggled. "It landed on one of the ropes and made the bells ring. What do you think happened next?"

Zizo stared at her.

"Well, the soldiers heard the bells and thought, by mistake, that it was time to begin building the city! It *wasn't* time to begin. It was just that the raven had landed on the rope and made the bells ring. But it was too late to stop things. 'Oh no!' cried the astrologers. 'Oh no!' cried the General. They were all so worried. 'Astrologers!' cried the General, 'wait for the night sky and look at the stars and the planets to see what can be done!' Again the astrologers did what they were told - they waited for the night sky and looked up. 'Look! Look!'" Amu pointed excitedly over Zizo's head. "'Over there!' they said. 'It's an omen!'"

The boy stared wide-eyed at her.

"Do you know what they saw, Zizo? Do you know what the astrologers were looking at?"

Zizo blinked and barely shook his head.

"You know what it is, Zizo. Think hard. Here's a clue: what's the brightest thing in the night sky?"

"The moon!"

"Not this time."

"A star!"

"No. It wasn't the moon and it wasn't a star. This time something bright was in the sky that could only be seen once every *fifteen* years! That's a long time, isn't it? That's almost three times as old as you!" Amu herself seemed pleased to have managed to hold the boy's attention. That, and she enjoyed a certain enthusiastic pride in her acting skills. She paused for effect, her hands by her sides, regarding the boy as if she were finished. She noticed the boy's half-eaten pastry and set his plate aside. She knelt in front of him, taking his little hands in hers, speaking softly.

"The astrologers told the General what they had seen; that they'd seen the brightest thing in the night sky for the first time in a very long time – for the first time in fifteen years. We've seen the planet *Al Najm Al Qahir*,[16] General! It's the brightest thing in the night sky in fifteen years! We're convinced it is an omen!' And do you know what the General did?"

Amu stood up and Zizo put his hands on his head.

"General Jawhar considered the words of the astrologers very carefully. And he looked at the work the soldiers had already done. He was convinced the omen was telling him to finish building the city but to name it on behalf of *Al Najm Al Qahir*. That would guarantee that everything would turn out well and everyone would have enough to eat and be healthy and happy. 'Al Qahirah!' shouted the General. 'We shall call the city *Al Qahirah!*'"

Zizo's eyelids were drooping and he teetered as if about to tumble off his chair. Amu picked him up and carried him to bed. "And that, Zizo," she whispered, watching him sleep, "is how the city of Cairo came to be."

---

[16] *Al Najm Al Qahir* is Arabic for the planet Mars.

# CHAPTER 10

# THE PYRAMIDS ROAD

**VIXY CLENCHED HER FISTS** and squirmed in her seat. "I want to walk." She ground her teeth at the absurdity of the barefoot donkey-boy and the jarring and clattering of their ridiculous wooden-wheeled cart. She grasped Amu's arm, imploring her with her eyes – "Amu, can't I at least get out and walk? And this blasted veil!" - she made to tear it from her face but Amu squeezed her hand.

"I beg you," said Amu under her breath. She glanced about fretfully. "We must ride in the city. To not be noticed. If they find out you have been discovered as a foreigner -"

Vixy relented, repulsed by the cart, by her ugly clothes, by the dusty, congested streets. She wanted to scream. The *niqab* over her face irritated her almost as much as the awkwardness of the cart ride. And the robe and head scarf she'd been forced to change into this morning at the *hammam*, that horrible public bath Amu had taken her to? Buckets to wash in and no privacy? - it was awful. It was all so preposterous, so ludicrous. If she was indeed a prisoner, a captive, she'd just as soon behave as one instead of complying with the charade of a disguise. Leave no trace – the hell with it.

She felt insignificant, trapped, torn away from everything and everyone she knew. Waves of panic swept through her. Keep it together, she thought; don't lose it. *Think.* What would Mr. Z. do? He would *think of something.*

Their cart trundled along, the boy guiding his donkey carefully through the bustling activity of vendors hawking their wares; of passers-by, people coming and going and the tumultuous hurly-burly Vixy had already, in less than two days, come to associate with this strange place. Cairo. *Eighteen eighty-one.* Again her panic assailed her and again she beat it back; the sense of loss and fear, the overwhelming disorientation - it made her want to die on the spot. Damn it all. Damn it all to hell - she wanted to cry and scream and run. But where? Where could she go? That fat bastard Bruggs was right. She *was* lost. Lost in time.

She felt Amu's hand pressing on her arm and clutched at it, tears burning her eyes. If not for this mysterious woman, she'd have gone crazy already. She'd wanted so badly to time-travel, to be a time detective; to complete her studies and become an archaeological anthropologist; to go on great adventures and accomplish great deeds; to go everywhere and see and do everything, to live as big and bright and beautiful a life as her heart would allow. She had so much left to *do.* This can't be happening. Marooned. Captive. Beholden to a pair of thugs.

She thought of her parents, of what it would do to them; what they'd be suffering when they knew she was gone. How in hell would anyone ever find her? No transponder. No way to send a signal. She squeezed her eyes shut, holding back the tears. God help me. She'd never prayed. Who was she praying to? The cosmos. Whatever god would help her.

The noise and dust and hustle and bustle faded as they approached the outskirts of the city. They passed the last of the low buildings and the street disappeared, unfolding without ceremony into the quietude of the open desert. The desert both frightened and comforted her – too vast, too remote but also free; free of the city's strangeness and filth; free of foreign tongues and the oppression of her captors. She scanned the horizon, her heart lightened by undeniable expectation – could she see them? There! There they were, the legendary pyramids! She couldn't take her eyes off them; couldn't resist the thrill of them - their astonishing antiquity, their spellbinding, indomitable, perpetually mysterious renown – all there, before her very eyes. It wasn't as if she'd studied them or had longed to encounter them over the years. It was rather as if they were the only things that seemed real in this crazy place. The pyramids existed in her time, too, after all - they were a link to the past *and* the future; to something she could hold to, to home. She looked to them as if her life depended upon it, as if by way of the pyramids she could survive until she found a way. Heaven help me, there has to be a way to get back home.

They'd stopped. Amu climbed from the cart and tugged at Vixy to do the same. It felt good to stretch her legs and back. She knew the pyramids weren't far off – perhaps twenty-some kilometers, but at this pace it would take them all day to get there. Meanwhile, it seemed as if they were waiting for something.

Nearby, a solitary date palm arched skyward and it was impossible not to notice the dark-skinned man sitting casually beneath it, his back against the trunk, his camel resting alongside him on the sand. He was smoking, gazing into the desert with an indifferent air. Their donkey-boy led the cart within earshot of the man then paused, adjusting the beast's harness and then rearranging, uselessly as far as Vixy could discern, the sundries on the cart, clearly vying for the man's attention. It was the camel, however, that seemed keen to acknowledge the boy's activity – that, or the donkey's presence - eyeing things imperially, chin raised. The camel grunted and the man tossed aside his cigarette.

"*Ala mahlak ya sadiqi.*"[17] Something about his Arabic made his voice seem both arid and exotic.

I wonder if he's a Bedouin, thought Vixy. And I've heard of camels spitting at people. She watched the boy trying not to watch the man. Were donkey-boys routinely impressed by Bedouins? It hardly mattered. What

---

[17] "Take it easy friend."

she really wanted was to walk up and ask for a cigarette. But she checked herself – she'd gone far enough in her cadet training to know it was unwise, if not improper in this part of the world, to say nothing of the proprieties of 1881, for a woman to take such an initiative - to approach a man and initiate a conversation, let alone smoke.

When the man's indifference remained impregnable, the boy's conviction seemed to fail and he ceased his fussing and stood quietly beside his cart.

"He's a proud boy," whispered Amu. "A fatherless boy struggles to teach himself how to be a man."

"You know him?" said Vixy.

The boy stroked the muzzle of his donkey. He did seem anxious, perhaps intimidated by the women. He reminded Vixy of all the shy, willful, painfully self-conscious adolescent boys of her youth.

"Bishoy!" said Amu. She continued in Arabic and Bishoy nodded.

Vixy tugged at Amu's robe. "What did you say?"

"I asked him if this Bedouin is the man we are to meet."

"Meet?"

"Yes. A Bedouin is to accompany us to the Plateau. But either Professor Bruggs or Monsieur Laron was to have met us here. And there is no sign of them."

Bruggs has my transponder, she thought. I know it. What if he's left us here? It was all she could do to conceal her panic.

"Bishoy!" said Amu, and again addressed the boy in Arabic.

"What did you say?" said Vixy.

"I told him to ask the Bedouin if he knew the whereabouts of Professor Bruggs and Monsieur Laron. But Bedouins are often arrogant and despicable to women. Even if this man has seen two European men outside the city he may not speak of it." Bishoy appeared tentative and Amu became impatient, furrowing her brow at him and gesturing, implying that he approach the Bedouin directly. "*Muḥāwala*, Bishoy."[18]

---

18  "Attempt," as in make the attempt.

Bishoy appeared to be gathering his courage for a moment, then did what he was told, striking up a tentative conversation. The Bedouin seemed patient with him, glancing back and forth between Bishoy and the women as he listened. Then he cut the boy short and strode directly towards them. Vixy endured a rush of anxiety.

Someone shouted and they turned to see another boy scurrying towards them, apparently having come from the outskirts of the city. He was waving his arms as he ran. "Bishoy! Bishoy!" The boy's voice was high and clear, like a musical note. He arrived in a cloud of dust and stood before them, breathless and wide-eyed. "*La mu'axza*,"[19] he said, his eyes darting towards each of them in turn. He addressed Bishoy, speaking hurriedly.

"*Tayyeb*,"[20] said Bishoy. "*Shukran*."[21]

"*A'fwan*,"[22] said the boy, glancing round at everyone and performing a short bow. He nodded at Bishoy then turned away, towards the city, still breathless, waving at them over his shoulder. "*Ma' al salamah*!"[23]

The Bedouin, meanwhile, had been standing beside them, watching the goings on, and now he addressed Bishoy. They conversed for a time.

Vixy tugged at Amu's arm. "What's going on?"

At the sound of Vixy's voice, the Bedouin's eyes widened and he stared at her, his apparent incredulousness only increasing as Amu translated to Vixy, in halting English, all that had been said; namely, that the boy from the city was Nabil, a fellow donkey-boy like Bishoy and a messenger for Bruggs and Laron.

"Professor Bruggs and Monsieur Laron, they are not coming," said Amu. "We are to go alone to the Plateau."

Vixy felt the pressure of the Bedouin's gaze and kept her eyes averted. Amu addressed him in Arabic.

---

[19] "Excuse me (begging pardon)."

[20] "Okay."

[21] "Thank You."

[22] "You're welcome" (as a reply to "Thank you").

[23] "Goodbye."

Vixy appealed to her with her eyes and furrowed her brow – a technique she'd only just discovered as a means to communicate beyond words and the confounding the limits of her veil.

The Bedouin had been watching her. "She asked me what we should do," he said in plain English. He stood for a moment inviting the women's stares.

"And from now on I shall speak English as a courtesy to you." He rubbed his chin without taking his eyes from Vixy. "My name is Hesso Ishaq. I have been awaiting that oaf Bruggs and his slimy accomplice Laron - "œil le Sang" – just as you have been. I never considered he would send women on his behalf. And led by a boy! They are scoundrels, Bruggs and Laron. Perhaps worse. But I mean to be paid and if they think they can find what they are looking for on their own, well...." He trailed off and clenched his jaw, a flash of anger in his eyes, his hand twisting at the hilt of the scabbard tucked in his belt. "The Pyramids Road is not safe for anyone, let alone donkey-boys and women. I will escort you back into the city and finish my business with Bruggs and Laron when I find them."

"œil le Sang," said Vixy. "That's what you call Laron? Is it French? What does it mean?"

"Blood Eye," said Amu.

"Blood Eye," repeated Hesso, turning to spit into the sand. "Yes. A Frenchman. And dangerous only because he is a coward. But enough of Laron. Who are you?"

"I am Amunet Rizk," said Amu. "I have agreed to help Professor Bruggs at his camp on the Plateau; to cook and translate."

Hesso narrowed his eyes. "And you?" He turned to Vixy. "You don't sound British. Neither do you sound exactly American."

"My name is Vixy Velure." She felt relieved to be talking openly. "I was born in Canada. And I've lived in America. I have my own reasons for finding Bruggs and Laron – they have something I want."

Amu grasped her arm, her eyes flashing as if Vixy was being foolish.

Vixy felt her pulse quicken – Amu was right, to be blurting intimacies to this stranger was a risk. But it was too late now. "If we're to meet them at the Giza Plateau," she said, "then I say we go. There is nothing for me in Cairo."

Hesso held her gaze. He withdrew a cigarette from within the folds of his robe, put it to his lips, struck a match and drew a long breath, allowing the smoke to curl about his mouth and nostrils. He regarded them all in turn – Vixy, Amu, then Bishoy standing patiently beside his donkey cart. He turned on his heel and strode towards his camel.

"*Yalla, Deloua, Yalla!*" [24] he said, coaxing the animal to its feet.

He led the beast a few paces away and it was then that Vixy noticed what appeared to be a line of leafy trees in the distance, disappearing into the haze of the desert, more or less in the direction of the Plateau. "What is it?" she said; "where's he going?"

Hesso looked back. "*Yalla, Yalla!*" he said, beckoning to them. "By the grace of God we'll take the Pyramids Road together. Come!"

Vixy, Amu and Bishoy looked expectantly at each other for a moment. Then the women climbed wordlessly onto the donkey cart, Bishoy tugged at the reins of his donkey and they set off, following the mysterious, En-glish-speaking Bedouin and his imperious camel away from the city. And so it was that together they began their journey to the pyramids.

---

[24] *Deloua,* meaning "spoiled child," is the name of Hesso's camel and *Yalla* means "Let's go."

# CHAPTER 11

# EAST OF EDEN

**MR. Z. TOSSED TWO SMALL PILLS** on the table and grimaced at them. There was a knock at the door.

Neutic set his papers aside and answered it, returning with a tea service that he set between them on the coffee table. "How is the arm, sir? Do those help?"

Mr. Z. washed his pills down with tea. "It's the awkwardness that makes me crazy. The sense of disability."

They returned to their reading, the morning sun angling into the room and the breeze swishing through the curtains. A quiet hour passed before Mr. Z. glanced at the time. "Noon," he said, poking into his pockets. He packed tobacco into his pipe and sighed at the loose piles of paperwork and textbooks cluttering the table. He diminished the handful of v-doc images with a snap of his fingers, glad to be rid of them. Something about working with electronic documents always exasperated him. "What do you say to a walk?"

Neutic tossed a sheaf of papers onto the table and sat back, rubbing his eyes. "Yes. I'm not getting much out of these reports. All this documentation and it just reiterates the classic Oriental themes. I guess I was expecting something more compelling, especially from the Eranos archives. Seeing as it took an act of Congress to get access. A lot of this is available on other databases."

"Yes, but I half expected as much. Nevertheless, I consider it worth our time to have discovered that image."

"And you're convinced it's more than a fanciful illustration; more than a mythologized image? But how can that be? I mean, if no one - no scholar, no scientist, no military intelligence, no thrill-seeking adventurer - has ever penetrated the Mothmen realm? There wouldn't be any record of first-hand encounters."

"Off-world assassination," said Mr. Z. "Or rites of initiation. Remember our discussion back at the T.E.? Just because nobody gets in doesn't mean the Mothmen don't get out. If the rumors are true, and I believe they are, then somebody, somewhere over the centuries has caught at least a glimpse of them. Vixy and I almost did, remember." He stopped to ponder the image. "It strikes me that the Mothmen are watchers. And a watcher is bound to get himself watched."

"Watchers?"

"Observers. Of oracle coins and hexagrams. Of omens. Of the changes and transformations in things in the yin, yang, Confucius, Tao, Oriental sense as we understand it here on Earth. The Mothmen seem to blend these various belief systems, at least in my opinion, and their apparent devotion to cleromancy would be the glue that holds it all together."

"Cleromancy?"

"It's just the word for the casting of oracles or the casting of lots, as they're called. With oracle coins, yarrow stalks or dice, for example. And of reading so-called signs in turtle shells or tea leaves. It hinges upon the idea that nothing in life is random, that divine intention or cosmic will or supernatural knowledge – especially in the context of the future - is revealed in what somebody else might interpret as a random event. We toss coins on a table with a question in mind and it's as if we've opened a window into how things are."

"Like magic. Or magical thinking."

"No. Cleromancy or divination is not akin to magic. Although they're both concerned with influence and gaining an advantage. Magic seeks to change the world to align with our behavior whereas cleromancy seeks to change our behavior to align with the world. One is mechanical, in a way, and the other is spiritual or at least metaphysical. They both take a certain scientific attitude towards things, regarding the world as figure-out-able, if you know what I mean. Magic casts spells, sprinkles potions, carves objects, what have you – it's a form of applied science akin to engineering, one intends to engineer or manufacture the outcomes. Cleromancy is rather a form of applied mysticism, of pure sight, that amounts to personal cartology – one seeks to map Nature or reality as it truly is, free of life's illusions and obfuscations, and find one's proper way within it."

"Okay," said Neutic. "Then what are the Molemen doing trying to engage in mind control? If that's what it is? Psi powers or whatever. That's neither cleromancy nor magic."

"You're right. It's just another technology. Which happens to be biological. Natural. Supernatural. Or super natural with a space between the words. You see what I mean? As in not otherworldly but super-worldly. Not extrasensory but super-sensory. Yoga falls into this category – the yoking of the mind so as to empower its effectiveness. Alternatively, yoga empowers the mind to escape its own biological limits, which is why it's sometimes referred to as a psycho-spiritual technology. But psi has to do with just another physiological capability – an ability we all more or less possess that has nothing to do with our particular spiritual perspective. Why are the Molemen using it? And why with such treacherous intentions? I don't know.

"All I can think is where it once may have been productive for the Mothmen to remain isolationist, to keep to themselves for hundreds and thousands of years, casting oracles and interpreting the changes and so forth, watching, minding their own business, perhaps now they're looking beyond their physical borders."

"But what are they looking for? Answers? New Ideas? And why now?"

"Perhaps a new perspective on their old ideas. Why now? Some kind of cultural strain, perhaps, some trauma." Mr. Z. ran his hand through his hair, pondering. "And something about the silence of it all strikes me as... I don't know. The utter lack of communication. Aggression implies the behavior of a culture who are convinced they *have* the answers." He poured more tea. "It strikes me that there could be a great deal more to all this than just the attack on the Professor." He waved away the idea and instead snatched a book from the table, opening it to one of his marked pages.

"This is Jean Clottes, an early twentieth century archaeologist concerned with Paleolithic imagery." He read aloud: "'A peculiarity of human beings – *Homo spiritualis* in the broad sense, beyond the material contingencies of survival that they share with other animals, is their ability to project themselves into the past or the future, to ask questions about themselves and of the world that surrounds them, to seek out and elucidate its mysteries and take advantage of them.'"[n] He tossed the book aside. "Guetti, on the other hand" – he picked up another book and flipped it open – "is determined to dismiss just such an experience, in favor of the so-called limits of metaphor." He cleared his throat.

> The essential hollowness of this "as if" thinking, of this process of continually and self-hypnotically reconstructing the illusion of order, is nowhere more clearly dramatized than in *Heart of Darkness* in particular and in the works of Melville, Conrad, and Faulkner in general. The capacity of such provisional metaphor to structure experience is shown here to be essentially artistic and, I think, essentially frivolous. It is not something upon which – when necessity requires – one can depend.[o]

"Frivolous! Not something upon which one can depend! Why, it's all that we can and *do* depend upon, not least of all in our time of need. And, again, what's an oracle coin? As I've tried to point out, it's a perfect example of a symbol – a symbol of a culture that an individual also identifies with on personal terms. And an oracle is an individual, inherently personal appeal to connectedness via symbols; to the possibility of divining one's future, a future that is ours for the taking. Or for our creating. It's a legitimate experience to feel oneself part of a larger whole. Anyway, my point is that symbols and metaphors aren't provisional. Rather, they're mythological. Which means they're essential. Except when none of it is working, when the symbols and the metaphors no longer seem to connect at all to reality. Then you experience exile instead of connectedness. And the Mothmen may be struggling with exactly that. Maybe their thousands of years of connectedness has disintegrated, I don't know. Maybe their mythology is no longer aligning with their experience. So they're looking elsewhere, looking out, looking to exert their influence outside the Mothmen realm, to see what can be done about it. Do you follow me at all, Neutic?"

Neutic frowned and scratched his head. "I don't know, sir, to be honest. Metaphors. Symbols. The coins. I swear I just read something about this." He selected a textbook and turned it over in his hands.

"What is that, Jung?"

"Yessir. Where he interprets selections from a patient's series of related dreams. I'd found it baffling, but now I think it has to do with what you're saying. May I read it to you?"

"Certainly." Mr. Z. stood chomping on his pipe.

It is all part of the banality of its outward aspect that the gold is minted, i.e., shaped into coins, stamped, and valued. By being shaped and named, psychic life is broken down into coined and valued units. But this is possible only because it is intrinsically a great variety of things, an accumulation of unintegrated hereditary units. Natural man is not a "self" – he is the mass and a particle in the mass, collective to such a degree that he is not even sure of his own ego. That is why since time immemorial he has needed the transformation mysteries to turn him into something, and to rescue him from the animal collective psyche, which is nothing but a *variété*.

But if we reject this unseemly *variété* of man, "as he is," it is impossible for him to attain integration, to become a self. And that amounts to a spiritual death. Life that just happens in and for itself is not real life; it is real only when it is *known*. Only a unified personality can experience life, not that personality which is split up into partial aspects, that bundle of odds and ends which also calls itself "man."[P]

Mr. Z. yanked his pipe from his mouth. "*Spiritual death*. There you have it! There you have the *peculiarity of human beings*; there you have *Homo spiritualis*, exactly. Let me see that." He snatched the book from

Neutic's hands. "Yes. *Life that just happens in and for itself is not real life; it is real only when it is known.* You've got it here, exactly."

Neutic frowned, unconvinced. "*Unintegrated hereditary units... the transformation mysteries....*" That's pretty much mumbo jumbo, isn't it?"

"Unintegrated hereditary units are the archetypes of the collective unconscious – perhaps Jung's most controversial but in the end most resonant and lasting contribution to psychology and for that matter mythology – it's the very thing that drives non-Jungians nuts. The idea that we literally inherit the architecture of our affecting symbols; that each of us is provided the outline of the imagery that we dream into existence. I liken the idea, simplistic as it sounds, to a coloring book: the outlines of the forms are there on the pages but colorless, lifeless. Available to us all but *unintegrated* – unconscious – until we take the time and devote the energy to coloring the images in, to animating them; to bringing them to consciousness. Then the images do their proper work; they help us instead of hindering us. We bring the shadow energies to light and we find that life isn't so much of a battle. It may remain mostly a mystery but not entirely so. But you have to believe that we are indeed wired to help ourselves."

"And the transformation mysteries?"

"That's a reference to alchemy – a philosophical and pre-scientific tradition which originated in Greco-Roman Egypt. But Jung interpreted it, also, as expressing the dynamic between our material and spiritual outlook. Expressing it in the form of metaphor, that is. It legitimized Jung's intuitions as a budding psychiatrist within the nascent field of psychology – with the difficulty he saw people having with negotiating their inner and outer lives; with the difficulties he himself experienced. Meanwhile, alchemy - the idea of transforming base metals into gold, something base into something precious - is merely a metaphor for transforming oneself from an unintegrated, uncentered, ungrounded and therefore ineffective and unhappy jumble of raw, archetypal architecture – a clock with its clockworks out of whack – into one's true self; the integrated, individuated wheel that rolls out of its own center." He gestured at the book with his pipe. "I'm mixing metaphors, there, I know, but it's our predicament, isn't

it? And it's a predicament that can be said to apply to an entire culture, like
that of the Mothmen, for example, as well as an individual." He laughed at
himself. "Listen to me pontificating. If we were in class this is where you'd
be justified in throwing something at me. As a matter of fact, I think I've
had that dream – where my students pelt me with erasers. Or tomatoes. I
get carried away, Neutic. Such is the nature of zeal. Meanwhile, as far as
mysteries, there's no mystery in what a fine day it is out there. Let's go - I
want to show you the grounds."

They strolled along, blinking into the sunshine, following a well-tended
footpath that encircled the Casa and meandered through the colorful gardens. There were clipped hedges and manicured trees and the occasional
stone bench or low wall that seemed to beckon one to sit and idle.

"It is like a college campus," said Neutic, donning his sunglasses.

"And a seminary and a public park all rolled into one."

Neutic nodded. It seemed to him that Mr. Z.'s vigor was returning
to him in waves. "It's meditative, absolutely. Except for a certain, I don't
know -"

"Vitality?"

"Something. There's a zing to the whole place."

"The climate has something to do with it, I think, and the drama of
the scenery." Mr. Z. turned and gestured into the distance. "I mean, look
at those mountains."

Neutic was struck anew by the Alps, raising his sunglasses as if to
experience their full impact. "Amazing." He returned his attention to the
grounds. "And all this" – he made a sweeping gesture – "The upkeep, for
one thing. And the expense. I mean, the maintenance of these gardens.
Yet one never seems to encounter a gardener or greenskeeper or laborer of
any type. It's as if they did all their gardening at night, or by way of fairies
or elves."

Mr. Z. laughed. "After Olga Froebe-Kapteyn died, in what was it - nineteen sixty-two, I think?" He held a flame to his pipe, puffing at it. "The Eranos lecture series and the campus itself fell into disrepair. Understandably, I suppose – Miss Froebe-Kapteyn had been struggling to maintain the place even with occasional financial help from the Mellons. Jung had died the year before and, well, the peak had passed. It was only by way of the PMC– their vision and diligence and, I don't know, their tenacious devotion to its value as an antiquity in its own right, you could say, that the donations and gifts were raised and the buildings and grounds were restored. And now maintained in perpetuity. The money also supports the annual summer lecture series."

They followed the path, their steps crunching quietly on the gravel, making their way amongst the lawns and gardens that immediately surrounded the main building, finally arriving at the entrance of Casa Gabriella where they paused, admiring the iron gate and its moss-covered stone gateposts.

"The annual lecture series remains stubbornly – some would say, admirably - sympathetic to esotericism and so-called rejected knowledge, such as it is." Mr. Z. puffed his pipe as he talked. "But not in an intellectually flabby, emotionally indulgent, otherwise counter cultural sense of naïve experimentation. Eranos respects scholarship." He laughed heartily. "There I go again, bloviating – I suppose it's obvious that I must be feeling better, eh?"

Neutic cocked his eyebrow at him. "Well, mythology, symbolism, metaphor, all these things, theorizing about them at least, it's all new to me. But the energy of this place - it's as if the past and the future have equal standing here, I guess; as if they're always playing off each other."

"That's high praise, I think," said Mr. Z., looking around. "For most of us the substance of life, its affecting symbology, its sacredness, has to sneak up on us, if it ever does. Places like this, I don't know, I don't want to make too much of the experience. It's certainly not the only worthy archive in the cosmos, not by any means. But not every archive possesses the mythological potency of this place – its own version of the zing, as you call it."

"No. Especially digital archives. I like to think I've more than a passing interest in databases and I have to admit I was one who didn't see much purpose in brick and mortar versions, except as museums. But clearly the physicality means something."

"So you've changed your perspective?"

Neutic looked round self-consciously and shrugged. "I guess the experience speaks for itself."

"I'd be happy to arrange for us to attend an Eranos conference, a *Tagungen* as they're called – if you'd be interested. Vixy might even enjoy it, too."

A silence fell upon them at the mention of Vixy's name.

Mr. Z. paused, puffing on his pipe, glowering past a low stone wall into the shady silence of the woods beyond.

Neutic shoved his hands deep into his pockets and kicked at a pebble.

They waited for what seemed a long while before Mr. Z. emptied his pipe, tapping the bowl against the gate post. He glanced at his transponder. "It's a forty-five-minute walk to Ascona, Neutic. Mostly along the lake – we can take this path. There's a damn fine tavern in town if you're up for a beer or two and an early dinner?"

Neutic raised his eyebrows at the idea. "Let's do it."

They'd been walking in silence, having followed the path deep into a stand of trees that obscured their view on either side. Mr. Z. unzipped his collar. "It's been too long since I've had any decent exercise, I can tell you. It's good to get the blood up, isn't it?"

Neutic's enthusiasm seemed to be flagging in comparison. "Those birds sound like they're nagging at us." He immediately affected a self-conscious laugh. "I'm sorry. It's not like I've never spent any time in the woods. My grandparents had a vacation house near a wood like this. I used to spend all day in it when I was a kid. Those are skylarks."

"A native species," Mr. Z remarked. He regarded Neutic discreetly as they walked along. He was such a reliably present young man. Attentive. Except mention of Vixy's name always seemed to unsettle him quite beyond the difficult nature of her predicament. As if... a pang of recognition struck him, and a sense of infinite compassion. He's in love with her, the poor boy. "Incongruous energies," he said as if to the trees. "One walks long and far enough and like any physical activity it can become a meditation. Energies shifting within the body. Not all of them pleasant."

Neutic trailed along, staring at the path as if he'd not heard a word.

Mr. Z. tried a different tact. "Meanwhile, I'm not convinced we've done our due diligence regarding the T.E.'s forensic results from the Olympic. The autopsy of the fifth terrorist, for example - the non-cadet, the one Vixy injured. There was something in the report about a tattoo on his chest but no photograph or description."

He hadn't finished talking before Neutic had retrieved his transponder from his pocket and begun tapping at it.

"Yessir, the one that killed himself. A tattoo. I'll ask the lab – there shouldn't be any reason they can't provide an image."

Atta boy, Neutic, thought Mr. Z. It hadn't occurred to him how much he was depending upon this young man's help. Moreover, how much of a vacuum Vixy's disappearance had created. In everything. That they had their work cut out for them was an understatement. "I've got some homework for you, too."

Neutic cocked an ear as he fussed with his device. "Homework? Yessir. Certainly."

"I'd like you to apply yourself to the *Book of Changes* – to read it through, to familiarize yourself with it as best you can, and quickly. Also, with Hellmut and Richard Wilhelm's explanatory lectures, *Understanding the I Ching*. All the stuff we discussed at the debriefing." He looked ahead, his strides purposeful. "We've got to squeeze as much information from these esoteric clues as we can. Otherwise, well...." He filled his lungs. "Frankly, Neutic, I don't feel I've been at all helpful so far. For all my talk;

for all my extrapolations and theorizing and expositions. Hell. I've not brought us a single tangible step forward."

"Not at all, sir," said Neutic. "You're here to recuperate. And an injury like that -"

"Ah! I'm dismissing you with my trademark one-arm wave, see?"

Neutic smiled.

"And I'm going off those painkillers for good, I can tell you, as of right now – they do nothing but cloud my thoughts. Air and sun and exercise are as good a tonic as anything."

It wasn't long before they emerged from the cool shade of the woods into the invigorating afternoon sun. In the distance was the quaint little town, its central clock tower surrounded by charmingly antiquated multistory buildings, their cheerful colors – bright yellow, red, pale blue, even a tasteful pink – an inviting contrast to the imperious, commanding background of the snow-capped Alps.

"Palm trees?"

"Beguiling, isn't it?" said Mr. Z. "And a little incongruous, too. It's hardly the challenging alpine climate one would expect with the Alps so close, is it? Apparently, it's the proximity of the lake that makes for the area's cool summers and warmer winters – the so-called Mediterranean climate."

"I can imagine that the weather alone would entice tourists," said Neutic.

"Oh yes. Some of them absurdly wealthy. Ascona is definitely a resort town."

They followed the broad Piazza Giuseppe Motta, its stone buttresses overlooking a congested waterfront, a jumble of dinghies and diminutive sailing vessels– toy-like things apparently designed for brief jaunts upon the water – boxed in shoulder to shoulder, rocking to-and-fro in the mild swells. At Contrada San Pietro street they turned away from the lake, making their way for a block or so in the general direction of the clock tower.

"Here we are." Mr. Z. gestured at a nondescript door that opened onto the sidewalk.

Neutic hesitated.

Mr. Z. looked up, following Neutic's eyes. "Right. No sign. Never has been. No name on the door, no address. Nothing but this brass door handle in the image of a fish - a trout, I think it is, now that I look at it." He bent close, scratching his head at the image. "It's been years since I've been here but unless they've changed proprietors -" He grasped the fish and shoved the door open. "If nothing else we ought to be able to get a lager at the bar. And I dare say some fresh fish from the lake."

They entered a low-ceilinged tavern. The sun had been bright, the breezes off the lake refreshing but demanding, too, and now the cool dimness of the tavern, with its wooden beams and rich aroma of pipe tobacco and old varnish seemed immediately convivial. They made for the gleaming taps at the back of the room and had just committed themselves to finding a place at the bar when an agreeable blonde waitress approached them.

"*Hoi zäme, wilkomme,*"[25] she said.

Mr. Z. brightened. "Thank you. Do you have a table?"

She smiled and led them to a booth just vacated, clearing the glassware and wiping the tabletop as they slid in across from each other. "*Kasch Du Schwitzerdütsch reede?*"[26]

"*Entschuldigung, nein,*"[27] said Mr. Z. "Just English."

"Okay," she said, smiling.

"Drinks for you?"

"*Sibe,*" Mr. Z replied.

---

[25] "Hi, welcome" in Swiss German dialect.

[26] "Do you speak Swiss German?"

[27] "Sorry, no."

When Neutic looked uncertain the waitress spoke up. "*Sibe* is a lager beer. Brewed for us here in Ascona." Her accent was strong but her English clear and confident.

"Yes," said Neutic, nodding. "That's fine."

She withdrew two small menus, mere quarter-sheets of paper from her apron, set them on the table and hurried off.

"What looks good?" said Mr. Z., donning his spectacles.

"I can't read the menu," said Neutic, "I ought to have asked the waitress."

"We could do that, but let's see if I can recognize anything. Ah, *Zürcher Geschnetzeltes* and *Rösti* – you must try it. *Zürcher Geschnetzeltes* is sliced veal and veal kidney in a cream sauce with demi-glace, white wine and mushrooms, and *Rösti* is akin to hash browns - authentically German-Swiss." Mr. Z. continued to examine the menu. "But if that doesn't suit you, then don't let me stop you, we'll ask the waitress what else there is."

A comfortable seat, the pleasantness of the tavern and the exquisiteness of being off their feet was already having its effect upon Neutic. "No, sir, I'm starving - all that sounds good. Even the kidneys."

Their waitress arrived with their drinks and a basket of crusty bread with butter, took their order and was off again.

Mr. Z. enjoyed a long draught from his tankard. He began digging into his vest pocket. "After a long walk it's like the alcohol goes directly to my knees. Which is heaven." He withdrew a pocket-sized, micro-vellum[28] book from his pocket and set it between them, waiting for Neutic's reaction.

Neutic leafed through it. "*Understanding the I Ching*," he said, looking up. "Hard copy." He set the book down and sat back, sipping at his beer.

---

[28] Micro-vellum is a type of polymer-reinforced, synthetic cellulose "paper." Its technological advantages over traditional pulped, natural cellulose products include minimal caliper and grammage, good opacity, appealing rigidity and high tensile and shear strength. Coating and polishing are not required to deliver high optical density in the printed image. Stability is archival grade. Environmental impact is comparatively low. Cost of production limits marketability.

"With due respect to your philological abilities," said Mr. Z., "especially in the digital realm, I typically prefer the printed page whenever it's available. You may have noticed. At least for research. Flipping back and forth, making notations - when it comes to anything beyond cursory reading I can't bear the electronic versions. I swear I go blind and my head hurts. And I know that makes me sound ridiculous."

Neutic nodded. "Not at all. I've no experience with bound books, though. Just handling this one, the tactile nature of the thing. It's all there, the information, of course, but it's a different experience. It seems substantial and fragile at the same time."

"Indeed. At least you didn't turn your nose up at it like so many of my students." He reached for the book. "Indulge me." He flipped through the book's pages, found his place, paused to enjoy a sip of beer and cleared his throat. "This brings us," he read,

> to the thing that makes the *Book of Changes* interesting to persons other than those consulting the oracle. Even if we shrink from approaching the book with the willing faith of an oracle seeker, we can still meditate on this image of the cosmos for its own sake and seek to understand it.[9]

He glanced at Neutic before continuing, measuring his interest.

> The mythological period from which the images of the *I Ching* stem is...primary and immediate, not yet muddied by the sediment which periods of great intellectuality usually leave behind in the individual psyche. This is why the images coined are so illuminating and so generally valid. And, in order to make the *Book of Changes* out of those images, King Wên had only to formulate them and put them into an ordered system harmonizing with the rhythm of the cosmos. Nor did he have to go far for this. The cosmos was not yet strange to him; it was not the subject of a specialized science; he lived in direct contact with its

law of change, and the images were at hand, out of the store of ideas offered by the time and a living tradition.[r]

Their meals arrived and Mr. Z. pushed the book aside. Neutic had already begun buttering a slice of bread and Mr. Z. was regarding his plate of food with an air of critical anticipation, his knife and fork poised as he leaned forward to appreciate the aroma.

The waitress regarded them with a bemused attitude. "*En Guete*," she said, and immediately translated - "Enjoy your meal."

Mr. Z. sampled both the veal and the potatoes, nodding his appreciation, inhaling noisily as he chewed his hot food, washing it down with a gulp of beer. He reached for a slice of bread and lathered it with butter before dabbing a corner of it into his sauce. "I've appreciated your patience so far Neutic. It might seem to you that we should be taking a more direct form of action; that regarding Vixy there's no time to be lost. And you'd be right. I'm as anxious as anyone to accomplish something tangible - to retaliate in some way. To make ourselves known to these terrorists with a show of force, some kind of support on behalf of Vixy, the Professor, Miss Morrison and the others." He chomped at his bread and enjoyed a mouthful of food from his plate. "But, I'm convinced our predicament points to something both smaller and larger than mere zealotry or so-called religious fundamentalism or spiritual extremism. The strange coins, the assassination attempt, the images of the hexagrams and Vixy's abduction; the ensuing silence – no ransom, no claim of responsibility, no proclamation of ideology." He shrugged, his mouth full. "All of it. What I mean is, if we keep pounding away at these things, these clues, however intangible they seem, the next step will come to us. Pressure and time, Neutic, pressure and time."

"You're convinced that nothing about the attack is politically driven?"

"Only if you consider a disintegrating cultural mythology to have political ramifications. Frankly, I'm not convinced that a political agenda alone would ever motivate a culture like that of the Mothmen to emerge from exile. Otherwise, they would have emerged eons ago. A cultural mythology, to be sure, is composed of four functions: a sense of awe or the divine, a cosmology that supports that awe, a sociology, yes, that establishes ethics and social norms and, finally, a supporting or otherwise pedagogical psychology.[5] Politics, at least to me, is merely an aspect of sociology. And typically expressed in monetary terms - the haves and the have nots. Meanwhile, the affecting image is what grips the psyche - the motivating factor within a culture, and for that matter the individual, is always mythological. Politics – wealth versus need – will incite no end of strife. But transform politics into mythological schism and you can start a war."

Neutic frowned as he chewed. "A war?"

"I can see Vixy rolling her eyes at me," said Mr. Z. He reached for his beer. "She has a way of checking my tendency towards both tedium and exaggeration." With that he swept his glass into the air: "Here's to Vixy; to getting her back home if it's the last thing we do."

They clinked their glasses together only to fall silent as soon as they'd drank.

"I have to admit, sir," said Neutic, "that I've been feeling a little out of my depth. A lot out of my depth, actually. As if I'm somehow lacking all around. I'm sorry I haven't been of more help. You and Captain Chase – the TDC in general – may have been better served with somebody more, I don't know... more erudite."

"Bosh!" Mr. Z. used his knife to push the last mouthful onto his fork. "I'm intending that you read that book. And I'd suggest you simply spend some time in the Eranos Library. Just read. Read whatever catches your fancy. As far as a focus, I'm confident it will help our cause if you put your mind to the idiosyncrasies of this particular wisdom tradition" – he tapped the Wilhelm text with the butt of his knife. "To Taoism. It's obviously tied to our dilemma. Anyway, you've a talent for discernment. On top of your abilities with information science. That's what it's called, isn't it?"

Neutic chewed his food. "Yessir."

"Anyway, with the databases and digital archives. The Captain hopefully has already recognized your value in that area. And I think you've a mind for mythography too, which is obviously my special interest and which I'm confident will undoubtedly serve you well, I'll leave it at that. Meanwhile, all this is to say that time detective work is a craft, and crafts can be learned, which is something I'm always trying to communicate to Vixy – that one can develop a skill in observation. Now, a *talent* for observation is something else entirely. And I'll admit it's more akin to a compulsion. You may not possess that compulsion, Neutic. But that you've found yourself knee-deep in something perhaps out of your comfort zone, is merely a classic introduction to the adventure. This might not be your life's work, Neutic, and then again it might be - it's all too early to tell. But *I'm* here to tell you that you're a part of this investigation hook, line and sinker. And I'm glad of it."

Their waitress returned. "Two more?"

They nodded.

The waitress moved on and Neutic's transponder buzzed and flashed on the tabletop. "It's the lab," he said, putting the device to his ear. "Hello, Robbie. Yes. A tattoo? Correct. Hmm. That's strange. Okay. Well, send it right away, will you? Thanks, bye."

The waitress returned with their lagers and Neutic waited until she'd gone. "That was the forensic autopsy technician from the T.E., the one who actually took the photograph of the terrorist's tattoo. For whatever reason it didn't get imbedded in the official report. He swore he included it. I don't know, he seemed convinced that it somehow disappeared. If it were anyone else, anyone less exacting and reliable, I don't know. Anyway, the body has been cremated but Robbie made a drawing of the chest tattoo from memory. He's convinced the location of the tattoo - over the heart, as he put it – is significant. Something about scarabs and Egyptology being one of his interests, I couldn't follow it all. Also, he noticed two other tattoos, apparently in the style of hieroglyphs – one on each of the man's forearms."

"Hieroglyphs." Mr. Z. frowned and sipped his beer.

"Here's the drawing." Neutic shoved the device across the tabletop. "The resolution leaves something to be desired."

Mr. Z. narrowed his eyes at it. "Hmm. Winged scarab. The ankh symbol on its back. But instead of the sun, the scarab is shown supporting the *taijitu*. A curious mash up of Egyptian and Chinese symbology."

"*Taijitu?* You mean that smudged circle thing?"

"Yes, otherwise known as the yin-yang symbol, at least in the Western context. The play of opposites. Black and white. Shadow and light. Feminine and masculine. The past and the future, for that matter - the interpretations of the idea are essentially limitless. The dots symbolize the portion of perceived opposites that exist within each other." He removed his spectacles and rubbed his eyes, as if the topic weighed upon him. "Show me the hieroglyphs."

Neutic tapped the device.

Mr. Z. studied the images for some time. Then he drained his beer, withdrew his money clip and swiped it through the payment kiosk. "We ought to be on our way if we're to get back to Eranos with light in the sky."

They stood on the sidewalk outside the tavern and squinted into the late afternoon sun.

"Sorry if it seemed like I cut us short in there, Neutic. The information about the terrorist and the tattoos and everything - we can discuss it on the way back."

They retraced their steps down the narrow street and turned west, making their way along the lakeshore. The water lapped against the shoreline and a humid breeze wafted off the lake.

Neutic suddenly seemed contemplative. "Mud and minerals – it reminds me of my grandparent's vacation house. Besides the woods, there was a lake. A tenth the size of this lake, maybe. But that's the smell of freshwater."

They made their way along the strand at a purposeful pace, out of step with the sauntering tourists. Before long, they'd left the village behind and arrived once again at the footpath leading into the woods.

"All is illusion," said Mr. Z, "let it go." His voice was strangely evocative, as if he were reading poetry. "All is in order; let it come."[t]

"That sounds Oriental," said Neutic.

"It's my translation of the hieroglyphs on the terrorist's arms."

Neutic was intrigued – such profundity was somehow the opposite of what he expected from tattoos on the body of a murderous criminal. "Then they were indeed authentic hieroglyphs? And the chest tattoo?"

"Ah," said Mr. Z. "An example of mythological syncretization: combining the scarab beetle with the ankh – Egyptian symbols of rebirth and life, respectively. And in the place above the scarab, a place normally occupied in Egyptian imagery by the symbol of the sun, we find instead the *taijitu*, the yin-yang symbol – expressing the play-of-opposites. The location of the chest tattoo? Over the man's heart? I agree with our man Robbie that it's relevant. Entirely apt. It was in dynastic Egypt, after all, that the heart of the deceased was left in place while all other organs were removed. The Egyptians believed the heart to contain the soul - and a scarab amulet endowed with words of power – literally inscribed into the stone - was placed upon the chest as magical protection. Protection in the sense of quieting the heart to prevent its betraying the truth of one's transgressions - one's sins, so to say. At the moment of judgment before Osiris and his host, which included a guardian monster. The heart of the deceased was weighed against a feather, the feather of truth. Too heavy and crunch! – the heart and the soul were consumed by the guardian monster. Such things as heart amulets weren't cheap, of course."

"People were trying to buy their way into heaven as far back as the Egyptians?"

"That, and to engineer it. You know the Pyramids – perhaps the costliest crypts ever constructed, at least on Earth, speaking of money – have been referred to by some as resurrection machines?"

❁

They penetrated deeper into the woods and a disquieting sense of foreboding crept over them, a vague oppression.

What is it about these woods? thought Neutic. He focused on his footsteps, on putting one foot in front of the other so as to keep his mind from obsessing on his trepidation. He recognized the chestnut and pine, knew trees like this as the most abiding, sheltering, even comforting things in his life, at least in daylight. And it wasn't as if he'd never spent any time in the woods at night. But he peered with foreboding at the darkening branches arching overhead. "Hettie," he murmured, suddenly struck by her image, the memory of her face.

"Pardon?" said Mr. Z.

Neutic walked on, seemingly oblivious.

Mr. Z. pricked his ears, waiting, resisting the urge to ask again. Let him be, he thought. I've been talking too much today as it is, overloading him. He whistled softly to himself – an incongruously cheerful snippet of some tune he couldn't place - which only seemed to increase his queer sense of uneasiness. He trudged along in silence for a time, aware of Neutic beside him in the dark and suddenly keen to return to the Casa.

"Our birthday," whispered Neutic.

"What's that, Neutic?" He tried to sound as accommodating as he could.

"I'm sorry, sir, yes. My sister and I – we're twins - I'd forgotten that today was our birthday."

Mr. Z. eyed Neutic carefully. "You're too young to sound so unhappy about it."

Neutic shook his head. "It was three years ago. She died – she was killed. Murdered. Alongside four others. They were all students at Parzival University. Something about a Jihadist raid or some such thing. She was studying medicine. She was twenty-two."

Mr. Z. couldn't believe he'd been so remiss, so unobservant as to not have been aware of such a thing. "I'm sorry, Neutic." He felt himself an incompetent, heartless fool - it only now occurred to him that he'd not taken time to read Neutic's file. "I had no idea. Here I've been yammering on all day and, well, I ought to have -"

"No, sir. No, not at all." Neutic stopped, regarding the path ahead blindly, as if consumed by his thoughts. His voice seemed distant. "Hettie wouldn't have liked a fuss being made. I remember she told me once – we were kids and I'd been going off about how I wanted to be rich and famous or something - and she said, 'I'm not interested in being remembered.' And I never understood what she meant by it, really, until now."

Mr. Z. found himself at a loss. "But *you* remember her."

Neutic nodded almost imperceptibly.

"Happy birthday, Herman. And happy birthday to Hettie, too. I would have liked to have known her."

Meanwhile, the woods themselves seemed to have become furtive, the still-ness almost eerie. No bird called or flitted within the branches, no squirrel rummaged amongst the fallen leaves. Night had fallen. It was then that Mr. Z. saw something over Neutic's shoulder. Or thought he did.

Neutic turned to follow Mr. Z.'s gaze. "What is it?"

"Nothing. A deer, I suppose." He nevertheless felt his heart quicken and his injury suddenly began troubling him, the whole of his arm aching to a degree that he grasped at his elbow. When he noticed Neutic eyeing him and the unsettled expression on the young man's face he felt com-pelled to muster some encouragement, motioning them ahead with a stoic thrust of his chin. "Let's get back."

They made their way in the gloaming, forcing themselves to remain unhurried, each man seemingly determined to project a mild bravado on behalf of the other, all the while craving a glimpse of the grounds surrounding Eranos, a view of lighted windows, even a glimpse of the lakeshore - some indication that the woods were coming to an end. And indeed, it wasn't a quarter of an hour before the forest seemed to relent, to open up and their path spilled onto the outskirts of the broad campus, the steadfast glow of the Casa's windows twinkling at them in the distance like a cluster of abiding beacons.

"Civilization," muttered Neutic, surprised at the intensity of his own relief. He sensed the dark vastness of the lake to their left and pondered the origin of the flickering lights visible here and there along the far shoreline – people merely settling in for the night, that's all, he thought.

Mr. Z., meanwhile, felt exasperated with his own nerves, at his having worked himself nearly to his wits end by way of an otherwise accommodating walk through a benign stand of trees. Enough of mixing painkillers and beer, he thought. The path turned north, rising a bit, and they came within sight, finally, of the well-lit entrance to the Casa and its broad, inviting porch.

"Whew," said Neutic; "I'm for putting my feet up." He hadn't taken another step when Mr. Z. slowed beside him, reaching out as if to bring them both to a stop.

"Wait, Neutic."

Neutic's heart skipped a beat.

"Do you see it?" Mr. Z. was whispering. "There. Something on the path. Between us and the Casa."

Neutic peered ahead. Indeed, not a hundred meters ahead of them, silhouetted against the illumined architecture of the Casa, was a shadowy, indecipherable shape, incomparably large. "What could it –?"

"Sshh...."

The shadow moved, appeared to be gliding towards them. Neutic felt his guts twist and his legs become leaden. "A bear, for God's sake?"

"That's no bear," said Mr. Z., and groped instinctively for his plasma pistol – like a fool he'd left the thing in the hotel safe! Meanwhile, the shape was closing on them. He shoved at Neutic - "Run!"

Neutic stumbled, collected himself and held his ground. He watched Mr. Z. step forward as if to face the thing, whatever it was – four-legged, immense, flying low over the ground like some hideous hellhound. He braced himself.

Mr. Z. stopped short, snatched the slender, hopelessly insignificant tactical arc-blade from his belt, raised it high and leapt headlong at the oncoming specter, hollering like a man possessed.

"No!" cried Neutic, lunging after him.

Mr. Z. slashed, the beast leapt, and Neutic prepared for the impact. Shockingly, the thing soared clear over their heads. They both ducked and whirled, saw its huge bulk drop onto the path behind them, soundless but for a spray of gravel clattering across the path as the beast sprung sideways, speeding like a shot across the campus lawn – unnaturally swift - barreling into the blackness of the trees.

Mr. Z. stumbled and fell, his arm hindering his balance. He struggled to get up. "Let's go!" He held out his arm and Neutic seized it, hauling him to his feet. "Don't look back, Neutic, don't look back and don't mind me – just get to the Casa!"

The words jolted Neutic back to himself and he redoubled his grip on Mr. Z.'s arm, hauling the two of them forward. "C'mon, Mr. Z. - c'mon, goddammit!"

They half-stumbled, half-sprinted arm-in-arm up the path and through the gate, breathless as they clambered up the steps of the Casa and into the light of the porch, bursting through the heavy doors and forcing them shut behind them. They collapsed onto the granite sanctity of the lobby floor and lay panting, staring wide-eyed at each other, winded and dumb with relief as if they'd outrun the devil himself.

# CHAPTER 12

# "That's an Order...."

**The space-train emerged** from the steam-clouded maw of the decontamination hangar and lumbered into the station, wash-water cascading from its bulk as if from the hide of an enormous mechanical pachyderm, pouring into the hot works of its underbelly and bursting into spitting gasps of vapor. Heralded by the indomitable engine, car after gleaming car rolled forth, groaning upon the rails, the polished, hyper-steel fuselage reflecting the sunlight, the faceted window-prisms sparkling. The onlookers flooded through the turnstiles, hastening to the platform, craning their necks to catch a glimpse of the disembarkation bays.

Always impressive, thought Cog. A testament to the power of Mole-man engineering. He loved watching the space-trains arrive, especially from the vantage of the VIP observation platform – probably the only true perk his job offered. This particular craft was about eight-hundred meters long and veritably aquiver from the torturous demands of hyper-dimensional travel. It wheezed and clattered and hissed, as cantankerous and noble as the age-old railroad steam engines. He loved those too. Especially anything manufactured in the iron era from the first galactic quadrant. Hmm. It occurred to him that he'd not received his latest edition of *Ancient Rails* – he could have sworn he'd renewed his subscription. Look at me. Too busy to keep track of my hobbies. He used to scoff at anyone who whined about work-life balance. Now? He felt more adrift with each passing day. This Giza project, the demands of it. He kept thinking he'd get his feet under him. And he hadn't. When it's over, when we get this thing done, I'm going to apply for my vacation and... he didn't know what. He watched the engine haul itself into the station, belch a plume of steam from its exhaust manifold and shudder to what seemed a reluctant rest.

"Welcome home, old girl."

An arrival bell rang out, echoing down the expansive, multi-level station and the crowd pressed closer. The bulkheads released, the bay doors opened and a cargo of pensive, travel-weary passengers burst forth, spilling onto the arrival platform of Mega City One.

Cog never tired of it – the sense of import and heroic action; of dangers overcome and worlds traversed; of engineering pageantry, as it seemed to him, at least. Especially trains like this one - one of the famed Hadron series. She was a classic. A beauty – such lines! Never again will they create such elegant, charismatic icons of hyper-dimensional travel; trains that evoked the courage and romance of their age. He regarded her at rest, her doors cast open, the last of her passengers scurrying off, the bustling crowds drifting towards the exits, oblivious to the travails of her cata-clysmic exertions, to the majesty of her accomplishment. She'd be retired soon, replaced and antiquated into a museum. Or scrapped. Just like me, he thought. And I've never even gotten myself off-planet. Fifteen years. Fifteen years of cloistered, top-secret toil within the bureaucratic confines of the Galactic Clock Project. He was capable of more than managing the Giza cell, he felt sure of it. But he'd never been one to aggrandize his accomplishments, solicit praise or otherwise attempt to bring attention to himself - he preferred to let the quality of his work speak for itself. Except it never did.

"Everybody gets tired of their job and wants a change," his wife was fond of explaining to him; "you don't think I enjoy fitting quad-links all day for twenty years, do you? But look at what we've got, what we've earned for ourselves; look at our home and the things we've acquired – most of our friends haven't done nearly as well. You've got a *good job*, Cog," she'd declare, always with the same emphasis. "Lieutenant Engineer. In the Giza Cell Project, of all things. Who among your peers can say that? We're doing well. We've just got to keep working and not get restless. Someday you'll get an off-planet assignment and we'll celebrate. Meanwhile, don't fret. Worry is wishing for what you don't want."

*Wishing for what I don't want.* Another aphorism he couldn't seem to fathom. He caught sight of General Ten-Square shouldering his way through the crowd, his arm raised and eyes gleaming – the man seemed uncharacteristically exuberant. Cog raised his arm in acknowledgment and hurried down the platform steps.

"Cog!" said the General, breathlessly hauling his bag onto the luggage cart – the General's bag was always impossibly heavy. "Cog, old man, we've done it!" He gestured towards the transporter lot and they hurried towards an open pod, squeezed themselves in and Cog set the coordinates. The door snapped closed and when it opened again after sixty seconds, they disembarked at their offices on the other side of city.

"Damn fiftieth floor," said the General, squinting into the glare. "And damn solar magnification dishes. What are we coming to? As if the sun isn't powerful enough on its own."

"Energy for everyone," said Cog in a sing-song voice.

"I hate that advertisement," hissed the General. "New World propaganda. Give me a practical subterranean facility any day."

They barreled down the corridor, Cog at pains to keep pace with the General – whenever the man returned from an off-planet assignment it was as if his adrenaline was at a boil. He swiped his hand across the DNA security sensor and thrust himself through the doorway before it had completely opened. Cog followed, standing at attention near the exit as he always did, following protocol to the letter, regarding the General with due attention as the man flopped into his desk chair in a breathless huff.

"It happened, Cog. I've been waiting to tell you." He clapped his hands together, his voice animated, his ears perked, belying the fatigue evident in his face. "The extension! We received it! Giza cell funding is secured through the end of the project. And! – you won't believe this but the Consulate General approved us for an increase of an extra *fifteen percent!*" The General relaxed into his chair with his hands clasped behind his head and his ears turned back, beaming.

Cog brightened, mostly at the thought of the potential for a respectable raise.

"We're going to make out well as a result of the restructuring and the new initiative," said the General, "just as I've been saying. The Giza cell is finally getting the recognition it deserves – the recognition *we* deserve for making it all happen on a shoe-string budget all these years. In fact – you should have seen it, Cog – the Consulate stood at the podium in front of the entire SnoGlobeCon and declared the Giza cell the number one strategic priority for the Galactic Clock Project. *Number one*, Cog. Amazing! All those years we've been the black sheep, always scratching and crawling and me attending these damn confabs with my hat in my hand and look – now we're front and center! Everyone, even the skeptics in the Freehold Committee are behind it, cracking open their damn coffers for once! At ease, Cog," – the General gestured impatiently at his guest chair. "Sit. We've got a lot of debriefing to do, beginning with this business of the Mothmen."

The General paused to retrieve two energy drinks from the cooler behind his desk, tossed a bottle across the room at Cog and invoked a faux toast. "To the Mothmen, always busy kissing their fingers at the moon." He tipped his bottle, then gulped at it, wiping his mouth with the back of his hand. "Cog, my man, they've finally managed to screw themselves, these spiritualist whack-jobs with their mind-games and mysticism and spooks and rituals and what have you – they've finally managed to screw themselves in public. The Mothmen have got their asses in a vise."

Cog did his best to appear bemused when what he really wanted was to call it a day and get home before his dinner got cold. Again. The Mothmen with their asses in a sling. Or did he say in a vise? Anyway, fine. But I'm tired. After all these years why can't it wait until tomorrow?

The General leaned forward and lowered his voice conspiratorially. "The Mothmen received a communication, Cog – an inquiry – from the Time Guard, of all things, that creaky old institution, asking if they knew anything about the assassination attempt at the Olympic Theater. And they had to acknowledge it, didn't they? They had to climb out of their hole or come down from heaven or whatever and listen because it's an official inquiry. And their leadership – their priests or sages or whatever they are, having consulted their sticks and coins and turtle shells and what have you...." The General rolled his eyes and threw his hands up. "Hell and blood, Cog, the point is these yogic morons, so proud and mysterious and puffed up in their cloistered superiority, they've placed our whole reengineering initiative, the whole damn CCP, at risk of discovery by all and sundry. All with their little debacle at the Olympic. And now the shit is hitting the fan. Now they've got the old farts at the Time Guard putting their fingers into everybody's business." He sat up and thrust his finger at Cog. "That's exactly the little speech I gave the directors of the SnoGlo-beCon, by the way. In so many words. Meanwhile, for all we know we'll have the Pangalactic Mythology Coalition – the damn PMC of all things, Cog – coming after us and then the whole damn universe will be asking stupid questions about things we couldn't make anybody but a Moleman understand in a thousand years. Here we are on the cusp of it, Cog, poised, our long-awaited implementation is at hand, my friend; and we've no time for the impossible politics nor the interminable pedagogy involved in attempting to convince and otherwise educate everyone in the damn universe that we've got their best interests in mind. Hell, half the reason our engineering is so effective is because three-quarters of the Cosmos have never heard of us. People say the Mothmen are a mystery, that we're a legend. Yeah, okay, we're a legend. But what we really are is *legendary*. Lead, follow or get out of the way, am I right? And sometimes you've got to drive from the back seat, to manage the hell out of your managers, as they say. Isn't that what you and I have been doing all along?"

"That, and avoiding death by committee," said Cog, submitting to the inevitability of his cold dinner. The General's face was blank – it was rare that he managed to say anything the General found at all compelling. He tried again. "But what came of it, sir?" The General raised an eyebrow at him, which was encouraging. "I mean to say, what came of all the discussion, sir, and the conferences and meetings and –"

"Well!" – the General puffed his chest out, blew on his medals and swiped at them with his handkerchief – "our leadership was steadfast; we stated in no uncertain terms that we should engineer a proper response on behalf of the otherwise flummoxed Mothmen priests; a properly official-sounding response, expressing incredulities and anticipated sympathies and so on, so as to acknowledge but deflect any suspicion on behalf of the Time Guard. It's not a smokescreen, it's just the way the geo-politics work, Cog; it's how the game is played at this level."

Cog nodded, sensing an inevitable exposition. "Yessir."

The General swigged from his bottle, slammed it on the desktop and indeed continued to hold forth. "The whole predicament begs the question, in my mind at least, as to what value the Mothmen are adding. This alliance, Cog; what's it doing for us? I dare say I'm all for declassifying the top-secret designation of the larger mission and otherwise allowing those of us in the trenches a legitimate level of influence, not merely an opinion, on the proceedings. He shoved himself away from his desk, his glide-chair drifting backwards, and spread his arms wide. "It's only at disingenuous gatherings like SnoGlobeCon, after all, isn't it, with everyone posturing and straining to put on airs of tolerance and cosmic unity and so forth that everyone gets carried away with playing nice and accommodating all the cultural idiosyncrasies that tie up progress; that tie up the engineering we're trying to accomplish." He stood up. "It's the same old story, isn't it? Getting stuck in the past? Fear of change. Roadblocks for the sake of, I don't know, self-serving agendas? Powerplays? People trying to keep their jobs at the expense of doing what's right?" He aimed a finger at

Cog again. "Enlightenment. Have you ever heard that word before, Cog? Enlightenment?"

"No, sir." Actually, he'd read about various contemplative ideologies, mythologies of enlightenment, as they were called in the old banned-books archives, but he'd always maintained that it was safer, from a career stand-point at least, to keep his occult dabbling to himself – his researches took place off-duty and outside his army office.

"The Mothmen can go ahead and get carried away with an idea like that," said the General, "and suffer the vicissitudes of un-engineered space-time for eons and eons and eons. That's their business. While we've been busy working our asses off, getting things done, doing the heavy lifting of the future, *doing* things to make the universe what we want it to be, what it ought to be. Willing it into existence."

The General was right, of course. The Molemen were right. But the General's brusque delivery and his truncated world view always grated upon Cog's more refined sensibilities. He believed in the Cosmic Clock Project with his whole being. It simply went without saying that they, as a race, were at the forefront of change and progress and the betterment of the Universe. Nobody else was capable of engineering space-time, it was that simple. Otherwise it would've already been done. He merely lamented the cosmo-political posturing his own culture seemed determined to inject into everything; the vainglorious aspect that tarnished, in his opinion, the otherwise immaculate utility of everything they sought to accomplish. Moleman engineering prowess was a birthright. History demonstrated that other cultures routinely squandered their abilities, their opportunities. Cultures arose, peaked, endured dissolution. Not us. "MPH, sir," he said.

The General chuckled and strode across his office. He faced the wall of windows with his legs spread and his hands behind his back, as if survey-ing the entire metropolis. "MPH. You're exactly right, Cog, my good man. Perhaps I'm nothing but an old windbag. But I'm right, too; absolutely on point in my own way. I believe in the Cosmic Clock Program. The CCP is my life. It's been *our* life, yours and mine, all these years." He glanced over his shoulder at him. "These twenty billion Molemen, Cog, they're relying on us; we've got a responsibility to them. To the entire Cosmos. If some of these lesser cultures regard us with envy and suspicion; if they consider us a threat, so be it. That's half the reason we work so hard to remain unseen, unobserved, to perpetuate the legend of our demise. So we can get our damn work done without any interference. Who needs the resistance, the argument, the endless compromise proposed by every damn foreign entity? He gestured at the cityscape with his arms outstretched, his palms open, wiggling his fingers. "It's good to be home."

Cog stood up, sensing the diatribe had concluded. The man could indeed wind himself up.

"Meanwhile," said the General, his voice hoarse from his exertions, "we've got our own work to do." He clapped his broad hands and rubbed them together vigorously, reestablishing himself behind his desk. "You're doing well, Cog. Keep it up. You and me and everyone else in the Giza cell project are going to see rewards - unprecedented rewards. I've been assured of that. Now," he said, implementing his military, business-like tone of voice. "Update me on Giza."

It took a moment for Cog to come back to himself – it was always a test of his powers of mental endurance and concentration to appear attentive during the General's rants. He took a breath, tapped at his device to update the data and launched into his report. "Five attained the plateau on schedule for his rendezvous with Bruggs and Laron. However, sir, apparently neither Bruggs nor Laron are in possession of the antiquity. Nor its coordinates. That is to say, Five reports that we've been lied to and that Bruggs and Laron have resorted to employing a Bedouin, of all things, as their guide. Supposedly to help them locate the relic."

The General inhaled noisily and rubbed his face. "Go on."

"As such, Five has been doing his best, short of breaking cover, to expedite acquisition."

"We can't suffer a delay, Cog," said the General. "Five must obtain the antiquity within the scheduled time frame or, frankly, there won't be one. We can't risk the zodiac passing out of congruence. We can't endure the loss of our advantage in reengineering the clockwork machinery, you know that as well as I do." He flopped back in his chair and frowned. "This is exactly why I'm tempted to run roughshod over the middling irrelevancies of our agreement with the Mothmen. That's a compromise position we cannot afford – it binds our hands, dammit."

"Compromise, sir? Regarding the Arrow of Time?"

The General nodded. "There's too much at stake now from the engineering perspective. I don't care what the hell protocol we've supposedly bound ourselves to with the Mothmen – the respect we're supposed to demonstrate on behalf of their belief system. It's their nostalgia, that's all it is. Nostalgia. Romance. Interpreting time as omnipotent and unidirectional. People are weak that way, always looking to the past when the answers are all in the future, out in front of us. Meanwhile, the bullshit divine imperative that blinds the Mothmen to the reality they claim to have apprehended is what is going to wreck this alliance, Cog, you mark my words."

"What if we asked for another extension, based on Five's report?"

"No," said the General. "I'm telling you, Cog, we just received the only extension we're going to get and the last of the funding to make it happen. And now it's all about results. Say goodbye to anything but clamping your ass to the existing implementation schedule. Do you hear me? According to plan. Five has got to find a way."

"But the complications at Giza might... it may...." Cog couldn't help stammering. He knew – for shit's sake he *sympathized* – with the difficulties Five was enduring. He'd spent more than his fair share of time in the field, after all. Not on a mission anywhere near as delicate and challenging as this, of course, but he'd put his time in, bucking up, sleeping rough, being away from home for years on end, toughing it out. He collected himself. "The rift in the CTA, sir – we've been warned of the potential consequences –"

"Political bollocks!" The General fumed. "Pseudo-scientific posturing!" He narrowed his eyes at Cog and jabbed his finger at the desktop. "So-called consequence research has always been funded, as you damn well know, by factions of the PMC and the T.E. All those likeminded – I should say *softminded* – academic types who are intimidated by the types of change they claim to embrace. Change like we make manifest. They're merely keen to perpetuate their own flabby institutions, Cog. Including the pesky Time Detective Cooperative."

"Contingent, sir."

"Pardon?"

"The Time Detective Contingent."

"It's all bosh," said the General. He looked hard at Cog. "Time is not, as the Mothmen and some of the folks on Earth like to believe, a vector. Relativity. Retro-causation. Indeterminacy. Block universes. Neither does any of that crap get it right. Bosh and more bosh. Any halfway competent engineer knows that time has no primal direction, let alone any degree of magnitude; it has no cosmic importance, let alone a divine one. Time is a tool. Eternity is what we make it. Earth is going to be our first demonstration of that, that's all. They drew the coordinate card and lost."

The General gulped the last of his energy drink, crushed it in his fist and flung the container at the waste basket – it bounced off the rim with a "clack" and rattled across the floor, coming to rest in the corner of the room. He stared at it and puffed his cheeks out as if he was deflating. From his exertions? From his travels?

It's weighing on him, too, thought Cog. It has to be. For all his grandstanding the General is as worried about Five and this mission as I am. Perhaps more so. He's the one who was close with Five's father. He's the one who pushed for Five's selection. He's got everything on the line.

"We've only a week, then, sir?" said Cog. "Seven days to acquire the artifacts? And then for Five to complete the repairs and the installation? All of it?"

"Less than that, Cog." He glanced at the chronometer. "One hundred sixty-four hours, eleven minutes...."

They watched the deciseconds tick down, the centiseconds speed past and the milliseconds rush past in a blur.

"We've no time to lose, Cog. No time at all to waste. That's an order."

Cog closed the door to his dreary, windowless office and slumped into his chair, the sound of the General's booming voice still ringing in his ears. The thought of initiating his next communication with Five, scheduled within the hour, whereby he'd be compelled to demand results from the young cadet at all costs, including threatening the lives of their conspirators, seemed a nearly impossible weight. More and more he'd come to interpret his own career ambitions as troublesome, as an unwanted threat to his sense of molemanity. He'd assumed his years of soldiering, such as they'd been, would have hardened him to the realities, the necessities of what had to be done when great change was undertaken. Instead, ironically, he'd become more attuned to a kind of tolerance; he was no longer convinced that absolutely everyone sought engineering as a salvation, as the means to an experience of being properly alive. Meanwhile, all these years of dutiful servitude seemed to be transforming him into exactly what he hated: an administrator – a soft-hearted, soft-minded, gutless bureaucrat.

He sighed at the framed image of himself astride the gangway of the very first Hadron to penetrate all four galactic quadrants. Hadron Engine Number One. Incredible. What a beauty. What a story! He'd wanted his wife in the photograph – they weren't married then – but she'd been determined to allow him his moment with the great train, as she put it. "You've waited for this practically your whole life, haven't you?" And it had seemed that way, after all those failed lottery applications year after year. The General had pulled the strings for him, even though he'd only been on the job a year. He felt a pang of guilt for having become so impatient with the old war horse. He enhanced the illumination of the image and sat back. It'd been so long since he really looked at it. At himself in it. *I was happy then. So happy. Me and the great train.* He sighed again, dimmed the image, and tapped his transponder.

"Five. Do you copy, Five?"

*"Both kinds of wisdom, straight and crooked, should be within the call of the king. If thou art not prepared to be cruel and to kill men as the fisher kills the fish, abandon every hope of great success."*[1]

# CHAPTER 13

# THE CROOKED WAY

**A DRY WIND FROM THE NORTH** howled across the plateau. Five stirred within his enclosure but did not awaken; not until a tendril of sand trickled into his collar. He groaned and half-opened his eyes. Hell, he thought. I feel like hell. His joints were stiff, his muscles sore. His hand had become alarmingly swollen. I can't do this.

His trek from Dahshur through the open desert had been arduous – twelve hours of intense heat, penetrating sunlight and strenuous lumbering across the shifting, blowing sands. He'd rested only briefly at midday and only then to hunker down out of sight of a small caravan that threatened to cross his path. He couldn't afford to risk being seen; he knew the experienced eyes of a Bedouin, to say nothing of their camels, would spy him from perhaps kilometers away. Moreover, his cloaking device had become unreliable, switching itself off and on again maddeningly until he was forced to dismantle it – grains of sand and a pernicious dust had somehow infiltrated its circuitry. Sand and dust seemed to infiltrate *everything* here, despite his precautions, despite the supposed impermeable seals engineered into the design of his equipment. Hell and blood, I'm tired.

He'd arrived fatigued at the Plateau and made directly for a spot between two of the three small secondary pyramids – the so-called Queens pyramids constructed along the southern aspect of Menkaure's tomb – and bivouacked. The last thing he remembered was hollowing out a place in the sand and crawling beneath his shadow-tarp. But sleep hadn't helped. *Beware the effects of hyper-dimensional travel fatigue, otherwise known as hyper-lag: they include psychological as well as physical sluggishness.* Blah, blah. He and the other cadets had prided themselves in brushing aside such dreary field manual advice. We're young. It's all attitude, they'd told themselves.

He rolled over and groped into his pack for a vitamin chew. *Do not be remiss in regularly consuming your vitamin chew, especially in advance of strenuous activity – it will help curb deleterious mental and physical effects.* Too late, he thought, straining to sit up.

He sat, chewing, and peered ruefully over the lip of his dugout into the silvery-blue night; into its alien, strangely beguiling emptiness. The immaculate silence seemed incongruous – it had been windy, hadn't it? I must have dreamt it. He checked the time. Zero four-hundred hours. Go time. The beginning of his mission proper. Acquire the artifact. Engineer the installation. Get home. It sounded simple enough. Yet here he was already a day and a night behind schedule.

"Mind the meridians, pay attention to the parallels and heed the hyper-meridians." He repeated the mantra quietly, almost unconsciously. Of course there were myriad ways the mission could've been made easier, more logistically efficient. Instead of trudging miserably through the desert, for instance, he could've hired a boat and drifted leisurely down the Nile from Dahshur. But he understood the space-time imperatives, his responsibility to leave no trace; to return to Mega City One just as he'd left it. That meant no unnecessary contact with the populace, no use of non-issued equipment, no increasing the risk of skewing the time-space continuum outside of mission parameters. No slip-ups.

Home. He felt as if he couldn't be further from it. He looked up, scanning the stars, looking deeply into space: Mega City One was out there; his planet, his sun, his moons. An ancient version, at least. He sighed. When I get back I'll be a Moleman engineer. I'll have done everyone proud and I'll have lived up to dad's legacy.

He switched on his headlamp and reached for his book, selecting a page he had marked:

> One has only to know and trust, and the ageless guardians will appear. Having responded to his own call, and continuing to follow courageously as the consequences unfold, the hero finds all the forces of the unconscious at his side. Mother Nature herself supports the mighty task.[v]

Mother Nature. No such thing. Except somehow the words buoyed him every time he read them. He flipped back through the pages, pausing at another passage.

> The figure of the tyrant-monster is known to the mythologies, folk traditions, legends, and even nightmares of the world; and his characteristics are everywhere essentially the same. He is the hoarder of the general benefit. He is the monster avid for the greedy rights of "my and mine." Self-terrorized, fear-haunted, alert at every hand to meet and battle back the anticipated aggressions of his environment, which are primarily the reflections of the uncontrollable impulses to acquisition within himself, the giant of self-achieved independence is the world's messenger of disaster, even though, in his mind, he may entertain himself with humane intentions. Wherever he sets his hand there is a cry (if not from the housetops, then – more miserably – within every heart): a cry for the redeeming hero, the carrier of the shining blade, whose blow, whose touch, whose existence, will liberate the land.[w]

Five closed his eyes and lay back, savoring the ominous thrill of the passage. The wind had picked up – he could hear it whistling softly, hissing across the sand – no, whispering, like a mysterious lullaby. He imagined it eddying between the stony monuments of the ancient plateau, imagined ....

"Five! Do you copy!"

He started at the sound and sat up, striking his head against the low-slung shadow-tarp. Damn! He fumbled for his transponder. Damn, damn, damn! He'd been laying atop his device. "Affirmative," he said, stammering; "Five here." He rubbed his face, dismayed at his incompetence. How long have I been out?

Cog's voice betrayed a measure of urgency: "What is your status, Five?"

"Bivouacked, sir. Queens Pyramids." He checked the time. "I rendezvous with Bruggs at zero seven-hundred."

"Make certain Bruggs delivers," said Cog. "The deadline is fixed. No delays, no exceptions – the strongest measures have been authorized; you know what that means."

Five's guts rolled. He knew. Except he didn't know if he could go through with it. Threatening a man's life. Lethal force. The ultimate leave-no-trace override. He was relieved Cog couldn't see him, sitting here, vacillating. He fidgeted at the closeness of his dugout. The glamor and excitement and novelty of the whole damn adventure seemed to have vanished, slipped through his fingers like this alien desert sand.

"Five?"

"Yessir. Copy that, sir. I understand. Strongest measures." He squeezed his eyes shut and clinched his fists. Get your shit together.

"Remember about Laron," said Cog; "he's unpredictable, more cunning than Bruggs. Perhaps desperate. Nevertheless, if Bruggs fails us, we force our hand with Laron. Play the two against each other if necessary, Five. Remember your training. *Rely* on your training. You've got to be ruthless. I don't have to remind you what happens if we fail. There will be no living it down, Five; not for you, not for me, not for General Ten-Square. Success is right there in front of us. Your success. Our success. The success of the Cosmic Clock Project. The success of our race."

"Yessir." His own voice sounded hollow. He somehow *felt* hollow, as if his confidence had evaporated. It's the hyper-lag, he told himself; it'll pass. He was relieved when his transponder suddenly vibrated and a message flashed across the display: "AT MENK VALLEY TEMPLE."

"Sir. I've just heard from Bruggs. He's arrived."

"Copy," said Cog. "Do you have any questions?"

"No, sir."

"I'm signing off. Good luck. Cog out."

The sudden silence seemed to hang in the air. He was on his own. He could hear himself breathing. Get moving. He peered out from the edge of his shadow-tarp into the predawn glow. The horizon was visible, as was the outline of the pyramid. The light was coming up; the landscape was coming to life. It was all happening with or without him. He felt his destiny somehow trying to outrun him and he hastened to stow his pack and decamp. He broke open a ration and shoved it into his mouth, washing it down with mouthfuls of energy gel, crouching in his hovel, chomping indifferently as he ran through his assigned tasks step by step despite his jangling nerves. Shit! Bruggs! He'd forgotten to respond! He snatched at his transponder, typing madly: "Copy. ETA 10 minutes."

Five considered foregoing donning the synthetic *tob* and *kufeya* – the dreadful robe and head piece, complete with *igal* he'd been lugging in his pack.[29] What were the odds of him being seen by anyone at this hour? *Leave no trace - minimize your impact in time and space.* Stick to protocol. Protocol will keep the mission safe. Listen to me, he thought, reciting training mantras. I used to roll my eyes at training mantras. He struggled to jam his ears beneath the *igal* – the headband that secured his *kufeya* – his injury made him clumsy enough without his heart pounding

---

[29] A *tob* and *kufeya* (optionally secured by an *igal* or camel-wool rope) composes the basic wardrobe of Egyptian Bedouin men.

and his hands shaking. Deep breath. He managed a shuddering inhale and fraught exhale. He was perspiring and he hadn't even exerted himself. *What in hell is wrong with me?* He straightened his headgear, adjusted his *tob* and immediately felt completely inauthentic, hopelessly contrived, a misshapen freak in comparison to a true Egyptian. *Any man of the desert would find him out at first glance. Get moving.* He forced himself to crawl from the dugout, brushed himself off, readjusted his garments and looked around. *Nobody watching. Nothing moving. Just the open sky, the monuments and the desert.* He kicked sand across his shadow-tarp, resisting his compulsion to get down on his knees and eliminate all evidence of his presence. *Just get moving – the shifting sands will obscure everything, no one will notice.* He tapped his transponder, reverifying the coordinates of the bivouac, did his best to steady himself and moved out.

He paused to examine at the eastern face of the Menkaure Pyramid – the sunrise had tinted the rough stones a pinkish hue – then looked east, down the length of the decrepit causeway, the jumbled, forlorn stones half-buried. When new, this had been a mortuary temple, walled and roofed. Now, it was a pathetic ruin. Some five-hundred meters away stood the Valley Temple, his rendezvous point with Bruggs. It all appeared familiar enough, more or less exactly as it was rendered in the training simulations.

He trudged alongside the rocky remains of the causeway, resisting his urge to hurry, determined to pace himself, to practice blending in. "Where are you, Bruggs?" he mumbled to himself, scanning the length of the rubble. There! A human, rotund, dressed in a dark suit coat; standing by the Valley Temple entrance. Nearby he spied another human, a slightly built Arab by the looks of him, in a white *tob* and *kufeya* and tending a camel. A dragoman, perhaps. He wrapped his *kufeya* closer round his face, snugged the *igal* over his ears and trudged towards them.

[*Bruggs speaks henceforth in German; Bab speaks in Arabic and Five uses his auto-translator to communicate in the language of each.*]

"Hello, Bruggs," said Five, surprising himself when his auto-translator emitted a spurious, incoherent squawk.

Both Bruggs and the camel flinched at the sound, the animal tugging at its rein so that the Arab had to calm the beast, cooing at it and clicking his tongue.

Five adjusted the squelch control – the damn thing had worked flawlessly when he'd packed it. He resorted to speaking more slowly and annunciating more carefully, a technique that sometimes improved the unit's response. "Hello, Bruggs." Coherent German, good. Bruggs nonetheless appeared baffled. "It's me, Bruggs. Five."

"Mister Five?" Bruggs' fleshy jowls quivered when he spoke. He compulsively smoothed the pockets of his dusty suitcoat and nodded warily. "Of course, of course. Good morning, Mister Five."

There were those who seemed at ease with the phenomenon of watching a man's lips moving out of synch with the translation of his words and those for whom it seemed a perpetually unsettling experience. Five considered himself one of the former and apparently Bruggs was one of the latter. He was a human from Earth's nineteenth century, after all, technologically challenged to say the least. Bruggs's discomposure nevertheless assuaged his own. Try using it to your advantage, he thought. "Do you have it?"

Bruggs withdrew a crumpled handkerchief and coughed into it, a wheezing, emphysema-like hack that strained the man's entire chest cavity. He wiped his brow. "Please, Mister Five, in due time." He gestured towards the entrance to the Temple. "Let us talk inside."

Five waited, observing Bruggs' affectations – his labored breathing, his clumsy, unathletic posture; the apparently permanent scowl on his face and his darting, black eyes.

The Arab secured the rein of his camel under a large stone and made to follow them.

Five paused. "Alone."

Bruggs looked perplexed then glanced at the Arab. "He is merely my dragoman."

Five didn't respond.

Bruggs shrugged. "Wait here, Bab."

Bruggs entered the temple and paused within the vestibule, turning to face Five while scanning the crumbling walls and rocky ground with a reverent, intense regard.

"The Valley Temple of Menkaure," said Bruggs. He appeared to relish the space. "Originally constructed of mud brick. However, there are indications of limestone in the structure of the pavement and column bases." He gestured casually at the debris. "This vestibule is flanked by two sets of four storerooms. The southern set opens into a long corridor that runs along the length of the temple, takes a turn to the north and meets with the distal end of the causeway. Here at the west end of the vestibule a doorway leads to the courtyard."

Bruggs looked at him expectantly and it occurred to Five that the man perhaps assumed that he likewise maintained an interest in Egyptology for its own sake. "Let's talk in the courtyard."

Bruggs bristled, tucking in his flabby chin, his posture stiff and haughty, then seemed to catch himself, stifling his irritation and leading them into the open. The rough-shod face of the Menkaure Pyramid soared upwards before them.

Five glanced to the north – the more ancient and imposing Khafre and Khufu monuments were still largely obscured by the morning haze but even partially hidden they rendered the Menkaure a bedraggled, disappointing cousin in comparison.

Bruggs, meanwhile, appeared transfixed by something at his feet, peering down past his belly, hands on hips, seemingly oblivious to the grandeur surrounding him. He inhaled a raspy breath and coughed quietly into his handkerchief, tapping a hewn stone with the toe of his shoe. "These are limestone slabs," he said. He gestured to the south. "Over there is a basin with a drainage system that empties under the pavement. At the end of this section, at the western end of the causeway, is a pillared hall containing six columns which once supported its roof. Beyond the hall is a sanctuary and to the south of that are smaller chambers, the niches where the famous triads of King Menkaure were found. I can tell you I would have liked to have participated in those early excavations. Fifty years ago already."

Again, Five waited. He felt as if they were both still taking the measure of each other. Bruggs' scholarship seemed authentic enough. But his aptitude for dealing in black market antiquities, which was the entire point, had yet to be proven. "We regarded the Kings of the Fourth Dynasty – Snefru, Menkaure and the others," said Five, "as able administrators. My father spoke well of the intelligence and vision of King Snefru in particular. They used to fish and hunt fowl together on the Nile. And of course Menkaure was a competent engineer in his way."

Bruggs appeared duly unsettled, scratching nervously at his belly and rubbing the back of his fat neck with his handkerchief. He removed his bowler and mopped his entire head, glancing sideways at Five. "Hmm, Indeed." He cleared his throat and glanced at the brightening sky. "It will be warm today, I should think." He shed his suit coat and draped it over his arm.

It's hardly warm, thought Five. He noticed how Bruggs' fleshy hands and fingers appeared as flexible as a child's and never seemed to cease fluttering about his person, smoothing first his suit coat and now the fabric of his shirt. "The artifact," said Five. "Where is it?"

"Yes, yes, well. It is... how should I say...? Nearby. I mean to say, we *almost* have it."

"Almost?" Five took a step closer to Bruggs.

Bruggs once again cleared his throat and a coughing fit ensued. When he'd recovered, taking careful, shaking breaths and re-mopping his flushed face and neck, his voice was hoarse. "Mister Five, you must understand. We – Laron and myself – we have only yesterday received word from our guide – a Bedouin as it happens who travels widely but is known as a reliable dealer in antiquities. He is to meet us here, on the Plateau, where he promises to deliver the artifact."

"You agreed to provide the artifact today."

Bruggs held up his hands defensively. "Today, well, yes, we shall do our best, but –"

"Today. That is the agreement." Five forced himself to speak slowly, half on account of the auto-translator and half on account of intending to maintain an air of imperious authority. "Today, Bruggs. Or you will not be paid. And we will engage other means."

Bruggs wrung his hands, nodding compliantly. "Of course, Mister Five, of course. But, indeed, regarding the issue of the fee. Given the effort we have been forced to undertake –"

"Money will be the least of your worries should you fail to deliver." Not bad, thought Five, surprised at his own daring. Emboldened, he practiced glaring at Bruggs. The man was clearly a feeble, self-important lout. Both Bruggs and Laron were, after all, nothing more than part-time criminals – petty thieves and opportunists. That this part of the mission had to depend on such incompetence was maddening.

Bruggs appeared rankled, his eyes narrowing as he looked Five up and down. "This posturing of ours is absurd. You must understand the delicacy of the situation."

"I'll be the judge," said Five. But, indeed, this play acting and games-manship was already proving exhausting. Isn't anything about this mission going to go to plan? "Where are you encamped?"

"Hmph!" said Bruggs. "South of the Western Cemetery, of course. Near the Petrie base of operations."

Bruggs's stubborn imperiousness was impossible. "Where *exactly*?"

"Why, as everyone knows, at the northeast corner of the Khafre Pyramid. I am director of the excavations."

"What about the girl?"

Bruggs huffed again. "Girl?"

"The one you and Laron kidnapped. Where is she?"

Bruggs shrugged and made an exasperated face. "Of what concern –?"

"She is a liability, Bruggs, and an unnecessary risk to our doing proper business. She is a time detective."

Bruggs' eyes flashed. "She is nothing. No one. A nobody. Perhaps of some pitiful value by way of...." He trailed off. "It does not concern you."

"Your bungling is unacceptable. You've placed the entire operation at risk."

Bruggs shrugged and his voice cracked as he raised his voice. "We have her transponder. The young woman is powerless here. Incapable of straying. Irrelevant."

"Show me your camp. Take me there."

"Now?" Bruggs scowled at his pocket watch. "I am sorry, Mister Five, but I have additional excavations at the Sphinx – I must inspect them this morning."

"Your problems are not my problems," said Five. "Our agreement is your primary concern."

Bruggs' stiffened, a little cloud of dust gathering at his feet, and glared at Five, balling his hands into fists. He strode away in the direction they'd come. "We will proceed to the Sphinx."

Five watched the man stumble along the causeway and disappear into the temple. Now what? Run after him? Threaten him? If he's lying about the whereabouts of the artifact – if he's been lying this whole time.... Five ground his teeth and trudged after him. The thought of a confrontation at this early stage seemed perilous. And he wasn't convinced he could manage it. Better to give it time.

"Bab," said Bruggs, "I am going to ride."

The dragoman tugged on the camel's saddle straps, then coaxed the beast to its knees.

Bruggs grasped at the saddle and clambered into it, a precarious enough operation that required a good deal of huffing and puffing from Bruggs and much effort on behalf of the dragoman to leverage the man's bulk. The camel, for its part, looked askance at Bruggs and snorted, reluctant to stand.

"Up, dammit," said Bruggs, waving his arms. "Up, up, up!"

The dragoman cajoled and the beast yielded, rising with the peculiar combination of awkwardness and grace that defined the nature of its species. Bruggs sat sweating and swearing.

"Let us go, Bab! *Yalla!* For the love of God!"

The dragoman tugged on the rein and the camel strode forth. Five fell in behind them, struggling against the lingering stiffness in his legs, the awkward drape of his disguise and the rising heat of the morning. It struck him that he might have difficulty keeping up. He trudged along fitfully, perspiring and unable to catch his breath before discovering he could more or less mimic the mindful fluidity of the camel's gait. Lift your foot, place your foot, glide. Lift, place, glide. Why hadn't he learned this in basic training? Come to think of it, he probably would have – he'd been exempted from so many of the requirements the other cadets had to endure that it had caused a controversy in the ranks. Leadership explained that it was the urgency of this mission that necessitated the exemptions and who was he to argue? *Take what's given,* his mother had told him; *don't do anything to inflame anyone's jealousy. Advantages come with a price.* And so on.

Meanwhile, the camel intrigued him. At rest, the creature appeared an improbably awkward, knobby-kneed, biological incongruity – an unsightly bag of bones brimming with a distasteful irascibility. But to watch it float across the sand was to appreciate the elegant efficiency of its design. *Ship of the desert,* he'd read somewhere. Indeed. They continued northeast, marching into the heart of the central Plateau until Five finally worked up his confidence and came up beside Bruggs.

"I have no time for the Sphinx, Bruggs."

Bruggs seemed determined to ignore him.

"Bruggs!" His auto-translator squawked and the camel started, coming to a halt then turning in circles, stomping its hooves, fighting the rein.

"Ack!" cried Bruggs, clutching at the camel seat and flailing his legs. "Bab! Don't just stand there!"

Bab was already doing his best to calm the beast, scurrying alongside it, clutching at the rein with one hand and camel's bridle with the other

– "Sshh! Sshh!" – until the animal relented, content to hold its chin high, snorting softly at the dragoman.

Bruggs appeared as if he couldn't steer the camel if his life depended upon it and carried on as if the situation were an unholy disaster. "Mister Five!" He was shouting over his shoulder. "A man must make a living! Coolies are as stupid and unreliable and infuriating as this lunatic camel! I surprise them with my inspections or I get no work out of them! Meanwhile, you are free, Mister Five, to go to the camp yourself!" He finally lowered his voice. "Bab, let us go – who is paying you, somebody besides me?" Bruggs gestured fitfully and kicked at the camel. "*Yalla, yalla*, go, go!"

Five brooded. This is impossible. They are a pair, exactly, this obdurate ass of a man and his spiteful, stubborn camel. What to do? But there was nothing for it, no point in arguing, at least not yet; not until he was prepared to do something about it.

It wasn't long before they'd crossed the open expanse of the Plateau and arrived at the haunches of the great Sphinx, at this point in history mostly submerged by millennia of drifting sand. He watched the coolies at their drudgery, the diggers with their shovels and hoes, the men and boys cradling flimsy woven baskets, hauling their sandy debris to the perimeter of the excavation, pitching it aside and circling back in a perpetual cloud of dust.

Five paused to watch Bab attempting to dissuade Bruggs from his proposed route down the slope of loose sand and gravel that comprised the excavation and rather circumambulate the dig – an obviously more practical route. Bruggs just barked at him.

"No! This way! We shall go down and up the other side!"

Bab relented, leading the camel, Bruggs pitched forward in his seat, clutching at it, attempting to counterbalance himself as both Bab and the camel plunged knee-deep in sand.

"Ack! Bab! You dog! You will be the death of me!" The three of them half-lunged and half-spilled themselves down the embankment, emerging from the modest avalanche they'd spawned at the bottom of the dig. A handful of the thirty or so coolies paused to glance over their shoulders at the spectacle.

"What are you looking at?" shouted Bruggs. "You are being paid to dig, not gawk! Dig! Dig!" He threw up his hands, inadvertently throwing himself off balance so that he was forced to once again clutch at his saddle. "Where is Laron?" That his shouting was ineffectual – who among the coolies could possibly understand him whether he yelled in English or German, after all? – merely seemed to further Bruggs's tyrannical posturing. "Confound it! Listen to me!" One or two coolies glanced tentatively at him but otherwise held to their task. "Confound it! Laron!" Bruggs bellowed and squirmed in his seat like a child, kicking at the camel's sides and gesturing in the direction of a rocky promontory across from the Sphinx, atop which were gathered a clutch of people, foreigners in European clothes – tourists perhaps – alongside their dragomen and a few camels.

Now what? thought Five. He ground his teeth at the growing unwieldiness of the situation.

"Up!" shouted Bruggs. "Get me to the other side!" The indefatigable Bab led the camel onwards, the coolies taking care to avoid them. Five watched man and camel and rider reverse the process, sand and gravel pouring down the embankment as they struggled, finally gaining the promontory in what seemed an exhausting, Herculean effort on behalf of all.

Five chose the level route around the excavation, in due time arriving in view of the foreigners but not so close as to draw their attention. Three middle-aged Caucasian women on camel-back, dressed in the heavy, overwrought clothing of the period. Two men stood casually alongside, perspiring in their dark suit coats and fanning their faces with their hats. A dragoman and several young Egyptian boys made up the balance of their little caravan.

The group had been chatting amongst themselves, gesturing casually towards the Sphinx, gazing absently across the Plateau but otherwise bestowing most of their unhurried attention upon a pale, angular, unhandsome man with a hawkish nose and deep-set eyes shaded beneath his broad hat. He was lounging on a folding chair near the edge of the promontory, facing the Sphinx across the gap of the excavation, his head tipped back so as to regard a pad of paper he held at arm's length, one end of a pencil pressed against his chin. He was attended by a young Egyptian, a coolie boy whose sole task, apparently, was to shade him by way of holding a frilly-edge parasol over his head.

One of the men spoke up. "Hail, and good morning to you!" He laughed. "That's quite a climb."

Bruggs huffed at them and retorted in a heavy accent. "Tourists!"

"We are indeed tourists," said one of the women unselfconsciously. "We've been several days coming down the Nile and now we're here for the Pyramids, of course."

"And the marvelous Sphinx," said another.

"Monsieur Blanc here is doing the scene justice, certainly," one of the men added.

"He's a brilliant artist," the first woman stated. "Monsieur Blanc, I don't mean to embarrass you."

The seated man nodded and regarded them mildly, as if engrossed in his drawing. "*Merci beaucoup*, Madam," he said, gesturing into space as if to acknowledge something unseen. "Alas, I'm working with only a pencil – my oils would do better to capture the light."

Bruggs spat. "*Monsieur Blanc!* Capture the light! Laron, you are a lazy fool! May I trouble your artistic sensibilities to perhaps do what you are paid to do and supervise the digging? Better yet, why don't you trade that pencil of yours for a shovel and join the coolies?" Bruggs' jowls quivered and his belly shook in cooperation with his bellowing. "Well?"

Laron rose from his chair in a huff and tried to compose himself, straightening his suit clothes, tucking his pad and pencil under his arm and performing an awkward bow on behalf of his admirers before shuffling down the rise in the direction of the work crew.

The tourists exchanged glances, fidgeting and fanning themselves but otherwise affecting insouciance to Bruggs's disagreeable air.

"*Yalla!*" said Bruggs, kicking at the camel. "Go, go!" He twisted in his saddle, glaring at the work of the excavation. "*Laron! œil le Sang! Oui, vous êtes surnom convient à votre laideur et votre incompétence français!*"[30]

Laron, thought Five. It figures. He ought to have recognized him.

Laron shrugged and turned away, sulking at the coolies. "*Mon Dieu! Mon Dieu!*" he grumbled; "*Une telle lout!*"[31] - I'm not your servant!"

"Lout?" bellowed Bruggs.

"Sshh, sshh," Bab cooed, stroking the camel's neck amidst the uproar.

Meanwhile, Bruggs had managed to turn the camel away from the dig and appeared ready to leave. Five skirted the promontory, hustling to catch up, relieved that he'd avoided confrontation with coolies or tourists or for that matter Bruggs and Laron. And finally heading towards the pyramids felt like progress. If Bruggs turns out to be lying about the artifact, well... he didn't know what. He put his mind to his walking.

They marched along silently, proceeding in the direction of the Great Pyramid, Five pondering the back of Bab's *galibeya* – the man's tailored, smooth-fitting Egyptian robe. He wondered about the dragoman's persistent tolerance, wondered what it would take – how far the man would have to be pushed – for him to contradict Bruggs, either on behalf of his unfortunate camel or himself. The tolerance of these so-called dragomen, these professional servant-guides, astounded him. Moreover, there was something about Bab's measured persona that went beyond the proclivities of his race and his vocation. A dragoman who never said a thing, never sold himself, never held forth on the mysteries of ancient Egypt, never

---

[30] "Blood Eye! Yes, your nickname suits your ugliness and your French incompetence."
[31] "My God, My God! Such a lout!"

patronized his employer? And the man seems to understand his share of English, perhaps even French or German, for that matter. His expression, the way he carries himself, it seems to me that he comprehends more than he lets on. Five tried to bring himself up alongside Bab.

# CHAPTER 14

# BREAD & SALT

**THE PYRAMIDS ROAD STRETCHED OUT** before them like a dusty promenade; the sinuous branches of the eucalyptus trees reaching skyward as if to appease the relentless austerity of the desert with their foliage.

Vixy, her veil unclasped, tramped alongside the donkey cart as best she could, unsteady in her sandals and on the uneven ground but determined to enjoy the sun on her face, the open vista of the desert beyond the trees and most of all, to think. She was footsore, thirsty and hungry but otherwise glad to be walking freely and unobserved – the road was virtually empty of travelers. She was also desperate for a cigarette. *The next time Hesso smokes....*

The road followed a murky tributary of the Nile, its waters uninvitingly stagnant. Beyond its muddy banks was a small village, what amounted to a humble clutch of earthen, mud-brick structures nestled amongst a handful of Royal palm trees. It looked primitive and poor, a pathetic outpost that amplified her anxiety, her desperate sense of exile. How could she be certain this marching into the desert wasn't taking her further from Bruggs, Laron and her transponder – if they even possessed it – instead of closer? What if they'd destroyed it? What if they'd sold it? What if whomever they worked for – they must work for somebody more capable than themselves – had knowledge of it; had already taken it? The irony of hoping that the bumbling pair weren't as reckless and incapable as they appeared was maddening.

"That is the village of Kafr," said Amu.

Hesso gestured for them to come to a stop. "Kafr, yes," he said, glancing at Vixy – he seemed perpetually intrigued by her. "Full of dragomen these days, trying to make money from the foreigners and tourists." He sighed and looked towards the pyramids. "We'll reach the Western Cemetery soon enough. We can rest here." He led them to a shady portion of the roadside and dug through his camel bags.

Bishoy likewise rummaged amongst the stores on his cart and offered a package to Hesso.

"Ah, good," said Hesso, "Bishoy has *dukkha*."

Amu enlisted Vixy to help her lay down a blanket and Bishoy set the food before them – Hesso's bread, nuts and dates alongside the *dukkha*. A water skin was passed round and soon they were enjoying a Bedouin picnic.

"What is *dukkha*?" said Vixy.

Amu seemed momentarily at a loss. "It is different for everyone who makes it. A mixture of nuts and spices" – she made a motion with her hands – "pounded together."

Vixy, ravenous, nevertheless forced herself to mimic the patience of the others and dipped her flatbread sparingly into the *dukkha* paste, nibbling discreetly. The water from the water skins tasted earthy and while she considered its source and thought that perhaps it should have been boiled before they drank it, she still found herself doing as the others did – what choice did she have? The dried dates were plump, rich and irresistibly sweet – redolent of caramel, raisins and black tea. Indeed, everything about the meal seemed flavorful and nourishing – satisfying far beyond its spare, peasant-like appearance.

Hesso withdrew his tobacco pouch and papers and rolled a cigarette, settling against a tree, peering absently into the foliage overhead. "They say the Pyramids Road was inaugurated by Ismail in 1869 for the comfort of Empress Eugénie of France." He glanced around at each of them before addressing Bishoy in Arabic – to Vixy it sounded as if he were questioning the boy.

Bishoy nodded, grinning. "*Aiwa*."[32]

"Bishoy has heard the story," said Hesso. He struck a match and held it to his cigarette. "And you, Amu, have you heard the tale?"

"When I was a young girl."

Vixy had been sitting alongside Amu but got up and resettled herself across from Hesso, cultural proprieties be damned.

Hesso puffed on his cigarette and regarded her with a wry smile. "The Empress offered the monarch acacia trees that were planted on either side of the road. The legend says the Khedive had schemed with the engineer to bend the road sharply at some point, hoping the empress, who was accompanying him in her husband's absence, would be thrust against him and press her body against his." He smoked, regarding Vixy with a sidelong glance.

"So, did his little scheme work?" Vixy looked him squarely in the eye and reached for his cigarette. "Did the Khedive get what he wanted?"

Hesso seemed taken aback at first, his eyes darting between Vixy, Amu and Bishoy in turn, then back to Vixy. His expression hardened and he frowned at her outstretched hand.

Just when Vixy thought he may have taken offense, that she'd indeed been too forward, his countenance softened and he offered her the cigarette.

"I don't know," he said, watching her smoke. "I seem to have forgotten the ending. I only know the acacias were eventually replaced by these eucalyptus trees." He grinned wryly and shrugged.

Vixy laughed - a short, pleasant, unselfconscious laugh that seemed to disarm everyone. She handed Hesso his cigarette.

---

32 "Yes."

Nevertheless, Amu reseated herself next to Vixy, at the same time making an obvious effort to look askance at Hesso. She squeezed Vixy's hand and widened her eyes at her.

Vixy squeezed back. "We're just talking. There's no one to see us."

Amu averted her eyes and smoothed her robe.

Hesso discarded his cigarette, stood up and sauntered towards his camel. He fed the animal a handful of grain and stroked her neck. "We'll pass through the Eastern Cemetery. And then across the north side of the Khufu pyramid to the Western Cemetery." He untied the beast and led her onto the side of the road.

Bishoy had already begun gathering up their things and the women helped with the blanket.

"And there," said Hesso, "unless I am an ignorant dog, I expect to find Bruggs and Laron."

Vixy looked into the distance, towards the pyramids. They shimmered in the haze and heat, looming larger and more distinct; still thrilling but no longer comforting. Indeed, they now seemed foreboding, as if encountering them would somehow tip the scales of her destiny. She hugged herself and sighed, a painful longing sweeping over her. A longing for home. For her mother and father. For everything about her missing life.

It was mid-afternoon when Hesso led them into the shadow of the Great Pyramid of Khufu. The mid-November sun was low in the sky – they were traveling along the monument's north face – yet to Vixy the shade was nonetheless a relief. She was relieved, too, at the disappearance of her nagging sense of trepidation. Approaching these ancient icons on foot, gradually, had given her the opportunity to acclimate to their impenetrable antiquity, their remoteness and immensity. Like the skyscrapers in Manhattan when she'd first encountered them, they seemed somehow fragile, vulnerable, evocative of the hand of humanity that built them instead of the indomitable permanence she anticipated. Awesome, certainly, but not in the way a mountain was, or a sea, or for that matter, the desert. "So old," she murmured, running her hand along the surface of the stone. The lowest course stood perhaps one and a half meters high, almost up to her shoulder. How many lifetimes of work to quarry, transport, shape and fit all this? The accomplishment was staggering, almost magical; the physical, human effort incomprehensible. The pharaonic zeal that must have initiated this work and the cultural endurance required to sustain it across generations – it bordered on lunacy.

But Egyptology had never been her area. Mr. Z., on the other hand, could speak to it, to the mythology. Something he'd said about the Nile Valley had always stuck with her. *What is visible there represents to this day merely a portion of the archaeological treasures that lay beneath the sands.* It was such unfathomable intrigue that had drawn her first to archaeology, then anthropology and, finally, to the study of archaeological anthropology. And here I am walking the sands of Giza exactly where and when it all began – in the time and place of the birth of professional archaeology on this planet.

Shellback. The phrase came to mind suddenly. I'm a shellback. It struck her that she'd crossed over. It was some ancient initiation thing, a rite of passage for mariners when they managed to cross the equator for the first time in their sail ships. At least that's what she'd heard in cadet training. Likewise, a time detective cadet became a shellback at their first HDT event. *Nobody ever forgets it*, they'd told her. In fact, there wasn't a mentor in the whole cadet program, including Mr. Z., who wasn't anxious to regale any so-called pollywog – what they called a cadet who'd yet to make their first HDT – about what it was like; how your first crossing would change you forever. She always rolled her eyes at it all – it seemed so old-fashioned and silly. But secretly she'd thrilled to the idea of it; dreamed of it, even – what her first HDT would be like. Now here she was a shellback and not by choice. What she wouldn't give to be a damn pollywog again. Or to not be a cadet at all. She didn't even remember the trip. Just the horrible arrival. The irony brought tears to her eyes. Yes, she'd crossed over, something she'd set her sights upon, that she'd dreamt of doing and instead... look at me. I'm a statistic. An HDT accident. Nothing but a castaway.

Amu had been watching her. The woman's deep reserve combined with her authentic compassion always made Vixy uncomfortable, as if Amu somehow always knew more than she shared, not just about Bruggs and Laron and her own life but about many things.

"Have you been here before, Amu? To the pyramids?"

Amu looked down. "No. I've lived within sight of them all my life, but I never ventured into the desert. Even as a child I had no desire to come here, to see the pyramids up close. They were just something that had always been there. And now, as a *dallālah*, my work is in the city. An unmarried Arab woman would have no reason to travel here."

"A *dallālah*?"

"A woman who, I don't know how to say it." Amu struggled with her halting English. "A woman who sells goods, who trades."

"In the markets?"

"No. I sell to women in their homes; women who do not go out; women of the upper classes. Of the *ḥarīm*."

Vixy raised her eyebrows. "So, you're in business for yourself? An entrepreneur?"

Amu appeared bemused. She struggled to pronounce "entrepreneur." "What is this word?"

"An entrepreneur is a person who works for themselves instead of for someone else."

Amu shrugged. "Women of the *ḥarīms*, wealthy women, cannot – are not allowed to go to markets. They must buy clothing, jewelry, whatever they need for themselves, from the *dallālah*. From women like me."

"Then why do you work for Bruggs and Laron? You don't make enough money as a *dallālah*?"

Amu didn't answer.

Vixy touched Amu's arm. "I didn't mean to offend you, Amu. Did I say something wrong?"

Hesso, Bishoy and the animals were some distance ahead of them and Amu slowed, leaning closer to Vixy and lowering her voice: "I have a customer – a woman who has become a friend to me. Sitt Khadījah. She told me of Bruggs because of what he pays. For work that is not difficult. Caretaking. Is that what you call it? Cooking. Cleaning."

Vixy nodded.

Amu shrugged. "I cook and clean and sometimes I help with the sale of antiquities." She'd pronounced the word "antiquities" with precise emphasis, as if she'd practiced it.

Vixy waited, intrigued.

"Sitt Khadījah is a wealthy woman. She knows others who are wealthy. Foreigners, especially. People interested in items from the tombs. And she has a child, a small boy whom I care for."

"She needs your help to care for him?"

"There are nursemaids in the home, of course. But Zizo –" Amu glanced warily at Vixy, as if she'd not intended to reveal the boy's name. "The boy's father...." She trailed off, seemingly exasperated.

"What is it, Amu?"

"The boy's father is not the husband of Sitt Khadījah."

They walked for time in silence. "There's nothing so unusual about that, is there?" Vixy asked.

Amu shook her head as if to dismiss the idea. "Egypt is changing. They speak of British Rule and this man from England – Cromer is his name – they say he will bring more British. So that Miss Khadījah is always hopeful that Zizo's father – a London businessman – will arrive to work here."

"Then he could care for the boy himself," said Vixy.

"He could make it safe, make it better, for the boy," Amu replied. "Provide for Zizo's future."

They'd arrived at the western edge of the Great Pyramid and emerged from shadow into the glaring sun.

"Amu," said Vixy, squinting and shielding her eyes at the light. "Is that your nickname?"

Amu looked puzzled. "Nickname?"

"Yes. I mean, you told Hesso your full name, but I don't remember it. You didn't call yourself 'Amu.'"

"My full name is Amunet Rizk. 'Amu' is what everyone calls me."

"Amunet Rizk," said Vixy, thoughtfully.

Amu's voice became distant, dreamy. "We are Copts. But my mother once told me, when I was a little girl, that I was named after a goddess."

"A goddess? What kind of goddess? Egyptian?"

Amu nodded. "My mother told me it means 'the female hidden one.'"

Hesso led them directly westward and into what appeared, at first, to be an otherwise vacant expanse of desert stretching to the horizon. He turned to wait for the rest of them. "There!" He gestured towards a billowing cloud of dust in the distance.

Vixy squinted at it. "What is it?"

"Digging."

Barely discernable were a group of what appeared to be Egyptian peasants – their garb the familiar simple robes and head wraps – a more or less chaotic jumble of men and boys hauling armloads of debris – sand and rock – from one place to another.

Bishoy seemed suddenly enthusiastic, speaking excitedly in Arabic.

Hesso laughed and it seemed Amu was smiling beneath her veil.

"What did he say?" said Vixy.

"Bishoy is explaining the excavation," answered Amu. "That the men, the coolies as they're called, are working to uncover treasure in the mastabas. Tombs that have only just been discovered."

Bishoy interjected with more Arabic and Hesso smiled and patted the boy's shoulder, winking at him. "He's excited because word has spread amongst the donkey boys in the city that more treasure is being discovered at the pyramids. And he's here to see it." Hesso regarded the digging and scratched at the back of his neck as if pondering it for himself. "It is said that this whole area may be an ancient cemetery."

"Mastaba?" Vixy recalled the word only vaguely from her studies. "You mean a tomb?"

"Yes." He made a sweeping gesture encompassing the broad expanse of desert surrounding the dig. "Mastabas are perhaps everywhere here. Rectangular tombs of mud brick and stone, with sides that slope like this" – he gestured with both hands – "and a flat roof. Five or six meters high. Beneath, underground, a burial chamber. At ground level, above the burial chamber, are rooms in which offerings were stored."

They watched the digging for a moment.

"What about Bruggs?" said Vixy. "And Laron. Do you think they're here, involved with this?"

Hesso nodded. "Talk in the streets – word of excavations on the Plateau travels quickly within the city and elsewhere. Men and boys alike are always keen for stories of treasure." He winked at Bishoy again and eyed Vixy staunchly. "But, yes, Bruggs. Perhaps Laron. But, Bruggs, certainly. Like flies and jackals, they are the first and last to feast upon the dead."

The dusty wind streamed southward in the direction of the pyramid of – what was it called? Khafre. Vixy struggled to recall what she knew about the geography of the plateau. The pyramids lay on the diagonal, northeast to southwest in chronological order: Khufu, Khafre – which only appeared larger than Khufu because its position on the plateau was higher – then the newest and smallest of the three, Menkaure.

They made their way closer to the excavation and Vixy discerned the rudiments of the process: the men were working in small groups, uncovering what indeed appeared to be a mastaba – the rectangular nature of the structure was discernable. Several men chopped at the ground with tools that resembled garden hoes –metal plates attached to the end of wooden poles. They dislodged the sand and rock and shoveled it into the waiting baskets of the others who snatched up their burdens and scurried to pitch the waste unceremoniously at the outskirts of the excavation in a ceaseless cycle. Great quantities of earth were being moved by hand, slowly but relentlessly, basketful by basketful.

"*Ya ibn el kelb!*" An Egyptian of imposing bearing was leaning on a staff and eyeing the diggers from the edge of the excavation. "*Ishtaghal, Ishtaghal, ya bint! Hawafi, ya shekh, hawafi! Ent ze hamir!*"

The diggers appeared to ignore him until one looked up and responded in an incongruously cheerful voice, "*Hader, ya sidi hader.*" The rest of the men laughed under their breath.

Vixy looked to Hesso to translate.

He laughed. "The foreman is telling them he has, as you say in English, his eye on them. He tells them, 'Oh, son of a dog! Work, work, oh daughter! Good day, oh sheikh, good day! You are like donkeys!' And the digger replies, '*Hader, ya sidi hader*' – 'Ready, oh my lord, ready!'"

Vixy donned her veil before coming within sight of the men and it struck her that it provided her a measure of protection against their glances, allowing her to observe the work more discreetly. But where in hell was Bruggs?

Hesso led them upwind of the obfuscating cloud of dust towards a section of the cemetery that had already been worked. It turned out that several mastabas had been exposed, each a uniform distance from the other, as if aligned in a grid, akin to little buildings surrounded by city streets. Vixy recalled images, ancient photographs she'd seen in the databases at University. But the images revealed hundreds of mastabas – a vast field of them, not merely a handful. Why, of course! She felt a fool. It's the same Western Cemetery in the photographs but long before it had been completely excavated. It will be years, perhaps decades, before all of this is explored and exposed. The realization that she was in possession of *a priori* knowledge – knowledge in advance of everyone here, knowledge of the future – struck her with all its import. She couldn't mention even in passing what little she knew about this place to anyone here - not to Hesso, not to Amu, not to Bishoy. Not if she wanted to adhere to anything like the leave-no-trace protocol that had been drilled into her since she'd begun her cadet training. *Even observation leaves a trace; your mere presence affects time and space.* It sounded silly and trite then and she'd taken the idea for granted almost as soon as she'd heard it like the rest of the cadets in her class. Sure, they'd endured the horror stories of consequence accidents introduced by the early HDT mistakes, but for the most part they assumed such concerns wouldn't apply to them, that such risks were from a different era of hyper-dimensional travel. Now? It seemed the ironies she'd was being forced to endure would never cease.

"Who is buried here?" asked Amu.

Vixy listened, eager for Hesso's explanation – for a Bedouin he seemed curiously learned in the ways of Egyptology.

"Priests or high officials. It is said some mastabas may be as old as the pyramids."

"Have you been inside one?" asked Vixy.

"No. Anything of value has already been plundered in ancient times, like so many other tombs." Hesso looked at the ruins intently and scratched his chin. "But there is always a chance that something valuable, some treasure, has yet to be found." He shrugged. "What else would attract the likes of Bruggs and Laron?"

Bruggs and Laron. Vixy's skin crawled. It figured that they were plunderers. Graverobbers as well as kidnappers. She wondered about their knowledge of HDT, of the future and how they were no doubt taking unholy advantage of their technology and foreknowledge. Hackneyed archaeology. Black market dealings in antiquities. Crimes against time. And what else? What was their connection to the Olympic Theater? Indeed, where and when were *they* from? Even if it was all about the money, it just didn't add up, nobody was getting rich off Egyptian antiquities. Not yet anyway. There had to be something more to it all.

And what about Hesso for that matter? For all his seeming straightforwardness and friendly bravado, he could be a mere rogue, an opportunist like anyone else, a Bedouin bandit. *Don't be swayed by appearances.* That's what Mr. Z. would say. Vixy tried to reexamine Hesso objectively and nonetheless found it difficult, as she always did, to separate her impressions and her intuitions from her observations. Hesso carried himself with the swagger of a young man but with a hint of the self-possession of someone older, more mature. His voice and face – his teeth and hair, noticeably – were youngish but perhaps he had money to avail himself of better food and medical care? His features were modest, well-proportioned, with hints of crow's feet at the corners of his eyes. A life outdoors would age a man's appearance, no doubt. Indeed, his hands, akin to the flesh of his face, appeared suitably weathered. His simple wardrobe gave nothing away – the course fabric of his robe was of the same dusky cloth as any other she'd encountered since arriving. He was moderately clean shaven – how did he go about it? There was no gray in his stubble or sideburns, his hair otherwise obscured beneath his head scarf. He was lean but not boney and at least a head taller than her. Finally, there was his savage, almost vulgar looking dagger with its elaborately carved handle, its sweeping sheath and curled tip. He kept it snug within his belt, almost always with at least one hand upon it. His eyes seemed dark but when she looked more closely she realized they were a tawny gold, it was only his black lashes and the way he tended to narrow his eyes that gave an impression of a more smoldering countenance.

"There he is," said Hesso, glancing over his shoulder at Vixy. "Bruggs. The fat scoundrel."

Vixy bristled. Bruggs had emerged, apparently, from inside the mastaba and stood wiping his head with a handkerchief, his bowler hat under his arm and otherwise clutching an object that consumed his attention. Beside him stood a curiously short, broadly built character completely shrouded in a Bedouin-style robe, his face concealed by his wraparound, otherwise awkward looking headdress. They watched Bruggs struggle to scale the sides of the excavation, huffing and puffing up the rough-hewn, make-shift steps towards level ground. He gestured towards a stoic looking Egyptian beside a camel which seemed to have appeared from nowhere - how could she not have noticed a camel?

"He has a dragoman with him," murmured Hesso.
The Egyptian, camel rein in hand, hastened towards Bruggs, received the object and hurriedly swaddled it in a piece of cloth before placing it into one of the camel's saddlebags.

"Wait here," Hesso instructed. He thrust Deloua's rein at Bishoy and scrambled down a gangway into the dusty, rock-strewn excavation, skirting the various workers and bounding straight up the other side so that he stood face-to-face with Bruggs. Vixy shaded her eyes against the glare. *Did he have her transponder?* Was it in one of the saddle bags? She watched Hesso gesture in their direction, watched Bruggs glance towards them. The two men appeared to be speaking heatedly for a moment then just as quickly turned away from each other, Bruggs making off with his dragoman and camel in the direction of the Khafre pyramid and Hesso hastening his way back.

"The man is a dog," he said, breathless. "Arrogant and stupid. Amu, he demands that you and Bishoy meet him at his camp – he wants his meals cooked and clothes cleaned. Bah! I told him no, that he'd forfeited his claim to you when he left you to fend for yourselves at the Pyramids Road. Forget all this. Whatever he's paying you, I'll better it until I can get you back to Cairo." Hesso looked hard at Amu. "Consider it seriously, woman, I am offering you a chance to escape from his clutches – nothing good will come of your dealings with him." He regarded each of them with renewed interest, as if his conversation with Bruggs had transformed his sense of responsibility towards them all.

"Are we to return to the city, then?" said Amu.

"We need to make camp," he said. "It's getting late." He pointed towards the Khafre pyramid. "You see the large tent? At the northeast corner? That is Petrie's camp. He is some Englishman whom Bruggs claims to be working for. But I think Bruggs is up to his own business more than anything. He is busy pilfering this mastaba, you can be sure of that." He grabbed the rein from Bishoy. "We'll make camp south of them – I'm not letting Bruggs out of my sight."

They set off and Vixy approached Hesso. "What did Bruggs say to you? Did he mention me?"

"He said you were an impoverished foreigner; that you'd gotten yourself in some kind of trouble and he was helping you, allowing you to work for him." Hesso appeared dubious. "But, Allah as my witness, I don't believe a word he says."

Vixy turned away. She felt desperate, stymied.

Hesso leaned close and spoke in a complicit tone. "I have not forgotten that Bruggs has something of yours. We can keep an eye on Bruggs together, can we not?"

Vixy chafed at her impossible position. She couldn't reveal anything about what was really happening to her. Neither could she reveal what little she knew about Bruggs – that he and Laron were apparently capable of hyper-dimensional travel; that they'd kidnapped her; that Mr. Z. and the Time Detective Contingent were searching for her across time and space and that her only hope of returning to her home in the distant future was recovering her transponder. Hesso would rightly consider her a lunatic even if she could tell him half of it. And what would it avail her, besides? How could Hesso or Amu or anyone here help her? She closed her eyes and tried to think, tried to hold on to something, tried to envision some sort of plan. Don't fall apart. Keep your shit together. What would Mr. Z. do? What would he say if he were here? Watch and wait. Be observant. Seek an opportunity. But what opportunity?

They trudged southward, avoiding as best they could the trailing dust from the excavation until they'd left the bleak mastaba field behind them and arrived at the pyramid of Khafre and the Petrie camp. There was the large canopy they'd witnessed from the cemetery – it sheltered an array of cluttered worktables burdened with what appeared to be maps, their curling edges secured against the wind with stones and all manner of dusty artifacts – shards of pottery and indecipherable lumps of rock. Several Egyptians resided at the tables, sifting through the rubble, wielding brushes and slender tools, painstakingly cleaning and sorting.

Their company ambled past the encampment and Vixy found herself looking longingly at the scene, desperate to experience anything approaching an aspect of civilized life as she recognized it. Here, at least, despite the archaic details, was something resembling a formal enterprise of educated archaeology. Things to read and analyze. Intelligent work to do. It was only a handful of days ago that she'd had her whole life ahead of her. The disparity was almost too much to bear. Look at me, trapesing through the desert like a servant or a Bedouin. If I don't do something to help myself I'm going to end up the topic of somebody else's research project – some accident report at the TDC or somebody's worthless discovery of bones millennia hence, another dusty corpse. No one will ever know what happened to me. She tugged at Hesso's sleeve. "Where are we going? I'm tired."

"We'll camp at the mortuary temple at the foot of the Khafre Pyramid. It's just ahead."

They were still within a stone's throw of the Petrie camp, heading southward towards the remains of the mortuary temple, when they came upon a severe-looking European of perhaps late middle-age attired in white shirtsleeves and khaki-colored slacks. It struck Vixy that he was barefoot. They watched him fiddling with a bulky piece of equipment atop a tall, wooden-legged tripod. He seemed keenly absorbed.

"Bloody hell," he said, straightening and flexing his fingers and scowling at the device. When he finally noticed them, it was with an air of indifference and skeptical, bug-eyed impatience. "Yes? Is there something you want?"

He had a British accent and a mass of dark, straggly curls. He sported a thick beard and his narrow eyes were set beneath a heavy brow, accentuating his inelegant wedge of a nose. He appeared both undeniably imperious and a shiftless castaway, all at once. He was about to return his attention to his device when Hesso spoke up.

"I am Hesso Ishaq. This is Miss Vixy, Amu and Bishoy."

"I'm not looking to hire anyone," the man said. He grasped something on the device and grimaced as if he couldn't manage to budge it. "Unless you're diggers. And you don't look like diggers to me. Except perhaps the boy."

They all stood watching him, each of them apparently at a loss.

"Otherwise, my *firmans* are all properly in place with Boghos Bey." The man bent down awkwardly to peer at the underside of the equipment. "And the coolies are legitimately under my charge. Otherwise you'll have to speak to my assistant, Professor Charles Bruggs, whom you should be able to find –" he glanced towards the camp. "Oh, I don't know, somewhere!" He sighed at the device and made to look as if he would strangle it. "Damn this thing!"

"No, sir," said Hesso. "We are not looking for work. Nor are we looking for Professor Bruggs." Hesso winked at Vixy. "We have business of our own and not with you. But may I ask, sir, is that a camera? Are you taking photographs?"

It never fails, thought Vixy - men and their inevitable interest in mechanical devices.

They waited but the man appeared to have forgotten about them entirely.

Hesso turned and shrugged. They'd all made to move on when the man spoke up.

"A camera? No, this is nothing of the sort." He squinted at Hesso. "If you're indeed a Bedouin, then your English is certainly good. You are a Bedouin are you not? And how is it that you've heard anything of cameras?"

"I am a trader," said Hesso. "I travel outside Egypt. And cameras? I have seen them."

"Indeed," said the man. He stood up and turned to evaluate them. "This device is called a theodolite. It's akin to, say, a telescope and, I don't know... well, it's akin to a dioptra or geometric square." He scratched his head and frowned, searching for a better explanation. "I'm measuring angles, both vertical and horizontal so as to survey – that is to say, map, in a way – the position and dimensions of the pyramids."

"Why?"

The man sighed. "Look here. Hesso, is it? My name is Flinders Petrie. I'm here from England to study these monuments – everything about them. Thoroughly. Precisely. Scientifically."

"And to dig for treasure," said Hesso.

How can this be happening to me? Vixy felt overwhelmed once again with the queer irony of her predicament, with the uncanny collision she was experiencing between legend and physical fact; between the thrill of her encounters and the desperation of her dilemma. It seemed there must be some way, for instance, to put her knowledge of this man Petrie to use. But there wasn't a way, there wasn't anything anyone, even Flinders Petrie, could do even if she were irresponsible enough to ask. She felt as if she were going mad.

"I'm studying these ruins – the pyramids, the Sphinx, the mastabas, all of it. I'm planning to excavate all through this Plateau, cataloguing everything I find and making an engineering survey, the results of which will be published in England. I'm a scientist." He studied Hesso for a moment. "That's not to say I'm not interested in antiquities for trade. You referred to yourself as a trader, did you not? Well, Hesso the trader, I should like to see anything you yourself may have collected. Or that you may know about, let's say." He returned his attention to his theodolite.

"We are merely passing through the Plateau on our way to Saqqara," said Hesso. This time he aimed his wink at all of them.

"Saqqara?" said Petrie, continuing to make his adjustments. "Well, you're a long way from Saqqara."

Hesso nodded. "That is true, sir. And we must be going so as to make our camp for the night."

"You'd be wise to stay clear of the coolies," said Petrie matter-of-factly. "I've no authority over them after dark, nor as soon as the digging stops for the day, for that matter."

Hesso appeared indifferent to any implication. "*Yalla*," he said, tug-ging on Deloua's rein. "Goodbye to you, Petrie."

✸

They trundled along the east face of the Pyramid of Khafre in silence, the shadows of the pyramids lengthening, the sands and stones reddening in the changing light, and Vixy enduring the longing that so often tugged at her insides at the setting of the sun. She was tired, thirsty and footsore. Amu had availed herself of the donkey cart ever since the encounter with Petrie. Bishoy, ever quiet and abiding, dutifully guided his donkey onwards despite the wheels bogging down in frequent patches of loose sand – he seemed determined to demonstrate his resilience on behalf of Hesso. And Hesso, for his part, along with his camel, seemed indefatigable, virtually immune to fatigue. Man and beast seemingly drifted across the desert like boats on a tide, buoyed along effortlessly.

Vixy's fatigue did nothing, however, to staunch her anxiety about spending the night in the desert. No decent meal. No soft chair. No bedroom. No bathroom. No change into comfortable, clean clothes. No privacy.

They'd come upon ruins – what amounted to a barely discernable, rectangular outline of jumbled limestone blocks, apparently the only evidence that anything like a so-called mortuary temple had once resided here. "This place is as good as any," said Hesso, and turned to his camel, speaking in Arabic to her and pulling her rein gently, drawing her down so that she kneeled on her forelegs then settled onto the sand.

It wasn't long before Hesso and Bishoy had unpacked the supplies and erected a tent made of dark, coarsely woven wool. It seemed large enough to accommodate several persons, albeit snuggly. Then they went about establishing a campfire.

"We have enough water for tonight," said Hesso, "but tomorrow we have to replenish the skins – there is a tributary at Giza." He spoke to Bishoy in Arabic and the boy nodded. Hesso tossed him two coins.

Bishoy's eyes widened. "*Alf šukr*,"[33] he said.

Hesso winked at him.

---

[33] Egyptian Arabic for "A thousand thanks."

Amu leaned towards Vixy and whispered a translation. "He's asking Bishoy to work for him, to get our water for tomorrow and to travel with him when his business here is finished."

Bishoy beamed quietly, redoubling his determination to get the campfire going and soon he'd established a crackling, pungent little blaze that drew everyone to it.

They gathered around it with their blankets, once again passing small plates of nuts, dates, flatbread and *dukkha* amongst themselves and drinking hot tea from the kettle that Bishoy tended. The air was growing cool, the evening coming on, and Vixy savored the food and rest. But she was no closer to getting her transponder back than when they'd left the city. That she'd be forced to risk everything and confront Bruggs and Laron alone or somehow find a way to steal back her device – everything about the prospect exasperated her. She sipped her tea and stared fitfully into the fire. Thoughts of home tormented her. The idea of recovering her transponder tormented her. What if Bruggs or Laron didn't have it? They *had* to have it. She had to get it. She had to send an SOS with it. There was no other hope of getting home. Stop fretting. She tried to buck up. Get some rest. Make it to tomorrow, whatever it brings. Don't give up. As if I've got any choice.

Hesso sat down beside her and offered his cigarette.

For once in her life she felt indifferent to tobacco. She was bone-weary, physically and psychologically exhausted beyond all cares. Numb. She nevertheless reached for the cigarette and immediately coughed at the pungent smoke. "It's strong," she said, wiping at her watering eyes. She coughed again. "I'm sorry, I'm not used to it."

"This is *Hodri*," said Hesso, "not the trash sold in the markets in Cairo. You see it's still green?" He offered her the open pouch. "Smell."

Vixy leaned close and nodded.

Hesso reached into his tunic and produced a kind of double-barreled flute. He settled himself cross-legged, licked his lips and began to blow.

To Vixy's ears the music was a breathy drone, hoarse and mournfully discordant – it reminded her of nothing if not an old-fashioned, slightly dysfunctional train whistle. Meanwhile, Hesso's fingers fluttered over the keyholes, the notes spilling forth, the fire glowing now in the heavy dusk, the stars emerging like icy pinpoints in the blue-black heavens. Drowsiness overtook her and she welcomed it, the strange sounds of the flute carrying her along as if the night were not the end of things, as if life and hope remained.

Amu, meanwhile, had brightened at the sound – the music seemed familiar to her and she nodded and clapped softly to a rhythm that Vixy couldn't fathom. Bishoy was the most enthusiastic of anyone, rummaging hurriedly through the donkey cart baggage until he'd produced a small drum. He plopped down besides Hesso with the instrument between his legs and tapped a syncopated rhythm, the two of them flashing earnest smiles at each other.

The intensity of their playing and likewise the energy of the music increased by degrees until at what seemed its most furious point, Hesso stopped, smiling broadly at Bishoy's drumming. "*Mish batal, Mish batal!*[34]

"*Aiwa!*[35] Bishoy," said Amu, still clapping to the boy's rhythm, "very good." She glanced at Vixy, leaning towards her encouragingly.

Vixy smiled and tried to find the beat, resorting to mimicking Amu's clapping.

Hesso had just returned the flute to his lips when they heard a man's voice behind them.

"*La mu'axza.*"[36]

Vixy caught her breath and glanced over her shoulder, startled to discover an Egyptian standing just within the light of the campfire. Beside him was the same short-statured, mysteriously shrouded, odd-looking character they'd seen accompanying Bruggs at the mastabas.

The man repeated himself, "*La mu'axza*" bowed and continued in halting English. "I beg your pardon. Sorry to disturb. I am Bab. And this is Mister Five."

---

[34] "Not bad, not bad," in Egyptian Arabic.

[35] "Yes," in Egyptian Arabic.

[36] "Excuse me, (begging pardon)" in Egyptian Arabic.

"You are with Bruggs," replied Hesso, flatly. "His dragoman. You were at the excavation."

"Indeed," said Bab.

Vixy hadn't noticed that Bishoy had departed until he'd returned with an armful of acacia branches and built up the campfire – it crackled and smoked with the new wood, a flurry of yellow-orange sparks soaring upwards.

"Mister Five wishes to speak to you." Bab held up a slip of paper and read from it: "My business with Professor Bruggs is finished. You and I may do business directly."

Hesso shoved his flute into his robe and stood up. "Business?"

Five scribbled something and handed another note to Bab. Bab stepped closer to the firelight, holding the note at arm's length and squinting at it. Meanwhile, Five thrust a larger piece of paper at Hesso.

"Mister Five explains that this is the receipt of payment between Professor Bruggs and himself. For the artifact."

Hesso frowned at the receipt and scratched his chin as he read it. He raised his eyebrows. "Artifact?" He shrugged. "So, you've done business with Bruggs. That doesn't mean anything to me. Who are you?" He addressed Five directly. "And why can't this Mister Five speak for himself?"

Five remained as he was, his face shrouded behind folds of his *kufeya*.

"Mister Five does not speak," said Bab. "He must write."

Hesso appeared skeptical.

Bab reached into his robes and produced a small pouch, hefting it several times to the unmistakable sound of jingling coins. Bab tossed the pouch and Hesso caught it, tipping the contents into his palm, glancing back and forth between the two men. Five jotted another note and handed it once again to Bab.

"Mister Five asks if you agree to conduct business with him for the artifact."

Vixy tried to ignore her rising uneasiness. If these men had been doing business with Bruggs and were now approaching Hesso, what of it? As long as it didn't entail Bruggs leaving the Plateau. Meanwhile, something

about Mister Five seemed incomparably odd – he was so strange, so dispro-
portioned. It was too dark and he was too obscured by his garments for her
to observe any details about his appearance, except his curious hands which
he kept mostly covered beneath his garment. They seemed enormous and
utterly out of proportion with his small stature. And she swore he was
wearing large spectacles – goggles of some type, even – otherwise shrouded
by his head scarf. His robe appeared too large for him, it dragged along the
ground, obscuring his feet – in fact, everything about his wardrobe appeared ill-fitting and cumbersome. That he was apparently mute seemed
the least unusual thing about him.

"One man's money is as good as that of another," said Hesso. "Yes,
Mister Five. We can do business." Hesso suddenly became gracious. "These
are my companions. Please. Sit." He gestured towards the place he'd left
vacant by the fire.

Bab and Five seated themselves, far enough outside the firelight that
Vixy could still barely discern their features. Five scribbled another note.

"Mister Five wishes to confirm that your cache contains a canopic
chest with four jars intact."

Hesso wagged his teacup at Bishoy and the boy filled it with steaming
liquid. Hesso blew on it noisily and sipped loudly. "Yes."

More scribbling.

"Old Kingdom?" said Bab.

Hesso nodded slowly. "Old Kingdom."

Five dug into his *tob*, hefted a pouch identical to the one Bab had
produced, coins clinking, and tossed it unceremoniously onto Hesso's
portion of the blanket. He handed Bab another note.

"What do you know of the images on the chest?"

Hesso snatched at the pouch, hefted it and stuffed it into his robe.
"Nothing," he said, shrugging. "Ancient Egyptian gods and goddesses."
He sat up and held his hands toward the fire, rubbing them together. "Isis,
Nepththys, Neith and Selkis. Those are the deities as inscribed. Meanwhile,
gentlemen, with all due respect, the price is double what you have paid."

Vixy was taken aback by Hesso's apparent deftness with Egyptology. That, and his apparent other life as a black market antiquities dealer. Here she was just beginning to rely on his authenticity.

Five produced another note.

"You have received half the price," said Bab. "You receive the other half when Mister Five receives the artifact."

Five gestured and Bab peered more closely at the note, holding it to the firelight.

"Providing the chest and the jars are authentic and completely intact. No exceptions."

Vixy shivered despite the heat from the fire. It was as if the intrigue between Hesso and these two men were sapping the last of her energies. She glanced at Amu and Bishoy – they sat beside each other, observing. Bishoy seemed fascinated, either at the money changing hands or at the men's discussion, or both, despite the language barrier. He sat hugging his shins, chin propped firmly upon his knees, focusing on their every move.

Hesso suddenly stood up. "It is a deal, then. *Šokran.*[37]" He gestured toward the fire. "Bishoy" – he looked askance at the boy – "tea for these men."

Bishoy moved to fetch the teapot but Amu waved him away. "Let me," she said.

Hesso sighed loudly, as if pleased, and rubbed his hands together. "You understand, Mister Five, that I require a reasonable period of time to retrieve the artifact. I've hidden it, of course. I can hardly carry such distinctive valuables about with me. Tomorrow, by midday, I will deliver it. Then we will conclude our business."

Mister Five scribbled and Bab dutifully read aloud. "Will another fifty percent convince you to deliver the chest tonight?"

Hesso looked askance at both Bab and Mister Five, then shook his head. "No. It is too late. I am tired. And I will not abandon my friends."

Amu poured tea for everyone in turn. Vixy brought her cup close to her face, inhaling the warmth and aroma. She watched the bronze faces

---

37 "Thank you" in Egyptian Arabic.

glowing in the firelight and sensed the dark peak of the pyramid looming behind them. She glanced up, struck by the brilliance of the Milky Way, brighter even than she remembered it from her home in Old Masset. "Hesso? Don't refuse the money on our account. We can take care of ourselves."

"No," he said, "the Plateau is not safe."

"What if Bab remained behind with us?" said Vixy. "How can you ignore such an offer?"

Hesso turned to Bab and addressed him in Arabic. "Bab, you are a Ma'aza Bedouin, are you not? Perhaps of the Khushmaan Clan? I recognize your speech and bearing."

Bab regarded Hesso with an air of mild dignity and responded in English. "I am Khushmaan, yes."

"The Khushmaan I have known," said Hesso, "are among the most honorable of men. It is said they abhor unjust violence and thievery. I walked with Sulimaan Silmi[38] and it would be on behalf of the Khushmaan honor that I would agree to leave the women and boy under your protection."

Unperturbed, Bab nodded his consent. "*Subhaan Allah,*"[39] he said; "I walked with *Hayy.* But be advised, I am no warrior, no fighter. I am old, anyone can see. And I must return to Bruggs at dawn."

"*Subhaan Allah,*" repeated Hesso, digging a hand into his *tob* and producing several coins. "You needn't work to protect my friends till dawn – I shall have returned with Mister Five and the chest when the moon is still low in the sky."[40]

"The honor of the Khushmaan Clan is a priceless thing," said Bab quietly, waving away the payment; "*Subhaan Allah.*"

"*Subhaan Allah,*" replied Hesso, and the two men shook hands. "Mister Five, can you ride a camel?"

Five nodded.

---

38 The phrase, "I walked with" (i.e., "I knew the deceased") is a routine utterance meant to show pride and respect amongst the Ma'aza.

39 "God be praised" in Arabic.

40 Moonrise on November 10, 1881, Cairo, Egypt occurred at 8:51 PM.

Hesso looked pleased. "Bishoy!" he said. "Bring us bread and salt!"

Bishoy did as he was asked and before long, Hesso was tearing at a flatbread, sprinkling salt upon it and offering it to Bab, who dutifully consumed it in a single bite, and another to Five, who merely nodded and held the morsel in his lap.[41]

Hesso clapped his hands together. "*Yalla, Yalla*, Mister Five," he said. "Come!"

They watched the strange man climb aboard the camel saddle – perched atop Deloua he appeared more diminutive and misshapen than ever.

"Bishoy," said Hesso, beckoning the boy. He spoke to Bishoy quietly for a moment and handed him something, gesturing at Vixy. He addressed the rest of them. "My friends, may Allah and our Bedouin friend keep you safe."

Vixy watched them leave, heading south along the base of the pyramid. She marveled at Hesso's endurance. The night suddenly weighed upon her and she shivered.

Amu sensed her discomfort. She motioned to Bishoy and he retrieved blankets from his cart. Amu draped one around Vixy's shoulders and the other around herself and sat down beside her. The fire was low, the coals hissing. Bishoy tended it with more wood, then knelt before them both and spoke to Amu.

"He says that Hesso told him to give this to you," said Amu.

Bishoy handed her a small dagger. Its handle was made of bone and when Vixy unsheathed it, its pointed blade glinted in the firelight.

Bishoy whispered something.

"Hesso told him it was small enough to fit your hand," said Amu. "And that he believed you would know how to use it."

"Thank you, Bishoy," said Vixy.

Her voice seemed to embarrass him and he looked round self-consciously before rushing off to get more firewood. He returned and sat some distance away from the women, whittling upon a stick with his own little pocketknife.

---

41 Eating bread and salt, even with one's enemies, signals no hostility.

Bab, meanwhile, had been tending to his camel. He returned bearing a bulky woven basket which he set upon the sand within the light of the fire. He sat down cross-legged beside it and Vixy noticed he held a small pipe, or perhaps a flute, one end of which was bulbous and reminded her of a gourd.[42] He removed the lid of the basket, put the pipe to his lips and began playing.

*It can't be.* The pinched, nasal trill of Bab's music was unmistakable – the scene was straight from some otherwise clichéd vision of the ancient Orient. Vixy turned towards Amu and they widened their eyes at each other. Bishoy appeared nonplussed.

Bab played quietly for a few minutes, his eyes gently closed, his fingers fluttering over the keyholes and his hand occasionally cupped over the end of the flute. He appeared to Vixy to be meditating instead of performing. The dry, throaty mournfulness of the flute was similar to that of Hesso's instrument yet somehow more penetrating. It droned on and on hypnotically and Vixy drew her blanket tightly around her, staring into the fire, listening drowsily.

Amu gasped and Vixy started. A dark shape arched and swayed above the basket in front of Bab. He continued to play, eyes closed, the flesh on his face gleaming with perspiration, his body rocking gently, rhythmically.

Vixy recognized the snake's telltale silhouette – the vampiric shroud of its hood and the diabolical slope of its wavering head. A cobra. Black. Blacker than the shadowy night beyond the firelight and hideously large. The beast swayed heavily back and forth, mirroring Bab's movements with a ghastly grace that was at once beguiling and repulsive.

The snake rose up menacingly, its body arched, poised as if to strike.

Bab ceased his playing and opened his eyes, the shadow of the snake flickering over his face in the firelight.

"*La'a!*" said Amu. "No!"

Vixy clamped her hands over her mouth, stifling her scream.

Bab moved slowly, deliberately, lowering the flute onto the sand and at the same time groping blindly beside him for something, his eyes never

---

42  The instrument, indeed typically carved from a gourd, is known as a *pungi.*

leaving the cobra. There was a pouch beside him and when his fingers touched it he deftly loosed something upon the sand. A tail twitched and a shape skittered away from the fire – a rat!

The cobra struck and Vixy recoiled at the thump of its impact and the sharp spray of sand. They watched the hapless rodent convulse in the snake's jaws, once, twice then hang limp, the rat disappearing gulp by stomach-churning gulp into the snake's gullet.

Vixy stared. Bishoy sat hugging his knees, his face twisted into an ironic half-smile. Amu, for her part, had covered her face with her hands.

Bab snatched the snake from the sand, the tail of the rat dangling from its mouth, and in what seemed a single motion swept the cobra back into the basket, secured the lid and carried it off.

"Praise God," said Amu under her breath.

Bab returned and stood quietly just outside the reach of the firelight. He placed his own blanket upon the sand and sat crossed legged, relaxed but dignified, staring into the fire as if nothing untoward had occurred.

Who is this man? – thought Vixy. Whomever he was, dragoman, yogi, conjurer, magician – he was apparently no fakir. But she was so exhausted now that none of it seemed to matter – this last bit of excitement had seemed to consume what little energy she had left. Thoughts of home overtook her, welled up within her; thoughts of Old Masset and her warm bed and her mother and father. She was tired, so tired; too tired to be afraid. The fire flickered and glowed, hissing and crackling quietly and an impossible drowsiness carried her away.

"Mr. Z.," said Vixy. They were face to face but he seemed to be looking through her. "*Mr. Z.*" Nothing. He was talking without making a sound – somehow she couldn't hear a word he was saying. His expression hardened, his eyes flashed as if he were furious – she'd never seen him so enraged – and now he was shouting, soundlessly shouting her name – she knew it, she could read his lips, but for the life of her she couldn't hear it. "*I'm *right here!"* She made to reach out and panicked when she couldn't move her arms. She watched him turn and walk slowly away across an unsightly slough of black, uneven rock – lava rock, she supposed – its surface ragged, rough, threatening, expanding. The ground heaved and she stumbled, crevices widened beneath her – fissures, yawning gaps, chasms....

She woke with a start. Then shouts and strident voices. She sat bolt upright, fully awake, looking wildly round the camp.

"*Sebni!*"[43] shrieked Amu. "No! *Matelmesnīš!*[44] You are dogs!"

Vixy threw aside her blanket and leapt up only to be knocked to the ground by the brute weight of a man, reeking of sweat and liquor, groaning and clutching at her with hands like iron. She cried out, gasped and struggled, his weight crushing her, holding her down. With a great effort she writhed out from under him, cried out again, and his strength seemed to double – he wrenched at her arm as if to tear it from her shoulder. The pain was shocking, infuriating, and she kicked and tore at him but he was on her like an ape. With all her might she thrust her knee into his crotch.

"Arghh! You Arab bitch!"

He swung at her – she saw stars and reeled, tasted the iron tang of blood. She kicked again, blindly, twisting free, scrambling desperately across the sand, but he pounced, snatched at her foot, hauling her towards him. She screamed and punched at his hands and arms and face, her fists raining blows, his heavy flesh seemingly numb, as if she were hammering against a tree trunk. He lunged upon her with his full weight, his breath acrid and suffocating, clutching at her neck, pinning her arms against the sand, digging his knee between her thighs, groping. She shrieked then fell limp, feigning collapse, and when his weight shifted she shoved herself out from under him and rolled, slashing at his eyes with her nails.

---

43 "Leave me alone!" (to a man) in Egyptian Arabic.
44 "Don't touch me!" (to a man) in Egyptian Arabic.

"Argh! You whore, I'll have you!" His arms and hands were like tentacles, she couldn't escape them. She kicked at his face and he grabbed at her foot. The knife! – she fumbled for it within the folds of her robe but he yanked her towards him and it flew from her hands. He stripped off his belt and whipped her, the pain blinding, consuming, her strength failing. He lashed her again and fell upon her, panting, growling, sweating, groping. She couldn't fight, couldn't move under his stinking, brutish, indomitable bulk.

"You're mine," he moaned, breathless, leaning hard upon her, fumbling with his clothes as she lay trapped beneath him. "Ah, yes," he breathed, "yes!" and reached to cover her mouth. She sunk her teeth deep into his flesh and he yanked his hand away, howling. He raised it higher as if to strike her and she fell back, too exhausted to defend herself, her mind blank with horror....

"Argh!" The brute writhed and fell away from her. "AIEE!" The nauseating snap of breaking bones shocked her. What in hell?

Mister Five stood before her, the fingers of his enormous gloved hand clenched around the assailant's shin like a vise. Her attacker squirmed on the sand, wailing, clutching at his mangled leg, "No, no...!" She watched Mister Five twist the limb and squeeze – the man's shrieking cut short when the leg snapped again, blood gushing from the torn flesh. Vixy turned her head away as the body collapsed in a heap, then peered at Mister Five. He retreated a step, arms at his sides, his face shrouded.

Vixy hauled herself across the sand and reached for her knife, strug-gled to her feet and stumbled towards the brute, spitting into his face. He writhed and moaned, semi-conscious, and she kicked him square in the teeth so that his head snapped backwards and he lay still.

Five took another step back.

Vixy held the knife in her fist and drove the blade into the assailant's neck, flinching at the spray of blood and collapsing onto the sand away from the corpse, her eyes squeezed shut, her body convulsing with sobs.

The rest of the camp was in turmoil. Bab lay face down and motion-less in the sand some distance from the campfire, his hands and legs bound behind him and his mouth gagged. Bishoy attended him, carefully cutting at the bindings.

Hesso was some distance away, assailing a disheveled man cowering at his feet. "Where is she? Tell me! By the devil I'll kill you like I killed the other one!" Hesso clutched the man's hair, bellowing at him, his dagger raised, the man wincing, grasping at Hesso's arm and squirming like a beseeching dog. "Answer me! So help me I'll split you open like a *melon!*"

"*Laa! Laa!*"[45]

"Hesso! Here!" Amu, breathless, fell upon Vixy, laying Vixy's head in her lap, staring hard into her face, her own eyes welling with tears. "She is here!"

The huge shoulder of the moon hovered low, yellow-gold, uncannily close, the stars blazing. Vixy saw Amu's bloody teeth, her blackened eye and swollen cheek. She had lost her veil and head scarf – her hair hung wildly about her shoulders and her robe was torn.

Hesso struck his prisoner in the jaw with the butt of his knife and the man collapsed. He rushed to kneel beside the women, seethed at the sight of their wounds, at the blood and their torn clothing. He clenched his teeth and his nostrils flared. He saw the body and Mister Five standing over it.

Bishoy appeared, his nose trickling blood and his lip swollen, bearing a full water skin.

Amu held the spout to Vixy's mouth, cupping her hand under Vixy's chin.

Vixy slurped at the trickling water, half drinking, half choking, her bruised hands shaking. Amu dampened a piece of her robe and wiped carefully at Vixy's face.

"Mister Five," whispered Vixy, her voice hoarse, her words slurred by her swollen mouth. "Mister Five –"

"Sshh," said Amu. "Sshh." She stroked Vixy's forehead.

Hesso looked perplexed. "Where is he?"

---

[45] "No, no!" in Egyptian Arabic.

Bishoy whispered something in Arabic and Hesso's eyes darted from Vixy to the corpse and back. He exchanged glances with Amu, the flesh of his face quivering with turmoil. "God help me I am to blame for this."

Amu cradled Vixy in her arms.

Hesso addressed Amu, his eyes fixed upon Vixy, his expression fraught. "Bishoy has told me all of it. The young woman, he says, she fights like a lioness."

Amu addressed Bishoy in Arabic. "Get us a blanket, Bishoy, and restore the fire. Hesso, help me get her into the tent."

Hesso carried Vixy in his arms, Amu beside him, tending to her, and lay her on a blanket inside the dark and quiet of the small enclosure.

"Sleep," said Amu. "I will not leave you."

Vixy lay still, her mouth and face throbbing, swollen; her neck raw; the lash marks upon her arms and chest ablaze. The savagery of the assault reverberated within her. She gazed blankly outside the tent with heavy-lidded eyes, transfixed by the gleaming quarter-moon,[46] by its uncorrupted purity; losing herself in the pale brilliance of its desiccated seas that hurt her eyes to look at. Such subtle, sweet pain saved her, the moon's remote eternity kept her safe, a sanctuary for her ravaged identity. "Thank you, Amu," she whispered, and her exile threatened to consume her so that she shut her eyes against it, against the pain in her body and the longing in her heart that no tears could quench. She held the image of the moon in her mind like a beacon; a beacon that was rising over her home just as it was rising here; a beacon and a pristine evocation of another time and place.

[46] In astronomical terms what is colloquially referred to as a half-moon (when half the face of the moon is visible) is more accurately termed a quarter-moon (one quarter of the total spheroid surface of the moon is visible). For Vixy, it is just prior to 11:00 PM on November 10th, 1881 and the moon phase is waning gibbous; she is seeing the moon directly east over the horizon at approximately 23 degrees altitude.

CHAPTER 15

# GOD'S EYE

**MR. Z. CHEWED ON HIS PIPE** and read through his work.

Eranos pivots upon discernment. The feast is not a smorgasbord; rather it was and remains an orchestrated improvisation akin to any memorable meal. As such, the lectures do not always succeed, the soufflé occasionally falls. More often, however, one dines famously. As to the selection of the scholars, the vision of Olga Fröebe-Kapteyn remains vital: a speaker at Eranos is one who "delves into the fullness of his inner visions and seeks to retain them in scientific form."[x] The subject matter, then as now, and as Tilo Schabert suggested in the twenty-first century, unfolds a cultural and methodological diversity of disciplines – Mythology, Buddhism, Chemistry, Biology, Physics, Library Studies, Philosophy, Psychology, Political Science, Mysticism, Neoplatonism, Gnosticism – within which our modern investigations into hyper-dimensionality and psi-studies, for example, abide in full flower.[y] Indeed, Eranos today continues to foster "a cosmos of knowledge wherein things, separated as they normally are, tend to come together."[z]

The modern academic of course, chafes at inclusion and cross-disciplinary scholarship. And Schabert was writing on the cusp of the venerable institution's mere one-hundredth anniversary. What of the vision of Miss Fröebe-Kapteyn's Eranos as it stands today, millennia hence? To be venerated is not to be vital, least of all imperative. Is the wisdom that resides here resonant, invigorating, immaculate in its timelessness? Or does it all appear rather long in the tooth? Writes Thackeray:

> His cousin was now of more than middle age and had nobody's word but her own for the beauty which she said she once possessed. She was lean, and yellow, and long in the tooth; all the red and white in all the toy-shops in London could not make a beauty of her.[aa]

Meanwhile, it was Rudolf Otto who suggested the name "Eranos" and it is Otto, of course, who is attributed with identifying the so-called numinous as the compelling component of all contemplative traditions, which he rather termed religions. He furthermore conceived of systematic theology as a science of religion, subdivided into the philosophy, psychology, and history of religions. Which, it can be argued, are merely several of the organs that make up of the body of mythology. So that, borrowing from Otto and proceeding analogously, the science of mythology would be divided into the philosophy of mythology, the history of mythology and the psychology of mythology. However, there is no science of mythology if we adhere to the idea of science being concerned with repeatable experiments that verify veracity of a theory. What would repeatable experiments look like, after all, when considering the veracity of the numinous? As such, I think Miss Fröebe-Kapteyn, while perhaps secretly holding out for a revealed science, rather intended to imply her preference for the intellectual rigor – that is, the method - that is routinely expected of anything deemed scientific. She appeared to enjoy and inspire the invested remove of scholarship – an invigorating paradox still readily available within these grounds – and its preference for analysis. In terms of the frequency and amplitude, so to say, of the numinous experience, it can be argued that mystics, artists, philosophers and scholars, in that order, exemplify the diminishing slope of the graph.

Hmm, thought Mr. Z. It's a start. He rubbed his face and sat back in his chair to finish reading:

Eranos, then, as a campus, is a polyglot and polygenetic wealth of symbols – the physical presence of the symbolic, of the objects that seek to embody the feast of the intellect and spirit. Tucked away as they are here and there upon the grounds, within its rooms, gathering spaces and sanctuaries, its plazas and meandering gardens, the symbols are as much a part of the feast as the speakers and their ideas. Context is challenged by way of enlivening juxtaposition. One encounters, for instance, this or that image of a bodhisattva or a Buddha residing upon an end table beside a totemic tribal figurine; or a mythologically ornamented Hellenic clay pot in service of a clutch of innocently flowering plants, or perhaps an elegant Egyptian bas relief tile gracing the backrest of a bench or the coined corner of a garden wall. Even your knife and fork will tell a story if you care to look.

He pushed his chair back and rose from the table, despairing. First drafts are unendurable. He flexed his bad arm at the elbow and wrist, made a tentative fist and rotated his hand in small circles. Better day by day, I suppose. No more sling, at least. But still weak, dammit, and sore all the way up to my neck. Hell. He sighed and dutifully performed his neckrolls, eyes lolling, surrendering to the dull ache and the curious tingling that penetrated all the way to his fingertips. He arranged his scattered books, gathered his papers into a folder, doublechecked that he'd saved his writing and logged off, compelled to scribble "Eranos Essay" across the top of his notepad before turning away from it all.

He glanced around the room absently, slave to his discontent yet mollified by the sense of having worked, of having written out his thoughts, of having respected the muse and accomplished at least something of his writing for the day.

A picture on the opposite wall caught his eye: a diminutive, intricate image that inspired closer inspection. Hmm. He touched the frame to expose the digital museum card. *The Knight, Death and the Devil*, 1513, by Dürer. A reproduction of a sixteenth century etching. Nearby he encountered *The Blind Man's Meal*, 1903, a Picasso that had initially struck him as so mawkish and ghastly that he'd been avoiding it since his arrival. Now he felt compelled to attempt to decipher it. Chilly. Dreary. Nocturnal. Cadaverous. No, wait. It struck him that perhaps the scene expressed not the viewer's perspective but that of the blind man himself – the realm of the man's active senses? What of the bloodlessness of the flesh? Perhaps luminosity, a shrouded awareness. The pale swirls upon the tabletop? His sense of its surface, its dimensions. The earthenware carafe, a comparatively vivid ochre. That's odd. And for that matter the bread, a pale buff color but color nonetheless. Ah! He's seeing these things, his sustenance, with his fingers and hands; experiencing the life in them with his mind's eye! Not pigment but energy; vitality amidst the crepuscular... no, undersea, hues. Undersea? Could Picasso have intended such archetypal symbology? Waters of the unconscious, indeed. Or the *subconscious*. A diminished awareness. Yes. He's eating, not being contemplative or visionary. It's we who are contemplating. Envisioning what it is to be blind when one isn't. What isn't tactile, flavorful, aromatic or audible recedes in the blind man's eye. Submerges. Into the depths of semi-awareness. He scratched his head.

A curious subject for a painting. Risky. Ambitious. He hastened back to his writing desk and scribbled a note: "Allow the images to do their work."

An odd little three-dimensional piece across the room caught his attention: a garish piece of predominately blue-green earthenware mounted on the wall. It resembled a grotesque, anemone-like sea creature, its bulging, green-glazed "eye" surrounded by six contorted tentacles. Earnest. Not quite unaccomplished. Crafty. It struck him as rather more primordial than artisanal. Biological. Also alien, vaguely monstrous. Yep. He read aloud from the card. "God's eye." That's what I thought. "Glazed earthenware. Unattributed. 21st century."

Hmm. He stepped back, focusing on the object, adjusting his position, experimenting with being drawn into it.

The remote viewing[47] sessions - RV as they called it - that he'd been a part of during his early days of training as a time detective had more or less followed the original tenants of the historical program – the settling of one's mind into its Delta level of awareness (1-4 brainwave cycles per second), recording so-called analytical overlay – AOL - or "noise," probing the intuitive ideograms and otherwise attempting to connect with the target. If an image is stable, he reminded himself, and clear in your mind's eye, then it is an AOL coming from your imagination, not actual intuitive data. Real data is fleeting and fades more quickly. Probe and reconnect often.

He hauled his writing table and then his desk chair across the floor, negotiating the furniture in the room and the rug on the floor, struggling with his lousy arm, until he'd rearranged his workspace directly beneath the God's eye. He collected several clean sheets of paper, sat down, tucked his chair in and began by writing Vixy's name at the top of a page. He inhaled and exhaled mindfully, fixing his gaze upon the God's eye, braving the trepidation that assailed him whenever he attempted to engage a session. He closed his eyes, holding the image of the God's eye in his mind, undertaking his preparatory series of deep, calming breaths, anticipating

---

47 So-called remote viewing is a technology first investigated with scientific rigor in the nineteen-seventies by the United States Central Intelligence Agency.

a condition of attentive relaxation, of blank, receptive awareness. Open, yet centered.

"Vixy," he said aloud, allowing the idea of her to flood his consciousness, to consume his awareness. When his hold on her slipped he opened his eyes and reabsorbed the image of the God's eye.

"Vixy." He projected himself outward, pouring his thoughts into the image on the wall while carrying the image of Vixy with him in his mind. Seeking her there. Where?

"Vixy." Images as memories of her. But not her. Merely imaginings. The present assaulted him – his surroundings, the nagging discomfort of his injury, the herky-jerky conveyor belt of his thoughts.

"Vixy." Deep breaths. Surrendering to the pull of the God's eye.

"Vixy Velure." Rushing forth. Vast distances. Flying overland. Flying up, into the space, into the black, into the white. Undifferentiated space. Then sands. Undulating sands. Images fleeting. Clear blue skies. Fleeting. Pale rock. Desiccated bones... fleeting. Dark door, dark tunnel... a passageway?

Falcon... river... black mud... a sense of rising... looking up... rising to the center... huge stones... rising, rising... flat surfaces... hewn granite... sands... blocks of stone... architecture of stone... scarab... gold... eyes... alluring eyes... female, black-lined eyes... towers... towering stone?... shovel... spade... dust... wind... a veiled face....

"She is here." A man's voice, strong accent, Arabic.

"Who is here? Where is here? Who are you?"

"The woman you seek."

"Vixy?"

"She is seeking you."

"Where and when are you?"

"Stop them."

"Stop whom? Stop what?"

"Power of gold. Alien."

"When? Where? Who are you? Is Vixy there?"

The God's eye. No. Slipping away. "When, what year, where are you?"

"I am Bawaba. 1881."

"What do you mean?"

"Khafre."

The connection failing, the presence slipping away.

"Wait!" Mr. Z. panicked. "Vixy! Wait!" The voice gone, the connection lost....

"Wake up! Dammit, Mr. Z, wake up, wake up!"

He opened his eyes. "Neutic." He was face-to-face with him.

"I'm calling for help," said Neutic.

Mr. Z. struggled to sit up, leaning on his elbow, surprised to find himself on the floor beside his desk chair. "No. No calls. I'm all right." He rubbed his eyes, rubbed his face, ran his hand through his hair. "I'm fine."

"What the hell happened?"

Mr. Z. shook his head.

"If I help you up, can you make it to the couch?"

He offered Neutic his arm, together they hauled him up and he slumped onto the couch, grasping his temples and shutting his eyes.

Neutic rushed into the kitchen and returned with a glass of water.

Mr. Z. sipped. Neutic sat on the edge of the couch beside him. "What happened? Did you faint? Do you remember?" Neutic looked Mr. Z. up and down. "You weren't answering my messages. The door was open, I'd only just come in to see if you – my God, Mr. Z., we ought to at least call the nurse."

Mr. Z. dismissed the idea with a half-hearted wave of his hand. "No. Just let me think. There's something...."

"What? What is it, sir?"

"Horses." He squeezed his eyes shut. "I smell horses." He shook his head. "Or a stable. A barnyard. Something farmy. I can't place it."

Neutic looked at him squarely. "Horses? Do your best to tell me what happened, sir, please."

Mr. Z. took another sip of water, then several gulps. "I tell you, Neutic, I could use something stronger than water."

"What's the last thing you remember? For God's sake, sir, I swear you were unconscious when I found you."

"Well," he said, scratching his head, "I don't think I was unconscious. Not exactly." He looked round. "My papers...."

Neutic got up and gathered the handful of papers that were strewn about the writing desk and the floor. "What is all this?" He looked cock-eyed at the scribblings. "Sir, with all due respect, you may have hit your head...." He handed over the pages and watched Mr. Z. shuffling through them.

"It has to be here."

Neutic frowned, watching him pour over his documents.

"My remote viewing session."

"Remote viewing?"

"Yes. Well, I suppose my methods actually incorporate several psi-related techniques. Extended mind, that kind of thing." He shut his eyes and winced, pressing his fingers against his temple. "I don't know, I must have become catatonic. I remember spiraling out, psychologically. Considerably beyond my means, I must admit." He blinked at Neutic. "Remote viewing is one thing, but astral projection or an out of body experience – that wasn't my intention. Nevertheless, I experienced something uncanny. A kind of interaction. I heard a voice. I mean to say, I was speaking with someone. A man. Arabic accent, I think."

Neutic eyed him skeptically.

"I'm serious, Neutic. It sounds ridiculous, I know, but... well, there was a man's voice and his presence, a sense of him, I don't know, it seemed like we were... I mean it seemed as if we were connected, but then not, because I don't know where we were. And then I lost it." He snapped his fingers. "Poof! – like that – and it started rushing away from me, or I from it, I don't know, all I can say is if it weren't for the God's eye...."

Neutic followed his glance. "God's eye."

Mr. Z. stared blankly, as if recalling something. "*Bawaba!* Neutic, that's it!"

"Bawaba?" Neutic frowned.

"The voice. The man's name. 'I am Bawaba,' he said. And I swear he spoke in an Arabic accent."

Neutic slumped into the couch, exasperated. "Sir, I don't understand. I mean, I don't get it. Any of it. This remote viewing session as you call it – what were you trying to do?"

Mr. Z. laughed ruefully. "I'm sorry, Neutic, you must think I've gone crazy. I was trying to find Vixy."

Neutic blinked at him.

"I was looking at the images here on the walls, the illustrations and paintings, I remember looking at this one and that one" – he gestured here and there at the walls – "and then the God's eye, this object here. Well, an inspiration hit me. Or desperation, one or the other, or both, I don't know – it just struck me that we've been getting nowhere in our investigation and I thought I might try something I haven't tried in quite some time. I figured it couldn't hurt. You never know what might shake something loose." He raised his eyebrows, puffed out his cheeks and exhaled, as if relieved. "I just didn't expect to be, I don't know, so... –"

"Overcome?" Neutic squinted at him. "I mean, sir, I still think it might be worth having the nurse examine you."

Mr. Z. shook his head. "Listen, Neutic. I tried to connect with Vixy, to locate her without physically leaving this room. That's what remote viewing is. RV as they call it. I used that damn God's eye as a focal point – you know, as an *affecting* and *effecting* image. The technique involves jotting down whatever fleeting things come into your mind – any images, scenes, information. Then you try to decipher it, to make sense of it within the context of what you were seeking to accomplish."

They stared at each other.

"I was desperate, I must admit. I'd been working and waiting, just as you have been, to come across something, to discover something, anything, regarding Vixy's fate. But there's been nothing. Nothing for too long. And

then our troubling encounter last night. That shadow monster. It seemed
to me... well, it seemed that momentum was turning against us, that the
trail was going cold. Drastic measures, you know?"

Neutic appeared thoughtful. "I understand, sir. Desperation. Me too."

"And believe me," said Mr. Z., "I do realize that I'm perhaps talking
to you now only by the grace of God, as they say. It occurs to me that
whatever happened with this session, which by the way is intended to be
a conscious experience" – he rested his hand on top of his head as if newly
astonished – "if this were rather akin to astral projection, well, I was well
out of my depth."

"It looked as though you were out cold."

"Well, as I'm saying, out from your perspective. There are stories of
shamanic flights, after all, whereby the shaman, lying there prone, is attended by a helper, a protector, someone to prevent even a fly from resting
upon the shaman's inert form so as to keep the cosmic channels, such as
they are, open; to ensure his safe return. It's a fantastic image but I can't
say I ever took such things seriously, as anything other than interesting
forms of self-induced psychological trance. But, Neutic, I can't help but
think that if you hadn't walked in and found me... I don't know what." He
scratched his head.

Neutic got up. "I think you're right about needing something stronger to drink. Me too."

"All that aside, Neutic, I've made a connection!" Mr. Z. leaned forward
eagerly, his eyes flashing. "She's *alive*, Herman. Vixy is alive, I *know* it!"

Neutic strode across the room to the bar. He returned with two
whiskeys and sat down across from Mr. Z.

"Look, here." Mr. Z. reached for his drink, sipped, then gestured at
his papers. "It says 'Bawaba.' That page on top. Look."

Neutic eyed Mr. Z.'s scribblings.

"Bawaba is the man who spoke to me during my session. I did not
actually encounter Vixy, never saw her or heard her voice." He frowned.
"Which worries, me, I can tell you."

Neutic squinted as he sipped his whiskey. He shuffled through Mr. Z.'s papers with growing interest until his skepticism seemed to dissolve. He read quietly, intently.

"I know it doesn't seem like much on the face of it," said Mr. Z. "AOLs – analytical overlays, they're called – spurious information – such things are to be anticipated in an RV session; one's imagination tends to run rampant and we get fixated on powerful impressions and strong images. One is instructed to discard or disregard such things as irrelevant, as cognitive noise because the stronger or more forceful the image the less reliable it is, the more potentially misleading. The mind is always somehow attempting to project its version of reality versus merely accepting input, versus focusing on perception. We're not computers." Mr. Z. waved his words away – he seemed impatient to make his point. "But this is no time to analyze the RV process. Fleeting strokes of the pen. The seemingly innocuous. The seemingly spurious. This type of thing, especially if it recurs in a session – that's exactly the stuff one is after. You see these dots here in the midst of my doodlings, for instance?" He held up a page and pointed to a set of converging lines. "Well, this is where I'm probing; something seemed to me especially potent, especially relevant, apparently. I don't remember doing it, but the method is to make a note, to literally press your pen point on it and attempt to spend more time with the intuition. Ideograms is what they're called, these recurring impressions. Link them together and we might arrive at something tangible, some legitimate clue. And here, look!" He pointed to something else on the page. "These numbers. I asked when and where Vixy was and I clearly heard this man Bawaba say 'eighteen eighty-one.'"

"Eighteen eighty-one, sir?"

"You're thinking eighteen eighty-one could mean anything, right? Anything from a street address, say, to an apartment number, to a quantity or distance or weight of this or that –"

"But you're telling me it's a calendar year. The year Vixy is in."

Mr. Z. affected an exaggerated nod and slapped his thigh. "Exactly. I'm convinced this Bawaba is referring to the year *eighteen eighty-one.*"

"By what calendar? I mean, we're using the Gregorian. But throughout history, haven't there been any number of calendars – Chinese, Islamic, Hindu, Jewish – how can eighteen-eighty-one mean anything in particular?"

"You're right. And it wasn't as if I had an opportunity to ask about it. I swear the last thing I remember is hearing this number eighteen eighty-one and then waking up on the floor with you staring into my face. But let's set the calendar question aside for now – we won't make any assumptions, we'll just proceed to analyze this stuff, these scrawls and scribbles one by one and see if we can't piece together something more." He closed his eyes as if to recall his experience. "His accent was Arabic, I'm certain of it. So, right there, we could be dealing with the so-called Hijri calendar."

"Bawaba," said Neutic. "A weird name." He scratched at his temple. "Do you think that's Middle Eastern, too?" He drained his whiskey and strode to the data console, tapping at it. "Yep. Egyptian Arabic."

"Yes. You see? There are clues in these scribblings – we've got to go through them carefully, the analysis can't be rushed; again, it's tricky to separate the wheat from the chaff, the legitimate ideograms from the spurious garbage." He stood up and scowled. "I need a shower and something to eat – whiskey for breakfast isn't going to get us through. What do you say to meeting back here in thirty minutes? I'll have some food brought up and we can attack this on a full stomach."

Neutic appeared bolstered by the idea. "Yessir. Meanwhile, I'll request a refreshed GID analysis on the year 1881." He hurried towards the door. "We'll start with the Gregorian calendar and hope we get lucky."

Neutic stood in Mr. Z.'s doorway and rapped on the doorframe.

Mr. Z. glanced up, chewing heartily, a forkful of fried egg, waffle and sausage dripping with maple syrup poised over his plate. He gestured for Neutic to sit. "The food just arrived and I couldn't resist, sorry. Help yourself."

Neutic tucked a napkin into his collar and dug in.

"What about the GID?"

"No luck, sir. They reconfigured the scan, ran another distillation on the data but nothing dropped out. Something about evidence half-life – that too much time has passed since the incident at the Olympic for any reliable ghosting to have survived."

"It figures." Mr. Z. shoved a few of his papers at Neutic. "Help me look these over again, will you?"

Neutic frowned at the papers. "What am I looking for?"

"Anything that relates, however obliquely. Patterns. Repetitions that might connect to other repetitions. I've sat here looking at the stuff so much I can't see the forest for the trees." He shook his head and gulped the remainder of his coffee. "I need a breath of fresh air, do you mind?" He tipped his head, gesturing towards the balcony.

Neutic already seemed to have immersed himself in the pages. "No, sir," he said absently, "not at all."

"Shit," said Neutic. "Holy shit." He looked up to find the room empty. He glanced at the time: thirty minutes had rushed past. He caught sight of Mr. Z. standing with his back to him, outside at the railing of the balcony. He leapt up and clamored past the screen door. "Sir, this business of 'rising, angling and converging at the center.'" He followed the writing with his fingertip. "And here, you've written 'stone,' 'sand,' 'blocks of stone, "architectural stone.'"

Mr. Z. puffed on his pipe. "Go on, Neutic, go on."

"River. Black mud. Sir, if these aren't, what do you call them – ideograms – parts of a recurring theme – then I don't know what is. You've written 'black mud' six times on this page alone."

"I know, Neutic." He shook his head. "But for the life of me I can't glean anything from it."

"And *rising, angling, converging at the center*. A river with black, muddy banks. What about a river that rises? Of course there's a lot about stones and hewn granite – blocks and architecture and so forth. And, look here," – he thrust the page at Mr. Z., pointing to a clumsy image – "you've drawn what looks like an eye, a single human eye. But stylized. And you mention eyes in here somewhere – alluring, black-lined, female eyes. What about Vixy's eyes?" When Mr. Z. didn't respond, Neutic's enthusiasm flagged. "I don't know, maybe I'm way off."

"No," said Mr. Z. He puffed quietly, thoughtfully, as if the ideas were compelling. "No, not at all, Neutic – you just might be on the mark." He gestured at him with the mouthpiece of his pipe. "Vixy's eyes." He grabbed at the paper. "Let me see this." He emptied his pipe, tapping the bowl on the railing and stuffed it in his pocket. He donned his spectacles and peered at the page. "I never saw Vixy, never heard her voice, remember? Only Bawaba's voice. But you said stylized. For shit's sake it's just that I can't draw a lick." He jammed his finger at the image. "Eyeliner."

Neutic looked baffled.

"Cosmetics, Neutic." Mr. Z. began pacing back and forth on the balcony. "Of course Vixy wears eyeliner."

"But nothing like that," said Neutic. "Right? I mean, lots of women wear eyeliner. But this is thick, dark, like something you'd see on stage, in a rock band or an opera."

"Something ancient, Neutic." Mr. Z. thrust the page at Neutic. "Tell me that doesn't remind you of something from *antiquity*."

"Cleopatra," said Neutic in a breathy voice, as if it had dawned on him. Mr. Z. nodded ominously. "Egypt, Neutic. A human eye? The eye of a woman? How about the eye of a god? A falcon-headed god. Existing on the banks of a river with black, muddy banks. A river that famously floods. Architectural stones that rise and converge. Like pyramids." Mr. Z. rattled the page. "It's the eye of Horus. The river is the Nile. The stones are the pyramids. Look here, the word 'scarab.' What's more Egyptian than that?" He slapped his leg. "And that damn odor!"

"Odor. You mean horses?"

"What about a camel? Bloody hell, why couldn't I make sense of this before?"

"Vixy's in Egypt, then," said Neutic. "Near the Nile River and the Pyramids. In the year 1881."

Mr. Z. nodded at him. "We've almost found her."

"Almost?"

"There are pyramids and stone monuments all up and down the damn Nile, for miles, even into Upper Egypt. Exactly *where*? And when? When in 1881 - what month, what day, what time? We need all that to set HDT coordinates. How in hell do we decipher that from an RV session? We can't."

Neutic regarded him staunchly. "What about the calendar issue? We've got to figure out what eighteen eighty-one means."

"Right. Check on it, will you? – start with the year of adoption of the Gregorian calendar in Egypt. Now we might finally get lucky."

Neutic swiped at his device and tapped away with his usual dexterity. "Eighteen seventy-five. Adoption of the Gregorian calendar in Egypt."

"Close enough. There's always a chance this Bawaba, if he's Muslim, could be referring to the Hijri – all manner of concurrent calendar usage occurs on Earth and everywhere else in the cosmos. Meanwhile, the Gregorian remains in play." He clenched his fist and pounded tentatively on the railing of the balcony. "This Bawaba character – he's critical, he has to be. He could be some sort of spiritual adept himself for all we know – how else would I gain such compelling access to him? But how to...? I don't know, Neutic. I tell you I'm feeling out of my depth entirely. Here we're finally getting somewhere, we're finally closing in on Vixy –"

"Perhaps Professor Wilhelm can help?"

Mr. Z. snapped his fingers at Neutic. "My boy, that's it! That's it exactly! If the Professor can't help us no one can."

Neutic tapped his device. "I'll put a request in to Captain Chase telling him what we've discovered – what we think we've discovered, anyway. Hopefully he can manage to interest the Professor –"

"Oh, she'll be interested, alright; I'm certain of it." Mr. Z. opened the screen door and they reentered the living room. "This calls for another drink."

"Meanwhile," said Neutic, "I'm curious about something. Forgive me, sir, but I can't help wondering how in hell you have any idea what a camel smells like?"

"Ah," said Mr. Z., chuckling. "As it happens, I've actually been to Egypt. To Cairo. As a young man in my early twenties. Let's just say I spent some significant time around camels – I'll tell you the story one day. Meanwhile, I'll never forget what a camel smells like again, I can tell you that."

A miniature cacophony of electronic chimes, bells and buzzing suddenly issued forth from both Neutic's device and Mr. Z.'s transponder and even the concierge panel on the wall.

"It's the Captain," said Neutic.

# CHAPTER 16

# CORRIDORS OF POWER

**"HOW'S THE ARM, Z?"**

"Much improved, Captain, thank you." Mr. Z. settled into an armchair across from Neutic.

"That's fine, Z, fine," said the Captain, rolling up his sleeves. "That's good news. And I've got more."

Neutic and Mr. Z. exchanged glances.

"Approximately two hours ago," the Captain began, "the TDC received a transmission – of entirely dubious authenticity, mind you – from what we believe to be Vixy's transponder. That's right. TDC forensics has been over it with everything they've got, with the proverbial fine-toothed comb. And I'm sorry to report they haven't come up with much. No provenance, no encryption, no proper coordinate tags and most importantly, no bio-link to Vixy's DNA – no proof-of-life. In other words, it wasn't an SOS. In fact, the data stream was so deteriorated, carrying so much noise that the technicians almost discarded it as dimensional ghosting. All this took place within an hour of the official downgrade in Vixy's SAR[48] priority – as a cadet–in–training she's not authorized for an extension of resources, not that I didn't run the request through anyway. Nevertheless, this signal buys us time. It's evidence. It keeps her out of cold case for another seven days and authorizes us to maintain the investigation at full throttle."

"No SOS," said Mr. Z. "No bio-link. In other words, Vixy couldn't have initiated the signal."

"Correct," said the Captain. "And you know as well as I do, Z, how damn well impossible it is that anyone could've breached the firewall in her device. They couldn't have turned the damn thing on, let alone transmitted."

"What if she were coerced?" suggested Neutic.

"No," said Mr. Z. "Impossible. Duress sensors would block any transmission. Likewise, any external augmentation to her physiology or biochemistry by way of narcosynthesis."

"Narcosynthesis?"

"The controlled administration of intravenous hypnotic medications," the Captain explained. "So-called truth serums. Psychoactive drugs and the like. TDC-issued transponders, even the less robust cadet versions like Vixy's, are designed with torture-proof fail-safes. Neither can they be activated by a corpse – the bio-link is animation dependent."

Neutic appeared mildly unnerved, shifting in his chair.

Mr. Z. withdrew his transponder and held it in his outstretched palm. "Any TDC-issued transponder is keyed to unadulterated, living DNA and the user's beta, alpha, theta and delta brainwave signature." He sat back and addressed the Captain. "The question is how somebody other than Vixy could've transmitted on her device, not why we can't effectively trace her HDT residue."

"Right," said the Captain. He rubbed his chin. "Except for the fact that Vixy's transponder hadn't been activated for HDT."

Mr. Z. frowned. "But I submitted the upgrade authorization months ago, sir."

"Ten weeks and two days ago to be exact – I authorized it the same day you submitted it and forwarded it according to protocol. Nevertheless, the upgrade for Vixy's device was not initiated. I've been through it all with my commanding officers and TDC administration, tracing the authorization trail. Something about the IT framework at headquarters being down for repair, bad timing, what have you - a perfect storm of gaffs. But it's all beside the point. Not that I haven't logged a complaint. Regardless, it got missed. Vixy's transponder, at the time of her abduction, remained in no-fly mode."

Mr. Z. put his hand to his temple.

"No-fly, Captain?" said Neutic; "as in –"

"As in no HDT. And this is the rub: a no-fly transponder is not configured to assimilate a full security package upgrade."

Mr. Z. was livid. "So Vixy's transponder remained essentially a training transponder, open to tampering. By someone like a terrorist with their own HDT technology; someone with sufficient technical acumen could... could...." Mr. Z. stammered.

"Possibly effect a transmission, that's right – I know where you're going with this, Z." "Which may explain the clumsiness or glitchiness of the transmission. Look, Z, I'm as unhappy about this as anyone. It's intolerable. Administrative snafus. A mistake like this has further endangered Vixy's life. Nevertheless, what we've got is a transmission from Vixy's transponder. Which is *something* versus the nothing we've been working with so far." He tapped at his control panel and a series of capitalized letters came up on the display which the Captain recited one at a time. "B. R. U. G. G. S."

Both Mr. Z. and Neutic stared blankly at the characters.

The Captain's tone was flat. "We also deciphered this."

Neutic typed the letters into his device and Mr. Z. scribbled them onto a piece of paper.

"From Vixy's transponder?" said Mr. Z.

"That's right. The letters came in sequentially just as I've read them, as if someone was pecking at the keyboard, hitting the 'enter' key after each letter. The two other associated transmissions have a data density far below that of the evidentiary threshold. 'R. A. N. S. M.' And one more, a third transmission in such bad shape that forensics isn't willing to classify it as legitimate; they say it's just as likely spurious as anything. The analysis and reconstruction could only generate three characters: 'G. E. H.'"

Mr. Z. looked vaguely startled. "Ransom," he said. He got up and began pacing slowly round the room.

"Yes," said the Captain, "Ransom. It fits with the scenario, anyway. The third transmission? Nobody knows what to make of it. A name? Initials?" The Captain threw up his hands.

"Or a location," said Mr. Z. "Excuse me, Captain. The first transmission: 'BRUGGS' – assuming it may be a name, or part of a name, a search came up empty in the criminal database?"

"Yes."

"What about relic attributes? Were there any attached to the transmissions?"

"That was my next item. Relic attributes are without a doubt nineteenth-century Earth. Which is interesting but hardly constitutes sufficient accuracy for a hard target search."

"No geological foci? No coordinates?"

"Nothing, Z. In the meantime, the TDC has set up a looped reply, but without foci, the signal pans globally. Add to that the time-slice of one hundred years – the nineteenth century – and our search field becomes enormous."

"No ping saturation?"

"Of course not," said the Captain. "I've requested it; but you know as well as I do, Z, there's no precedent for saturation pinging – the Leave-No-Trace legislation is stronger than ever against so-called signal pollution – hell, the irony isn't lost on me that it's something we've all been battling in support of all these years – to keep the meridian, parallels and hyper-meridians clear – and now it's the very thing working against us. And again, Vixy's status as a cadet-in-training means we can only do so much anyway – the resources are limited. These dribs and drabs are all we've got, gentlemen."

Mr. Z. was standing before the God's eye, his back to Neutic and the display console. "G, E, H."

"Sir?" said Neutic.

Mr. Z. spun round. "Neutic. Search the alternate English spellings for the Egyptian city of Giza – G, I, Z, A – as it appeared in Gregorian calendar year 1881."

"Egypt?" said the Captain.

"Yessir. I'm thinking specifically of a spelling I recall from a study of the pyramids within the Plateau by Flinders Petrie. If I'm not mistaken the name of the city within that text is spelled, 'G, I, Z, E, H.'"

Neutic brought up a virtual keyboard and began tapping. "Yessir, Gizeh with the letters 'e' and 'h' is a common spelling, especially amongst European Egyptologists of the time, apparently. The Flinders Petrie publication is entitled *The Pyramids and Temples of Gizeh*, published in 1883 as it happens, with that exact spelling."

"I'm missing something here, gentlemen," said the Captain. "There might be any number of locations we could contrive to utilize the letters 'g,' 'e,' and 'h.' And what is it about Giza and the year 1881, anyway?"

"Bear with me, sir," said Mr. Z., "but Neutic and I have spent the morning reviewing the data from my remote viewing session – remote viewing in coordination with extended mind – and, well, it's my preliminary conclusion, corroborated by the tattoo found on one of the terrorists and the evidence you've just presented to us that Vixy is alive in Giza, Egypt in the year 1881."

"Remote viewing?" said the Captain. "Experimental psi methods? In your condition? Dammit Z! You of all people should realize how reckless that is. To say nothing of your lack of objectivity. What good is your data? You're biologically compromised – physically weakened and medicated. And of course, you're impossibly biased – too emotionally close to Vixy and the case for the data to be considered legitimate, anything more than projections. You know that."

Mr. Z. sat quietly, for a moment, staring blankly at a spot on the floor, as if he'd anticipated the Captain's reaction.

"Believe me," said the Captain, "I understand the sense of urgency, the idea of the trail going cold. I get what drives any man with half a gram of integrity to want to do something about it. But, hell, Z, RV remains an unauthorized investigative technique. Anybody sticking their nose into the TDC playing around with stuff like that – like the damn oversight committee that breathes down my neck every month, for example – would be happy to slap us with a violation. And then you'd be looking at insubordination." He drummed his fingers on the tabletop. "Do you understand what I'm saying? You can lean too hard on a friend, Z."

Mr. Z. spoke in a measured tone. "Yessir. It was impulsive. Outside protocol. Nevertheless, I believe I may have stumbled upon something. Some*one*, actually. I communicated, briefly, with a man, no doubt Arab judging by his accent, who indicated his knowledge of Vixy's whereabouts – *the woman you seek is here*, he said. When I asked where and when, he provided the number eighteen eighty-one. Which we're convinced is a calendar year. Moreover, based on other data from my RV, we'd surmised the Nile valley as the probable geography. That is, sir, until you provided the additional clues which narrow the probable locale to the vicinity of the Giza Plateau."

"I'm going to indulge you, Z, for the sake of argument. But I'm not here to allow my TDs to transform an investigation into their personal experiment, no matter how desperate the situation. I repeat: I'm not condoning your methods." The Captain allowed his words to hang in the air. "Now. How do we know this so-called Arab man himself isn't one of the terrorists? How do we know, for instance, that you weren't under the influence of the same psi phenomenon inflicted upon the Olympic Theater cadets?"

"Was that the determination?" asked Neutic. "At the Olympic?"

"That it was a psi attack?" The Captain shook his head. "No. That is, there still hasn't been any determination at all. Frankly, this sliver of evidence involving Vixy's transponder is the only damn thing that's come out of any of it." He sighed at Mr. Z. "Which is why I'm indulging you, Z."

"I can't speak to the veracity of my RV data, sir, let alone my application of extended mind techniques. I don't claim to be in the league of a Professor Wilhelm when it comes to psi - perhaps I'm vulnerable to an outside influence. I only know that Neutic and I focused on the fleeting and the repetitive and did our best to remain objective. Which is impossible, I realize that. But I wasn't looking to encounter anyone. Besides Vixy, that is. Let alone a man with an Arab accent named Bawaba. Yes, he provided his name. I was focusing on Vixy and this man interceded. The experience was all pretty unwieldy, I admit. It could have been hallucinatory. Outside of my data I could have imagined it all. Perhaps I literally dreamed it."

"I found him flat on the floor in his room, Captain," said Neutic. "He was unconscious. Or close enough to it not to be dreaming I can tell you." Neutic looked hard at Mr. Z.

"I don't want to know, Neutic," said the Captain. He was holding up his hands defensively. "I don't want to know the details of what went on. You didn't participate in an unauthorized RV or extended mind or otherwise parapsychological experiment, do you understand me? You were helping Mr. Z. recuperate. Do I make myself clear?"

A silence ensued.

"Then there are the tattoos, Captain," said Neutic. "Namely, the tattoos found on the body of one of the terrorists – the one who killed himself at the Olympic."

"What do you mean?" said the Captain. "There's nothing in the postmortems about tattoos on any of the terrorists. If this was part of Mr. Z.'s RV then –"

"No, sir. No, not at all. This was something we discovered yesterday that was somehow left out of the report – for whatever reason photographs of the body went missing, a strange thing in and of itself, sir, as I'm sure you'd agree. Regardless, the technician who took the photos, an acquaintance of mine as it happens, was able to recall the images – the designs were on the terrorist's chest and arms and without question they convey Egyptian iconography – a winged scarab over the man's heart and on his arms... well, I'm not an expert...." Neutic trailed off.

"On the man's arms were hieroglyphs," said Mr. Z.

"Hieroglyphs?" said the Captain, incredulous. "And why haven't either of you informed me?" He narrowed his eyes at both of them. "For

God's sake, gentlemen, is there something about the sound of my voice, about me asking that both of you lay low there at Eranos that inspires the opposite... I don't know..." – he struggled for the word – "*behavior* – that makes you two think you're better off being cowboys? Perhaps we all – the TDC, the T.E. and the PMC– ought to turn this entire investigation over to you both?"

Mr. Z. cleared his throat and winked discreetly at Neutic.

"I'm forwarding the images to you now, sir," said Neutic, typing into his console.

They watched the Captain peering closely at his display as he talked. "Meanwhile, Neutic, I trust Mr. Z.'s aversion to institutional bureaucracy, as he sees it, isn't becoming too seductive on your behalf." He leaned closer to the images. "These tattoos. They're authentic? You've researched the translation?"

Mr. Z. appeared engrossed in his own thoughts.

Neutic spoke up. "All is illusion; let it go. All is in order; let it come." He was regarding Mr. Z. "Isn't that what you said? Mr. Z.?"

Mr. Z. came back to himself and looked squarely at Neutic. "Power of gold. Stop them. Khafre."

"What?" The Captain frowned.

"Sir?" said Neutic.

Mr. Z. put his hand to his head and sat bolt upright. "Blast it all! I've been witless! I'm sorry, Captain. Neutic. Both of you, I apologize. It just came to me. I mean to say, I just remembered it. What this man Bawaba said. *Power of gold. Stop them. Khafre.* I never wrote it down. We scoured my notes and – hell!" His enthusiasm seemed to overtake his impatience with himself. "There's more. At least I think there is. This evidence. It connects to more evidence. To do with the Molemen, of all things."

"Z," said the Captain, "you're making me crazy. The Molemen? What in hell are you talking about?"

"The intelligence we'd uncovered. That the Molemen race had survived the cataclysm they'd endured – their dying sun – that they'd engineered their way out of it."

"And propagated the legend of their annihilation. That's not only old intelligence, Z, it's *ten years* old. And for Christ's sake, it's top secret."

"Sir, I don't see... I mean to say, Neutic, he's as close to this investigation as anyone. Are you telling me we can't authorize –?"

The Captain rubbed his head, his voice heavy with exasperation. "I'm not telling you anything, Z, because it clearly wouldn't matter if I did." He shook his head and gestured as if to keep things rolling. "Get on with it, Z. Tie it all together."

"Our evidence, as you recall, sir – and I'm repeating this for Neutic's benefit - was pointing towards the idea that at the time of the annihilation, of their sun going nova, the Molemen had already commenced several decades of unauthorized research into time-suspension technology; into the engineering of space-time stoppages – so-called progression rifts and all that. On a planetary scale."

"They couldn't just request authorization for the research like anyone else?" asked Neutic.

"Certainly. And they could've asked for help, too. From any number of galactic humanitarian organizations that support emergency emigration strategies for planetary refugees. But they didn't. Their sun died, their planet disintegrated, and by the time news of the holocaust reached galactic media feeds, everyone thought it was the end of them. That they'd vanished. And they did. They'd vanished via their HDT prowess into another world. They'd evacuated their entire population and transported everything attached to it in a cosmic swap – a wholesale planetary evacuation and emigration."

"An unmatched feat of engineering," said the Captain.

"I don't understand," said Neutic. "Why the secrecy? To what end? What motivates a race to propagate the legend of their disappearance, of their annihilation?"

"Now you're talking like a time detective," said Mr. Z. "Motive. What motivates *anyone* to engineer their own disappearance?" He waited, eyeing Neutic expectantly. "What would they seek?"

"A chance."

"A chance for what?"

Neutic spoke carefully. "To be born again."

"Indeed." Mr. Z. seemed pleased. "But why?"

Neutic shook his head. "I don't know. There could be any number of legitimate reasons, or illegitimate ones...." He trailed off.

"We don't know either, Neutic," said the Captain. "Nobody does. In fact, the TDC were just getting our heads around the intelligence data when everything went to hell; when all our evidence was dismissed."

"Dismissed?" said Neutic.

Mr. Z. was determined to continue. "In their quest to save themselves the Molemen would've scoured the cosmos for a new planet, a new home – vacant, yet hospitable. Vacant, because there's no evidence that they ever sought to invade or otherwise appropriate or even request refuge on a populated planet. It must have been an incredible exploratory effort. Meanwhile, they naturally encountered cultures unlike their own – they *must* have. Vast numbers of them. And one of those, I'm convinced, was that of Earth."

"A conclusion likewise dismissed," said the Captain. "By the GTA – the Galactic Transparency Alliance, of all things. They took a few days to supposedly examine our data, cited the TDC for breach of planetary security protocol and confiscated it. All our investigative work, that is. We had to relinquish everything. Otherwise, they refused to comment."

"The summons, Captain," said Mr. Z. "The red-level that brought Vixy and me to the T.E. You said it was an HDT anomaly; that the Time Guard had performed an analysis on an anomaly in the Ghost Impression Database, spurred by a report by the Consequence Research Project."

"Yes. And the TDC had been assigned the investigation. And ever since, you've been keen not on the Molemen but the damn Mothmen as having something to do with the oracle coins and the attack at the T.E. So what are you driving at, exactly?"

"I'm just thinking out loud, sir, bear with me." Mr. Z. got up and paced the room. He shoved his pipe into his mouth and chomped on it, puffing at the empty bowl, his brow furrowed. "This is for your edification as much anything, Neutic." He continued to pace, as if the pacing were helping his thinking. "Correct me if I'm mistaken at any point, please, Captain. The GTA contributes annually to the funding for Consequence Research. And it's my understanding that any time-suspension project, initiative or research of any type – anything to do with scientific experimentation upon the Cosmic Time Architecture – requires a three-point authorization by the GTA, the GIA and a special concession from the Time Guard. Otherwise it risks adjudication by those authorities as a time crime of the first magnitude."

"That's right," said the Captain.

Mr. Z. sat down with an air of resolution. "Our data, then – the data the GTA squelched – revealed a rift in the area of the Giza Plateau in the 4th Dynasty – two-thousand six-hundred to twenty-five hundred BCE or so."

Neutic tried to restrain his astonishment, his glance darting between Mr. Z. and the Captain. "Regarding Vixy, then," he blurted, "and this Bawaba character – are we implying some sort of Moleman connection?" He couldn't hide either his skepticism or his impatience. "*Power of gold. Stop them. Kaffer.* The Consequence Research Project report – the ghost-impression anomaly. The summons of Mr. Z. and Vixy to the T.E. It's all tied to Vixy's kidnapping? With her being in Egypt in 1881?"

"Khafre," said Mr. Z.

Neutic appeared flummoxed.

Mr. Z. spelled the word out. "He's an Egyptian King, a pharaoh from the fourth dynasty, Old Kingdom. Builder of the second largest pyramid in the Giza complex. I'm sorry, Neutic, the information I came across involving the Molemen only just now seemed to fit. It was ten years ago the last time the Captain and I had anything to do with that investigation."

"Hmm," said the Captain. "It's still one hell of a stretch, Z. A verifiable Molemen presence in Egypt. That would lend credence to the theory, or the legend, that they interfered with the Pharaonic period of development, the so-called Old Kingdom period in particular; that they had something to do with influencing the engineering of the Pyramids."

"Incredible," said Neutic.

"Direct manipulation of Earth's future," said the Captain. "And a time crime of the first rank with incalculable permutations to the Cosmic Time Architecture."

Neutic's astonishment percolated. "I don't even want to ask whether either of you think the oracle coins – or whatever they are – and the attack at the Olympic have anything to do with this anymore. The Mothmen. Mind control and all that. The Professor, for that matter."

"Which only points out that we've got far too much theory and not anywhere near enough hard evidence, gentlemen. This investigation has got to start generating facts. Z, I cannot run with your RV data nor the conclusions you're drawing – no matter how compelling – unless we get something definitive. As in proof of life of Vixy Velure. To say nothing of her validated HDT coordinates. We've got seven days. And then the rug will be pulled out from under this investigation.

"Meanwhile, Z. And this is off the record...." They watched the Captain tap his console. The "scramble" icon appeared beneath his image and "no transcription" scrolled across the bottom of the display. "This is all going to require further analysis. To say the least. Unofficial analysis. Which is to say I'm willing to take your RV data and present it to Professor Wilhelm. For review, let's call it. Officially, I'm requisitioning additional resources towards narrowing Vixy's coordinates. That is, I'm going to push for nothing less than a Hyper-Dimensional Drift Net across the Giza Plateau in the year 1881. Not that I'll get it. With nothing but my own reputation to wager into the bargain. And some debts I'm going to call in within the powers that be, as they say. But I need time, Z. I need time if I'm going to get the Drift Net deployed. And these tattoos, the hieroglyphics and the scarab – I've got to run them by our symbology department and get an authorized translation from the Egyptology experts at the T.E. – if your translation differs we can discuss it at our next confab." He glanced at the time. "Zero eight-hundred tomorrow morning?"

"Zero eight-hundred, Yessir," said Mr. Z.

"Sit tight, you two. Is that understood?"

They nodded.

"Signing off."

Neutic collapsed into the couch and sighed as if he'd been holding his breath.

Mr. Z., alternatively, stood up. He looked anxious, clutching his pipe in his good hand and making a fist with his bad one, rotating it and grimacing. "I could use some fresh air, Neutic. What do you say to a walk around the grounds, perhaps down to the lake?"

# CHAPTER 17

# NET OF GEMS

**MR. Z. BURST THROUGH THE CASA'S DOUBLE DOORS** and onto the broad porch, paused briefly to take in the view and bounded down the steps, spilling into the sunshine as if he were newly free. Neutic paused to lean on a porch pillar, watching him from above.

"Ah, what brilliant weather!" Mr. Z. scratched at the back of his neck and stretched his arms out, yawning as he talked. "You know, Neutic" – he looked back – "there's something about meetings... or getting out of one – that makes me feel like I've survived an illness." He employed a deep knee bend and stood up, hands on hips, looking out expansively as if from the prow of a ship.

"Right," said Neutic. "Me too." He followed as they made their way through the manicured garden, squinting into the brilliant sunlight, content to absorb the rugged beauty of the mountains, the clarity of the sky and the fresh, sweet-scented, invigorating breeze. The sparkling lakeshore beckoned. He found himself envying Mr. Z.'s blithe perspective. That they were following the same path upon which they'd rushed back to the Casa that fretful night seemed strange; strange in the context of this luminous afternoon, but stranger still that Mr. Z. had yet to comment on the incident, as if it hadn't happened. Maybe it's just as well. Perhaps I'm being morbid, he thought. Yet he found it difficult to regard their headway, such as it was, in the investigation as anything substantial. He couldn't rid himself of a nagging sense of guilt, as if Vixy's circumstances made their own seem frivolous – what did their so-called progress amount to if Vixy remained lost? That, and the Captain's imposed restraints or, more accurately, his *restraint* regarding Mr. Z.'s evidence on behalf of Vixy's whereabouts seemed stifling.

Mr. Z. looked askance at him. "What do you make of the debriefing?"

Neutic hesitated, determined to say something apt. "I don't know, Vixy's transponder and all that, on the one hand it seems like fantastic progress and on the other hand, well, it seems like we got a talking to, if you know what I mean." He shrugged and cringed at his negativity. "But I don't know, maybe it's not my place."

Mr. Z. laughed. "No. It is. You're as invested in this as any of us. Nevertheless, the Captain certainly makes a point of establishing the rules of engagement, doesn't he? He ought to, after all. He's got a job to do. And it's my fault, Neutic. I get carried away and the Captain had every authority to charge me with misconduct and he didn't." He plucked a leaf from a low-hanging branch and tossed it aside. "And it's the kind of thing I suppose I wouldn't recommend for anyone pursuing a career, not just within the TDC. You can be right and still be out of a job. It gets tricky." He gestured dismissively. "Ah, do as I say, Neutic, not as I do. How's that for a worthless old adage?"

"How about this one?" He was determined to sound lighthearted. "Institutions are like ships at sea. They take a long time to turn."

"They certainly do. And don't get me wrong – I'm not disparaging the Captain." He'd filled his pipe with tobacco and stopped to light it, puffing as he talked. "Nor the TDC. Heavens no. It's just that, oh, I don't know – I swear I don't intend to be contrary. It's just my damn impatience that makes me blind to a more agreeable method. The Captain is a good man. You'd think I'd learn."

The path diverged, continuing eastwardly into the forest on its way towards Ascona and, alternatively, spilling down the hillside towards the blue-on-blue allure of the shimmering lake and the chiseled grandeur of the mountains beyond. The sun was warm on their faces and they made their way enthusiastically to the water's edge, the surface rippling in the breeze, lapping noisily against the jetty, the gulls tipping their slender, pointed wings towards the swollen lake, their cries rising and falling, reflecting off the water's surface.

"Has Vixy ever been here? To Eranos?"

"No." Mr. Z. twisted his expression into a rueful half-smile. "I dare say she'd be impatient with the privileged atmosphere, with the affluence. And bored. 'It's nothing like the ocean,' I can hear her telling me."

Neutic smiled to himself and kicked at a pebble. "What do you think the odds are, sir, of us finding her, of getting her back?"

"She's resourceful and shrewd, Herman, as you may have already gathered. And tough. Strong. Strong-willed. But inexperienced. Though I'm not sure experience would help anyone in her situation. Whatever her situation is, for God's sake, I don't know. From our end, without a hyper-dimensional trajectory vector or even a detectable cosmic wake or echo – either of which the TDC would've immediately traced – the odds, I'm afraid to say, are long. Very long. There's no precedent for a so-called recovery under such circumstances."

"What happens to someone...?" He trailed off. "I mean... I don't know what I mean."

Mr. Z. put his foot up on the railing and picked at a fleck of paint. "They become lost in time." He squinted into the distance, across the water in the direction of the mountains. "But what does that mean – that's what you're asking, I know. I dare say we've all thought about it, Neutic. Becoming an HDT castaway. What it would be like. What we'd do. Horrible. A fate worse than death for some, I suppose. And then perhaps the bravest souls make the best of it; somehow make a new life from it."

Neutic shoved his hands into his pockets and they both looked out over the lake.

"I've been away too long," said Mr. Z. "Me and this blasted recuperation business, this injury. I've got to get back into the thick of things." He emptied his pipe against the railing, the low ring of the wood upon the metal like the chimes of an old clock. "Let's head back."

They'd returned to the place where they'd had their ominous encounter with the shadow shape. This time Mr. Z. paused, examining the trail itself, following the creature's path, as he recalled it, all the way across the lawn to the edge of the trees. "You know, Neutic, there are any number of recorded examples of the appearance of an unearthly, wolf-like animal – upon battlefields, for instance, or prior to environmental cataclysms or critical points in cultural history. And they're generally interpreted either as projections of psychological trauma – hallucinations – or as literary tropes developed by the authors of the stories to lend supernatural import to otherwise historical events."

Neutic likewise pondered the scene. What had seemed so portentous and menacing the night before now struck him as impossible – the trees stirred in the breeze, the sunlight dappled the path, birds sang and the campus seemed nestled serenely within the abiding, idyllic landscape.

Mr. Z. followed Neutic's gaze. "The wolf is often symbolic of fear. And also of the past. The past that drags away all that you've acquired. Alternatively, it can symbolize justice. Judgement. Cosmic balance. It's also a herald of death." He puffed on his empty pipe. "And of course as a species, the wolf is a preeminent hunter – a ruthless, yet not indiscriminate predator."

"I'll tell you, sir, I don't know what it was. You say a wolf of some type. I'm more comfortable believing last night was some sort of shared hallucination. I mean, we were tired, or at least I was. We'd had some drinks, we'd walked a long way in the dark...."

Mr. Z. looked into the distance for a time, facing the breeze, shading his eyes with his hand. "Indeed. But I saw something else, Neutic. Something strange before we even got close to Eranos."

Neutic waited, uncertain whether he wanted to hear what Mr. Z. was going to tell him. "Something in the woods, sir, wasn't it? I remember. You were looking over my shoulder at something, I knew it."

"The logic that whatever it was in the woods was a Mothman, perhaps the same mothman who planted the coins in my cruiser at the diner in New Jersey, well, it's not impossible. That would be unsettling enough. But this... this thing that came at us from the Casa. I don't know. I must admit the resemblance wasn't exactly point for point. Not at all. This thing seemed... different. Wolfish, is all I can make of it. Which is what has me thinking that way. But as you say, we were tired. It was dark. It was all just damn shadows in the dark."

"A Mothman." Neutic frowned, astonished. "Following you all the way here, to Eranos? But how –?"

"Oh, believe me, I don't know how or why or anything. And I've no proof, of course; it's just an intuition. Something about the way it moved in those trees. Stalking us. Watching. But I'll tell you if the shadow in the woods and the shadow at the Casa were the same thing, we'd be dead, Neutic. A Mothman assassin wouldn't have allowed us to get into the open, let alone go flying past us at the last second." He stuffed his pipe back into his pocket and glanced sideways at Neutic. "I think whatever it was that came at us from the Casa, wolf or otherwise – I think it saved our lives."

The images flooded back and Neutic relived something of his unspeakable dread – the unsettling look on Mr. Z.'s face in the woods, the image of the shadow-thing poised just beyond the reach of the porch lights of the Casa, the silent menace of its approach, its leaping overhead and bolting away."

Mr. Z. stood rubbing chin, his expression mildly fraught, as if he were reliving it, too. "I swear I think that shadow shape at the Casa was waiting for it. Waiting for the mothman to make its move. And if I'm right...." He shook his head dismissively. When he made to move on, Neutic spoke up.

"If you're right, what, sir?"

Mr. Z. stopped. "I don't know, Neutic. There are things in this world, in this cosmos... mysteries. Connections." He shrugged. "If I'm right then we're fortunate to be standing here talking about it, that's all. And to still have a chance to help Vixy."

Neutic followed Mr. Z. towards the Casa's entrance. He recalled what Mr. Z. had alluded to in the cab ride from the airport to Eranos – it seemed an age ago to him now – when they were discussing the Mothmen as presumed assassins and Mr. Z.'s knowledge of an investigation and a controversy. *I have my reasons,* he'd said. *But all of this is just between you and me, for now, okay?"* He bit his tongue and trudged onward. Don't think so much, right, Hettie?

The Eranos library was a grand room with wood paneled walls, long, broad tables adorned with reading lamps and tall, straight-backed chairs that seemed to invite hours of mindful, patient research. A magnificent, vaulted ceiling with ornate crown moldings soared above them and, at the center of everything, an enormous chandelier – a beguiling work of bejeweled, multifaceted art glass that evoked both a cascade of shattered ice and an impenetrable constellation of stars. There were opulent and expansive oriental carpets, luxurious drapes and an impressive fireplace, its carved stone mantel sweeping upwards. Between the floor-to-ceiling bookcases hung paintings of the nineteenth and twentieth century symbolists – Klimt's *Death and Life* was prominent, for example – but there were works by Gaugin, Whistler, Moreau, Toorop, Bonnard and others. Opposite the fireplace, far across the way, occupying its own niche, loomed an enormous illuminated globe, perhaps six meters in diameter, its lower quarter sunken into the floor and surrounded by a broad, transparent, structural glass ring that allowed the viewer a glimpse of its underside. Mr. Z. was drawn to it.

"Are you familiar with this, Neutic? This marvelous globe?"

Neutic followed. "No, sir."

Mr. Z. stood admiring it. "Do you notice anything about it? That is, besides the outlandishness of the thing?"

"Well. It's turning. I think. Very slowly, isn't it?"

Mr. Z. nodded and when he swept his hand over the globe's surface it seemed to awaken, illuminating from within. "Yes. And it's ever so slightly tilting, also. The whole thing is designed to reproduce exactly, proportionately, the revolution of the Earth and its axial tilt."

They stood watching the continents and seas drifting past, their parchment-textured hues evoking the muted colors of ancient cartography.

"You know, you can select any time period in the Earth's history, reproducing continental drift, glaciation, the rising and receding of the oceans, the changing in the coastlines, to say nothing of the limitless cartographic options – every historical period down to the day."

"This must be the control panel," said Neutic. "What if I type in the year 1881? Gregorian." When he tapped the last entry, the colors of the globe transformed, the borders of nations redefined themselves and the coastal boundaries of the continents mildly receded, commensurate with the appropriate sea level.

"Let's see now," said Mr. Z. He'd donned his spectacles and tipped his head back to peer through them. He gestured so that the globe rotated according to his influence, mirroring his movements, then walked his fingers across the globe's surface until he'd found it. "Egypt. And here. The Giza Plateau."

A sonorous ringing distracted them and they turned to look.

"The grandfather clock," said Mr. Z. "Over there in the far corner. Striking the quarter hour."

Neutic peered at the surrounding books in their bookcases, followed them with his eyes around a portion of the room. "These are all real, I assume?"

"Indeed. Digitally archived, of course, but these are paper and ink and cloth and leather – real bookbindery, past to present. The cataloguing technology – the information science of it – is routinely updated."

"Pan-galactic access?"

"The digital archives, yes. The hardcopies – the books themselves, no. Non-circulating."

Neutic nodded. "I'm surprised they allow any handling at all. I mean, we can pull any of these and read them?"

"Absolutely. It's a trade-off, I suppose, between maintaining a museum – protecting the books as priceless relics – and allowing them a life, some interaction with interested scholars." He watched Neutic stroll amidst the shelves. "Why keep them, right? Or, why upkeep them?" He regarded the imposing collection himself with a kind of friendly reverence. "Well, they add something to life, I think. Something tangible. Something...." He trailed off.

Neutic glanced back at Mr. Z. and couldn't help but be struck by the way the man appeared to become part of the architecture and contents of the room, as if he belonged in it. As if he were at peace within its immense learnedness or physical history or beauty or perhaps its abiding wisdom. He couldn't quite describe it. They strolled and paused, strolled and paused, examining, contemplating, each man to himself, and Neutic reached out here and there to caress a book's spine or to tilt his head at an *objet d'art*. "And there are more books in the so-called stacks?"

"Oh, millions more. Literally. The stacks descend, I can't recall exactly, something like a kilometer beneath this building. It's all here, virtually the entire mythological archive of this planet and many others – I don't know where the Eranos librarians are in their acquisition program." He glanced over his shoulder, gesturing at the shelves, an air of wistfulness about him.

"Words on paper, sir," said Neutic. "Unwieldy, fragile, clumsy. The format is impossible in terms of scholarship, I would think. I mean, I can't imagine trying to find anything, trying to work with anything. Literally pulling texts and paging through pages. That said, it's like being in any museum, I suppose. It's humbling and evocative of the past, of the eons of human endeavor. It's centering and grounding and sort of wild and unnerving all at the same time. Why keep them? You tell *me*, sir. You seem at home in here."

"Hmm?" Mr. Z. was peering up at the shelves.

"I said you seem at home here. Like you could be a caretaker of all this yourself."

Mr. Z. stopped and reached into his vest coat for his pipe, hefted it, then put it back again. He flexed his injured arm, clenched and unclenched his fist, and rubbed his shoulder. He looked around the room as if taking it all in at once. "It's time, Neutic."

"Time?"

"Time for me to go."

Neutic didn't know how to respond.

"There's nothing for it, I'm afraid. Somebody has to be on the ground if we're going to find Vixy. And it can't wait. Not for any drawn-out investigation and bureaucratic series of manpower requests and approvals and authorizations."

Neutic pulled a chair away from one of the study tables and flopped into it, leaning forward with his elbows on his knees, staring blank faced at Mr. Z. "You don't mean...?"

"I initiated an EIB." He'd been staring up at the books and turned, having anticipated Neutic's apprehension. "An Emergency Immolation Beacon. It amounts to a self-destruct command to Vixy's transponder."

"Self-destruct?" Neutic felt the floor and the walls shift, as if everything was closing in on him. He sat up. "I... I don't understand."

"An EIB is the only thing that will override the security buffers, all the physiological fail safes and force her transponder to transmit an unrestricted, trans-hyper-dimensional signal burst."

Neutic could only look at him expectantly.

"It's akin to a tracing flare. With the unfortunate caveat that, like a flare, it's a very brief signal. Powerful, but brief. And you have to be looking for it."

"You're telling me that Vixy's transponder has transmitted its HDT coordinates?"

Mr. Z. nodded.

"And destroyed itself in the process?"

Mr. Z. pulled up a chair and sat across from Neutic. They were almost knee-to-knee. "*These* are the coordinates." He handed Neutic a slip of paper. "I need you to keep them to yourself for a time. You'll know when the time's up. Otherwise, this is another one of those do as I say, not as I do moments, I'm afraid."

Neutic stared at the slip of paper in his hand as if he couldn't fathom it. "Won't the TDC driftnet pick them up? I mean, the Captain said –"

Mr. Z. shook his head. "I have the coordinates because I was looking for them. As Vixy's mentor, my transponder can initiate and receive her EIB. But nobody else at the TDC can. Because they're not looking. You see, an authorized EIB requires coordinated signal scanning at the moment of immolation. Such a widely disseminated signal begins powerfully but quickly weakens – you can imagine the energy required. So-called driftnet scanning won't catch it – the analogy of a fish net is apt, one's mesh has to be fine enough to catch what one is fishing for besides having some idea where to fish to begin with. And even if the net is cast in the right area, if the mesh is too large. A lot gets through."

"So, I suppose the EIB wasn't authorized. And you're not going to go about getting an authorization because –"

"Because it's too late, Neutic. Look here, as the Captain indicated, the TDC can deploy only a limited amount of resources on behalf of a lost cadet. The Captain is doing all he can. And all irony aside, Neutic, time is of the essence. The trail indeed goes cold. As cold as outer space. No ransom notice, no claim of responsibility from the terrorists – it indicates they're either incompetent and bungling or they don't consider her the kind of high-value hostage worth protecting, worth keeping. Besides, if Vixy's captors have the capability to transport her to nineteenth-century Giza we have to assume they can take her anywhere." He looked hard at Neutic. "Somebody has to do something."

"But the signal, sir. Maybe the terrorists are listening? Or the immolation will have panicked them. What if this Bruggs is one of the terrorists and he –"

Mr. Z. dismissed Neutic's protestations with an expression of infinite forbearance. "Understand me. The EIB has been initiated. We've got the coordinates – you and me – and Vixy's last means of communication has been cut off. *I've* cut it off. And now the clock really starts ticking. Because who knows if she'll remain anywhere near these coordinates." He stood up and returned his chair mindfully to the tableside. "The responsibility is mine, Neutic. Entirely my own. And I've got to go. Now."

They stared at each other.

"What if we *both* looked for her? I can go with you. The Plateau covers how much territory? It has to be more effective with at least two us –"

Again, Mr. Z.'s expression deflated Neutic's argument.

"I'm sending you home." Mr. Z. placed his hand on Neutic's shoulder and looked into his face. "Back to the T.E. I've already requested your reassignment based on the threat posed by our encounter with the Mothman assassin. That's exactly how I worded it. And, besides, you can assist Captain Chase more effectively from there, with all the resources of the T.E. available to you."

Neutic bristled. He pushed his chair back and stood up. "But we don't know for certain. I mean, I can't just go home. Not now. With all due respect, sir, you need all the help you can get. And the damn mothman, or whatever it is –"

"The mothman absolutely will not stop, my boy, until I am dead. And because of me – because of your association with me – your life is in danger."

Neutic paced back and forth, his exasperation like a burgeoning weight around his neck.

"You've got to go back," said Mr. Z. "To the T.E. If I should fail, you've got to be there. You've got to be *here*." His eyes were imploring. "For Vixy."

"Sir," said Neutic adamantly, "I'm going with you."

Mr. Z. walked heavily across the room to stand once again before the globe. He reached for his pipe and puffed on its empty bowl, as usual. "You know, a library somehow always invites the idea of a good smoke. At least to me. But it's bad for the books." He looked to Neutic with a wry smile and winked at him. "There's a lot you can do to help. Foremost is using your skills to research all you can about everything that we've been encountering. You know about Mothmen. But there are the Molemen involved, now, too. And when you said a motivation for disappearing is a motivation to be born again, well, the Egyptians knew a thing or two about being born again. Born again to a new life. The pyramids themselves, after all, have been referred to now and again as resurrection machines." He nodded as if to hammer in the point. "Observations. Connections. Those tattoos on the terrorist's body. I swear it's some sort of cult and who knows if it doesn't have some connection to the investigation. And the attack on Professor Wilhelm – her vision of the hexagram. And my own oracle from the coins. There are forces coalescing out there, Neutic, like I said, that go beyond Vixy's abduction. The incident at the Olympic has yet to reveal its full import, I feel it in my bones. The investigation has to continue at full bore."

There was a library ladder positioned nearby – the type that rolled along rail guides mounted above the bookshelves. To Neutic's surprise Mr. Z. leapt towards one and scrambled up a few rungs.

"Dante, I think it is," said Mr. Z. "*Vita Nuova*." He was leaning over past the ladder, eyeing the books. "Ah!" He hurried down to the floor, pulling the library ladder noisily along its track and then bounding up it again. "Here!" His voice bellowed across the room. He half-dangled there, poised upon his perch like some tree monkey – his feet on the rungs, clinging to the ladder with one arm and other thrust out, holding a book aloft. He flopped the book open with one hand.

Neutic approached the ladder. "Sir, your arm; maybe you should –"

Mr. Z. leaned out further, his pipe still clenched between his teeth, and began reading aloud, "Here is a god stronger than I who comes to rule over me... Now, your bliss has appeared... Oh, wretched me! for I shall be disturbed often from now on."[ab]

Mr. Z. climbed down and handed the book to Neutic with an earnest, sympathetic grin, his eyes glistening. "But there's a more liberal translation

I read somewhere that I like better. 'The spirit of my eyes said, *You behold your delight*. The spirit of life in my heart said, *You behold your master*. And the spirit of my body said, *Now you will suffer*.'"[ac] He returned his pipe to his pocket, his voice low and abiding. "And to suffer, Neutic, including suffering for the love of a woman, is to know you're alive."

# CHAPTER 18

# ENGINEERING THE COSMIC CLOCK

**NOW I'VE DONE IT.** Five made his way beyond the dim firelight, approaching Hesso's camel with the mixture of self-assurance and cautiousness he'd learned from watching Bab and Hesso manage their animals. Even if I'd killed that man myself I'd hardly have left a more significant time-trace. What was I thinking? What came over me? Meanwhile, he couldn't get the image of Miss Vixy, as they called her, out of his thoughts. Why should he be concerned with her well-being? Why should he care at all about any of them?

The canopic chest was strapped high on Deloua's back. He tugged gently on the beast's rein and, whispering, tried his best to mimic the phrase Hesso and Bab used when they wanted the camel to lay down. Deloua flared her nostrils at him, twitched her ears and blinked. When he tugged again she jerked her chin up, yanking the rein from his hand and curling her lips to expose her ramshackle teeth. He stroked her neck and tried again, cooing softly. He was relieved when she kneeled, then tucked her hind legs beneath her, resting quietly.

Five worked as quickly as he could to untie the box, the clumsiness of his injured hand making Hesso's knots difficult. He lowered it to the ground and glanced around warily – the camp was in an uproar, with more and more Egyptians arriving, likely from Petrie's group. He dislodged the lid of the chest and peered inside, hands shaking, his heart pounding. He hefted a jar. No, too light. He hefted another. Again, too light. What if none of the jars...? Yes. This one, much heavier. As he finally held the relic in his hands, he replayed the night's traverse of the desert towards the Zawiyet el-Aryan necropolis.[49]

The tranquility of the alien night had soothed his nerves and when Hesso led them deep within the bowels of the Unfinished Pyramid[50] he'd thrilled to the idea that he'd entered one of the secret spaces his father had known.

They'd located the corridor entrance and descended into the cramped, unadorned tomb, its empty granite sarcophagus eerie in Hesso's flickering torchlight. Hesso's cache lay within a fairly ingenious niche he'd constructed in the wall, its opening disguised amongst the joints and dimensions of the limestone blocks. The authenticity of the box was easy to recognize - its vivid imagery and hieroglyphs surprisingly intact for its age – and his concern became the integrity of the four canopic jars that lay inside. [51] Particularly the one he sought as his prize.

---

[49] Located approximately four kilometers southeast of the Giza Plateau. The Unfinished Northern Pyramid of Zawyet El Aryan, also known as Pyramid of Baka and Pyramid of Bikheris, are descriptions used to describe the large shaft which comprises part of an un-finished pyramid at Zawyet El Aryan. It is dated by mainstream scholars to the early or the mid-4th Dynasty (2613–2494 BC) during the Old Kingdom period.

[50] If finished, the pyramid would have been very nearly the size of Khafre's pyramid. Walls near the pyramid, made of fieldstone and clay, are similar to those found around the Giza pyramids. Within, a long, sloping corridor leads to a shaft about 21 meters (69 feet) deep. The bottom of the shaft was paved with huge blocks of granite and limestone. There was a massive granite sarcophagus in the form of an oval tub, with an intact cover, but no body within. Citation: touregypt.net, 12.30.2015.

[51] Five's canopic chest resembles the so-called "Shabti Box of Paramnekhu," Dynasty 19, reign of Ramesses II, 1279-1213 BCE, Thebes, Tomb of Sennedjem, Maspero excava-tions, 1885-86 in the collection of The Metropolitan Museum of Art, metmuseum.org/

*You see?* Hesso had whispered to him. *All the jars are intact.* He'd carefully lifted each one partially out of the box. "This one is very heavy – I've been tempted to break it open to discover what's inside."

Five's heart had skipped a beat when Hesso mentioned breaking the jar open – it had been all he could do to restrain himself. He'd nearly shoved Hesso aside, ready to run off with it up the corridor on his own. Instead, he'd waited, even helping the Bedouin strap the relic onto the camel.

"Where is Bruggs!"

The shouting thrust Five out of his reverie. It sounded like Hesso.

"So help me if that fat lout has had a hand in this...!"

Five's heart quickened. He needed to complete his escape. He suddenly felt indifferent to the camp and the humans – even Miss Vixy – and keen to return to his hovel with his prize. He rose, clutching the jar in his arms, glancing back once more at the camp as he hurried south, relieved beyond measure to be on his way. He was tired, hungry and thirsty – his hand ached and what he wanted most in the universe was a hot shower and a change of clothes, even a bath in the Nile would suffice. He wouldn't be getting any of it. But his heart was light – the most tenuous, unpredictable part of his mission was over – he'd acquired the jar! He hurried along, the noise of the camp diminishing in the distance and then proceeded to stumble repeatedly, maddeningly, in the loose sand and stones. Pick up your feet, dammit! He slowed a bit, trying to step mindfully, efficiently, anticipating holing up in his bivouac and transmitting his success to Cog.

It wasn't long before he'd rounded the corner of the Menkaure Pyramid and found himself addressing the featureless area of sand where his bivouac ought to be. He fine-tuned his orienteering coordinates, got down on his

art/collection/search/544703.

hands and knees and felt for an indication of his shadow-tarp. There! He cleared the sand, peeled back the tarp and set about re-digging the hovel's proportions – every nook and cranny of his tiny abode had either caved in or suffered a pernicious infiltration of sand and small rocks. Argh. Was there no rest? He reestablished the hovel's dimensions – shored up the walls, dusted off his pack, shook out his bedding, hunkered in and finally re-secured his shadow-tarp. [52] He stripped off his *tob* and *kufeya*, tore into a ration and an energy gel and slumped onto his slumber pad, exhausted. His anxiousness to communicate with Cog gave way to the exquisite safety and silence of his freedom – freedom from being watched; from enduring examination and suspicion; from speaking and being spoken to; from having to act the part. He propped himself up and stared through the moonlit dimness at the jar, content simply to be with it. How he longed to capture an image of it as proof of his success! But a captured image was a heinous time-trace – number three or four on the violations list. Right behind injuring an indigenous being.

He rummaged through his pack for his headlamp and sonic hammer, held the tool firmly against the jar and pulsed it – there was an audible "crack" and the clay fractured, sloughing away at the pressure of his hands and exposing the unmistakable luster of gold – gold! He'd done it. Retrieved the golden ball. Released it by his own hands from millennia of shrouded oblivion. He blew the dust from it, his pulse racing, almost overcome by a sense of his father's presence. His father had machined it in the age of Snefru, here on the Giza Plateau. He buffed its lustrous surface carefully – its high polish beguiling.

He doffed his headlamp and aimed it at himself, peering at his own reflection, the ball's curvature distorting his features wildly. Dad must have looked at himself in it just as I'm doing. He must have admired his work, just like I am. A breeze penetrated the shadow tarp and cooled the moisture

---

[52] Shadow-tarp fabric is designed to blend, akin to the skin of a chameleon or octopus into the color value and to some extent the texture of its surrounding environment and it is semi-rigid, capable of providing minor, temporary structural support in certain applications. Moreover, it is waterproof and windproof. Its structural dynamism relies upon the application of a relatively weak electric charge; Five's device is sufficient to power it.

on his cheeks. He blinked away his tears, taking pleasure in reciting the object's physical attributes:

Diameter: 75mm
Mass on Earth at sea level: 4261 g (9.39 lb.)
Density: 19.3 g/ml

He ran the thumb-print analysis, enduring a twinge of anxiety in the fraction of a second before the results displayed. Nothing to fear, of course: a perfect match. Now to forward his confirmation. He typed carefully, a thrill passing through him as he tapped the "send" button: "02:05AM, 11.11.1881. COMPONENT ACQUIRED. BIVOUACKED. STANDING BY."

Cog would be asleep and Five didn't have any reason to anticipate a response until morning, which suited him perfectly as he felt capable of at least several hours of uninterrupted slumber. He shed his trek uniform, set aside his gloves, took care to "wash" himself with a series of body wipes – ah, the refreshment! – pulled his thermal foil about him and finally laid his head down. It seemed he'd just closed his eyes when his transponder pulsed:

"!!WELL DONE!! CONFAB 6:30AM GIZA TIME."

"Copy." He yawned despite his excitement, unable to take his eyes off the display and sent his reply. Well done! He lay staring at the message, savoring it. Meanwhile, a few hours of blessed sleep. He sprawled onto his bedroll, the ball in the crook of his arm and his transponder beside him so he could peer at Cog's message as his eyelids drooped and his mind became quiet and still. He'd done it. He'd arrived and endured everything – endured Bruggs and the desert and the camel and the camp and even his own bungling - and found the ball. He breathed deeply, shut his eyes and plunged into sleep....

05:58AM. The laser lathe passed over the whirring surface of the ball and shut down. Shit. He felt a pang in his guts and perspiration beading on his forehead. A malfunction? After only a single pass? He should have checked sphericity last night. No, wait. He examined the machine carefully. Everything functional. Five sat back and marveled at the numbers on the display:

$$\text{SPHERICITY (Y)} = 9.9998 \times 10\text{-}1 \text{ ORIGINAL}$$
$$\text{SPHERICITY (Y)} = 1.0000 \text{ CORRECTED}$$

Wow. He scratched behind his ear, rubbed his head and sucked at his coffee lozenge. His father's work really *was* that accurate. It was true, then. Mission data supported the conclusion that his father's laser lathe had failed, that he'd been forced to perform the sphericity task manually. It was a feat that some engineers – his father's detractors – considered impossible. Which only served to help amplify the legend. His father, for his part, never officially endorsed nor denied the story.

*Your father said the outcome of the mission was all that mattered,* his mother had told him; *and he disliked being singled out from the other engineers. When he said, 'We were all just doing our jobs,' he meant it.*

Five rolled his shoulders and lolled his head from side to side, trying to assuage the dull ache in his muscles. Almost done. He hadn't noticed the encroachment of the desert's pale, pre-dawn glow – the prospect of a new day somehow enhanced his nagging fatigue. He yawned and stretched again. Three hours of sleep a night was going to catch up to him eventually. He squinted at the bleak horizon. "Coffee changes everything," he said, tunelessly humming the theme from an advertisement that seemed to run continuously at the cadet barracks. He was suddenly irascible – his close quarters, the strange light, even the silhouettes of the pyramids –affronted him. The alien nature of everything seemed heartless.

I want to be done with all this. I want to be home. He thought of his mother and their small subterranean apartment; the glistening city lights he enjoyed contemplating during his train ride home each day; the smell of cooked dinner when he walked through the door. He'd hurry to change out of his uniform and sit at the kitchen table, hungry and tired and eager to discard the day's trials and troubles with good food and, later, a good book.

Meanwhile, his joints ached and his hand throbbed. He'd been working at his calculations for hours and was disappointed to find himself becoming susceptible to the effects of Earth's slightly less oxygenated atmosphere – a miniscule discrepancy that he'd been instructed some cadets suffered from and some didn't. Oh well, apparently he suffered. Along with my mediocre eyesight, flat feet and lousy ways with numbers. Inferiorities. Any of which would have eliminated him from the cadet program if not for his pedigree. He'd never forget the bitterness and vehemence of a few of the more accomplished cadets – the way they looked at him askance and whispered to each other shamelessly whenever he failed. That, and the wicked ruthlessness of many of the cadets' parents – the semi-public controversy they seemed determined to incite; their cruel insults and vicious protests. His mother called it "character assassination." Cog called it "professional jealousy." He'd wanted to quit more than once. The baleful politics of it all had been almost too much to bear and if it hadn't been for his mother's support and his father's legacy he would have. In the end, despite Cog trying to convince him it was "increased mission efficiency," he knew his transport date had been expedited as much by the looming public relations issues. He'd even heard rumors of threats of lawsuits against the Giza Cell Program brought on by his selection.

"Astronomical refraction," he murmured, and chided himself. What self-respecting Moleman engineer talks to himself so much?

He broke open a ration and chewed while scanning his data package for the details of Earth's specifications, as much to try to relax himself as anything. It was always this way: he'd become anxious before undertaking the engineering – the calculations and applied theory seemed somehow daunting until he immersed himself in the work. It wasn't impossible stuff, he just never seemed completely at ease with it.

He glanced at the sunrise. Astronomical refraction, for instance, explained why the sun was appearing to break the horizon this morning

– refraction by the Earth's atmosphere was responsible for the illusion. It likewise explained why the sun, whenever it appeared to be setting, had in fact already passed below the horizon. He warmed up his intellect by conjuring up more data: astronomical refraction of the light from a star, for example, equals zero in the zenith, less than one arc minute at forty-five degrees apparent altitude, and still only five point three minutes at ten degrees altitude. It dramatically increases, however, as altitude decreases, reaching nine point nine minutes at five degrees altitude, eighteen point four minutes at two degrees altitude and thirty-five point four minutes at the horizon, all values effective for ten degrees Celsius, one-hundred-one point three kilo Pascals in the visible part of the spectrum.

Ah, data. The numerical details centered him. Every good Moleman enjoys data – it was a truth that made him feel as legitimate and capable as any other cadet. He glanced at his standard operating procedures:

> Earth's axial tilt and orbital eccentricity explains why its sun, as viewed from a fixed coordinate on Earth, will not be in the same position in the sky at the same time each day. The north-south component of the so-called analemma is the sun's declination and the east-west component is the equation of time. The diagram of the sun's apparent meandering takes the form of a slender figure-eight.

Elementary stuff. Even Earth's Babylonian astronomers were compensating for the equation of time as far back as their first millennium CE when all they had were sundials.[53] What could fifteen minutes here or there in an Earth year matter to such backward people? He recalled asking an instructor the question and the response had stuck with him. *Compensating for what you don't understand is the opposite of engineering.* And he'd thought, first, what *is* the opposite of engineering? And then

---

[53] A sundial references "apparent" solar time; i.e., the time that's kept with reference to the sun's actual position in the sky. A mechanical or electronic clock references "mean" solar time. The difference between apparent and mean solar time is known as the equation of time and can amount to over fifteen minutes annually.

what does it mean to compensate for something you don't understand? Because he certainly identified with the idea of compensating for things he didn't understand. Even when he couldn't put his finger on an example. It rather amounted to his experience of life in general. Meanwhile, regarding engineering, the Babylonians' interest in celestial bodies was strong enough to force them to acknowledge the difference between two physical phenomena – the reliability of the motion of the sun versus that of the stars and acknowledge an error. And then work to resolve it in technical terms. It seemed to him that that qualified as a legitimate form of engineering. Or at least applied science. But what were they putting their faith in – the sun or the stars? Or the gods? Or the mysterious relationship between them all? The sun dial kept screwing up when it came to helping them understand the motions of the stars, while the stars themselves did nothing to keep them warm or provide sufficient light or make the crops grow. Confounding contradictions everywhere, it must have seemed. Hence, mythology? Utu, or Shamash – whatever the Babylonian's called him – for instance, was a sun god, wasn't he? – riding his sun chariot across the sky each day? Anyone could easily assume such a task involved some variability in the timing of the route, and there you have a reconciliation of the data. And a vivid story, to boot. Which probably did as much to assuage the anxiety over the mystery of life as anything since no one thing ever seemed sufficient to explain it all. And that's how he felt.

He snatched his galactic sextant from his pack, unsealed his shadow tarp, cloaked himself and crawled from his bivouac. He aimed the instrument here and there across the sky, noting the measurements in his head as they downloaded automatically into his mission database. Satisfied, he scurried into his hovel and pondered his next task; namely, that of verifying and integrating the strength of Earth's magnetic field – the force which powered the diamagnetic levitation of the ball – into the clockwork machinations of his pending build-out. He'd been twiddling with his mag-gage when his transponder vibrated. Shit, it's zero-six-thirty already?

He fumbled with the device. "Copy, Lieutenant, this is Five."

"Good morning, Five," said Cog. "Did you get much sleep?"

Five didn't have an opportunity to respond before Cog launched into his agenda.

"You're to be commended, Five. I repeat, *commended* on your excellent work reclaiming the ball. We're only twenty-four hours behind goal, still within mission tolerances."

Five felt his heart swell at the praise.

"But the schedule doesn't allow for any let up. Let's review your S.O.P."

"Regarding the tight mission schedule, sir," said Five, "I'm prepared to dispense with the S.O.P. review to help expedite things." Unpleasant silence followed and Five hastened to fill it. "Otherwise, sir, I'm fully prepared to begin as you see fit."

"Protocol, Five," said Cog. "Let's stick to it. We'll leave improvisation for when there's no other alternative."

"Yessir."

"First item: Sphericity Lathing."

Five followed along dutifully. "Check."

"Astronomical Refraction."

"Check."

"Vectoring Earth's magnetic field."

Five squinted and rubbed his head. "Pending."

"Pending?"

"Yessir. Sorry, sir." He was behind, he knew, but if not for this blasted debriefing, well, he'd have time for the calculations.

"Then let's work through it step-by-step. Build-out depends upon complete adherence to specs and iron-clad procedural integrity, you know that."

"Yessir." Me and my three hours of sleep, he thought – if I'd had the stamina to work through the predawn hours I'd be done with the protocols.

"When the installation inside the Pyramid is complete, run your maglev[54] trial and stream the data no matter what time it is – I'm on call around the clock from this point. All eyes are on us, now, Five."

---

[54] "Maglev" is jargon for Diamagnetic Levitation. Gold, like many substances, is diamagnetic – that is to say, it repels or opposes an applied magnetic field by way of altering

They worked dutifully for an hour, entering data and performing intense calculations before Five's fatigue once again threatened to bog him down. He rubbed his eyes and pressed his palms together, being careful of his thumb, attempting to stretch his fingers until the muscles and tendons burned exquisitely. He tapped lightly upon his injured flesh: tender but not unduly swollen – no infection.

"Items one through nine, check," said Cog. "That's it. Well done. As it stands, you'll have several hours to rest before the build-out."

"Yessir." Five muted his transponder and enjoyed a profound exhale, glad to finally be rid of the pesky S.O.P.

"Equipment status?" said Cog.

"A.O.K."

"Provisions?"

"A.O.K."

"Good. It's time to formalize the estimate for final build. Let's see, you're scheduled to penetrate the Great Pyramid[55] at twelve-hundred hours, complete the framing at fourteen-hundred-thirty hours and finish calibration by fifteen-hundred."

"Yessir." Five peeled back his shadow tarp and peeked out. The tedium of the prep was maddening. The desert beckoned. He felt anxious to decamp. At the same time, he endured a strange sense of not being capable of recalling much of anything about his training, as if he'd fallen from the sky and everything around him was new and different. It's just nerves. It'll all come back to me when I get going.

"Mission risk decreases from here on out, Five."

"Yessir."

"All the more reason to redouble your adherence to protocol. Repeat after me, Five. Complacency kills."

---

the motion of its electrons to counter the applied force (an object at rest tends to stay at rest). A key scientific reality that Five is to exploit in constructing his component of the CC is that diamagnets may be levitated in stable equilibrium in a magnetic field without power consumption.

55  The Pyramid of Khufu.

"Complacency kills, sir." He's proud of me, I can hear it, despite all the professional mumbo jumbo. He's pleased that I'm doing well. He's stood behind me all through it, from the beginning. Even when things looked black, even after I'd botched two rehearsals in a row.

"Any questions before I sign off?"

"No, sir. Thank you, sir."

"For what, Five?"

"For the help, sir." The words sounded silly. "I mean... nothing, sir."

"Ten-four. Good luck. Cog out."

"Whew." He tossed his transponder aside, cloaked himself and clambered stiffly from the bivouac. He meandered around the Queens pyramids, trying his best to shake off his fatigue, to acclimatize and pre-pare for the work ahead. He closed his tired eyes and raised his face to the sun, welcoming the penetrating relief of the diffused radiation, allowing the fading warmth to melt into his flesh, surrendering to drowsiness. He shuffled back to his bivouac, sealed his shadow tarp and flopped onto his bedroll.

11:15AM. Five awoke from a dreamless sleep, struggling to orient himself, his heart pounding with an uncanny sense of urgency. Where am I? The hovel. Giza. Damn, he thought, it's late. He'd intended to doze, not pitch into an oblivious slumber. He rubbed his temples, adjusted the polarity of his shadow-tarp and peered out. Empty blue sky. He felt displaced and disagreeable; dispassionate and anxious and irritable all at once. What's wrong with me? This is supposed to be the most important day of my life. "Circadian disruption," he mumbled, and dug through his supplies for a body wipe, soothing himself with the cooling evaporation of the cleanser on his face, neck, underarms, crotch. Wake up, dammit! He inhaled deep-ly, exhaled forcefully – anything to get the blood and brain going.

He placed the ball carefully on his bedroll – that it seemed heavy for its size was an attribute that always struck him as compelling; so much so that during the interminable months of training with the dupe,[56] its weight was the thing, even more than its appearance, that motivated him to maintain the illusion of it as significant. The dupe's *appearance* was contrived but its *weight* was real. This is a special object. It's different. You only had to feel it. Hence he was glad, early on, to discover that Earth's gravity mirrored exactly that of Mega City One – Earth was smaller and denser, of course, but that the ball's heft would be familiar to him here had assuaged some of his anxiety over the inevitable acclimation challenges. What he hadn't expected, however, was the power of the real thing to invoke thoughts of his father. As if somehow, in some weird way, it *was* his father. Pharaonic tombs were filled with a hoard of objects. And, of course, almost every culture in the cosmos prepared their dead with at least a token example of their possessions in life. It struck him that while it symbolized wealth to some – being buried with treasure – what it really had to do with was... the word came to him: symbols. The object symbolizes the possessor. The entangled identity of it all. Perhaps one believes we require planetary possessions – material things – in a next life, like the Egyptian pharaohs did? Or perhaps those left behind need a keepsake, something more tangible than a memory to help hold someone dear to us in our hearts? The thing is imbued with the person. The thing evokes the person. The thing *is* the person. Again, entangled identity. Can you destroy a thing without at least a twinge of anxiety that symbolizes someone else? Effigies. Voodoo dolls. He peered at the ball. Just a machined, metal sphere. And yet, his father had touched it, labored over it.

He tried to review his procedure. *Wait to lock the gravitational core trajectory until you get inside Caviglia's Chamber.* Ugh. He couldn't bear looking at any of it again. He picked up his sextant, peeled back a corner of the shadow-tarp and aimed it straight overhead, triangulating in the infra-red spectrum, firing a nano-beam and waiting for the device to calculate a preliminary warp value. All this preparation and I'll have to do most of it over again in the chamber, anyway.

---

56  Slang for "duplicate."

He removed everything from his pack and reloaded it piece by piece, reciting his checklist as he went, leaving the ball for last. "I'll get to you in a minute." Was he going crazy talking to the damn thing?

He recalled something Cog had said during another late meal one night at the canteen. The day's training had been arduous and it was the first time Five had noticed fatigue in the older man, his face drawn and lined, the rims of his eyes swollen and red. They'd eaten in silence, hardly looking up from their food.

*We're out of our element, Five,* Cog had said. *Literally.* Then he'd begun a meandering recitation about gold, reading aloud from his device, something he'd obviously referenced often, in a tone that was dreamy and far away, as if the words were a tonic to him:

Gold, perpetually lustrous, immune to corrosion, exceptionally malleable and a preternatural conductor of electricity. On Earth the metal is also a potent mythological symbol, the planet's many cultural iterations having transmuted its physical attributes into the symbolic powers of immortality, eternity, immutability, even divinity. Egypt, especially during its Pharaonic period, worked to master the rendering of gold's arresting, evocative beauty and to enliven its divine import within the context of their art – the essential symbols of their fantastical mythology, entombing their pharaohs within solid gold coffins and otherwise garnishing their sepulchers with any number of gold bangles and aesthetic treasures. Stone may have indeed defined its monumental architecture but the heart and soul of ancient Egyptian culture was gold.

It had struck him as lyrical as much as technical and he'd asked Cog about it – where he'd dug up the information.

Cog had sat back with his arms over his head and dismissed it all with a diffident shrug. *The Oxford Galactic Dictionary. It's just always struck me as incredible, awesome in a way, that gold is the only substance – the only one yet discovered – that remains incompatible with HDT technology. That only gold can't travel through time.*

Gold can't travel through time. He sealed his pack. He'd never thought about it. But the idea had stuck with him; that there was a substance immune to corrosion – ageless in that way – and also incompatible with HDT. Both eternal and timebound. "Big deal," he murmured, hefting the ball into its diamagnetic suspension frame. "It's just an x-ray reflector." He crouched within the hovel, brushing crumbs of sand from his uniform before shouldering his pack. He looked about, re-inspecting his bivouac for the umpteenth time. Quit stalling. *Let's go.* He engaged his cloak mode, scrambled from the hovel and glanced at the sun. Forty degrees altitude, I bet. He was feeling more himself just being outside and on mission. He kicked sand over his shadow tarp, took his bearings and set off west along the base of the Menkaure Pyramid.

He rounded the corner of the monument and paused, peering around for a sign of onlookers – it was never wise to put too much faith in his cloaking device – then scurried north, the ground cooler in the shadow of the pyramid's western face. Pausing again at the northwest corner, he hastened across the open distance to the southwest corner of Khafre's Pyramid, likewise hugging the monument's western face as he trekked. He continued in this pattern, pausing to scan the open space between pyramids, scrambling to the southwest corner of Khufu's western face, hustling north, until at last he arrived at the corner of the Great Pyramid with nothing in front of him but inconsequential desert. He crept east into the morning light, hugging the pyramid's northern face until he arrived at the disheveled mound of shattered limestone, loose rock and sand that spilled away from the pyramid's main entrance. He scrambled up, disparaging the noisy cascade of stones and sand and the tell-tale dust that trailed behind him. *Be careful, dammit. Complacency kills.* Attaining the summit, he crouched low, peering around. What in hell?

On the other side of the entrance mound, further east at the far corner of pyramid, was a large cluster of Egyptians, apparently focused on some activity at the group's center. He glanced up. It remained for him to scale the two meters of stone that separated him from the pyramid's entrance.[57]

But what of the strange activity below? Petrie's excavation work was taking place at the mastabas, not here. What could be so compelling as to draw all these workers? He couldn't make anything out - whatever was going on was obscured by two black umbrellas held aloft, shading something in the center of the gathering.

Let it alone. He checked the time: fourteen minutes behind schedule. Get moving. Besides, any distraction that diverted attention from his own doings was fortuitous. He scrambled up the short distance over the Pyramid's face to the floor of the so-called forced entrance. Breathless, he paused in the threshold to adjust his trek lenses and collect himself. There was nothing more for it, this was it. He breathed deeply – his last breath of fresh air – before plunging into shadow to descend into the monument's heart.

The dreary, dusty confines of the tunnel oppressed him – never during his training could he manage to acclimatize himself to the simulated lousy air and harsh, naked rock. That, and the manner in which the otherwise brilliant beam of his trek-lenses somehow diffused uselessly into the darkness a pitiful few meters in front of him, as if the light were no match for the black depths. And here the reality was dead on as miserable. Keep moving. You've practiced this dozens of times. It's no different than the simulations, no different than the dress rehearsals. He tasted the dust in his mouth, smelled the dank, stifling air, endured the closeness of the stones. Subterranean this was not – no comforting aroma of earth, no moist

57   This is the so-called forced entrance established by Al Mamun, the Abbasid Caliph (governor of Cairo) in 832 CE. It is located approximately 4.5 meters (fifteen feet) below the original entrance. In 1881, a large pile of stone and rubble debris from the excavation existed directly below the entrance, serving as a makeshift earthen ramp of sorts and this is what Five has scrambled up as an approach to the forced entry above him.

soils, no micro or macro organisms, no life. A tomb, indeed. He coughed. Breathe. There's plenty of air. Don't look back. Don't turn around. Just keep moving.

He descended furtively, listening intently – the chances of encountering anyone were virtually nil, the tomb itself was empty, the tunnel uninhabitable. But complacency kills, complacency kills – he ran the mantra through his mind to keep himself focused. It occurred to him that his trek-lenses were too bright, heightening his anxiety – he knew that! Dimming them was an immediate relief. "Acclimatization for fuck's sake," he murmured. Shut up. Quit bitching. Use all your senses. Keep moving.

He encountered the smooth floor of the original descending passageway and felt his confidence burgeoning – everything was as it should be, things were going to plan. He descended steadily, the masonry floor just over a meter wide and the walls just over a meter high, giving way after approximately sixty-seven meters to a floor of hewn rock. There's the well. He looked up, the beam of his headlamp disappearing into the impenetrable blackness of a narrow, semi-vertical, overhead passage, the so-called "well" that Caviglia had discovered connecting the tunnel to the Queen's and King's tombs above. It meant Caviglia's chamber itself was near. He plunged deeper, peering ahead anxiously. There! Where the floor became level – the chamber would be just beyond.

And it was. He stood poised in the entryway, scanning the cramped, roughly hewn, unfinished tomb. Pure bedrock. He'd travelled approximately 115 meters at a downward slope of twenty-six degrees to reach this terminal room and was therefore situated at some considerable depth, sandwiched below the pyramid's base and above the high-water mark of the Nile – a geologically secure location that would easily withstand the onslaught of the nuclear detonations scheduled to annihilate the desert. Moreover, and critically, this chamber, akin to the King's and Queen's chambers far above, was positioned exactly beneath the pyramid's apex which in turn was aligned with Polaris, the so-called North Star in Earth parlance.

He scrutinized the walls and ceiling, his light lurching across the unfinished, deteriorated constructions of what the ancient Egyptian architects had intended to be a tomb chapel. Entering the chamber, he used his extension rod to affix an illumination pod to the ceiling, banishing the disorienting blackness and sepulchral shadows in favor of a more or less abiding general illumination. He looked about. Every aspect was familiar, every corner, nook, cranny and stone; every contour of the walls and floor – it all matched exactly the reproduction, the stage set where he'd spent so many long hours training back home. He'd memorized the details of the space: fifteen meters long, nine meters wide and five meters high, the far side of the chamber displaying the unfinished and disheveled preconstructions of the chapel steps that rose perhaps a meter above the main floor. Abandoned by its builders and repeatedly ravaged by heedless excavations of any number of would-be tomb-robbers, the space existed as a hapless and somber dead-end; an insignificant footnote to the alluring pharaonic chambers that lay above.

Five rubbed his hands together, anxious to begin work, and knelt before the so-called "pit" in the center of the chamber's main floor. Perhaps a meter in diameter, it plunged several meters further, straight down into the bedrock. He leaned over the opening, directing the beam of his headlamp into the shaft and was encouraged by a view of the bottom. Good, no rubble to clear out. He pointed his laser-rule down the hole: five meters, as expected, more than enough room. He carefully unpacked the diamagnetic frame assembly and set it aside. "There you go, my friend," he whispered. The ball gleamed at him, despite the dim light, as if it somehow lived for the light. He felt a curious pang in the center of his chest – it suddenly struck him that this remarkable object – his and his father's precious golden ball – would never again see the light of day. He dug into his pack for his tools, unloading the remainder of his equipment. C'mon, get to work.

He began with an x-ray plumb reading, verifying the anticipated alignment of the center of the pit with the apex of the pyramid and beyond to the pole star. The laser-rule made short work of establishing the location of his support struts, his anchors found good purchase in the bedrock floor, ceiling and walls and he found himself moving quickly and efficiently, reproducing the choreography of the engineering – the step-by-step construction and assembly that he'd practiced over and over during his long months of training.

Within an hour he'd completed the lattice architecture and his dimensional analysis revealed spot-on tolerances. He stood back to admire his work, wiping sweat from his brow. He removed his gloves and opened a packet of degreasing wipes, meticulously scrubbing his hands from wrists to fingertips and back again with the mindful intensity of a surgeon. Now for the ball.

He secured the diamagnetic suspension frame to the guide cables and lowered the device in precise increments with his micro-winch, his eyes glued to the readout of his gravitron machine. It was always at this point in the procedure, with the ball and frame out of his hands, the thing descending out of sight into the pit, that he experienced a needle in his heart, as if everything was poised on the brink of disaster. A slip would indeed be ruinous – he'd damage the surface of the sphere, perhaps mangle the frame and be forced to retreat all the way back to his hovel for repairs. He squeezed the brake lever on the micro-winch, pausing the ball's descent so as to wipe away a trickle of sweat from his forehead. He blew on his hands to dry them, took a deep breath and released the winch again, easing the ball down, lowering it deeply into the pit. His muscles began to ache. Breathe. This is where he'd too often hold his breath and, with his blood oxygen plummeting, twitch or lose his touch and drop the damn thing. So breathe, dammit. Meanwhile, the drop-and-lock, as it was called, had to occur in a single run or he'd have to haul the assembly up and start again with the alignment, calculations and everything. "Come on," he breathed, "*Come on, baby....*"

He heard a soft click and a series of electronic "beeps." His gravitron flashed green. Yes! His heart was pounding and he dared not even sigh with relief. *Six degrees of freedom!* Perfect. Radioisotope generator efficiency? Within tolerance. Suspension frame correction performance? Likewise.

Diamagnetic link with the Earth's magnetic field? Established. He peered into the pit for a last look. The ball would do its work indefinitely, without further energy input, by way of the engineered stability of its natural dia-magnetic attributes.

He'd done it! Mission accomplished. As of this day, this moment, by the work of his own hands, the inaugural component of the Cosmic Clock Project lattice was in place! Engineering the other seven lattice points throughout the cosmos would follow, to be sure, but this was the first – it would always be the first. And the first was what would be remembered. Now to get out. The only thing left was to get home.

"Easy," he whispered, "easy, now." He retreated from the mouth of the pit on his belly, gingerly avoiding the support struts. Whew. He re-packed his tools and scanned the chamber. Clean. He'd left nothing behind. He shouldered his pack, snatched the illumination cell from the ceiling and made for the passageway. At the threshold of the tomb he initiated the false-wall – the radioisotope generator powered space-shift that would blind access to the chamber until the annihilation rendered the ruse irrelevant.

He stood poised in the sweltering, claustrophobic heat, aiming the beam of his trek-lenses up the sloping passageway. What am I waiting for? All that was left was to return home a success, to return home a Moleman Engineer. Perhaps even a hero. Like his father. His heart swelled. He'd dreamed of this. Why now did it seem he was leaving something behind when he knew for a fact that he wasn't? What's the matter with me? This is all I've ever wanted. Get going.

He ducked away from the entrance and scrambled up the passageway. Within twelve hours the schedule of cataclysmic nuclear detonations would commence and this planet's existence within space-time would be irrevocably severed. Planet Earth would be stilled, all life within it sacrificed for the greater good. Including *his* life unless he managed to evacuate and get himself off-planet. He'd be a hero all right, but a dead one. "Twelve hours," he muttered. "Twelve damn hours." So move your ass. He trudged up the incline, sweating, filthy, breathing hard. He had to get out of here. He had to get home. There was no time to lose.

# CHAPTER 19

# YELLOW ARROW

**VIXY CRAWLED TO THE OPENING** of the tent and sat in the glare of the rising sun. She could hear Hesso and Amu discussing something. Despite not understanding the Arabic, she picked out the names "Bishoy," "Bruggs" and her own. Her throat was parched and raw and she couldn't move a muscle without wincing.

Bishoy noticed her first. He'd been kicking at the charred remnants of the campfire, an armful of blankets under his arm and the teapot in his hand. He hurriedly tossed the blankets on the donkey cart and hastened across the sand with the teapot.

"She's awake," said Hesso, speaking English. In a moment all three of them were kneeling before her on the sand, watching her sip tea.

"We'll eat," said Hesso, "then Bishoy and I will finish breaking camp."

Amu tipped a portion of hot water onto a cloth and dabbed at Vixy's face, careful of her wounds, then helped her from the tent.

The women watched Hesso and Bishoy fold the wooly fabric, collect the poles and work to secure the whole affair onto Deloua's back, Hesso pulling sharply on the camel's strappings. He patted her ribs then waved the women towards Bishoy's cart where he'd arranged dates and some bread on a clean handkerchief. They ate in silence, enjoying the last of the tea, watching the sunrise.

Vixy struggled to chew her food but she was desperately famished and stood sucking dates and bread crust, wincing when she swallowed.

When they'd finished, Bishoy completed the packing and Hesso produced his tobacco pouch and cigarette papers.

An air of uncertainty hung about them and it seemed to Vixy their little caravan was on the verge of breaking up. What would she do? The idea of tracking down Bruggs and otherwise trying to find her transponder seemed impossibly remote, as if the context of her life had changed forever.

Nevertheless, Hesso struck a match and offered her the cigarette. She took it, wincing as she filled her lungs, gasping at the sharp aching in her ribs. When she handed it back, he paused, glancing at the bright dab of blood on the paper where she'd put the cigarette to her lips and looking hard into her eyes. Their fingers touched and Vixy averted her gaze, longing for her veil, ashamed of her injuries. She let her hand drop away.

No one spoke. Deloua stood chewing her cud and the donkey twitched his ears.

Hesso drew deeply on the cigarette, once again offering it to Vixy. She declined and he tossed the cigarette aside. "Well. Why are we all behaving as if this is goodbye?" He looked round at them. "We shall return to Cairo together if nothing else."

To Vixy, leaving the Plateau amounted to abandoning all chance of returning home – she'd be resigning herself to becoming lost in time, to somehow, crazily, attempting to build a life in 1881 Egypt. She couldn't fathom it. Only slightly less absurd was her remaining behind at the Plateau in search of Bruggs and her transponder. "I need to find Bruggs," she said, almost in spite of herself. "I don't know how or why, really."

"He took something from you," said Hesso flatly. He regarded her thoughtfully, a mixture of tender pity, anguish and resolute esteem clouding his face. "We will help you find it."

The words had only just left his mouth when there was a commotion in the distance, in the direction of the Petrie camp – a series of urgent, incoherent shouts and a general clamor that echoed across the Plateau. They craned their necks in the direction of the Great Pyramid. A thin cloud of dust had arisen near the monument's northeast corner.

Hesso gathered Deloua's bridle. "*Yalla,* everyone – let us see what is going on." The suspicion in his voice seemed to galvanize them. "Miss Vixy, Amu, will you walk or ride?"

"I'll walk," said Vixy.

Amu removed her own veil – it seemed one of the few pieces of her clothing that had not suffered damage from the night before – and secured it loosely over Vixy's face. Vixy didn't protest, merely grasped Amu's hand as they hastily gathered up their robes.

"*Yalla,*" said Hesso, and set off, leading his camel.

Vixy hobbled along, arm in arm with Amu, struggling bravely to keep pace behind Deloua. Bishoy and his indefatigable donkey, cart in tow, brought up the rear. once again rattling over the stones and struggling through the patches of deeper sand.

They came quickly enough to the Petrie camp, vacant except for the papers and pottery and tools strewn about the tabletops. Further along, the ruckus was ongoing – a disorderly conglomeration of coolies milling about in the blowing dust, talking loudly and gesturing wildly. Others sat some distance away, scratching their heads and staring out into the desert as if nonplussed. No one paid heed to their arrival.

"Wait here." Hesso handed Deloua's rein to Bishoy and they watched him shoulder his way into the most congested part of the crowd.

It struck Vixy that she'd not seen Bab since the trouble last night. And where was Flinders Petrie for that matter, let alone Bruggs? She made to plunge headlong after Hesso but Amu clutched at her elbow.

"Miss Vixy, no!" Amu drew a swath of her headscarf across her face as a makeshift veil.

"No, Amu," said Vixy, pulling herself away; "I've got to see for myself." She moved through the men, averting her gaze from anyone who stared at her, forcing her way through until she'd reached an impassable knot of Egyptians with their backs to her, two of whom held umbrellas up as if shading something against the late morning sun. Vixy ducked so as to peer through the men's legs. Someone lay motionless on the sand – a man in black trousers, the fabric riding up his shins in an unseemly, disheveled manner, his frayed black socks drooping. A dusty shoe lay upside down next to his foot. She tapped one of the men on the shoulder and when he turned she made to angle her way past. But the man reached his arm across her chest and grabbed her shoulder. She gasped at the pain and several coolies turned to scowl at her. "Let me go!"

"Let her be." It was Hesso's voice speaking English then Arabic. "Let the woman through."

She stepped forward. Hesso knelt beside the body of an obese man lying flat on his back, the man's face obscured by a shabby cloth - a makeshift shroud. It can't be, she thought. Beside Hesso was Flinders Petrie himself, his arms folded across his chest and his expression grave.

"Miss Vixy has been looking for this man, Bruggs," said Hesso. He gestured for her to come near.

It was with a mild shock that she beheld the body up close: arms akimbo, torso twisted, fleshy belly partially exposed beneath a rumpled shirttail. The disheveled suit jacket, slacks, shoes and socks were all coated unnaturally in dust. One hand reached out in an awkward fist, the other, partially buried in drifted sand, lay twisted into the shape of a macabre, disjointed claw.

Vixy knelt beside the body, waving fitfully at the swarming flies. "May I see his face?"

Hesso appeared dubious.

Petrie put his arms behind his back, shifting his weight from one foot to the other. "I don't know who you are, Miss, but I don't recommend –"

"Show me, Hesso." She reached for the cloth herself and Hesso grasped her arm.

"It's him."

"I know. I just want to see."

Hesso grasped the corners of the fabric and partially lifted it.

Vixy steeled herself. The handful of forensic pathology sessions she'd been required to attend as a cadet, often in the company of Mr. Z., had not only made her squeamish but had often unsettled her for days. *It takes getting used to,* he'd suggested; *set your emotions aside and focus on the circumstances of the body, on your observations.* She peered staunchly at Bruggs's face for a moment then nodded for Hesso to cover it. Something about the way his torso was twisted made her curious to peer beneath his shoulder. "Blood. Pooled beneath him on the sand." The men murmured and crowded closer.

"Back!" said Petrie; "stay back, all of you!"

She tugged on the sleeve of Bruggs' suit jacket so as to examine his wrist and peered over the body at his other arm. The jacket sleeve was nearly torn away, exposing the white shirtsleeve at the shoulder. "No abrasions on his hands or wrists. He struggled, but it seems to me he was stabbed in the back." She glanced at Hesso, Petrie and the rest of them.

The coolie's murmuring became louder.

"Quiet!" said Petrie. "All of you!"

They hushed and Vixy continued.

"He's been here a while. The body's stiff." She pulled discreetly on the fabric of Bruggs's jacket sleeve to indicate the resistance. "Rigor Mortis sets in within three or four hours." She looked at the body. "But it can last for twenty-four, or more – it all depends on the physiology and the ambient conditions - so who knows when it happened."

Petrie cleared his throat. "Well, then. It must have been last night." He adjusted his hat and cleared his throat again. "Otherwise... well, I suppose someone would've noticed...." He trailed off, seemingly at a loss. "Regardless, the police will have their work cut out for them when they arrive – I've sent for them but there's nothing I can do to hold these men here."

"And a murderer wouldn't hang about, regardless," said Hesso flatly. "If any of these men saw anything, you are right, Petrie, getting the truth out of them isn't anything to do with any of us."

Vixy began patting Bruggs's pants pockets.

"What are you doing, Miss?" said Petrie. "I don't see how there's anything else to know about this situation -"

"Bruggs had something of mine," she said, looking hard at Hesso. "Something he stole from me."

Hesso nodded at her. "Yes, Petrie, she has a right to look."

"Burnt flesh," she said, "do either of you smell it?"

Petrie scowled. "Burnt flesh?"

Hesso nodded. "Yes."

Vixy tentatively lifted the lapel of Bruggs' suit jacket and looked away, gasping.

"Bloody hell," said Petrie, staggering back. He winced, waved his hand as if to clear the air, coughing into the crook of his arm.

Hesso caught his breath and stood up, glaring at the wound.

Vixy covered her mouth and nose with her head scarf and threw the lapel further back, peering askance at the place where Bruggs' shirt pocket ought to have been. All that remained was a fist-sized patch of charred fabric and blackened, sticky-looking flesh.

The crowd of men closed in again, muttering, their voices rising.

Petrie addressed them loudly in Arabic, waving his arms at them: "Quiet, all of you! Stay back! Clear the air!"

Vixy reached slowly towards Bruggs's ravaged chest.

Hesso looked askance at her. "What are you doing?"

She paused, her hand hovering over the spot, her fingers quivering, then she gritted her teeth and used her fingertips to pry something from the wound, smothering the object in the folds of her robe. She shuddered, leapt up and made to shoulder her way through the crowd.

"Vixy!" said Hesso, leaping after her.

She pushed past the onlookers, clutching her veil across her face, her eyes wet with tears, stumbling fitfully across the sand to where Amu and Bishoy waited with the animals. She threw herself onto the ground beside the wheels of the cart, the camel and the donkey stamping their hooves at her.

Amu rushed to her side.

Hesso was breathless when he caught up to her. "In the name of Allah, woman! What have you done?"

Vixy buried her face in Amu's arms and sobbed.

"What's happened?" said Amu, looking fiercely at Hesso.

They heard shouts and a greater commotion – a group of staunch-looking men had followed them.

"Let's go," he said unequivocally. "*Yalla!* Now! All of us!" He made to lift Vixy in his arms as if she'd become an invalid.

"Come, Vixy," said Amu, trying to help her to her feet.

But it was too late – Petrie and two of his sturdier supervisors had stormed up to confront them.

"I demand to know what that woman has taken from the body," said Petrie. "Professor Bruggs was under my employ. Whatever objects are on the man's person, they are to be considered evidence for the police." Petrie appeared exasperated, gesturing towards Vixy. "And for God's sake who *is* she?"

Petrie and his grim-looking Egyptians crowded closer.

Hesso glared back at them, standing his ground with his back to Vixy and Amu, one hand on the handle of his dagger and the other thrust out defensively. "Bishoy! My saber!"

In a flash, Bishoy had retrieved the blade from Deloua's side and hurled it handle-first across the donkey cart at Hesso who snatched it from the air and shook its broad, curved blade. He glared at the men. "She travels with me. That is all you need to know. That, and if you know Bruggs, you know he is a scoundrel and a thief. What he took from her is no one's business but her own."

"My good man," said Petrie, "calm yourself, no one here is threatening anyone with any harm. You said your name is Hesso – did you not? I recognize all of you from yesterday outside the camp. As leader of this

excavation and the official employer of these men – most of them, anyway
....” He turned and gesture at the gathering crowd, his face flushed. He
took off his hat and wiped his brow. “I say, sir, I’m not about to allow
anything to leave here without the police first having a look. There needs
to be a proper investigation. A man has been murdered, for heaven’s sake!”

Hesso lowered his blade yet stood his ground. “And I say to you, then,
Petrie, where’s your other man? Where’s the Frenchman? Laron? Where’s
œil le Sang?”

“Blood Eye,” said Petrie, sighing fitfully. “I know the name but nothing of the man. Except that he is... *was* a companion of Bruggs’s. Laron
was not under my employ. Meanwhile, I demand that you return what
this woman has taken. Let’s have it.” Petrie took a step closer to Hesso and
thrust his hand forward, palm upwards.

When Hesso pointed the blade of his sabre at Petrie, Bishoy’s donkey
brayed and Deloua became skittish, the boy struggling with the camel’s
bridle.

Petrie’s men bristled, reaching for their own weapons.

“Call off your dragomen dogs, Petrie,” said Hesso.

The Egyptians puffed their chests, their faces gleaming with perspiration, a stiff breeze whipping up whorls of dust that swirled around the
men’s feet.

“Here!” said Vixy. She leaned against Amu, her arm thrust out,
clutching the wadded-up portion of her robe. “Take it!” She shook the
thing at them. “It’s mine. Bruggs stole it from me. But it’s of no use to me
now.” She turned away, sobbing quietly, pitiably.

Petrie stepped past his men, furrowing his brow at the object.

Hesso stood poised, as if determined to hold the others at bay.

Petrie leaned closer, his voice low, unthreatening. “It’s a pocket watch
of some sort.” He produced a handkerchief from his shirt pocket and used
it to grasp at the object, peering at it closely, turning it this way and that
in his hand. “How in heaven’s name it came to be scorched like this is...
well, it’s beyond me.” He regarded Vixy with an expression of guarded
curiosity. “Young lady, clearly you are not Egyptian, despite your garb.

And why Bruggs had any interest in stealing something from you is, well, in my opinion, it's all quite suspicious. But I'm not the police. Nor am I a detective. Nor am I, frankly, interested in having anything more to do with this until the police indeed arrive, if they ever do. I'm not foolish enough, after all, to think things operate here as they do in London."

"It's just something that was made for me," said Vixy in a low voice. "It's mine, that's all."

"And you shall keep it," said Hesso, snatching the object from Petrie, raising his sabre at the encroachment of Petrie's men.

"No!" said Petrie, waving his men off. "Enough!" His exasperation seemed to have reached its limit and he turned to address the coolies. "Back to work, everyone. Back to work or you won't see a day's wages. There's digging and sorting to be done. Meanwhile, there's nothing here for anyone besides the police – let these vagabonds have their piece of junk."

The heat of the day was rising and most of the Egyptians seemed to be losing interest in the diminishing intrigue. They began drifting off.

Petrie, for his part, looked askance at Hesso, once again appearing to try to take the man's measure. "Hesso Ishaq – I remember now." He shook his head. "And there was that skirmish last night, somewhere near your camp, wasn't it? My men wouldn't speak of it."

Hesso glared at Petrie, determined to hold his tongue.

Petrie, exasperated, adjusted his hat and spoke as if to himself. "A man's death is enough to deal with on top of the responsibilities of my work." He addressed his dragomen sharply. "Get the men to work at the mastaba and have someone attend the body until the police arrive." Then to Hesso in English: "Be assured that I will inform the authorities myself as to what's gone on here. And there are enough witnesses, certainly, to identify all of you when the time comes." He gestured weakly at them and turned to go.

Hesso handed his sabre to Bishoy. He stood watching the backs of Petrie and the dispersing coolies. "This man, Petrie, like every other Englishman, was only interested in making certain we didn't make off with one of his precious artifacts. And as for the authorities – the Cairo police are at least as corrupt as the city politicians who employ them. If they arrive before tomorrow afternoon it will surprise me. By then the body will have been pulled apart by jackals and half eaten by beetles." He sheathed his dagger and straightened his robe. "Meanwhile, we need to leave the Plateau. All of us. We can go our separate ways when we get to the city."

They'd been plodding along in silence in the direction of the city, the plateau and the pyramids fading into the distance behind them, when Hesso slowed down to encourage Vixy to catch up. "I'm taking Bishoy with me to Alexandria. Amu has her trade here in the city. Will you stay with her?"

"I don't know."

"What will you do? Where will you go?" He handed her the handkerchief containing the transponder.

She took it, gazing absently into the distance as she walked, detached, profoundly resigned. "I don't know, Hesso." She had a mind to fling the transponder, what was left of it, into the desert – what could any leave-no-trace protocol mean to her now? Meanwhile, the idea of Hesso and Bishoy swashbuckling across the Mediterranean seemed romantic and quaint. And it only amplified her sense of slipping away from things, from everything, from her own fruitless life; of being forced to surrender to the nightmare of her fate. *An Emergency Immolation Beacon – it had to be.* The thought had assailed her from the moment she realized it was her wrecked transponder on Bruggs's body. She clutched at the thing, digging her fingers into the handkerchief as if to strangle the hard impossibility of it, as if she could squeeze her own last drop of bitter hope from it. An EIB – *what else could explain it?*

They'd been approaching the Pyramids Road and when they finally entered the shade of the first eucalyptus trees the relief seemed to heighten

Vixy's exhaustion. "I'm tired. Can we rest, Hesso?"

He led them to the side of the road beneath the trees, each of them assisting with what had become the routine of deploying their blankets and provisions. Bishoy unharnessed his donkey and led the animal to the shallow tributary beside the road to drink. Hesso offered his camel some grain and helped Amu and Vixy lay out bread and dates and a water skin. A warm, torpid breeze rustled the leaves overhead and the pale desert seemed to thrum beneath the unyielding midday sun. They'd been silent, as if the time and distance and events that stood between this meal and their first on the Pyramids Road together precluded any conversation.

"I've got to leave a sign," said Vixy. "Some kind of signal. So they can find me."

Amu grasped her hand and squeezed it fretfully, a pained look in her eyes. Hesso appeared mildly perplexed. Bishoy pretended not to hear them, stroking the neck of his donkey.

"Find you?" said Hesso. "What do you mean?"

Vixy hesitated. "I need to tell you who I am, Hesso."

Amu squeezed her hand again, whispering sharply in her ear. "*No, Miss.*"

Vixy shook her head dismissively. "No, Amu. It's time. It's the only hope I have."

Amu lowered her gaze.

Vixy looked Hesso square in the face, her chest heaving with resolve. "I'm from the future. From another time and place." Her words hung in the air between them like some awkward confession. "I was kidnapped by Bruggs and Laron. They brought me here. With an HDT –" – she shook her head, correcting herself – "with a time machine."

Hesso rubbed the back of his neck, peering at her from under his brow, a mixture of incredulity and curiosity on his face. "Kidnapped. Yes. I suspected they were more than thieves."

Vixy blinked at him, still hesitant. "They brought me here from the future. Bruggs and Laron. I don't know how they did it but they must have... they must have had..., oh, I don't know how to explain it!"

"You said they had a time machine," said Hesso. There was a wry glint in his eye, the hint of a droll smile. "I heard you."

"I'm being serious, Hesso." She shook the transponder at him. "Laron himself might have one of these. He has to have one, or something like it."

Hesso withdrew his tobacco pouch and poked his fingers into it.

"I know it sounds crazy. What I'm saying sounds crazy. But it's true. It's absolutely true. In the future people can travel through time and space and *I'm* from the future. This is my transponder. My time machine. Or it used to be. This is why I had to find Bruggs, because he'd taken this from me – he was keeping me trapped here, a hostage." She tore away the handkerchief, made a half-hearted attempt to wipe away the encrusted carbon and whatever else – burned fabric and cooked flesh? – and held it before him. "It's like a radio."

Hesso ignored it and finished preparing his cigarette. Amu looked away and Bishoy stood beside his donkey, searching their faces.

My God, thought Vixy. She knew full well that even if radio waves had been discovered already in 1881– she couldn't remember exactly – they weren't a commonplace technology let alone anything a nineteenth century Bedouin would understand. She was standing here violating every precedent of HDT ethics. But there was nothing for it. What else could she do? "It's like *lightning*. Time travel is like travel on a flash of lightning. Can you imagine that?"

Silence. Blank stares. Hesso lighting his cigarette.

Vixy put her face in her hands.

"I know nothing of time machines," said Hesso. "I know nothing of traveling by way of lightning in the sky. I only know, Vixy, that somehow you are not what you seem. Since the first day I saw you, with Amu and Bishoy, you seemed to me different than anyone, any woman I have ever met. And now you tell me that you are from the future, from another time and place. Praise Allah, somehow I am not astonished; not as astonished as perhaps I should be. I don't know why." He touched her shoulder and she looked up. "You are trying to get home. That's all. Who doesn't know what it means to try to get home?"

"The trees," said Amu, her voice earnest. She was suddenly animated, gesturing down the length of the eucalyptus trees. "We can mark the trees somehow, so that they'd know you were here. If someone is coming for you, looking for you, they might see it was you. Everyone going to and from the pyramids takes this road."

"Yes," said Hesso. "That's good. We will carve something into the bark. A message. It must be bold, yet simple. I'm no wood carver. What would your friends recognize? That no one else would? A secret sign."

They stood looking at each other, vexed.

Hesso approached the nearest tree trunk and carved a "V" into it.

Amu cocked her head. "Larger, Hesso, to see it from a distance," she said.

Hesso lengthened and deepened the slashes and stood back.

Vixy looked uncertain. "Wait. Repeat the mark. Carve another 'V' beside it, but lower. My last name – my surname – also begins with the letter 'V.' And an arrow pointing toward Cairo."

Hesso worked skillfully enough with his knife, steadying the blade with his free hand. He stepped back, turned to them and shrugged.

Vixy shrugged, likewise. The marks seemed so arbitrary, so insignificant and futile. "There's nothing else to be done. I don't know."

Hesso led Deloua onto the road. "We'll mark every tenth tree or so as we make our way to the city."

The tiny village of Kafr came into view and it seemed to Vixy as if years had passed since they'd stopped on the road across from the humble enclave for their first meal together. There had been an air of mystery and intrigue to everything she'd witnessed then – despite her despair everything had been new and infused with adventure. But now? The little huts seemed shabby and meager, filthy and destitute. Even the Pyramids seemed diminished, their mystery gone.

Just then she noticed a man on a camel emerge from behind one of the village huts. He wore a white *tob* and seemed incredibly familiar. Rider and camel approached the muddy banks of the tributary, the camel sloshing through the water, negotiating the moist earth along the shore. "It's Bab!"

Hesso brought them to a halt and Bishoy, along with Amu riding in the donkey cart, clattered up behind him. They all watched as Bab guided his camel directly towards them.

Vixy watched Bab ease his camel down and dismount with some difficulty. He'd been riding almost sidesaddle with one leg folded in front of him. Now he leaned on a cane. Otherwise he appeared at ease, regarding them with an abiding smile and a brightness in his eyes. It struck her that besides Laron, and the curious Mr. Five, if anyone knew anything about Bruggs' murder it might be his dragoman. A chill ran through her. Could Bab himself have killed a man?

"*As-salamu a'laikum,*"[58] said Bab.

Hesso responded with an air of suspicion. "*Wa a'laikum as-salamu,*"[59]

"I have been waiting for you," said Bab.

"Waiting?" said Hesso. The two men regarded each other. "Why? What are you doing here?"

Bab reached out to stroke the neck of his camel. "I live here. And I've been waiting to tell you something."

They waited, watching Bab searching their faces calmly, patiently. He stood with both hands on his cane. "The ruins inspire treachery. But I don't have to tell any of you." He paused as if to allow his words their effect. "Meanwhile, men like Mister Bruggs...." He shrugged. "And

---

[58] A common, informal Arabic greeting, akin to the American "Hello" or French "Bon jour," that translated means "Peace upon you all" (*As-salamu* = peace; *a'laikum* = upon you all).

[59] The response reverses the Arabic words and adds a prefix "*wa.*"

Monsieur Laron? Well, you see the outcome. There was nothing to be done. I had been lying awake that night. The pain in my leg would not let me sleep. I heard them arguing. They often argued, what of it? But then a strange silence. Despite my leg I felt compelled to... to... how do you say...? Investigate. I find Mister Bruggs laying there upon his back."

"You're saying Laron killed Bruggs?" said Vixy.

"I heard no one else," said Bab. "But who can be certain?"

"A man like Bruggs had no friends upon the plateau," said Hesso. "You left without telling anyone?"

Bab nodded.

"The police will be looking to question you," said Hesso.

Bab shrugged again. "Perhaps. Perhaps not. No matter. Meanwhile, as I said, I have been waiting for you. I have something for Miss Vixy. News – is that the word in English? Then I shall be on my way."

"What is it?" said Vixy.

"Mister Five. He has emerged from the Great Pyramid and is on his way to Dahshur."

They all turned to look at each other, even poor Bishoy who was understanding nothing.

"What do you mean?" said Hesso.

"Perhaps Amu and Bishoy would allow me to accompany them back to the city," said Bab. "Lame as I have become, I can perhaps still provide some assistance." He performed a short bow.

"Mister Five?" said Vixy. "You said Dahshur? I don't understand. I don't understand you at all. And what makes you think all of us aren't on our way to Cairo?"

Bab tipped his head and hobbled closer, leaning forward a little on his cane. "Miss Vixy." He peered at her intently. "Time is – how do you say? – time is short. I must tell you that a man – his name is... I do not know exactly. In England they say 'zed.' But you are not English." He paused. "Zee." Bab had elongated the pronunciation. "He is in search of you."

Vixy felt herself blanch and she swooned, grasping for Hesso's arm.

He caught her around the waist.

Amu leapt from the donkey cart and scurried towards her. "Bishoy! *Mayya!*"[60]

Bab seemed suddenly obdurate, unyielding, bearing down on her despite her condition. "Meanwhile, perhaps you have noticed something strange about Mister Five? Something not of this world? This Earth? Something as you say, alien?"

Vixy gasped, tried to collect herself. "Who are you?"

"Bab! Please!" said Amu. "Miss Vixy, drink." She held out the water skin.

Vixy brushed it away.

Bab stepped back, raising his hands as if in defense, as if acquiescing. "Who am I? Merely a man. A man who listens. And sees." A faint, incongruous smile hung upon his lips and he regarded them with an expression of resolute patience. "Have faith in your friends, Miss Vixy." His tone had become distant. "What you seek is indeed seeking you." He turned to dig through his camel's saddle bag and held out a rectangular wooden box, small enough to fit within the palm of his hand. Its top was perforated with small holes.

Vixy hesitated and Bab pressed the box into her hand. She felt something skitter within it, something alive, scratching at the wood. It was all she could do to keep herself from dropping it instinctively.

"By the devil, what is that?" said Hesso.

"For Mister Five," said Bab. "A yellow arrow, of sorts."

Hesso scowled and snatched the box away from Vixy, prying at it.

"No!" said Bab.

Hesso relented. "Why not? What is it?" He tossed it on the ground and made to stomp on it.

Vixy stared desperately at Bab, tears stinging her eyes. "No, Hesso. Wait."

Hesso let the thing be.

"Mr. Z. He's looking for me? You've seen him? Where is he?"

---

60  Arabic for "water."

Bab shook his head. "I have seen him, yes. But not in the way you know. Whether he is here now or not, I do not know."

"I don't understand," said Vixy. "Who are you? You've seen Mr. Z. but can't help me find him?" Her voice was ragged with anger.

Bab once again stroked the neck of his camel. "That is all that I have learned. It is all that I know. Mister Five is on his way, as I have told you. To Dahshur. His goal is the Red Pyramid. He is trying to get home. Just like you. But you must stop him. Stop *them*." He made to remount his camel, struggling with his bad leg.

Hesso helped him up. "What are you telling us?" said Hesso. "That we're to run off in search of Mister Five at the Red Pyramid? In the name of Allah, of what concern is Mister Five to any of us?"

Bab shifted himself in his saddle. "Find Mister Five. You must do this thing. I have told you all I know."

Bab unstrapped one of his camel bags and tossed it at Hesso. "Go with her, Hesso. Here is water and food – take it." Bab turned his camel round and set off in the direction of the city.

Hesso seemed incredulous. He stared at Vixy, shaking his head, holding Bab's camel bag as if it were ridiculous.

Vixy fell to her knees. "I don't know what to do."

Amu came to Vixy's side and grasped her hands in hers. "Listen to this man. Do what he asks. Bishoy and I will return to Cairo with him, just as he says. You and Hesso will ride to the Red Pyramid. Whatever it is that is happening, you have to... you must..." Tears welled up in her eyes. "There is nothing but Émile Laron and danger for you in Cairo, I know it." Amu's eye's flashed and she gathered her robes about her. "Thank you, Hesso. Thank you for helping us. Tell Bishoy you will be back for him. Come, Bishoy." She gestured to the boy.

Bishoy looked to Hesso.

Hesso spoke to the boy in Arabic and pressed a coin into Bishoy's hand. Bishoy nodded bravely and brought his donkey cart forward, helping Amu climb onto the cart. They started down the road, Bishoy and Amu,

290 • TIME CRIME

Amu glancing back at them, the cart trundling along, until she finally turned away.

"In the name of Allah," said Hesso, "I don't know what to make of any of this." He picked up Bab's little box, stuffed it into Bab's saddle bag and strapped the bag to the camel. "Down, Deloua, down." The camel knelt. He grasped Vixy's arm and motioned at the seat.

"But I can't," she said. "I've never ridden -"

"What do you say in English?" Hesso picked Vixy up and in a single motion hauled her onto the camel saddle. "There is a first time for everything? Hup, hup, Deloua!"

"Oh my God!" said Vixy, clutching at the seat, terrified as the camel lurched to its feet, stamping and snorting.

Hesso scrambled up behind her, his arms hugging her hips, grasping the rein in front of her. "Hang on here and here," he instructed.

Vixy clutched at the saddle. "This is crazy. I can't do this!"

"*Yalla, Deloua! Yalla!*"

Deloua strode forth.

Vixy stiffened, clutching harder at the saddle and grabbing at Hesso's arm.

"Don't fight the camel's motion. You are doing well!" Hesso kicked lightly at Deloua's flanks and they set off at a faster pace.

"Why so fast?" said Vixy, struggling to manage the change in Deloua's gate.

"The Red Pyramid is perhaps thirty kilometers distant," said Hesso: "Perhaps three hours at this pace."

"I'll never make it," said Vixy.

"You will, but you've got to trust somebody besides yourself. If not me, then at least Deloua. Look straight ahead into the distance, it will help you find your rhythm."

Vixy did as she was told, looking out. It was thrilling, in a way – the ground rushing past, the wind in her face, the view of the desert from so high a perch. And whether Hesso's words had dismantled her defenses or whether she was just tired of being afraid, or both, she relaxed her grip on the saddle, relaxed her legs clamping onto the sides of the camel. She sighed with relief, allowed herself to roll and sway with Deloua's fluid stride – there *was* a rhythm! The eucalyptus trees sped past, the desert opening out in a manner that took her breath away, made her feel undone and despite everything, she laughed, laughed into the wind, blinking at the tears streaming from the corners of her eyes.

Hesso laughed, too, and shouted above her shoulder, "They do not call the camel a ship of the desert for nothing!"

Five engaged his cloaking device and scrambled from the passageway, momentarily blinded by the daylight despite the auto-compensation of his trek lenses. He squinted and blinked, manually adjusting the polarization, crouched low and scanned the Plateau. The cluster of Egyptians had dissipated. All that remained were two men upholding the umbrellas. He still couldn't make out what it was they were shading. Another relic? It hardly mattered. He scurried down the loose embankment, dislodging another cascade of sand, rocks and jagged shards of limestone. He watched his cloud of dust stream away in the breeze. Don't get sloppy now. Don't get careless. Leave no trace.

He broke into a light jogging pace, careful to mind his steps, retracing his route along the northern, then western, faces of Khufu, scurrying across the open space to Khafre, keeping tight to the stone, crossing to Menkaure, hugging the stone again, his fatigue lightened by a burgeoning sense of his accomplishment and thoughts of home. Home! He resisted the urge to break into a run. It's six hours on foot to Dahshur. Pace yourself. Nevertheless, his heart felt light, his body strong – he could endure anything now.

He worked quickly to decamp, dismantling the shadow tarp, shaking the sand and dust from his bedroll and double-checking his inventory.

He used his hands to refill the depression that had constituted his hovel, toiling for a time at attempting to eliminate all evidence of his presence and finally abandoning the work. Let the winds and shifting sands take care of the rest. It's over. His work was done. If only he could HDT from here – the idiosyncrasies of the technology demanded that he depart from the same coordinates as his arrival. He hefted his pack, double-checked his bearings and took a last look round. Goodbye, pyramids. Goodbye, Giza Plateau. Moving out.

He set out almost due south at a modest pace, glad for the wind at his back. "Damn," he murmured. His cloaking device flickered and he tapped the interface. Then it failed entirely. "Shit!" He possessed neither the time nor the patience to troubleshoot the thing, let alone dismantle and repair it. Damn dust! He'd have to risk it. He unshouldered his pack and dumped three quarters of its contents onto the sand before finally wrenching his wadded up *tob* and *kufeya* from the bottom of it. Argh. The idea of donning his disguise, sweating it out under the bulky fabric and cramming his ears into the *kufeya*, exasperated him. "Screw it," he mumbled; "I'm not wearing *this* piece of shit." He crammed the headpiece back into his pack along with everything else, threw the *tob* round his shoulders and set off again, muttering to himself. "What's gotten into me? Calm down. Pace yourself, cadet." He enhanced magnification and scanned the desert. No man or beast in sight.

He marched along, across the open desert, despairing at the burgeoning heaviness in his legs but determined to make good time, refusing to surrender to the symptoms of his nagging exhaustion. The Plateau receded behind him, the sun low in the west. Altitude? Twenty degrees. Heading? Two-hundred-thirty-five degrees southwest. No moon until... let's see... no moon until approximately twenty-two-hundred hours – I'll be home by then! He plunged into the barren landscape with renewed vigor, playing catch-me-if-you-can with his lengthening shadow, allowing it to spur him onward.

❄

The torching afternoon sun made Vixy feel dry as a stick. And drowsy – her head bobbed and she couldn't keep her eyes open. Meanwhile, she'd begun to feel every one of Deloua's strides in her aching muscles, in her bones. The thrill of their departure had evaporated amidst the blowing sand and parched, unsheltered landscape. She was saddle-sore and miserable, fantasizing about cool baths, clean clothes and a soft mattress. She fancied leaping from the saddle and plunging naked into the Nile.

"There!" said Hesso, his voice hoarse. He gestured into the distance.

Vixy squinted, struggling to discern anything at all within the featureless desert.

"Below the horizon, due south: that's the Red Pyramid."

She shaded her eyes. "Whatever it is, it's not red."

"Ha! It isn't. Only sometimes, when the sun is just correct...." Hesso drew back on the rein and Deloua slowed and stopped.

Vixy's only desire was to dismount. She tried to slide from her seat.

"No," warned Hesso, his arm round her waist. "Wait – you would not be the first inexperienced camel rider to sprain their ankle, or worse, by jumping off." He slid off Deloua's back and grasped the camel's bridle. "Hold on tightly to the saddle and lean back. She will kneel onto her front legs first." He tugged on her rein, "Down, Deloua."

Sure enough, the camel knelt.

"Now her back legs – lean forward."

Vixy slid easily onto the sand and the firmness of it under her feet was exquisite. She peered into the desert and sighed fitfully. "What are we doing? This is crazy."

Hesso was likewise scanning the featureless expanse. "By the grace of God, if he is traveling from the Plateau, I think we are bound to see him."

Vixy tried to stretch her back and aching hips. Her behind and the inside of her thighs felt raw. "Who knows? - Bab himself might be crazy."

Hesso offered Vixy a water skin then busied himself examining the contents of Bab's saddlebag. "Hmm. Dates, flatbread... and this!" He held up a handful of something that looked to Vixy like beef jerky.

"Dried meat?"

Hesso sniffed. "Lamb." He used his teeth to tear off a bit, offering the rest to Vixy. "It's good quality. If Bab is crazy, he at least prepares fine provisions."

Vixy chewed absently on her jerky and watched Hesso offer Deloua several handfuls of grain and a slurp of water from his cupped hand. They shared a flatbread, a handful of dates and sipped at the water skin. Finally, Hesso produced a cigarette and they smoked it together, gazing into the far distance, each of them savoring what had become their private ritual. The dry southerly breeze tugged at the edges of their garments and caught wisps of Vixy's hair. She brushed the strands away from her eyes with her fingertips.

Hesso glanced at her, his eyes emerald gold reflecting the late afternoon sun, his face lean and dark. He seemed a part of the desert, part of its wilderness and mystery.

"Time travel," he said. "I believed that Mister Five was just another antiquities collector. Strange looking. Mute. But I swear most men in my business are strange, in their way. And if they have money to pay for what they want? And Bab, to me he was nothing but an old dragoman. But here Mister Five is... I don't know what he is. Or why he must go to Dahshur to get home. For there is nothing there but ruins. And Bab, while he looks like any other Egyptian, any dragoman, he is apparently also a magician. Or perhaps a sage. To know what he knows." He offered Vixy the last of the cigarette. "And did you know Mister Five left behind his canopic chest and three of the jars? I found them on the sand beside Deloua that night in the camp. After all the effort and money spent. To discard a thing like that. When he did not haggle with me over the price I should have suspected he was not what he seemed." He shrugged. "But it makes no difference. I hid the objects near the camp. I can sell the chest again easily enough, though an incomplete set of jars is not worth nearly as much."

They were silent for a time.

"This Mister Five, perhaps he can help you get home?"

"I can't imagine how." Alien indeed, she thought. She should have known; she should have been more observant. She ought to have suspected something. From the beginning she'd been too absorbed in her own difficulties to pay heed to anyone else. What would Mr. Z. think of the mess she'd made of things? What would he have done instead? She imagined him standing beside his air cruiser. He was holding the door open for her just as he was when they'd left for the T.E. They'd talked about Molemen. "Oh my God." The realization struck her like a shot.

"What is it?"

"He's a Moleman." Vixy put her hand to her mouth.

Hesso returned his attention to the desert.

"Aren't you going to ask me what a Moleman is?"

"If you told me what a Moleman was would it matter? Mister Five could be Ramesses the Second for all I know or care. Next you are going to tell me that Mister Five is from somewhere beyond the stars, perhaps – beyond space and time or some such thing." He smiled affectionately at her. "Like you."

"Why are you helping me, Hesso?" She couldn't seem to measure the depth of this man. Neither could she discern exactly what they had come to mean to each other. She only sensed an openness. And that her sins, such as they were, seemed to fall away from her in his presence. Along with any firm idea of who she was or what she was doing. Still, she longed to return to everything as it once was; to know everything as it once was; to know herself as *she* once was. Oh, to be home again with her plans and her life laid out before her. It made her frantic to realize she no longer understood what that meant, that everything about her old life and her place in it was becoming strange to her. Was Mr. Z. really searching for her? How could she know? What could she do? She watched Hesso repacking Bab's bag and hitching Deloua's saddle straps. "Hesso?"

His back was to her. "Yes, Vixy?" He was busy tucking the saddle straps into place. When she didn't respond he turned to find her staring at him. He looked at her expectantly, his brow furrowed and a gleam of concern in his eyes.

Her voice was heavy with emotion. "*Why are you helping me?*"

*It is, as al-Hallaj told us, the agony of the moth that is trying to reach the flame and become the flame and burn away his separate entity by union with the flame....* [ad]

# CHAPTER 20

# THE AGONY
# OF THE MOTH

**CAPTAIN CHASE SIGNED THE RELEASE,** sighed wearily, and stood waiting for the cell block door to open.

"Sorry, sir, just a second – the face recognition, it usually works fine, except –"

The Captain readjusted his eye patch and did his best to stay still for the camera, wherever it was. "No sweat, Lou, it's my eye patch, that's all. I can't remember the last time I was down here in the holding tank but the rest of the T.E. has been on DNA scan forever. Try it again."

Lou's frown seemed to encompass his whole amphibious face and he floated stiffly in his work tank, blinking his bulbous eyes at the controls and displays. "Budget issue is what they told us, sir."

There was a loud clack and the door rolled open. "There it goes, sir, go ahead."

The Captain stepped towards the vestibule.

"Excuse me, Captain?"

The Captain paused.

Lou drifted closer, grasping the edge of his tank, and raised himself up. His great eyes glistened at the Captain, his long, yellow-green lips tense. The tank's filtration system bubbled quietly. "Sorry, sir, but, I just wanted to tell you that, Mr. Neutic, you know, when he said he was turning himself in – that he was reporting a time crime and all that, and that he was responsible, well, we went through the motions with the paperwork and meanwhile I got a hold of Bull, seeing as we're family, you know. I mean to say, sir, we all know about Mr. Neutic working for you. And what a good man he is. Anyway, when I talked to Bull, he said to just keep it on the down low until you got here and not to put him in with the rabble, you know what I mean, sir."

The Captain nodded. "That's fine, Lou, you did right. And thanks for getting me his statement before putting it in the system. I owe you one."

Lou nodded. "Don't mention it, sir. Not at all." He swished to the opposite end of his work tank, tapped at his console and the inner cell block door swung open. "Straight ahead, sir, end of the block, Solitary Suite 6. I cleared you at the release gate, you can take him out that way."

The Captain trudged down the long, spare corridor. The institutional whiteness of it all made everything seem hard and dreary. The floor, ceiling, walls, the heavy-looking cell doors with their tiny windowpanes too high to see in or out of – everything white on dingy white. How does anyone endure confinement like this? He started feeling breathless and claustrophobic – he could've taken the tram down to solitary, after all. But he needed the walk. And time to think. Where in hell was all this going? For the life of him, the harder he worked, it seemed, the less that got done. Except for more problems. There was never a shortage of those.

Meanwhile, he couldn't shake an image from his head. It was from a dream he'd had the night before. He never remembered his dreams. Except there it was, the scene of him sitting in the middle of the street he grew up on, a ground-car parked beside him and a glimpse of his childhood home across the way. It was as if no one were around - no one in the car, nobody on the street, nobody in the house - and when he tried to recall it, the house, that is, it seemed dark, empty. He didn't have any sense of how old he was in the dream – was he a kid or the age he is now? What in hell was he doing there? What struck him most, though, were the leaves. Yellow-gold-colored leaves, zillions of them, blowing across the street in a strong breeze. More like a wind. Autumn, he supposed. But why all the leaves at once, and why all the same damn color? The last thing he remembered about it was looking deeper into the neighborhood, trying to figure out where all the leaves were coming from, and seeing a line of trees – tall ash or maple – virtually identical in size and shape, going on forever, it seemed; their black branches almost denuded of foliage by the wind.

The door was open and the Captain walked in. Well, stepped in. With one stride he was practically in the middle of the cell. Concrete floor, concrete walls, concrete ceiling, all white. The stainless-steel shitter and tiny sink on one side. Neutic on the other, bent forward on the edge of his cot, his elbows on his knees and his head down. His suit jacket and necktie were draped over the mattress and his shirt sleeves were rolled up. Even in prison the kid looked smart.

"C'mon, son. Let's go."

Neutic grabbed his clothes and stood up, his expression stern, a day or so worth of stubble on his jaw. "Yessir."

They ambled in silence towards the release gate, pausing beside the empty guard office window and stepping onto the footprint images imbedded in the floor, waiting for the face recognition and the green light, the clack of the locks and the door rolling open.

There was a tram waiting on the other side with its doors open. "I'm sitting," said the Captain, and flopped into a seat. "I've had enough walking."

They sat shoulder to shoulder, the station lights whizzing past the windows, the tram car swooshing through the tunnel.

"You know, Neutic, I spent a night in the clink once. When I was young. Out late with a couple buddies of mine – we used to drink the bar dry and then sometimes we'd get bored with the jukebox and the lack of girls and instead we'd get rowdy and stupid and try to raise hell. And this one night we thought we were hilarious throwing beer bottles through the windows of a vacant old warehouse and took off and ran straight into a cop. Apparently, the warehouse wasn't vacant. Anyway, fingerprints, mug shot, surrender your belongings, the full catastrophe, including your shoelaces - we were too stupid to figure that one out. One of us mentioned getting a phone call. 'None of you are getting any phone call,' says the cop, 'unless it's to your parents, and I'm pretty sure they ain't gonna wanna hear it. Because I've already talked to them. That's right. We're good friends now. And I've explained how you're all sleeping it off nice and cozy with the rest of the city's delinquents.' Or some such thing. Anyway. Good man. Lesson learned."

"I'm sorry, sir," said Neutic. "I'm worried about Mr. Z., I can tell you. And I didn't know what else to do. He wouldn't take me with him. And he said I'd know when to let somebody know about what he was going to do. That he was sending me back to the T.E. And I guess I just, I don't know, I just...." He trailed off. "I hate that I've let everyone down. That I let *you* down. I hate that Mr. Z. had to go it alone, to help Miss Velure. I hate the whole thing, the case going cold and all that." He shook his head.

The Captain sighed a long, hard, deliberate sigh and looked absently at the tunnel lights and tram stations zooming past.

Neutic couldn't tell if the man was angry or disappointed or exasperated or didn't give a shit altogether. At this point any reaction would make sense, he supposed.

"I knew the situation I put you in with Mr. Z., Neutic. I expected you to help the man and learn from him at the same time. And help me with the investigation, of course. I knew we were in a serious jam with the Vixy thing. The lack of evidence and the timeline on the cold case and the complexity of the whole damn boondoggle. I knew the risk of all that. But the way this case just keeps spiraling into a larger and larger..." – he gestured futility with both hands, letting them fall into his lap – "I don't know what. A damn mess!" He glanced at Neutic and let out a wry laugh.

"You're not going to believe me, but it all turned out like I expected. With Mr. Z., I mean. Or half expected, at least. I learned a long time ago you don't get any degree of talent – real talent in anything – without a compensating dose of bullshit."

Neutic couldn't help grinning a little at the Captain, at the man's rough wisdom and forthrightness.

"But that poor young woman. What she's going through. What her family's going through. Neutic, I swear, I'd have done just what Mr. Z. did – I'd have gone after her come hell or high water myself." He looked thoughtful. "Well, I like to think I would've." He fell silent and they both sat staring at nothing and listened to the sounds of the tram.

Soon enough, it screeched to a halt as a feminine voice blared over the loudspeakers, too loud, too cheerful. "Time Detective Contingent Headquarters, Ground Floor."

They hustled onto the platform and the Captain paused to check the time. "We've got an hour and a half until the Special Council. We're going to meet up with Professor Wilhelm in the private auditorium down the hall from my office – I've got authorized invites from Ganesh for all three of us. Whatever's going on with the PMC and whomever else to do with this investigation, we're going to find out."

"Are you sure you want me there, sir?"

"Don't be getting on my nerves, now, Neutic." He led them up the station steps, picking up his pace with each step as if the urgency of it all was once again settling in, driving him onward. Neutic followed closely behind. "You're going to snap out of it, straighten up and do the goddamn job I hired you for, you hear? Mr. Z. can take care of himself, you'd be surprised, I can tell you. And Vixy?" They reached the top of the flight of steps and followed the corridor leading to the Captain's office, Neutic hustling to come up beside the Captain. "Well, we're going to use the ninety minutes we've got before the Ganesh thing and you're going to fill me in on goddamn everything you and Mr. Z. were up to at Eranos. Every last goddamn detail, you hear?"

"Yessir," said Neutic, shoving his arm into his suit jacket and strapping his tie under his collar. "Absolutely, sir!"

"Greetings, everyone. On behalf of the Pangalactic Mythology Coalition, I am Mircea Ganesh, Legate of the PMC's Myth-Realm Integrity Wing and special envoy to the Time Guard Contingent. I am here to communicate a matter of utmost urgency related to the investigation of the recent Olympic Theater terrorist attack, heretofore classified as a localized time crime under the jurisdiction of the T.E. and TDC with support from the PMC but which has been upgraded, as of this morning, to both pangalactic and imminent threat status. Per the requirements of the Galactic Transparency Alliance under subtitle 1132 of the Galactic Law Statutes, this means that a Special Council comprised, at a minimum, of members of the GTA, GIA, PMC, T.E. and TDC is mandated to ascertain next steps and distribute an official communiqué to all affected nations – including non-member nations – the cosmo-political and cosmo-economic impact of which, as we know, risks inciting anything from peaceful, grassroots level protests and disruptive public demonstrations to war mongering and overt military machinations. Decisiveness and delicacy both, then, must be the hallmark of these proceedings.

"Each of you should have received this morning the file 'The Agony of the Moth.' This amounts to the declassified portion of the intelligence collected by agents of the GIA during a recent intragalactic, pan-stellar dragnet designed to detect evidence – primarily interrupted soft x-ray radiation spectrums – of white dwarf consumption. For those who do not know, white dwarf consumption, or harvesting, as it is also referred to, is extremely rare. White dwarfs themselves, also called degenerative dwarfs, are dying stars of masses similar to that of Earth's sun that have exhausted their nuclear fuel, cooling over billions of years while retaining a very hot core with a density surpassed only by a neutron star – a typical white dwarf is the same size as Earth but two-hundred thousand times denser, its gravitational force capable of literally shredding nearby planets. While a white dwarf is a relatively common astrophysical occurrence – it will be the fate of Earth's solar system, for instance – the consumption, harvesting or harnessing of its energy is extremely difficult and known to be concurrent with nefarious Hyper-Dimensional Obfuscation Fold activity, or HDOF.

"How so? An HDOF flattens space-time upon itself, a feat that requires vast quantities of energy; quantities of such unwieldy magnitude that HDOF engineering demands both isolation from populated solar systems and direct proximity to the energy source itself, conditions ripe within the proximity of solar systems undergoing a white dwarf phase of disintegration.

"And, indeed, independent, double-blind forensic analysis of the dragnet data on behalf of scientists at both the GIA and T.E. revealed soft x-ray interruption and white dwarf levels of energy consumption – potential white dwarf harvesting – at undisclosed super-galactic latitude and longitude coordinates over a period of several months within the last Gregorian calendar year. Moreover, certain clusters of data coincided with evidence of sympathetic HDOF frequency and amplitude signatures indicative of same-source engineering. Four such HDOF signatures have been verified. That is to say, four HDOFs were likely engineered by the same entity or entities for the same purposes.

"Note that the celestial coordinate system employed during the drag-net itself is classified top secret for the purposes of this Special Council. The location of the Fold, meanwhile, has no bearing on the application of Galactic Law nor the contents of our proposed communiqué. Neither have Fold coordinates been shown to reliably coincide with the coordinates of the source engineering – an HDOF is not akin to either fingerprint or breadcrumb evidence, so to speak; it does not identify the user or users but rather demonstrates circumstantial evidence of clandestine, perhaps criminal activity.

"That said, following a vary laborious and expensive dismantling of the HDOF architecture, it has been concluded that the heads of state of two non-GTA-participating, non-T.E.-member cultures operating within the cosmo-political realm of influence of the GTA and PMC – namely, the Molemen and Mothmen – have engineered clandestine gatherings, code-named SnoGlobeCon, that have convened on at least four occasions, the content of which describes illegal HDT research and development.

"Which brings us to 'The Agony of the Moth,'" an otherwise elementary introduction to the science of hyper-dimensionality and its application to HDT. The basic science of HDT technology has, of course, been in the public domain for several centuries, even as the deployment of the technology has from its inception remained highly regulated. However, the results of an Origin Analysis upon this document implicates both the Molemen and the Mothmen in a violation of the moratorium upon unauthorized HDT research and development by non-GTA members. By extension, such unauthorized, unapproved activity transgresses Galactic Law.

"I refer you to the document itself, namely, page three which begins a very introductory, I'm told, discussion and mathematical demonstration of velocity-based and gravitational time dilation."

Captain Chase swiped at the virtual doc. "Can you see it, Professor? Shall I magnify?"

"No," said Professor Wilhelm. "I can see it. And I didn't understand it the first time I saw it, so it hardly matters. It's like a page from a mathematics textbook. But this Ganesh character intrigues me – I want to hear him talk this through." She gestured dismissively at the image.

Ganesh scrolled through the document, pausing at the paragraph headers. "Here we have a diagram that illustrates the simple geometric method for deriving the time dilation observed by two bodies in constant relative motion to each other. Some of us may recall this stationary and moving mirror example from our school days – the photon is seen bouncing back and forth between the mirrors. In the stationary reference frame, the photon travels the distance D and in the moving reference frame, the photon is moving horizontally as well as vertically, hence the greater value of D – the photon must travel further in the same amount of time. All this coincides with the principles of invariant light speed and relativity – the two reference frames, one stationary and one moving, are equally valid pictures of the universe and we are not in fact describing two separate events with two different values for elapsed time - one here and one there – but indeed a single event.

"As we scroll down we see the calculations for time dilation based on the Pythagorean theorem and simple algebra giving us the well-known Lorenz factor ratio: delta t-prime equals delta t over the square root of one minus v-squared over c-squared. Further along, the Twin Paradox is addressed – that we observe time slowing down for all objects we're moving relative to - and so on, until towards the end of this section we arrive at the combined effects of mass and motion time dilation.

"I dare say I'm not a scientist, let alone a mathematician, "but I can assure everyone that the veracity of the mathematics and technical descriptions have been vetted by our scientists. The remainder of the document discusses in greater detail the more formidable aspects of the science as well as the technological requirements for exotic matter and negative mass-energy – the foundations of metric engineering and wormhole design that we are more or less familiar with today.

"Which brings us to the conclusion. Which is a remarkable one." Ganesh closed his virtual doc and readdressed the camera. "It presents hitherto unknown solutions for the difficulties of back-reaction and, most ominously, the navigation of the redshift horizon."

The Captain tapped the mute button. "Yeah, yeah, Ganesh." He slouched in his chair, rubbing his face. "So, Z was right. Back-reaction. Redshift horizon. I swear it was over a year ago Z came to me with the idea that the Molemen, of all things, were up to something like this. He convinced me to help him with the analysis and get the conclusions published and it's these same bureaucratic asshole gatekeepers at the PMC and everywhere else we submitted it that wouldn't listen to us." He glanced at the Professor. "Excuse my French, Professor."

"Not at all, Captain," said the Professor.

Neutic watched her flash her large eyes and pull her hair back from her face, the fine bones in her wrists and hands, the tasteful bangles she wore, and her well-manicured fingers an interesting contradiction to the

Captain's coarseness. The woman's beauty, in person, especially, struck him as remarkable. She was perhaps younger than his mother but then again, perhaps not. And how was it that she suffered her lameness – was it an injury or was she born with it? Beyond all that, she seemed formidable if only because of the sharpness of her intelligence or something about the power of her mind that seemed always to be operating behind the scenes, or the scenery, as it were, of her inarguably authentic charisma.

The Captain sat up in a huff. "I need this Ganesh fellow to just get on with whatever it is he thinks we don't already know."

Ganesh continued as if on cue. "Yes. Unquestionably remarkable. In fact, according to scientific experts within the T.E., the level of engineering involved is, in a word, revelatory, and implies that the Molemen have harnessed the technology to penetrate, traverse and potentially manipulate the expanding region of space-time or, more accurately, that portion of potential cosmological reality that the universe expands into - that which it generates *as* it expands. In short, it appears the Molemen have shattered conventional hyper-dimensional science and engineered a new physics. More spectacularly, they have gained mastery over the past, present and future.

"Be assured, the GTA, Time Guard, T.E. and PMC have issued joint sanctions against both the Molemen and Mothmen calling for public disclosure of their science and cosmo-political intentions and allowing for immediate on-site access to their technologies by inspectors from each of the organizations represented here today. Please reference your information packages for the full documentation of the transparency transgression cited within the mandate of Galactic Law.

"What else, then, is to be done? What is the responsibility of this Special Council? What ought to comprise our communiqué? To begin with, I'm proposing a root cause analysis aimed at discovering the motivations of the Mothmen and the Molemen and the nature of the crime against time that is unfolding before us. Why are these two otherwise culturally disparate civilizations cooperating? Do the Mothmen somehow identify with the Molemen having salvaged their civilization in the face of the tragedy of their dying sun? Are they impressed with the technology? The Mothmen sun is not dying. But their culture – perhaps it is. Otherwise, why is their cooperation hinging on subversive Moleman HDT experimentation? What's in it for each of them? That is to say, if the Mothmen seek HDT technology from the Molemen, what do the Molemen seek in return? Anything? What do they want from each other?

"Meanwhile, the GTA nations have been advised to secure their time-space borders and activate their defense protocols at the Orange Level – pre-military preparedness. And the evidence within the HDOFs – the evidence we've obtained regarding all four of the SnoGlobeCon gatherings themselves - is undergoing a root cause analysis in mythological as well as technological contexts. What little we know of the Mothmen ideology – its aversion to time-space manipulation and its overt spirituality, for example – seems to boldly contradict that of the Molemen, which is a culture keen to advance their technological prowess virtually without bounds. However, things change. Cultures transform. For any number of reasons. The PMC, of course, is best situated to analyze the mythological contingencies, which we naturally believe to encompass all the others. We are reminded, therefore, specifically, of one of the most steadfast truths identified by comparative mythology scholarship. I quote:

> The image of the cosmos must change with the development
> of the mind and knowledge; otherwise, the mythic statement
> is lost, and man becomes dissociated from the very basis of his
> own religious experience. Doubt comes in, and so forth. You
> must remember: all of the great traditions, and little traditions,
> in their own time were scientifically correct. That is to say, they
> were correct in terms of the scientific image of that age.[ae]

"The Mothmen, then, have perhaps established for themselves a new mythological age based upon new science – the science of the times, in so many words, the science of the Molemen, ironically enough, which at this point, frighteningly, has outstripped even our own. The PMC has coined the term 'Mythological Revitalization Initiative,' hereafter MRI, to encapsulate the behavior of a culture undergoing a peak period of otherwise proactive transformation – that which amounts to a wholesale 'overhaul' of their spiritual, cosmological, sociological and psychological mythological functions.

"In short, it may be that the Mothmen are reaching out, for perhaps the first time in their deeply mysterious history, to preempt what they arguably regard as the End Time, a cosmologically mandated, otherwise inevitable end of a world age that would, in classic mythological terms at least, demand a wholesale decline and disintegration of their civilization. Ostensibly in preparation for its rebirth in a new form. This cycle of creation and destruction defines the world view of untold numbers of cultures throughout the cosmos. Recall Greece's Hesiod, Norse Ragnarök, Christian Six Ages, Hindu Yuga, Buddhist Three Ages, Mesoamerican Five Suns, etcetera as examples merely from our own planet.

"But what if a culture refuses the outcome? That is, what if the Mothmen have rejected the perceived inevitability of their cultural disintegration and have taken action to prevent it? What if they have initiated an MRI? Furthermore, what if that MRI isn't localized? What if the Mothmen, for the first time, seek cosmo-political influence beyond their borders?

"Allow me to summarize the position of the PMC. Namely, that there are in cultural terms only two interpretations of time: namely, a cyclical one and a linear one. Time cycles or it progresses. Time is a circle or an arrow, so to say. These are the world views. What if a culture, then, decides to reject its mythologically resonant cosmology – namely, the outcome of it and engage in an MRI? What if it desires to keep the beginning and the middle and reject the end? The end being a legitimately fearful one?

"That is to say, what if the Mothmen recognize their decline, their cultural weakening, and seek to empower, re-empower or reinvent themselves via incorporation of a new technology otherwise anathema to their beliefs? If you can't beat them, join them – it's a trite aphorism with a ring of truth to it. For the Mothmen to reach out to the Molemen, or vice versa – we can only begin to fathom the details of this dynamic – it would seem a desperate, perhaps illogical, even preposterous gambit. At least for the Mothmen.

"For the Molemen, in the un-official opinion of the PMC, are the most unpredictable, cosmo-politically obstinate, ethically dubious, mythologically unsympathetic and technologically intimidating engineering experts – geniuses – in the universe. Molemen engineering is unmatched and now in fact poised to allow them to rule the cosmos. Hence, a Mothman-Moleman alliance is a categorical threat to the CTA. It demonstrates a time crime of pan-galactic proportions. It threatens the well-being of the universe and everyone in it."

"Excuse me, Mr. Ganesh," said the Professor.

Ganesh looked surprised. "I'm sorry? Did somebody -" – he frowned at his monitor – "oh, yes, Professor Wilhelm. I'm sorry, did you have a question?"

"No," said the Professor. She scooted her chair closer to the table, seemingly keen to take her time and did not acknowledge Ganesh's pointed gaze. "I don't have a question. Rather, I would like to clarify the position of the PMC on the subject of time. On behalf of which, it seems to me, sir, you've allowed yourself some liberties."

Ganesh sat stiffly.

"There is a third world view. Some cultures, yes, interpret time as cyclical, as in a sense recurring, whereas others indeed regard it as linear, as you say, pointing most often towards a form of enlightenment or potential, human potential, an ultimate age. But the third world view that we must consider as a possibility on behalf of the Mothmen, for example, is epicyclical."

"Epicyclical," repeated Ganesh.

"Indeed." The Professor finally glanced at him. "Akin to the rotation of a planet, say, within its larger orbit around a sun. Or of a solar system orbiting the center of a galaxy."

"Well, yes," said Ganesh, "those are cycles within cycles, but still a cycle overall."

"Unless," said the Professor, "one considers the movement, the linear progression, of that planet's solar system and its galaxy within the context of the expanding universe."

Ganesh blinked at the screen.

"So that time is an arrow pulling the cycling ages along with it." Here the Professor seemed to relent in her otherwise obliquely barbed remarks. "But this is no place for a debate. Let me volunteer, then, Mr. Ganesh, in my dual capacities of influence within both the PMC and the TDC, to lead an analysis of the mythology - of the motives in the form of cultural imperatives that may underlie these SnoGlobeCon events."

"Well, in that case, certainly, Professor, you are more than welcome to assist -"

"Assist, yes, Mr. Ganesh, and to lead, as I said, the analysis of the Fold data in comparative mythological terms. In fact, I'm looking forward to presenting our findings first off, as the lead topic of the next Special Council. We can assume that will appear on the agenda you're going to be forwarding, can we not?"

Mircea Ganesh nodded. "Yes ma'am. I'm sorry, yes, Professor, indeed." He removed a handkerchief from his jacket pocket, wiped his brow and drank from his water glass.

The Captain, for his part, seemed bemused. "He seems to have run out of things to distract him from getting to the heart of the matter," said the Captain, "to anything new. If he *has* anything new. Otherwise this so-called Special Council is going to become just another –"

Just then the image changed, panning back as if the camera operator suddenly intended to get a wider view. They watched someone enter the frame and lean down to speak urgently into Ganesh's ear. He nodded, the messenger hurried away, and Ganesh began again, the frame once again closing in on his face. He was preternaturally distracted, unable or unwilling to address the camera for a moment.

Finally, he collected himself. "My sincere apologies. Developments compel me to break at this point. Let's say we resume at half past – that's twenty minutes. Again, thank you for your attention to this point," and he got up, his fingers pressed to his earpiece, his papers tucked under his arm.

"Mr. Z. should be here."

Professor Wilhelm's voice snapped Captain Chase out of his focus.

"Only if he's not allowed to comment." The Captain glanced wryly at Neutic. "Neutic knows I'm only half serious, Professor, I apologize."

"Hmm, well, I'd be interested in Mr. Z.'s impression of Mr. Ganesh, I have to say. But perhaps I ought to apologize for giving Mr. Ganesh a little bit of a hard time. He's a fairly new hire to the PMC and while I don't know much about him, it seems to me he's risen very rapidly through the ranks, as they say. And I didn't appreciate his, well, I've said enough."

"Liberties," said Neutic.

The Professor smiled. "Yes." She sighed as if to clear the air. "Captain, I think Mr. Neutic ought to run interference for us when it comes to Mr. Ganesh."

The Captain seemed lost in thought, slouched in his chair, his arm outstretched indifferently on the tabletop.

"Captain?" said the Professor.

He looked up. "Hmm? Oh. Yes. Neutic. He can run interference, certainly." He tapped his fingers on the tabletop and sat up, rubbing his face.

The Professor regarded him closely. It seemed to her that the strain of the last twenty-four hours had taken its toll on the Captain's health. The news that Mr. Z. had initiated a rogue HDT to nineteenth century Egypt, coupled with the surprise of the Special Council, was indeed much to endure on top of the Olympic Theater investigation itself. She noticed his eyes were red-rimmed, his countenance drawn, haggard. She considered asking him how he was holding up but decided against it. "How long have you been with the TDC, Captain? I understand you're retired from the military?"

The Captain responded flatly. "Nineteen years. I'd planned on re-enlisting. I liked the Army. And I'd been toying with the idea of becoming a military lawyer. But it didn't work out. The TDC turned out to be more up my alley, anyway."

The Professor raised her eyebrows. "That's interesting. And Mr. Z., how long has he worked for you?"

The Captain furrowed his brow and scratched chin. "Ten years? Thereabouts." He sighed and sunk back into his seat, glowering. "There's unconventional and then there's Mr. Z." He shook his head and shut his eyes as if he were exasperated. "But the man gets things done, I'll give him that. I've never met a more uncompromising –" He sighed heavily. "Hell, he's my best TD. And he's right, you know, as much as I hate to admit it, regarding the EIB."

"How so?"

"We'd never have obtained authorization to EIB Vixy's transponder. Let alone the authorization or funding for a search and rescue mission. Her status doesn't warrant it. I hate the protocol as much as anyone but limits have to exist. If the TDC devoted all their resources to every cold case file, well, there wouldn't be any TDC. Cadets-in-training and their families, they're made fully aware of the risks prior to enlistment." The Captain had begun toying with his transponder.

"Any word?" said the Professor.

"Hmm?" He turned toward her blankly.

"On your rogue charge? On Mr. Z.'s status? Has he been located or tracked?"

"No. Nothing. Not yet."

The camera once again panned back and a large, forthright-looking man with a broad, fleshy, ruddy-cheeked face and bushy, lamb-chop-style side-burns strode into the frame, reluctantly taking the chair. He ran a kerchief over his gleaming bald pate and cleared his throat.

The Captain, Professor and Neutic exchanged wide-eyed glances.

"What the hell is the Viceroy doing here?" said the Captain.

The Viceroy's voice boomed. "Hello, everyone. For those of you who do not know me, I am Jarok Kamelian, Viceroy of the PMC. Unfortunately, Mr. Ganesh will be unable to return as he has been called away on urgent business. Without full membership participation, then, tonight's Special Council must be terminated. All of you will be contacted regarding a rescheduling. On behalf of the PMC, I apologize for the gross inconvenience. You are invited to submit inquiries via electronic media. Good day." He rose hastily and disappeared off screen before the image went blank.

The Captain tapped at his transponder. "Let's get out of here. Our own TDC confab starts in a couple of hours anyway. He rose and lolled his head, stretching his neck, his voice strained from the exertion. "First the Olympic Theater. Then Vixy. Then Mr. Z." He sighed heavily. "Now, we can add this mess between the Molemen and Mothmen to the agenda. And we can't even manage to convene a Special Council to help resolve it. Neutic, I need to find some damn strong coffee, I'm not kidding. Otherwise, I swear I'm going straight to the bar across the street. Professor? Needless to say, we're still going to need your help."

# CHAPTER 21

# THE ROLLING IRON BALL

**EMPEROR CHANGPU**[61] rested quietly upon his favorite couch, absorbed in his reading. Old furniture. Old books. They were his solace. And guidance. The couch, its railings crafted expertly of intertwined roots, burnished by centuries of use, comforted him simply by way of its humble rusticity. It spoke to him of the wisdom inherent in the earth. The book, by comparison, was ancient - thousands of years old – an off-planet text he'd stumbled across one evening as he wandered the deep halls of the vast Imperial Archives. He'd been confounded by its title, *The King and the Corpse,* in which this Zimmer fellow retells the myth of King Conn of Ireland and Queen Eda of Brittany whose marriage "was a union so perfect that it equaled that of Heaven and Earth." He turned the synthetic paper page.

> The historians declare that the perfection of their character and conduct was reflected in the blessings of their reign: "the earth produced exuberant crops and the trees ninefold fruit; rivers,

---

61 The meaning of Mothmen names mirrors that of the Chinese. Changpu, then, implies, "forever simple."

lakes, and the sea teemed with choice fish; the herds and the flocks were unusually prolific."

Such descriptions of natural abundance are not unusual in the legends of beneficent reigns; for when two faultless rulers conform to the divine law of the universe and guide their people by their own model conduct, they bring into operation the quickening power of perfection. The consummate king and queen make manifest together what the Chinese term *Tao:* the virtue of the universal order. They make *Tao* manifest as *Teh:* the virtue of their own proper nature. And this virtue is self-effulgent. Its influence penetrates like magic into the vital centers of everything around them, so that even the spirit of the land appears to be affected. Harmony and beatitude go out from it. The fields produce, the herds multiply, and the cities thrive, as in a Golden Age.[af]

Emperor Changpu closed the book, clutched at the couch rail to help haul himself up and strode to the window. He leaned forward with his elbows on the windowsill, looking out. If only life could be as orderly and well-pruned and handsome as the Imperial orchards. The dark, damp trees seemed to gather the mist about their trunks like noblewomen gathering their robes. Ah, the peach blossoms. Ah, the plums. Ah, the pears, all in bloom. And the cherry blossoms – the people's favorite. Such delicate, effeminate beauty. He himself, meanwhile, preferred the knobby old apple trees, awkward and unpretty even in bloom. So difficult to tend. Reluctant to produce fruit. But oh, the fruit when it came! The biting tartness and brilliant sweetness – if one could make wine from the autumn sunlight it would taste no better than the flesh of the Imperial apples!

But it was only spring. And spring was late. The gray sky seemed low, the forlorn blossoms shuddering at each gust of chilly wind, the petals scattering onto the saturated earth, incongruous against the cruel patches of snow. The rolling iron ball came to mind, something he'd read about elsewhere in that curious book. In the story, a strange, human-headed bird assigns King Conn the guardianship of a rolling iron ball. Easy enough to discern, such a symbol, thought the Emperor. That of Nature. And one's true nature. The iron ball, comprised of inherently worldly components, rolls along on its own, like Nature does, and we eschew following it at our peril.

But what of other men, other races? If they are of Nature, as they must be – behold the sagacity within that alien book of his, after all - what of their true nature? It seemed as if he'd been studying the idea for a lifetime and that many more lifetimes would bring him no closer to an understanding, to disclosing the mystery of why men differ so within their natural sameness.

The Emperor drew his vestments about him and shivered. "I do not like to see the blossoms being torn from the trees. It is like a betrayal."

"We *are* betrayed," said Advisor Feng.[62]

The Emperor started at the sound of Feng's voice but did not betray his surprise. He squinted at the leaden sky. Feng too often managed to sneak up on him and interrupt his meditations. "One would think the heavens were displeased."

"Your Excellency," said Feng, "did you not hear me? We are betrayed. Betrayed by the Molemen. Because of their incompetence and stupidity, we now suffer the prying attentions of the cosmos."

The Emperor turned his back to the window and shuffled towards the dais; the clack, clack, clack of his wooden sandals on the stones accentuating his stiff gait. He paused upon the landing of each step, Feng at his side, supporting his elbow, until he'd attained his throne and sat down.

"What is the status of our initiate?"

"Unknown, your Excellency," said Advisor Shan.[63]

"Still no word...," the Emperor trailed off. He frowned. "Ping's[64] disappearance coincides with my vision of the animal avatar." He scratched

---

[62] Feng means "sharp blade."

[63] Shan means "mountain."

[64] Ping means "stable."

at his chin whiskers then smoothed them against the fabric of his robe. "Twenty-four hours and no word." He inhaled deeply and exhaled loudly, puffing his cheeks and furrowing his brow, his expression dark. He eyed each of his advisors in turn, his hand on the hilt of his sword. "Presumed dead."

He looks like a catfish or a ridiculous monkey when he does that, thought Feng. And he's perhaps as dull-witted. Must emperors always be such fools? He affected his most attentive, compliant tone. "Pardon me, your Excellency, but we cannot be certain."

"Certain enough, I'd say," said Advisor Chung.[65] The old warrior stood with his legs apart, leaning with both hands upon his cane, the position that best eased the pain in his bowed legs – so many years upon the horses. He addressed the group. "With all due respect, the court has rather relied upon the Emperor's visions to our advantage for longer than Advisor Feng has been alive." He bowed his head at the Emperor.

Feng bristled, biting his tongue, tapping his folded fan against the palm of his hand once, twice, then clutching it tightly. "I apologize, your Excellency. It is not my intention to dismiss the importance of your sage-like visions. But without valid, scientific verification of the transponder data, well, initiate Ping may still be –"

"You insist upon placing your faith in the Molemen technology, Feng," said the Emperor sharply. "Meanwhile, the earthling, Mr. Z., survives. Under the protection of the wolf, no less. We continue to underestimate him, do we not? This so-called time detective?" He eyed his advisors. "We dismiss the oracle at our peril. A two-headed hawk was foretold. And all my advisors – Feng, Chung, Shan, Ru,[66] Ming-tun[67] – all of you, dismissed it as impossible. As a misinterpretation by the Empress. Wilhelm, each of you agreed, was the hawk. Z. merely the means to her. And therefore a suitable test for Ping. Well, Z. has turned out to be more than a suitable test for young Ping. Anyone with the power to summon such a beast – the wolf – it surpasses even the skills of our priests." He dug his fingers into the ornamental armrests of

[65] Chung means "intelligent."
[66] Ru means "scholar."
[67] Ming-tun means "intelligent, heavy."

his throne – carved heads of lions with broad, snarling visages in the Oriental style – and glared at each of them. "Ping has failed. *We* have failed. Again. Why? What is the source of our incompetence?"

Advisor Chung met the Emperor's gaze. Shan, Ru and Ming-tun avoided it.

Feng, keen to stand apart from the others, glared at all of them, clutching his fan tightly. Cowards. Hypocrites. Struggling to protect their puny positions. Not a leader amongst them. Besides Chung, the Emperor's favorite. And Chung was old. And as ruined as warped wood. Chung of the watery eyes and knees as decrepit as those of the Emperor's – must all old warriors hobble about so disagreeably?

"Indeed, your Excellency," said Chung, "we are suffering now for endorsing the Molemen prerogatives, knowing as we did that theirs was an agenda so contrary to our own." He directed an unsubtle glance at Feng and watched the younger man straighten. Look at him, he thought. He does his best to ignore me and only enhances his own impudence.

"Prerogatives, indeed," said the Emperor. "We have become entangled in a loathsome compromise with heathenish brutes, ignorant of the Way."

"Nevertheless, your Excellency," said Feng, "the compromise expedited our acquisition of the technology."

"HDT, indeed. And now we are condemned to suffer the intrusion of the unenlightened masses, to endure the peering eyes of the spiritually vacant whom the Mothmen have done well to eschew for millennia. Now, not only the hubristic Molemen but the misbegotten beings of Earth pry into our lives – cultures for which the Arrow of Time is a triviality, a plaything, an irrelevancy and not the divine imperative we know it to be. In so doing it is we ourselves – Mothmen at least as much as Molemen – who have transgressed the Way, who have violated natural law, who have tempted fate and thus hindered the changes."

I would lop off their heads, thought Feng, all of them; standing there biting their tongues, feigning their loyalty, accomplishing nothing. Likewise the Emperor with his tired body and tired ideas. The changes? Nonsense words from an ancient text. A text that other backward, ignorant planets besides that of Earth have misinterpreted as wisdom instead of frivolity. Oracles? His reliance upon the superstitions of his wife is what has hindered our recovery, let alone our advancement. Mythology is a lie. He compromises the supremacy of the Realm by way of contaminating the future with the past. He sees nothing of the universe with his face in a book and his mind on worthless divinations. He is blind to the changes with his eyes wide open. The only changes to divine are the hard facts.

"We covet the wealth and power of another nation and by so doing relinquish our own," said the Emperor. "Observe our failure at the T.E. The Professor lives. We who nurture the power to yoke the mind were thwarted. And now Eranos. Again, failure. The superior man does not doggedly pursue the way that has proven inauspicious."

The Emperor scowled and stood up, gathered his vestments about him, repositioned his sword and tightened his sash. He descended the dais and stood upon the last, broad step. "Advisors Shan and Ming-tun, ready the hyper-dimensional transport. Advisors Chung and Ru, coordinate the selection of a higher-level initiate – a proven assassin. Intercept the time detective Z and kill him. Fail me again and you all will appease the Way with your lives. Except you, Advisor Feng."

Ah, thought Feng, finally I'm regarded with due respect. He cultivated an air of superiority as he watched Shan, Ming-tun and Chung all bow, side-by-side, retreat several steps and turn to hasten from the room.

"Wait," said the Emperor. "All of you."

They stopped, turned and bowed, heads down.

The Emperor glanced at Feng.

"Your Excellency?" Feng stood tapping his fan against his open palm, his chin cocked slyly in the direction of the others while he narrowed his eyes at the Emperor.

"You, Advisor Feng, will attend the SnoGlobeCon as planned. Except this time Advisor Chung's assassin will accompany you." The Emperor waited until the silence compelled them to glance up. "See to it, Chung." The Emperor held them all in place by merely raising his finger, returning his attention to Feng. "Advisor Feng, use your influence to gain access to the leadership sanctum. Confiscate the remaining strategic intelligence and technological data of the Molemen engineers and kill them."

Feng looked astonished. "Kill them? Your Excellency, please. Interpretation of the hyper-dimensional technology requires continued political cooperation and strategic diplomacy, otherwise –"

The Emperor silenced Feng with a gesture of his hand. "For someone so enamored of the hard facts, Advisor Feng, there are none harder and better to appreciate than those of men's deaths."

Feng blanched and nearly dropped his fan.

The Emperor had already stepped down and was making his way towards the door, clack, clack, clack across the ancient stones, pausing to peer once again through the courtyard window into the orchard. He sighed, his expression wistful, his voice low. "A forbidding spring. Cold and windy. My poor blossoms. It will require all the skill of the Imperial gardeners to ensure the trees shall still bear fruit."

*And so every one of us shares the supreme ordeal – carries the cross of the redeemer – not in the bright moments of his tribe's great victories, but in the silences of his personal despair.*[ag]

# CHAPTER 22

# VAULT OF HEAVEN

**THERE IT IS! TWO KILOMETERS DISTANT.** Five pried his trek-goggles from his face – he could almost discern the Red Pyramid without them.

The sun had set an hour ago and the moon wouldn't rise until twenty-one-hundred forty-five hours, at seventy degrees east-northeast. No matter. He was frankly glad to be alone with the stars. Home was out there. And he wanted so desperately to be home. He even looked forward in a way to the unpleasantness of the wormhole, to the familiarity of the technology, at least; to anything associated with his departure from this miserable planet and the interminable wasteland of this confounded desert.

He forced himself to get up, draping himself in the shadow-tarp. Shrouding himself in the open desert was a clumsy solution but with his cloaking circuitry down what else could he do besides dig a shallow burrow and lay low? No more bivouacs. Too much exertion. Save your strength. He tried to stretch his legs but doing so only made his muscles seem somehow more depleted. Get moving. He shook out the tarp, folded it and stuffed it into his pack, surprised to discover his book laying on the ground. "That's right, you idiot, of all things leave your damn book behind." He blew the dust from the spine and the edges of the pages, smoothed his hand over the cover. With all its scuffs and scrapes it looked as travel weary as he felt.

He stuffed the book into his pack and adjusted his *tob* – best to remain at least semi-disguised as he approached the Pyramid. He scanned the desert, allowing himself a tinge of sentiment: this place and time – he'd never experience it again. Too bad the leave-no-trace protocol permitted no unauthorized photographs. *An HDT memory is not like normal memory.* More wisdom from his cadet training. *It's more akin to a memory of a dream,* they'd been told; *the images more remote and difficult to retain than even everyday experiences. As the years go by it becomes more and more like it never happened to you.* Maybe. Maybe, too, he ought to write it all down when he got back. Yes. The idea bolstered his resolve and he gathered himself for his last push, donning his trek goggles and tightening his pack straps. It was then that he noticed something moving across the desert to the southeast. He adjusted his magnification. Approximately a kilometer distant. A camel and two riders. A man behind and a woman in the saddle. He increased resolution. "Hell and blood," he muttered, "it can't be."

The ragged, deteriorated architecture of the Red Pyramid came into view. To Vixy it appeared humble and inelegant, entirely lacking the charisma of anything on the Plateau. "It definitely looks like a ruin."

"There's something out there," said Hesso, gesturing towards the otherwise empty desert; "somebody on foot. Do you see?"

"I see *something*." She peered out, trying to focus in the low light. "Wait. Yes." She and Hesso exchanged glances.

"He can't be more than a kilometer off," said Hesso and kicked at Deloua's ribs. "*Yalla!*" The camel snorted and lurched into a ground-covering trot. "*Yalla*, Deloua!"

She watched the lone figure, curiously short and broad, wearing an ill-fitting *tob*, striding hard across the sand. That's him, she thought, it has to be. Unmistakable except for – she squinted hard into the starlit night – *ears?*

He redoubled his pace, hurrying along – *maybe they haven't noticed.* He fumbled with his cloak control – switching it on and off, smacking it against his thigh – *just when he needed the damn thing most!* What were they doing out here – what was anybody doing in this part of the desert? He shed his pack and made to shift through his gear for his *kufeya*. It didn't matter. They were practically upon him. Of all things, the irony of it, to be discovered in the last hour, so close to freedom. *Don't panic. No need to tell them anything. What will they make of my looks? Just keep moving. Get to the Pyramid, get to the HDT nexus. There's nothing they can do to stop me.*

"Whoa!" Hesso brought Deloua up short, the camel fighting the rein as he leapt clear. "Easy!" Deloua settled and Hesso reached to help Vixy dismount. She slid into his arms and onto the sand. And suddenly there they all were, the three of them and the camel, virtually face to face, regarding each other warily in the open desert.

Look at them staring at me. I'm a fool for not wearing the *kufeya.* He ran his hand over his ears and tried to move on.

Hesso jumped in front of him. "By the devil." His eyes were wide, his astonishment making him appear almost childlike with wonder. He glanced at Vixy then back at Five.

Vixy smoothed the folds of her robe as if mustering her courage. How could she not have understood that Mister Five was... it seemed impossible. "You're a Moleman."

Five waited, staring back at her, waiting for something to come to him – some plan, some solution. How would he rid himself of them? He glanced at Hesso, at the camel, then Vixy. *Think.* When he reached towards his neck to engage his auto-translator, Hesso stepped forward protectively, his hand on the hilt of his knife.

Slowly, thought Five, do everything slowly, deliberately. He lowered his hand.

"Moleman," said Hesso flatly. "Praise Allah, I have never seen the likes of it."

"Hesso," said Five. "Miss Vixy." He nodded as a kind of affected courtesy.

"You can speak?" said Hesso, his voice tinged with suspicion. "But your voice –"

"He's using an auto-translator, Hesso," said Vixy. "It's a machine that translates what he's saying from his language into ours."

Hesso looked dubious and exasperated at once.

"Excuse me, please," said Five, "but I must be going." Again he tried to move on and again Hesso blocked his way.

"No," said Hesso.

Five remained silent, determined not to indulge in conversation. He held out an absurd hope that this ridiculous encounter would play itself out harmlessly. If only he could think of something to do about it.

My God, thought Vixy, is this what a Moleman really looks like? She'd seen images – illustrations, supposedly authentic photographs, but nothing could have prepared her for this, her first face-to-face experience with a member of an alien race. Besides the Moleman's absurdly large, pan-shaped ears – ears that wavered and twitched expressively, seemingly in all directions, that seemed attuned to everything at once – were his enormous, goggled eyes. And his face: roundish, with a stubby nose, his jaw and the lower half of his mouth obscured by something that resembled a kind of chin-guard. His lips were full and ruby-red even in the bluish light of the night sky. But it was his flesh – the flesh of his face and neck that astonished her – it was unnaturally pale, ghostly white and strangely radiant – at certain angles a luminous, red-tinged aura seemed to emanate from it. A shiny tassel of thick, black hair cascaded from between his ears onto his forehead. "Mister Five," she said, as if speaking his name would somehow make sense of him.

He blinked at her.

She glanced at Hesso. Then back to Five. The Moleman seemed as much at a loss as she and Hesso.

"In the name of Allah," said Hesso, "you must convince me I am not dreaming. This is Mister Five?" He rubbed his chin fitfully.

"I don't know what to say," said Vixy, addressing Hesso and Five at once.

"This is indeed a fascinating coincidence," said Five. "But I must be on my way."

"To the Red Pyramid?" said Hesso.

Calm, thought Five, be calm. Don't reveal anything. But how could they know his destination? His mind raced. What else did they know? He shifted his pack. "Let me pass. Please."

Hesso stood his ground. "You shall *not* pass. Who are you? What are you doing here? What do you want with the Red Pyramid? Why did you leave the canopic chest behind at Giza? And three of the jars?" Hesso glared at him. "Why?"

Questioning me, thought Five. What to do? The Red Pyramid, so close. He felt panicked. "I must go. Please. Both of you. Why will you not allow me to proceed?" He reached behind him for his defense kit.

Hesso withdrew his knife, the curved blade glinting. "By the grace of God, Mister Five, I advise you to remain where you are."

"Hesso!" said Vixy. It struck her that this Moleman must have a transponder of some type. If he were trying to get home – it was crazy, but was there a way he could help get *her* home? She tried to recall Bab's imperative. *Stop him*, he'd told them. "Answer him, Mister Five. Explain yourself." She went to the camel and reached for Hesso's sabre. "Here, Hesso."

Five placed his hands at his sides and forced himself to speak slowly, calmly. "Forgive me. In my haste, I have been inconsiderate." He glanced back and forth between them, keen to make eye contact, trying his best to follow rules-of-engagement protocol as he'd learned it, though he frankly

328 • TIME CRIME

felt compelled to... no, not yet. "You may call me Five. That is my proper name. Regarding the canopic chest and the jars? I had no use for them."

"But you nonetheless kept a jar," said Hesso. "And it is impossible for me to believe, looking at you, hearing you talk – well, you are no collector of antiquities. You are not human. What do you want with such a thing as a canopic jar?"

I can't kill them. I won't kill them. "Please, is there something I can do for you?"

"Yes," said Vixy. "There are exactly three things." It was as if the preposterousness of the situation – being face-to-face with a Moleman in the Nile Valley in 1881 – had reawakened her intuitions as a time detective. Observe. Draw a person out, get them to reveal themselves. Intimidate as a last resort. It was as if Mr. Z. were there beside her. Can you sweet talk a Moleman? "Number one," she said, "you can explain what you're doing, here, why you're on Earth in 1881 Egypt." Too harsh. Her damn nerves. She tried to soften her tone, whatever good it would do. "Number two, what do you want with the jar? Three, I want you to help me get home, to help me get back to the future. You've got HDT resources – a transponder, some device, you must have. Show me."

Five flexed his hands, opening and closing his fists.

"Well?" said Vixy. She turned to rummage through Deloua's saddle bag, thrusting Bab's box at Five. "Here. You remember Bab, don't you? Bruggs's dragoman? Well, he's the one who told us that you were on your way to the Red Pyramid. That you were trying to get home. He told me to give you this. Take it."

Five remained with his hands at his sides. Bab? He'd been careful never to reveal anything to the man - how could he possibly have discerned his plan? And what could he possibly want to give him? They all know too much. All of them. The sense of everything unravelling was a torture. But none of it mattered. He had to go, that's all. He had to get home. He was about to reach for his defense kit when Vixy tossed the box at his feet.

"You saved my life," she said. "In the camp. Why?"

Five moved slowly and carefully to unfasten his pack, pausing when Hesso stiffened, holding his hands in plain sight to calm the man, finally allowing the pack to fall from his shoulders onto the sand. He removed his *tob*, wadded it up unceremoniously and stuffed it into his pack. "I no longer possess the jar. Just as I no longer have need of this disguise." Then he stooped to retrieve the box, being careful to make all his movements deliberate. He regarded it for a moment, his ears twitching at the faint scratching within. He slid the lid open and shook its contents onto the sand.

Vixy flinched.

Hesso furrowed his brow at it.

"Scorpion," said Five. "Death-stalker."

The little beast raised its stinger as if on cue and scurried backwards.

"A yellow arrow," said Vixy. "That's what Bab called it."

Five blinked at her.

A slip of paper suddenly fluttered from the box and drifted across the sand towards Hesso. He snatched it up, his tone ironic. "More scribbling between the moleman and the dragoman?" He peered at it, turning it back to front, and addressed Vixy. "It's nothing but a single word. Written in Arabic."

"What does it say, Hesso?" Vixy reached for it.

"Deliverance," said Five, clenching his fists.

Hesso stared at Five, taken aback.

Vixy's glance darted back and forth between them. "Hesso?"

"He's right."

Vixy and Hesso regarded Five anew. Free of his disguise, he appeared even more alien: humanoid yet utterly unfamiliar in proportion. His most remarkable feature, besides that of his large head, outsized ears and mysterious, luminous, pale skin were his enormous, gauntleted hands – they seemed to dominate his physique. The strange gloves extended up his forearms to the elbow, their oddly industrial sturdiness and synthetic sheen belied by their apparent suppleness – they seemed to function more like a second skin of sorts. He was otherwise attired in a kind of pantaloon style pant suit or jumper, the fabric adorned with broad, horizontal stripes.

330 • TIME CRIME

His chest and arms were sturdy, muscular. While his belly bulged forth like that of a Far East Buddha, drooping a bit below his otherwise high waist, giving the impression that he hadn't a groin to speak of, nor hips for that matter, unless somehow his leg joints attached in the vicinity of his ribcage, if he indeed possessed one. His voluminous slacks – the pantaloons, such as they were – rode high above his frilly hosiery and surprisingly diminutive, almost delicate feet, shod in what appeared to be incongruously slight slippers. The effect was of a beguiling clash between industrial, workmanlike utility, and exotic, vaguely androgynous elegance.

"I am sorry, but I cannot explain the canopic jar. Neither can I explain the arachnid. Nor the note. Most importantly, I cannot explain my presence here. Nor my intentions. Least of all am I capable of considering your interest in my HDT resources. All of it is my own affair. You must allow me to leave you in peace. You must allow me to be on my way."

"Deliverance," said Vixy, straining to keep her desperation in check. "What kind of deliverance?"

Five waited. Deliverance. The word troubled him. Bab himself troubled him, now more than ever. When they'd talked, briefly, on the miserable trek from the Sphinx to the mastabas, the man seemed to communicate only in symbols and riddles. *The hindrance has passed*, Bab had said, apropos of nothing. *Your deliverance has come.* This before he'd even mentioned needing help finding the relic. *The task of deliverance acts as a weapon against all that is false and low. Even in your own heart. Yellow is the measure and mean, the arrow the straight course. Hence, your reward.* Reward for what? And what did any of it have to do with Miss Vixy and Hesso? Dammit, as if he didn't have enough to worry about. He tried to force it all from his mind. Stick to the mission. Just get to the Red Pyramid and get home.

"Dammit, Five," continued Vixy, "I don't care about whatever it is between you and Bab. All I know is that you arrived here by way of hyper-dimensional transport and you will return to your own planet, your own space-time by the same mechanism. Your transport coordinates – your HDT nexus – is somewhere near the Red Pyramid, which is where you're headed now. You're going home. I want to go home. I was kidnapped by Bruggs and Laron and brought here and I've no way back. Bruggs is dead and I don't know where Laron is nor the whereabouts of their HDT equipment. I'm stranded. Lost. I don't belong here. I need to get home, just like you. You can help me. Please. You saved my life once. Why can't you help me again?"

"It is not my mission to help you. Moreover, you are a time detective."

Vixy endured the flat tone of the translator's voice box like a slap across her face. She stepped closer to the Moleman, her eyes flashing. "How would you know? And what of it? Why should time detectives concern you?"

Hesso grasped her arm and came between them.

"No, Hesso," she said, yanking her arm free. "What have you done, Five? What are you doing now? Why are you trying to get home? The Molemen Engineers, what have you to do with them? Answer me!"

Hesso turned to address Five himself. "You are unforthcoming, Five. It is as good as lying to us. This is *my* country. *My* time. *My* home, you see." He drew himself up and grasped the hilt of his saber. "Your plans, whatever they are, as of this moment have changed. You will return with us to Cairo and we will find Bab and both of you will explain yourselves to us or, God forgive me, I shall take you away from here by force and the consequences will be your own doing."

A discordant electronic squawk startled everyone, including Deloua – the camel flinched and lunged away from them, Hesso running after her, struggling to snatch her rein. "*Ala mahlak ya sadiq!*"[68] She reared at him, her lips curled back and her eyes wild. "Deloua!" He ducked from her flailing hooves, alternately giving ground to her then digging in, doing everything within his power to control her. "*Deloua!*"

Meanwhile, garbled voices issued forth from somewhere on Five's person, the language otherwise unintelligible, alien. At the same instant Five's auto-translator seemed to be attempting a spontaneous translation into English, spewing forth an almost incoherent mishmash of garbled

---

[68] "Take it easy friend."

verbiage and electronic static until a burst of something intelligible caught Vixy's attention: "Detonations at Giza... less than twenty-two hours.... Western Desert."

Five snatched at his pack, tearing at the closures, apparently desperate to get at the source of the communications. He flailed at the contents, flinging clothing and equipment across the sand. Another crackling voice, perhaps two broke in, the auto-translator blaring:

"Yessir.... Hold on.... Five. Five, do you copy? Dammit, Cog, the signal is open – abort the transmission, abort, do you hear? The signal is open!"

Five tore at his auto-translator and the communication and noise was cut off. He cast his pack to the ground indifferently, the disheveled contents strewn about him.

Hesso was still struggling with Deloua, the camel's eyes wild with fear. "Vixy, help me with her! Hold the rein, let me grab the bridle!"

Vixy snatched at the rein and held tight as Hesso leapt at the camel's bridle, grasping it tightly in both hands, using all his weight against her, digging his heels into the sand, cooing to her, *Ala mahlak ya sadiq,*" until finally the animal relented. Hesso stroked her neck, placed his hand gently upon her muzzle. The camel grunted softly, seemingly becalmed.

"My God," said Vixy, breathless.

"She is okay," said Hesso, speaking softly, stroking her. "The sound, it terrified her."

When they returned their attention to Five he was attempting to regather his things, shuffling about on the sand, brushing and shaking the objects free of dust and grit, replacing them one by one into his pack. When he'd finished he sighed heavily, fell to his knees and looked skyward, his shoulders slumped, as if beseeching the stars themselves.

"Detonations," said Vixy. "Giza. The Western Desert. Less than twenty-two hours. What does it mean, Five?" She glared at him. "What in the name of heaven are the Molemen doing here? What are *you* doing here?"

Five stared blankly past them.

"Answer me!" said Vixy. "Answer me or so help me...."

Hesso put his hand on her shoulder. "Vixy." He was watching Five intently.

Five sighed heavily. "There is nothing anyone can do to stop it."

"Stop what?" said Hesso. "Praise Allah, what are you talking about? Detonations. You mean explosions? An attack? A war? Here? Against Egypt?"

"Not a war," said Five. "An annihilation."

"Annihilation?" said Vixy.

"A cosmic rift," said Five.

"Do you mean to say the Molemen... that they've?" – Vixy couldn't help stammering – "That you've come here to destroy –"

"No one will suffer," said Five. "They will have no knowledge of it. Therefore, no fear. Instantaneous annihilation." He looked at them. "Suspension of space-time. The Earth will be stilled for eternity."

"You are crazy," said Hesso. "Insane." He looked desperately at Vixy. "All of this is crazy."

"Why?" said Vixy, raising her voice at Five. "Why do it? What do the Molemen want?" Five's indifference was making her hysterical. "What is it? Why won't you tell us!" She was almost screaming at him and then it struck her. "It's to do with the Pyramids, isn't it? Whatever it is, whatever you've come for, whatever you've done, whatever you're doing it's here, in this place, isn't it? Hesso," she said, struggling to calm herself. "You're right, Hesso. I think Five *is* crazy. And besides that, he's just a pawn, just a common soldier. He's nothing but a common terrorist." She spat the words out, her eyes flashing. "And now his mission, thanks to us, has become a suicide mission. Because he's not going to get home. Not if we can help it."

A knife glinted in Vixy's hand as she approached Five.

"Vixy," said Hesso; "Vixy don't...."

Five endured the words that fell upon him like a venomous rain, silent and still before the point of the dagger in Vixy's hand. Caustic, vicious, wounding words that seemed to crush his heart. Pawn. Common soldier. Terrorist.

"Vixy, stop," said Hesso.

"Earth must die so that all other civilizations may live." His pride emboldened him and the words seemed to come of their own accord, a recitation that came from deep within him. "Earth is to become, by way of the happenstance of its position in the fourth cosmic quadrant and its peculiar geophysical nature, the inaugural component of the Cosmic Clock Lattice. The engineering is miraculous, the technology, beautiful. We – the Molemen Engineers – have discovered the means, after millennia upon millennia of engineering, to control the fate of the cosmos, to control space-time; to engineer it according to our will, and our will alone." He stared back defiantly at them. What was left to hide from them? What trace would be left, what effect could it possibly have on anything now?

"By Allah you shall stop this thing," said Hesso – he withdrew his sabre – "or you shall die at my hand here and now."

Five stared Hesso in the face. "Allah. Ahura Mazda. Abraxas. Brahma. Buddha. Christ. Krishna. Vishnu. Yahweh. The Self. The All. The One. The Ten Thousand Things. The Way. The Tao. The Mystery. The Void." Five's goggles glinted in the starlight. "I know the names of your gods. But I came to Earth to complete my mission, to become a Moleman Engineer, like my father."

What happened next astonished them, for Five seemed to suddenly collapse under an unseen burden. He bent his head down and began teetering, swaying from side to side, wringing his hands together, the strange fabric creaking. They watched him throw his arms about himself, his giant hands clutching at his own shoulders, his body shuddering.

Crying, thought Vixy. I swear, of all things, he's sobbing. She struggled to believe it, to comprehend what was happening to this creature, this alien, to all of them. Everything up until now had skirted the unreal – her improbable trials, her kidnapping, her being lost in time, the assault, the EIB, the nightmare of it all. And now this terror - the supposed annihilation of the Earth at the hands of some megalomaniacal alien race long thought vanished. And Five its herald, such as he was. Five, who saved her life, suffering here on the sands of the Egyptian desert, enduring his own personal agony, an agony akin to her own.

A final astonishment came by way of the camel. In her unhurried, languid manner, she drifted towards Five. Towering over him she lowered her head to sniff his face. She sniffed at his ears and hands and nudged his fingers gently, almost tenderly, with her snout. She breathed on him. When Deloua began wrapping her lips around Five's goggles, he removed them, revealing his remarkable, enormous, glistening eyes. He sat back, slouched on his heels with an air of exhausted surrender. Deloua raised her head and stood over him, abiding and serene.

Hesso put away his saber and knelt before Five, peering carefully into the moleman's face, resting his hand lightly on Five's shoulder. He spoke quietly. "They say God has one hundred names, my Moleman friend. And that the hundredth is known only to the camel."

Vixy's heart ached, and she put her face in her hands. She lowered herself onto the sand beside Hesso, folding her legs beneath her, her head bowed. And so it was that the three, or rather the four of them – man, woman, moleman and beast – were bound together for a time beneath the vault of heaven, poised upon a catastrophe they could not fully fathom, suspended within the abiding grace of their agonized atonement.

# CHAPTER 23

# RESCUE FROM WITHOUT

**DENHA'S**[69] **STRIDE WAS LONG AND POWERFUL,** his ground-covering efficiency impressive. "A very good *jamal*,"[70] the salesman had declared. Indeed, with the green lushness of the Fayoum Oasis already out of sight behind him, Mr. Z. was confident that if he rode through the night, breaking once or twice for short rests, he'd make the Giza Plateau sometime after midnight.[71] He'd packed meager provisions to minimize the weight – a small sack of dates, a few crusts of bread and less than ten liters of water between them – he'd be driving Denha hard but it would have to do. Meanwhile, he could only hope that Vixy wouldn't stray too far from the

---

[69] "Denha" is a Syriac word (Syriac encompasses the four main church families of Eastern Christianity) meaning dawn or sunrise. Denha refers to the public manifestation of the Trinity at the Baptism of Jesus and in the Coptic Church, in the first millennium, Denha was celebrated on the banks of the Nile.

[70] A male camel is known as a *"jamal"* (the generic name for a camel), a female as a *"naga"*, and a young camel as a *"warh."* Citation: jordanjubilee.com.

[71] Animals that trot move legs that are diagonally opposed at the same time whereas a camel paces - moving both legs on the same side of its body at once. Pacing speed for a camel is 8–12 km/h (5.0–7.5 mph) on level ground. The distance between the Fayoum Oasis and Giza is approximately 100 km. Sunset on 11.11.1881 is 5:07pm, sunrise on 11.12.1881 is 6:23am (citation timeanddate.com).

coordinates transmitted by the EIB. She's willful, tough-minded, resilient and stubborn, he thought. And she'd have been pursuing her transponder and whomever had taken it from her to her last breath.

Meanwhile, he'd placed both Neutic and Captain Chase in intolerable positions; he'd abused their trust and opened them to accusations of complicity in a bald-faced violation of the TDC's own HDT authorization protocol. Career suicide wasn't the half of it. He'd abused his own rank to gain an emergency HDT authorization to get here, a time crime in its own right and a shameful irony for a time detective. But what did any of it matter in comparison to Vixy's life? He had to do it and here he was, no time for second guessing. She's at the Plateau. She's alive. She *has* to be.

The sun was poised just over the horizon behind him, burnishing the otherwise bleak landscape with hues of lavender, pink and gold, beautifying the desert beyond words – a transformation of the land at sunset that was as vivid as his memory of it. Yes, his memory of it!

He'd fancied himself an accomplished camel-rider then, so many, many years ago. A young man fresh out of university, trying to see the world on a shoestring, as carefree as he'd ever be, swashbuckling through north Africa – Morocco, Tunisia, Algeria, Libya and Egypt – countries so impossibly modernized they'd all but lost their air of romance and antique mystery. But the famous Khan El-Khalili bazaar in Old Cairo enchanted him – active since the fourteenth century! – its exotic vibrancy, the wealth of strange goods, the fantastic architecture and imagery of Medieval Egypt – it still revealed intimations of an ageless magic, at least to him. He'd lingered a few weeks in Cairo until he was virtually penniless and attached himself to a caravan, an authentic, old-fashioned caravan maintained by a tribe or two of stubbornly traditionalist Bedouins, God bless them, traveling to the Fayoum. The idea of a real oasis had seemed so romantic. Along the way, he'd learned to ride a camel, and soon after he'd arrived, on a whim and to earn a handful of guineas, he'd entered a camel race – what a rash and raucous thrill!

Now? The thrill was gone. He'd been riding only a few hours and he already felt tired and saddle-sore. No matter. Denha, by contrast, seemed to be reveling in the challenge, pitching his head forward with each rhythmic step, straining against the rein as if he indeed comprehended the urgency of their task.

"I know this book," said Vixy. "It was published here, on Earth, in the twentieth century." She glared at Five. "What do you want with it? Why do you have it? It couldn't possibly –"

"Nineteen forty-nine by the Gregorian calendar, to be precise," said Five. He was staring at his hands laying limp in his lap. He looked up. "The year of publication."

Vixy looked incredulous. "Nineteen forty-nine. That's fine. But I asked you, what is a Moleman doing with an English language, comparative mythology text published decades into the future – relative to now, that is – on a planet you're here to destroy? You've brought this across space and time. Legally? To what end?"

Is she suspicious or furious? thought Five. Human behavior hadn't been his strong point in training. But she's a time detective, so, perhaps both. He shook his head absently, struggling against a second wave of anxiety. What's happening – what's happening to *me*? It all seems unreal. Incomprehensible. All of this. To be so close to my coordinates, to my return, to home. And now this impossible delay, this conflict. How to escape it without... without what? – killing these humans? The unendurable irony made him want to laugh. To save this woman, as she believed he had, then murder her? All his stealth, all his commitment to the leave-no-trace protocol, all his training and it's come to this? He watched the sand eddying aimlessly. "It's my book, that's all." He grasped a handful of sand and tossed it aside. "A talisman, I suppose."

"My God," said Vixy, "who in hell are you? I mean, what Moleman...?" She trailed off.

Hesso eyed them both. "There is still time, perhaps," he said, "to do something to stop it. The war. Or the destruction. Or whatever it is you said, Five, that is going to happen. There must be something that can stop it."

Five laughed to himself – at the absurd innocence and earnestness of Hesso's plea. "Don't be foolish. This planet will die."

"There must be something!" Vixy said. "You can call off the detonations, cancel them, somehow. Why not? You've a communication device haven't you, a transponder? That's what we just heard blaring that message, wasn't it? Those were the voices of whomever you're reporting to, aren't they? It can't be too late to stop it, Five. You've got to help."

"It's too late. It's beyond my power to stop it. Once I established pre-functionality of the clock component, the engineering moved beyond me. I do not have the authority. I do not possess *any* authority." He shrugged, shaking his head. "I am dead. We are all dead. But the mission lives. The annihilation will come and the clock component will activate."

Vixy stood over him. "What do you mean, Five? That you're just going to allow it all to end with you?" She shook her head at him. "You want to get home but you can't unless you stop this thing. We can't let you. We can't. It's one thing to sacrifice yourself for some selfless thing, some altruistic, noble cause, and another thing entirely, something hideous, to die on behalf of a genocide you had the power to prevent. It's not even death you've sentenced us to, it's something worse, isn't it? We'll be trapped, all of us, forever; everyone on Earth, including you; trapped in some eternal rift in time. It's unspeakable. Inhumane. Wicked. It's a time crime beyond anything...." She threw up her hands at him. "You can't. You can't be so irresponsible. So heartless. So evil. You can't allow it now that you... that we... dammit, Five! You saved my life!" She shook his book at him. "It's all in here, isn't it? The story you yourself have lived – that we've all lived."

Five stared blankly at the sand.

"Well, isn't it?" Vixy thrust the book at Five like an accusation. "*The Hero With a Thousand Faces*. That's you, and me, and Hesso and everyone! Everyone committed to the affirmation of life, to the freedom to live, at least. Isn't it, Five? Isn't that you, too? Unless maybe you've chosen its opposite." Her expression was stricken, her eyes wild with despair. "What about it? What about this book? Why do you have it? Adventure, trials and return with a boon the world needs – the world that is the entire cosmos, not the world of any particular race. Is that what it means to you? Do you even read it?" She flung the book in front of him and turned away, wrapping her arms around her shoulders and burying her chin in her chest, shutting her eyes against it all. "You've never read it. If you did then you've never understood it. No Moleman could possibly understand it."

Her words struck him like blows. Yes. He wanted to say yes to everything; to tell her that he understood exactly the things that she understood. And that he lived for all of it with his whole heart. And that he'd thought, somehow, that his race, the Molemen Engineers, did too. But he was wrong. He knew that now. And everything was ruined.

The starlight illuminated the desert with a furious intensity and he looked up. The arresting brilliance of the Milky Way, like a broad river of light flowing from horizon to horizon, seemed almost within reach.

Five watched her. The breeze stirred the hem of her garment and teased at a lock of her hair. There was something about her. Impossibly alien. Unknowable. Yet, somehow, since he'd first encountered her... dammit, he couldn't figure it out, couldn't discern what it was!

He was no killer. He knew that. He'd *always* known it, despite agreeing to the risks of the mission, to the end game contingencies. He'd been trained to kill and he'd chosen to pretend it wouldn't happen, that he'd never have to do it; that sticking to protocol and leaving no trace and completing the engineering would be enough to accomplish the mission and get him home. *Accomplish the mission and get him home.* The words seemed hollow and selfish. Yes, that's all he'd really cared about. *His* mission. *His* home. Getting all that he thought *he* wanted. Being who he thought he wanted to be. Here he'd believed he was doing right, exemplifying his father and the Moleman race. But it was a lie. He was no Moleman Engineer. He read banned books. And he struggled at everything a Moleman Engineer like his father found not only straightforward but fulfilling. He could never explain the things that fulfilled him. Not to his father, his mother or Cog or General Ten-Square or anyone. And his race, for all their perceived magnanimity, perhaps they'd gotten it all wrong, too. Perhaps this alien woman – what she symbolized... he didn't know anything anymore. Except Mega City One was not his home. He didn't belong there. Not anymore. And he could not go through with it. He could not complete the mission.

"Perhaps there is something." His own words astonished him. Yet he felt compelled to continue, as if the solution were playing itself out in his head as the spoke. "The targeting of the weaponry. The warheads. If the engineering of the component were dismantled, if the diamagnetic architecture of the ball were...." He stood up, buoyed by a surge of energy. "If I can return to the Great Pyramid in time."

"The Great Pyramid," said Hesso. "Why?"

Five spoke quickly, eager now to explain. "Everything depends upon the engineering of the clock component. Inside Caviglia's chamber beneath the Great Pyramid. That is why I am here. That is what I came to do – to retrieve the relic and engineer the component. The ball – the golden ball was inside the relic, the canopic jar. That is why I needed it, because the ball –" He interrupted himself. "It doesn't matter. The targeting of the annihilation depends on the clock component, it depends on my work in the Pyramid. Within Caviglia's chamber. Destroy my work and –"

"Destroy your work and stop the annihilation," said Vixy, rushing towards him. "Can you do it?"

Five nodded, too taken aback to answer; too taken aback by what he heard himself saying and by the flush of hope he saw in Vixy's face. He began stammering. "I... I don't know. I don't know if there is time enough."

"How much time do we have?" said Vixy.

Five glanced at his transponder. "Perhaps five hours."

"That's time enough," said Hesso. "We're near Saqqara now. It's four hours to the Great Pyramid on foot; two hours at Deloua's fastest pace. With a burden – two people riding – we might be there in three. We'll take only water."

"That leaves an hour inside the pyramid," said Vixy. "But what's to prevent them from initiating the detonations without the architecture of the ball, without the component? What is the ball and what is it for?"

Five shuffled here and there across the sand to retrieve his things and stuffed them one by one into his pack while he tried to explain. "The ball is a solid gold sphere" – he paused to cup his hands together, demonstrating its dimensions – "it's an x-ray reflector, engineered to operate in conjunction with Earth's magnetic core as a node, a four-dimensional node or axis point, the first of eight lattice points that defines the architecture of the Cosmic Clock." He shouldered his pack and looked to the camel.

"Lattice points?" said Vixy. "You mean to say there are other planets –?"

"Only speculatively. None of them are confirmed besides the Earth; the Earth was to be the first. I could explain it all, but I fear we should proceed immediately so as to provide a margin of error –"

"Yes, we need to leave," said Hesso. "Down, Deloua." The camel knelt and Hesso helped Vixy into the saddle. "Vixy can ride until we get to Saqqara – she can wait for us there, in the shelter of the monuments."

"What?" said Vixy. "Why can't I –"

"We can't all ride – I'll be driving Deloua too hard as it is," said Hesso. "And you'll be safeguarding Five's – what do you call it?" He annunciated the next word carefully: "Transponder." He held his hand out to Five. "Mister Five, you understand the precaution."

Five held back. His transponder was his last connection to home; it seemed a part of him – relinquishing it seemed impossible.

"Mister Five!" said Hesso, shaking his hand at him. "It ensures that you return to help Vixy get home."

Five produced the transponder but paused again before handing it to Hesso. "The login security is biological," he said, "keyed to my DNA. It won't function without me. My return was to be a boomerang transport – that's why I had to return to the Red Pyramid coordinates and not attempt an HDT from the Plateau."

Hesso snatched the transponder and thrust it at Vixy. "Nonetheless, she will keep it." He turned his full attention to the camel. "*Yalla*, Deloua; *Yalla!*" He strode forward, pulling on the rein, speaking softly into the animal's ear. "We have the ride of our lives ahead of us, my friend." The camel lurched forward and they set off at Hesso's brisk walking pace. Five did his best to keep up.

Vixy looked down at the two of them, her body lunging back and forth to the rhythm of the camel. A Bedouin and a Moleman. And me up on a camel with the world coming to an end. She turned her face into the ceaseless northerly wind. If only it were just a dream, she thought; if only everything were just a terrible dream.

Approaching as they were from the southeast, they came to the Saqqara Necropolis and the crumbling rubble that represented the Pyramid of Unas. The ancient Step Pyramid was visible in the starlight, a short distance to the north. "Here are some of the oldest Egyptian pyramids," said Hesso, helping Vixy down from the camel. "It's quite a large burial site that was once associated with Memphis."

Their powerful, shared sense of urgency did nothing to assuage Vixy's reluctance to say goodbye to Hesso, to not be left behind. What if something went wrong? What if she never saw him again? And still she depended on Five's help to get home. "Hesso," she said.

Hesso was stripping the saddle bags from Deloua. "We'll be taking only water, like I said. And if Deloua struggles, we'll have to discard that, too, to save weight."

"Hesso," she insisted, her voice fraught.

Hesso dropped the saddle bags and frowned at her. "What is it?"

His eyes on her made things worse. She turned away, staring hard into the desert, into the darkness that separated them from the distant Plateau.

"Watch for us," he said. He pressed his tobacco pouch into her hands. "Look at me."

She turned. She glimpsed his longing, felt his resolve, understood his courage as their own, together. Then he climbed atop Deloua and reached for Five, hoisting him onto the camel's back.

Five clutched at the saddle as Deloua rose from the sand. "Look to the northwest," he said to Vixy, "to the Plateau. Look for a flare. Green, if we are successful." He looked to Hesso. "We have exactly three hours."

"Hold on tightly, Mister Five," said Hesso, kicking at Deloua's sides. "*Yalla! Yalla*, Deloua!"

The camel galloped away and Vixy, despite herself, ran after them until she could no longer see the trail of dust drifting into the desert behind them.

Hesso cupped his hands round Deloua's muzzle, coaxing her to drink. "She's been run too hard," he said flatly, stroking her face.

Five dug through his pack for an energy gel, tore it open and gulped it down, glancing at the waning gibbous moon. Altitude, twenty-five degrees. Heading, eighty-five degrees east. Moonrise was almost exactly two hours ago. They'd made good time but the tedious work ahead of him, the dismantling of his engineering within the Pyramid, seemed daunting. There were any number of things he could do to disable the functionality of the system, all of which seemed to cloud his thoughts, to distract him from the task of reentering the Pyramid. One thing at a time, he told himself. "The chamber is beneath the center point of the Pyramid, below ground level. The air will perhaps be bad for you."

"I will go as far as I can," said Hesso. "Do you have a lantern?"

"I can light our way." Five made to climb the entrance mound with Hesso behind him. After some furtive scrambling they found themselves before the tunnel opening. Five ducked in, switching on his trek lenses and turned, unthinking, to regard Hesso, flooding the man's face with light.

"Argh!" Hesso turned his face from the glare.

Five deflected the beam with his hand and turned away. "Follow me."

They'd descended perhaps halfway when Hesso coughed. "By Allah!" he choked, "you are right, the air!" He coughed and coughed into the crook of his arm. "Horrible!"

Five turned but Hesso waved him on impatiently, grimacing, gasping, holding the back of his hand to his mouth. "No, do not stop, I can breathe well enough." He glanced behind him into the pitch black and gasped, stumbling, leaning against the tunnel wall, clutching at it, panic welling up within.

"Do not look back, Hesso!" said Five; "look only ahead" – he grasped at Hesso's arm, shaking him. "Look towards the light." He turned and pointed. "Look straight ahead, we are almost there."

Hesso struggled to collect himself, clenching his jaw, swallowing hard at the dusty, cloistered atmosphere. He nodded fitfully. "Let's go."

They trudged forth, finally arriving at what appeared to be a dead end, the false entrance to the chamber, whereby Five removed his pack and began fumbling with his equipment.

"Where are we?" panted Hesso, his voice hoarse, his face and neck shiny with sweat.

The wall ahead of them seemed to distort and flicker, Five's light dancing over the surface as if reflected in a warped mirror.

Hesso groped at the tunnel wall and staggered back. "Argh! What in heaven?!"

"An illusion," said Five. He tapped his transponder and the wall disappeared.

Hesso stared wildly at the opening.

"We are here," said Five. "This is the chamber." He led them inside, attached a lamp pod to the ceiling, just as before, and negotiated his way past the filigree of support struts that surrounded the pit. He could vandalize the system in a number of ways, any of which might cripple its functionality but to disrupt the ball's diamagnetic suspension architecture, to unsettle its gravitational alignment would assure a permanent catastrophic failure that no remote intervention could avert. "I am going to cut these struts," said Five. "You can help by placing the pieces into my pack – nothing can be left behind."

Hesso wiped his brow and nodded.

Five severed a joint in the frame then twisted and pulled on the strut, snapping it free. Within a few minutes he'd dismantled the outer structure and approached the pit, laying on his stomach and reached deep towards the diamagnetic suspension frame and the ball itself. He aimed his laser scalpel, fired, and the ball dropped into the dark void below.

Five clamored to his feet and helped Hesso finish collecting the struts. He snatched his light pod from the ceiling, plunging the sepulcher into darkness and hefted his pack. He pushed past Hesso, aiming his headlamp into the tunnel. Now he was a saboteur. Now he really *was* a kind of terrorist. And a traitor. General Ten-Square and Cog would be forced to initiate a series of contingency protocols, the most severe of which he forced from his thoughts. "Come."

"Is it done?" said Hesso, "have you stopped it?"

"I have done all I can."

They emerged from the tunnel and scampered down the pyramid's face onto the rubble.

Hesso lay prone, coughing. Sweat streamed down the sides of his face and his brow was smudged with dirt and dust. He managed a wry smile. "Grave robbers. The Great Pyramid has been pillaged once again."

"Stand clear," said Five, digging into his pack. He held his arms out, turned his head away and twisted his hands together – sparks, hot gas and thick smoke sputtered forth so that Hesso flinched, his arm held up to protect his face.

"By the devil!"

There was a violent hissing, an arresting whoosh and when they looked up the thing seemed already halfway into the sky, a bright speck of light arcing upwards, trailing a plume of noxious, whitish smoke. They heard a "crack!", saw a flash of brilliant light and witnessed the entire Plateau – the pyramids, the mastaba fields, the Sphinx, everything – bathed in greenish illumination; a wavering, flickering, otherworldly transformation of shadow and light held them transfixed. No sooner had the flare achieved its apogee than it began drifting, trailing its curious squiggle of exhaust like some devilish, fuming, flickering star, silently adrift; unravelling its queer magic as if dangling from some cosmic string attached to the very dome of Heaven.

Then it dimmed, winked feebly once, twice, then vanished, unforgettably, leaving behind a remarkable, aching, emptiness – an impossibly dark stillness – and an acrid whiff of smoke.

Hesso stared wide-eyed at Five. "Incredible! Vixy *must* have seen it!" He stood up and spread his arms wide as if encompassing the entire Plateau. "And everyone else from Cairo to the Fayoum!"

"What in hell?" Mr. Z. struggled against Denha's rein. The camel veered off, lunging away instinctively from the streaking flash of light that arced skyward and burst into an astonishing green brilliance. "Easy boy! Easy!" Mr. Z. pulled back fitfully on the rein, clutched at the saddle and clung hard with his knees to the camel's sides, desperate to keep from being thrown. Denha circled, snorting, tossing his head and stamping wildly at the spectacle before finally gaining his composure and coming to a stop.

Mr. Z. watched, spellbound; watched the thing burn steadily, saw the pyramids silhouetted as if by an ominous, revelatory beacon, the eerie glow filling him with an overpowering sense of urgency and dread. "Vixy," he whispered. He kicked at the camel's sides and lashed at its haunches with the rein, "*Yalla!* Denha, *Yalla!*" They broke into a gallop and hurtled across the desert towards the looming pyramids.

Hesso and Five watched cadres of Egyptians spilling from their tents within the Petrie camp, some gazing upward, astonished, others covering their heads and scurrying for cover, reeling as if afflicted.

"The whole Plateau is awake!" said Hesso. They'd scrambled down the heap of rubble onto the desert floor. He returned his attention to Deloua, his hand on her neck, peering at her face. She lay on the sand at a queer, unnatural angle. "She may not recover. Lesser camels have died under the strain she's endured. "Up, Deloua. Up, my girl." Deloua lay still for a moment, seemingly indifferent to or incapable of rising, then, with what seemed a noble effort, struggled to her feet. "I won't drive her any harder. We may have to return to Saqqara on foot unless she recovers. She needs a week's rest." He scowled at the noise issuing from beyond the pyramid's northeastern corner. "This way – there is less chance of being seen along the western face."

Five followed blindly, his heart heavy, weighed down by his betrayal, impossibly exhausted. He was no better off than the camel. Return to Saqqara on foot? He trudged along until the effort became ridiculous and he stopped. Why? Why go on?

"Come, Five!" said Hesso, hissing at him under his breath. "Come! Your transponder. You must help Vixy get home. We must return to Saqqara. Mister Five, you must not despair, not now."

They'd just rounded the corner of the Great Pyramid when they caught sight of something to the west – an incongruous trail of dust.

"By the devil," said Hesso, "what now?"

Five adjusted his trek goggles. "A man. Driving a camel."

"Driving like I've never seen," said Hesso, staring. "Outside of a camel race, at least – he's riding like the wind!"

They watched man and beast come galloping, virtually storming towards them out of the Western Desert, the rider hunched low on the animal's backside, arms outstretched, legs forward, the fabric of his *tob* and *kufeya* flying wildly behind him, clinging with one hand to the saddle and lashing at the camel's ribs with the rein.

Hesso gripped the hilt of his sabre.

Now it all unravels, thought Five.

Camel and rider thundered to a blustering halt before them, the camel rearing back, nostrils flared, its ribcage heaving. The rider dismounted in a cloud of dust, leapt from the camel, and stumbled slightly before regaining his legs. Then he stood calmly, brushing at his *tob* and coughing mildly at the dust.

"Gentlemen," said the rider. He choked once, snatched at a water skin hanging from his camel saddle and drank, wiping his arm across his dusty face. "That was quite a sight."

Hesso let go of the hilt of his sword, glanced at Five and tugged on Deloua's rein, making to continue on in spite of the newcomer's surprising presence. "*Yalla.*"

Five followed.

"Pardon me," said the rider, "but I'm looking for someone."

Hesso and Five kept walking.

The rider raised his voice. "A young woman. A foreigner."

Hesso made to quicken their pace, encouraging Deloua in a quiet voice, "*Yalla, yalla.*"

"Her name is Vixy."

Hesso took another step or two and stopped. Five waited.

"Your camel seems tired," said the rider. "As tired as mine. Perhaps you've likewise been riding hard?"

"Who are you?" said Hesso. "What do you want?"

The stranger led his camel a few paces towards them and stopped, stroking the beast's shoulder. "I've told you. I'm looking for a foreigner. A young woman. She speaks English. Her name is Vixy. Vixy Velure."

Hesso waited, glaring at Mr. Z. "You ride like someone running a race. Yet you are no Egyptian. I asked you who you are."

Another pause ensued as they took the measure of each other.

"My name is Z. Mr. Z."

"Vixy," said Hesso. "What do you want with her?"

Mister Z., thought Five. Where have I heard that name? It was General Ten-Square who'd said it – he'd virtually spat the words. *An enemy of the Molemen*, he'd told him, *that's all you need to know.* "You," said Five.

Mr. Z. glanced at him.

"You are from the future."

Mr. Z.'s camel flinched at something moving behind it – a shadow in the night, creeping towards Mr. Z.

Five reached for his neuro-toxin dart and crouched low, aiming. "Duck!"

There was a sound like a sharp puff of pressurized air and Mr. Z. tumbled face-forward onto the sand. Someone or some *thing* clad in shapeless, billowing garments leapt over him with astonishing agility directly into their midst and stood poised, slashing the air with a kris[72] in each hand, the wavy blades cruel, lethal; the pale, blue-toned flesh of the creature's face twitching – a hideous mask with slit eyes, two stubby fangs and a horrible, ribbon-like tongue that lolled and flicked unspeakably, wickedly.

Five blinked and in that span Hesso was upon the thing, the blade of his saber ringing upon the outstretch daggers of his unearthly foe. The force of their collision drove them apart, Hesso a split second slower than his opponent in regaining his feet. The thing leapt at him with an unnatural, lightening quickness. Hesso rolled aside, deflecting the blow with a sweep of his saber before scrambling to his feet, flailing, holding his ground against the thrusts of the knives. Their blades locked together hilt to hilt, their faces almost nose-to-nose until Hesso suddenly gave ground, falling back, using the attacker's inertia to his advantage so that it stumbled forward, tumbling head-over-heels overtop Hesso's outstretched knee. Hesso wheeled and slashed, the thing dodged and kicked, leaping clear of Hesso's blade amidst a wild fury of limbs and weapons. There was a cry and the two fell apart, Hesso stumbling backwards, collapsing upon the sand, his opponent staggering back, falling, laying still.

Five and Mr. Z. both rushed to Hesso's side. Breathless, his chest heaving, Hesso tried to raise himself up but fell back, clutching his abdomen. At the same time, the attacker gasped and Five, drawing his own small knife, made for him.

---

[72] The kris is an asymmetrical dagger, famous for its distinctive wavy blade. Both a weapon and spiritual object, kris are often considered to have an essence or presence and to possess magical powers.

"No!" said Mr. Z. "Stay back – that's a Mothman assassin!" He began to tear at the fabric of his own robe. "We need bandages...."

Hesso clutched Mr. Z.'s arm, straining. "Too late for me," he said, his voice feeble. "Too late." He grimaced.

Five threw his pack down, rummaging through it for his first aid kit.

Mr. Z. gripped Hesso's hand and bent towards him. "Hold on, man, *hold on*."

"Vixy," gasped Hesso. "Saqqara. Help her." He went limp in Mr. Z.'s arms.

# CHAPTER 24

# WAR

"**We lost him between Saqqara and Dahshur, sir.**" Cog stared at the map projection in disbelief, as if he stared hard enough something would change.

"That was six hours ago," said General Ten-Square. He clenched his fist and rose from his desk. "And the component failed two hours after that?"

Cog squinted at the sub-display and scrolled through the data. "More or less, let me check...."

The General paced back and forth behind his desk and wrung his hands. "What does it matter now?" He snatched a sheet of paper from his desk and shook it at Cog. "*This* is all that matters! A directive to abort! Signed by Commander Halcyon himself! After all our work! On the threshold of success!" He crumpled the paper in his fist, looked wildly at Cog and flung it across the room.

"There's a chance, sir," said Cog, "a chance that Five is making repairs; that whatever happened he's fixing things. There might still be time." The hollowness in his words tasted bitter.

"Time?" The General glanced over his shoulder at Cog. "*Ten years* is time. Ten years of work. Ten years of my damn life, living and dying this blasted project. Ten years...."

"What about Five, sir? His transponder is still transmitting. That means he's alive."

The General glowered at Cog. "Alive? Then he's a dead man walking. The bombers have been scrambled. The drones are programmed. The clean-up is all that's left." His voice was flat. "We'll never live this down, Cog." He hung his head. "I swear I knew it was over as soon as we lost communication."

Cog's blood ran cold. Everything was slipping away. It didn't seem real, the magnitude of the disaster, the sheer cataclysm of their failure. "But... but, sir, I...." All he could think of was Five, alone in the desert. Lost or injured or both. He grasped at his temples, staring blankly. "It ought to have been me. Not Five. I ought to have –"

"Dammit, Cog!" The General glared at him. "Pull yourself together. We've only got one job, now; one job as soldiers. To leave no trace, Cog. No trace." He glanced at the time. "And to take our punishment. Let's go. Let's not keep the Commander waiting."

"Sir," said Cog, "the HDT event at the Fayoum, and the indication of a transport shadow behind it. The data is commensurate with that of Five's event horizon. Sir. What if...? What if perhaps Laron? Or this so-called Mr. Z.?"

The General adjusted the collar of his uniform and snugged the knot of his tie. "Hmph!" He shook his head, his face twisted into a disparaging scowl, as if he were about to spit. "We should have chosen more carefully. Let the cleanup drone take care of Laron. And Mister Z.?" He dismissed the idea with a brush of his hand. "Ridiculous. He and the TDC are nothing but incompetent meddlers. Humans, bah! An earthling couldn't possibly –" he threw up his hands. "Argh! Let's go. It's time to try to salvage what's left of our miserable careers."

❄

"Look at all this," said the General. "It must be the entire Army, Navy and Air Force leadership in here." They stood in the broad doorway of the conference room, astonished at the crowd of officers, the chaos of conversation and heightened urgency. A young aide pushed past them and broke into a run in the hallway. The Captain had to raise his voice to be heard above the din. "This is no court-martial hearing. What in the name of sun and moon is going on?"

For a moment Cog was convinced they'd stumbled into the wrong room. He watched the Supreme Commander and his various protégés clustered on the small dais at one end, the Commander himself seemingly engaged in at least several conversations at once. Otherwise, there may have been a hundred officers and their assistants crammed into the space, at least half of whom Cog didn't recognize. They were talking and gesticulating all at once, barking orders into their transponders, scowling at their notes and throwing fretful or expectant glances towards the dais, as if awaiting the Commander's word.

They'd only just begun trying to squeeze themselves past the threshold when Commander Halcyon himself stepped to the podium.

"Attention!" His voice boomed and he pounded his fist on the lectern. "Attention!" The room became hushed, all eyes on him. He waved away an advisor who was clawing at his elbow and cleared his throat. "We have been attacked. I repeat, Mega City One is under attack. There has been an air assault by the Mothmen – yes, the Mothmen – launched upon our Coral Bay Space Base."

Dead calm pervaded the room and Cog felt as if he'd been struck in his guts.

"Two galactic carriers have been damaged as well as four destroyers – one destroyer down with all hands. Our ships are trapped in sub-orbit; all flight decks are dysfunctional. Our fighters, what's left of them, are launching a counterattack from Meridian Field as we speak. Report to your battle stations! I repeat: report to your battle stations – this is not a drill – we have declared war against the Mothmen!"

# CHAPTER 25

# No Way to Say Goodbye

**Mr. Z. gently undid Hesso's headdress,** folded it carefully and used it to cover the man's face. The Great Pyramid towered over them, steadfast, abiding. He looked about him. The mothman's body lay untouched several meters away, a crumpled figure, a fold of the creature's garment undulating in the mild breeze.

Five crouched beside Mr. Z, aiming his med-scanner at the mothman. "Zero bio. Dead."

Mr. Z. frowned and pricked his ears. "Voices?"

"There is a camp on the northeast corner," said Five. "Excavators. Petrie's archaeologists."

Mr. Z. looked to the bodies. "We need to bury them."

Five blinked at him.

"Or perhaps move them into a mastaba if we can. But damned if we've the means to carry them any distance."

Five rose and strode towards the massive stones at the base of the Great Pyramid. He knelt in the rocky sand and plunged his powerful hands into the earth. Within moments he'd excavated a shallow, makeshift resting place. He stood up, his hands at his sides as if prepared to continue his work, examining the ground on either side of the grave, then turned towards Mr. Z. as if at a loss.

"Separate graves," said Mr. Z.

Five moved several meters to the south, knelt and toiled at the earth. When he'd finished they gathered Hesso's body, laid him to rest and carefully covered the grave. When they had lowered the mothman's corpse into the ground Five paused. He plucked something from the folds of the mothman's clothing and held it up between his thumb and forefinger, taking care to smooth the synthetic flights.

"It must have snagged within the folds of his tunic," said Mr. Z., squinting at it. He watched Five insert the dart carefully into a sheath on the shoulder of his uniform. "Still lethal?"

Five nodded.

When they'd finished covering the mothman's grave, Mr. Z. sat down heavily with his back against the base of the Pyramid. He brushed the sand from his hands and wiped his brow. Five handed him his water skin and sat down beside him.

"This man Hesso," said Mr. Z., grimacing and rubbing at his elbow. "A nineteenth-century Bedouin. To have done what he did. Slain a Mothman in hand-to-hand combat." He glanced at Hesso's grave. "He saved my life. And perhaps yours as well." He offered the water skin to Five but the moleman waved it away.

"Can you find your own way to Saqqara?" said Five.

Mr. Z. rose slowly, nodding. "Yes. But what about you? You're a moleman. From the future. We need to talk. We have much to discuss. We can ride together."

Five didn't respond and Mr. Z. brought his attention to his camel. He stroked the beast's nose and patted its neck, his voice low, "You're tired, Denha, but we've one last trip to endure."

"It is best that we go our separate ways," said Five.

Mr. Z. cinched his saddle straps and secured his saddle bag. He placed a handful of grain under Denha's muzzle then cupped his hand and offered the animal a few sips of water. He looked askance at Five. "What is your name?"

Five waited, gazing blankly in the direction of the graves. He hefted his pack and turned to look far into the Western Desert, adjusting his trek goggles. "Seventy degrees, thereabouts. Maybe one-hundred thirty degrees or so southeast of the meridian."

Mr. Z. followed Five's gaze. "The moon?"

"A waning gibbous," said Five. "Not unattractive, in its way." He cinched his pack straps.

Mr. Z. climbed into the saddle. "Hup, Denha!"

Meanwhile, Five had brought Deloua beside Denha, reaching up to hand Mr. Z. her rein.

Mr. Z. appeared dubious, looking Five over carefully before reaching to accept it.

"My name is Five."

They looked hard at each other for a moment.

"Where are you going, Five? Why are you here?"

Five stepped away. "There is nothing to fear, Mr. Z." He strode off unceremoniously in the direction of the Fayoum.

"Five!" said Mr. Z. He watched the moleman walking into the open desert, such an insignificant figure against the vastness of the terrain. My god, Vixy, he thought; what have you endured here? "Five!"

The moleman turned.

The two of them stared across the desert at each other and Mr. Z. considered riding out to him. There's nothing for it, he thought. Nothing except finding Vixy. They regarded each other for a moment longer until the moleman turned away and Mr. Z. put his heels to Denha's ribs, pointing the beast in the direction of Saqqara.

The camels lumbered onward, Deloua's rein taut, her neck outstretched as if she were struggling to keep up.

"Whoa, Denha," said Mr. Z.

He untied Deloua's rein and sat squinting into the distance. It's out there somewhere, the Step Pyramid, it has to be. Just keep moving. He let go of Deloua's rein and waited, struggling to convince himself to move on without her.

Meanwhile, the image of Five walking alone into the desert nagged at him. He's either returning to his HDT nexus or... no, it didn't make sense that his transport nexus would be in the middle of the desert. What has happened here? It struck him that the moleman, for whatever reason, seemed strangely... he couldn't find the word. Isolated? Resigned? To just walk away like that, somehow knowing I wouldn't follow him. And the Bedouin? It was if they were traveling together.

He sipped from his water skin and rubbed his face, wiped the grit and sand from his eyes. The horizon was brightening, the stars fading, the moon lowering into the southwest, bone-white against the pale horizon.

It's likely Five is just a foot soldier. He has to be – a moleman doesn't just show up on the Giza Plateau in 1881, let alone in the company of a Bedouin, unless there's a larger plan, a chain of command. He recalled Bab's warning: *Annihilation. The power of gold.* He shook his head at his conflicting thoughts. *Can you find your own way to Saqqara?* An uncanny thing to ask. He knows Vixy, somehow. He knows me. He was willing to help me. A curious thought struck him. What if Five was still helping him? Helping Vixy? Buying them time, perhaps? That green flare.

He sighed and drank again. It was as if each revelation merely begat another mystery. And another magnitude of monstrous foreboding. Gods above and below, what's coming? What in hell have the Molemen done here?

"Hup." He nudged Denha's ribs with his heels. The camel grunted, stepped forward and stopped. Mr. Z. glanced behind at poor Deloua. She stood with her head to one side, her eyes averted as if she'd resigned herself to go no further.

Mr. Z. turned away, making his voice hard. "Let's go, Denha. I'm sorry, but we've got to let her go." He kicked his heels but Denha remained recalcitrant. Or exhausted. He raised his voice and kicked harder. "*Yalla, Denha, we've got to go!*"

He was about to resort to lashing at the camel's backside when he caught sight of something in the distance, a shadow on the desert. Dammit it to hell, he thought, for forgetting my trek goggles. He sat up tall in his saddle, straining into the burgeoning light. There! Someone on foot. My God, yes! He kicked at Denha with renewed enthusiasm, lashing at the beast's hindquarters – the camel groaned and broke into a pace. Deloua, for her sake, with her companions pulling away, began again, trudging slowly but dutifully behind.

Mr. Z. squinted hard into the distance, high in the saddle, his expression fervent, rocking to the camel's strong pace, driving Denha onward. *Yalla, Denha, yalla!*

Vixy stopped when she was certain they were coming towards her, certain they'd seen her. But there was something wrong. Where was Five? And the rider... it's not Hesso. Who, then? Then it struck her and she hurried onward, hardly aware of her feet upon the sand, hoping against hope. My God! Oh my God! Her heart leapt. I'm dreaming. She broke into an awkward run, gasping, her hand to her mouth, her fingers trembling. I'm dreaming...!

Mr. Z. pulled back on the rein, "Whoa, Denha, whoa!" Vixy stood a stone's throw away from him, stock still, her hair fluttering in the wind, the fabric of her long, dark robe trailing away from her. She seemed at once indomitable and stricken, both a part of the harsh immensity of the desert and heartrendingly vulnerable, fragile.

He leapt from his camel and strode towards her, looked into her sun-bronzed face, into her kohl-lined eyes, her cheeks glistening in the morning light, stained with black tears.

*The Master said: To bless means to help. Heaven helps the man who is devoted; men help the man who is true.*[ah]

# CHAPTER 26

# THE RETURN

"**WHAT ARE YOU WAITING FOR?**" said the Captain; "bring them in."

"We can't, sir," replied Tech One. His hands darted here and there over the control panel; he twisted knobs, flipped switches, manipulated levers and strained against the inoperative control stick. "The coordinates are corrupted."

Tech Two typed furiously, looking askance at her display as if the data were in a foreign language. "I can't clear it. There's too much holographic noise."

The Captain leaned over the technicians' shoulders and stared hard into the HDT arrival monitor. It was blank. "What's going on?"

"The Tractor-Gyro," said Tech One. He tore the earphone from his head, rose halfway out of his seat and reached up towards the access panel emblazoned with fluorescent letters: MANUAL OVERRIDE.

"Wait!" said Tech Two.

Tech One paused, his fingers hovering over the security seal. "What? Why?"

Tech Two looked like she'd seen a ghost. "What if it's just static build-up in the sensors? Like last time. Engineering will think we're idiots."

Tech One scowled. "Look at that nonsense on your display. If you can clear it and reboot the Gyro, then –" he gestured fitfully at her display – "well, you tell me!"

Tech Two hammered at her keyboard then pounded at it. "It's frozen!"

"What are you waiting for?" said the Captain, "do the override before it's too late."

Tech One tore away the security seal, twisted the lever with a sharp flick of his wrist and thrust it forward, engaging the mechanism with a clack and a dull mechanical thud. "Start hauling!"

Tech Two stripped away her headset and leapt from her seat. She unhinged the inertia brake and the heavy wheel of the Gyro-Helm – perhaps three meters in diameter – groaned slowly into position. "C'mon, c'mon," she murmured.

Tech One engaged the hydraulic winch components and the helm's imposing bulkhead shuddered. Indicator lights flashed to life. "Locked!"

Tech 2 donned her gloves and threw herself upon the wheel, grasped it with both hands and pulled, straining. She fell back, her face shiny with perspiration. "It's jammed! I can't! –"

Tech One rushed to helm and they both heaved at it.

"Captain!" Professor Wilhelm rose from her observation cubicle and hobbled across the floor, her cane clacking on the granite.

"They're on the far curve of the meridian," said the Captain, "trapped between parallels, drifting into Elsewhere."

"Elsewhere?" said the Professor. "Outside the space-time cone?"[73]

The Captain stood hunched over Tech One's control panel, hammering at the keyboard. "I'm aborting all spurious traffic, locking down the HDT Highway." He threw a lever and an alarm wailed, lights flashed.

---

[73] In special and general relativity, a light cone (or null cone) is the path that a flash of light, emanating from a single event (localized to a single point in space and a single moment in time) and traveling in all directions, would take through spacetime. This view of special relativity was first proposed by Albert Einstein's former professor and is known as Minkowski space.

He rushed to the helm, straining side-by-side with the technicians to free the wheel. "Argh!"

"It's no use!" said Tech Two.

"Mind the wheel!" said Tech One, "both of you!" He wrenched a sledgehammer free from its wall mount and raised it high above his head, staggering under its weight, sweat streaming down his face, the cords of his neck bulging. "Stand clear!" With a mighty effort he struck against the Gyro's heavy turnbuckle and the metal resounded like a bell, the high-tension cables yowling in protest.

"Again!" said the Captain, "harder! Give it to me!" He snatched at the hammer, raised it and struck the turnbuckle a massive blow. Nothing. He raised the hammer again but before he could strike, a metallic screech assailed their ears and the wheel shuddered, shrieked and turned free, sending the technicians sprawling. The Captain pounced on the helm wheel, grappling with it, pulling hand-over-hand like a sailor in a storm-ravaged ship until the Tractor-Gyro gained momentum, whirling back to life.

The Gyro's ferocious velocity filled the room with a subsonic rumble, the floor resonating with its inertial power. The technicians scrambled to their positions at the control panel.

"What's happening? Where are they?" said the Professor.

"The Gyro can only suspend them," said the Captain, wiping his brow. "If the HDT monolith can't re-coordinate...."

Tech One stared into his monitor and shook his head. He strained against the control stick then yanked his hands away in frustration. "Dammit to hell!" He turned to the Captain. "The suspension will disintegrate; they'll lose the geodesic, become trapped outside the event cone. We'll never get them back."

"Lost in Elsewhere?" said the Professor. "What do you mean?"

"Elsewhere is nowhere," said the Captain. "It's a technical term for the region outside space-time – beyond the reach of our influence. Mr. Z. and Vixy will be neither here nor there – they'll be lost beyond the boundaries of the Cosmic Time Architecture."

"How long before the suspension disintegrates?" said the Professor.

"Four minutes," said Tech Two, leaning over to type furiously into Tech One's keyboard, her fingers a blur. "I'm trying to bypass the breech in the monolith, but...." She shook her head and redoubled her concentration on the display.

"But there won't be anything to bypass if we can't reclaim the coordinates," said Tech One.

"What *are* the coordinates?" Everyone's back was to her, the technicians and the Captain all focused on the control panel. She slammed the tip of her cane upon the floor.

The technicians and the Captain all flinched and glanced wildly at her. "Give them to me!"

The Captain nodded at the techs. "Do it."

Tech Two recited them in a clear, calm voice, her eyes once again locked upon her display: "Meridian: 4.8 by 41.0 by 101.332 by 114.7. Parallel: 60.6 by 232.4 by 889.9 by 892.0. Hyper-meridian: 202.4 by 777.4 by 1002.6 by 1433.0." She tore away the data-slip and handed the coordinates to the Professor. "But they're drifting as we speak."

The Professor snatched at the slip and hobbled stiffly across the room, the alarms blaring, the Gyro motors thrumming beneath the floor of the control room and the helm wheel spinning first one way and then the other, lurching spasmodically with each failed re-coordination of the HDT signal. She positioned herself before the vacant arrival bay and leaned hard on her cane.

The Gyro mechanism revved as if threatening to pull itself apart and the helm suddenly stopped fluctuating. An indicator strobe on the arrival bay flashed to life.

"What the hell?" said Tech One.

The Professor's eyes were unseeing, fixed, her vision inward, her posture unyielding.

"RPMs are doubled," said Tech Two.

"I'm not doing anything!" said Tech One, his hands poised above his controls.

"Helm stabilized," said Tech Two. "You must be doing *something!*"

Tech one stared desperately at his display. "There they are!"

"My God," said the Captain. He glanced over his shoulder at the Professor. "She's bringing them in."

"Re-coordinate!" said Tech One, scrambling to enter the data. "Lock the trajectory!"

"Locked!" said Tech Two, "but they're out of sequence – they're coming in too hot, the angle of reflection is too steep. They'll be torn apart!"

Tech One gripped the control lever with both hands. "Absorbing. Compensating. Synchronizing degrees of freedom. I've got them – here they come – brace yourselves!"

The Captain rushed to the Professor's side. Her face glistened with perspiration, damp strands of hair clinging to her jaw, cheeks and neck. She gasped, her cane clattered to the floor and she fell back, collapsed into the Captain's arms. They lay there, bathed in the light of the arrival strobe.

"Incoming!" shouted Tech One.

The Tractor-Gyro groaned and screeched to a halt, the force of its deceleration quaking the superstructure of the control room – the absorption springs resounding upon their stops with a thunderous BOOM! Fog condensed in the arrival bay, the platform scintillating. Ventilation fans roared to life. Two bodies lay sprawled on the floor of the bay – naked, motionless.

"The singularity!"[74] hollered the Captain, turning his face away. "Don't look at it – sever the boomerang!"

---

[74] Within the context of astrophysics, a singularity is a point in space-time, such as a black hole, at which matter has infinite density and infinitesimal volume and the curvature of space-time is infinite. Also called gravitational singularity. Also, the author entertains a mythological reference; that is to say, a singularity as theophany – the appearance of a deity to a human. A particularly dramatic example is the witnessing of the Hindu *Vishvarupa* (Universal form, Omni-form), encompassing all aspects of the universe, the infinitude of being, the play-of-opposites (beneficent and wrathful, light and dark, etc.). This form is described as terrible and only people blessed with divine vision are deemed capable or worthy of withstanding the sight. As such, an HDT arrival sequence is understood to encompass both science and the reality of mythology (spirituality, cosmology, sociology, psychology), if only as a precaution – not everything about HDT is understood therefore risks are significant - and the Captain, well-versed in HDT theory, follows protocol and averts his gaze lest he risk madness or annihilation.

Tech One pounced upon the void brake and yanked. "Severed, sir!"

The alarm went silent, the warning lights dimmed, the fans shut down and a single strobe flashed ominously above the bay. Dead calm.

"Where's the goddamn crash team!" hollered the Captain.

"On their way, sir!"

The control room doors burst open and four medics rushed toward the bodies.

A medic kneeled over Mr. Z., scanning, checking pupils. "I've got vitals."

The other tended to Vixy. "Me too."

"Blankets! Stretchers!"

Mr. Z. and Vixy, unconscious, were swathed in decontamination blankets, laid on gurneys and wheeled from the room. The two remaining medics attended to the Professor and the Captain.

"I'm fine," said the Captain, waving away the scanner. "It's Professor Wilhelm...."

The Professor lay still in the Captain's arms, the medic pressing a bio-scanner over her heart and positioning a neuro-gage against her temple. She checked her pupils, put her hand to the flesh of the Professor's neck. "She's cold as ice," said the medic. "Administer oxygen, get a thermal pack over her thoracic, will you? I'll get her shoes off."

The medic rubbed the soles of the Professor's feet with her hands, driving her knuckles deeply into the flesh. "There's been some bio-chemical trauma but she's not comatose. This can often re-excite the nervous system."

The Professor struggled and half-opened her eyes.

"Professor," said the Captain. "Thank heaven."

Professor Wilhelm blinked, glanced fretfully at the medics and around the room and tried to sit up. She was shivering. "Where?" She put her hand to her head.

"Breathe deeply, ma'am." The medic wrapped a blanket around her. "Let's get you onto the stretcher."

"Captain," said the Professor.

"Don't speak," said the Captain.

"Mr. Z... Vixy."

"They're here," said the Captain. "They're okay. You brought them home."

*Here Phaëthon lies: in Phoebus' car he fared, And though he greatly failed, more greatly dared.*[ai]

# CHAPTER 27

# THE FALL OF PHAËTHON

**FIVE OPENED HIS BOOK:** "Freedom to pass back and forth across the world division from the perspective of the apparitions of time to that of the causal deep and back – not contaminating the principles of the one with those of the other, yet permitting the mind to know the one by virtue of the other – is the talent of the master."[aj] He flipped to the end: "And where we had thought to find an abomination, we shall find a god; where we had thought to slay another, we shall slay ourselves; where we had thought to travel outward, we shall come to the center of our own exis-tence; where we had thought to be alone, we shall be with all the world."[ak]

Five closed the book and smoothed his hand over the tattered binding. He closed his eyes, desperate for the comfort the words usually brought. They seemed just words now. He tried to think of home but his mind raced. He listened to his own breathing; listened to the wind, to the hissing sands. He opened the book again, turning to the frontispiece – to the inscription he'd read a thousand times: *To my brave son. Be who you are. With love, mother.*

He adjusted the polarity of his trek lenses and looked about him. Dawn. No sign of anything. No drones. But they would come; it was only a matter of time.

One-hundred kilometers separated the Giza Plateau from the fringes of the Western Oasis. In four and a half hours he'd covered twenty of them. He hadn't slept since... when? He felt empty. Exhausted. Hardened to his fate. Yet, if he could keep going, make them work to track him down.... He swallowed the last bite of his ration, tore open his last energy gel and gulped it down. Only one SAMM[75] left. Maybe the other one had done its job. After all, given what he knew of the single-minded, programmed stupidity of an assassin drone there was a chance he'd drawn it off target. He started to laugh and choked instead, grimacing at the dust deep in his lungs. The so-called clean-up. Mission control would see to it, that's for certain. No evidence would remain. They'd seek to kill the humans – Miss Vixy and Mr. Z. – just to do it. If they had to send a hundred drones they'd make sure nothing was left behind. I wonder if it was General Ten-Square who had given the order? And what of Cog?

How had it come to this? Everything upside down. Me running like some hunted animal from my own people. To save a pair of aliens? To save a doomed planet? There was no saving anybody or anything. The Cosmic Clock Program wouldn't end with this, with his little fiasco. Someone else will take my place. The job will get done. Meanwhile he was going to die. And soon. He was going to die a traitor's death. He thought of his poor mother and his heart ached. He'd betrayed everyone. He'd betrayed himself. If only he'd had time to think it through, maybe he'd have done things differently. But there was no time now. No time at all.

Get moving. Make them earn it. He emptied his pack, dumping his tools, the installation equipment, the scrapped struts, his *tob* and *kufeya*, his empty ration wrappers. He shoved the SAMM into the sand. Even if it missed the drones, the debris from the explosion might keep them busy, delay their tracking him down. They'd at least have his little mess to clean up. He kicked at a strut, watched the wind catch hold of his disguise and

---

[75] Surface-to-Air-Missile-Mines.

drag it across the desert. His book and the box that Vixy had given him lay at his feet. He sighed heavily and picked them up. No. Not yet. He thrust them into his pack and shouldered it. They're mine. Mine to the end.

He found he could keep a good pace on the sand despite his fatigue. The effort focused him, got him out of his own head, helped keep his mind off the inevitable. Meanwhile, he held his finger poised over the SAMM trigger. He couldn't out-think the drones; any action he took would merely fall within a predictable strategy they were programmed to neutralize – they knew what a fugitive would do, what *he* would do, better than he did. He counted one, two, three and squeezed the detonator button, enjoying the fantasy of the drones crashing into the desert, the smoking wreckage. They'd only send more.

He started out again, continuing due west, half-trotting when he could, walking when he became too winded, occasionally stumbling across the sand in the general direction of the Fayoum Oasis. The sand seemed to suck the strength from his legs and he fell. He lay still for a moment, except for his gasping, and an image invaded his thoughts – Miss Vixy and Mr. Z. in Saqqara, at the Step Pyramid. He struggled to his feet. I wonder if they made it?

Cog sat alone in his dim office, staring blankly, ignoring the flickering tracking blip on the display of his transponder, listening to the soft pinging that indicated a detonation. That's two. His SAMMs are gone. He swallowed hard, fighting back tears. Five. He was running. Detonating his mines. Following fight or flight protocol to the end.

He couldn't have betrayed us. He couldn't have betrayed *me*. Something must have gone wrong... terribly wrong. But how? Why? Why did he sabotage the installation? Maybe it wasn't him. Maybe it was someone else. Maybe he was under duress? Contact him. Ask him.

No. He'd been through it all with the General, belaboring all the possibilities, haranguing all the facts, readdressing all the speculations.

He'd been over it and over it at the hearing, over it and over it in his own head. The General was right. They ought to consider themselves fortunate to have been reassigned a post on the front lines. Death in battle. The only dignity left to them. Two old soldiers, that's what we are, relegated to obscurity within the ranks. He thought of his wife. Poor woman. How he wished he could be a disappointment only to himself. He downed the last shot of whiskey, grimaced at it and disabled his transponder. He sighed as if it would be his last, leaned back in his chair and stared into the darkness.

Five bent almost double, his hands clutching his knees, gasping for breath. He spat and coughed, wiped his brow. Pressure waves. He froze, pricking his ears. Or was it just the wind? Or my damn heart pounding? Don't look back. Don't turn around. There, straight ahead. What's that? An outcropping. What the hell? Some kind of ruin? He hauled himself up, started again, focused on the strange jumble of rocks or stones, whatever they were, stumbled and fell. Legs failing. Dehydration. Exhaustion. He tried to spit again and couldn't. I could just not get up. I could lay here and wait for it. No. He struggled to his knees. No, not in the open – I won't die in the open.

It took what seemed an eternity for him to reach the outcropping and when he came closer he saw it was indeed some sort of crumbled ruin, its whitened limestone bricks mostly scattered, half-buried beneath the sand. A cluster of sprawling, twisted acacia branches jutted from the base of what appeared at a glance to be the disheveled remains of a low wall. He knelt down, dug out a few large handfuls of earth and kept digging, excavating down, down – compelled to follow the vein of natural rock face he was exposing. Perhaps the builders had used it for a foundation? He dug, working furiously to keep the sand from falling in on itself.

He'd unearthed half a meter or so of rock when he discovered the edge of what turned out to be a thick slab of natural stone. He could perhaps hollow out the earth beneath it. In a final, exhausting burst of energy, he tunneled out a hiding place, flailing at the sand, rocks and small stones, flinging the material up and away so that the wind caught it, driving a billowing plume of dust across the desert. He dug and shoveled until his arms and hands and shoulders ached, until his strength gave out and he tumbled into the makeshift hovel, breathless, his chest heaving, crouching beneath the overhanging rock, surrounded by sloping walls of earth, peering out at a sliver of blue sky.

What's that? Rumbling. He held his breath. Pressure waves? Drones? Rivulets of sand and small stones trickled down the sides of his excavation. A shadow passed over the opening of his hovel. If it were drones I'd already be dead. A long, low growl penetrated the earth. Someone, something out there, panting. He shuddered, an uncanny fear welling up; a gripping horror assailing him. He grasped at the hilt of his knife, squeezing hard to stop his hand from trembling. "Father...."

# EPILOGUE

**THE BEDOUIN CROUCHED TO PEER CLOSER** into the shallow space beneath the outcropping. "Look at this, Mehdi[76] – someone has been digging. Ha! What fool would dig for antiquities here?"

Mehdi did his best to examine the signs, scratching at his scraggly beard. "These are animal tracks. A dog, or a jackal." He frowned at them. "No, too large. What do you think, Saleh?"[77]

Saleh was looking elsewhere, squinting disdainfully at something in the sand. "The ruins are windswept, you fool – you see mysteries where there are none. Look, here." He bent to wrest it free and held it aloft by its corner – a tattered book, a handful of pages tumbling from its broken spine and scattering in the breeze.

Mehdi snatched at a page. "It might be English, I think."

"How would you know? Hmph!" Saleh tossed the book onto the ground and kicked at it.

---

[76] Mehdi is an Arabic name that means "rightly guided" or "guided one."

[77] Saleh is a common Muslim name meaning "pious, righteous, virtuous."

"It might be worth something at the Fayoum," said Mehdi. "Or in the city."

"Leave it. If it were worth anything to anyone besides the devil it wouldn't be here."

Mehdi skulked among the exposed stones. "These are strange tracks, I am telling you, Saleh. I have heard tell of men who saw a large animal, the size of a water buffalo, fleeing across the *wadi*[78] after sunset, faster than a man could run. The next morning, they looked and found no tracks."[al]

"You and your fables. Perhaps it's the work of *afariit*?" He sauntered a few paces away from the ruin then glanced back, smirking. "Or *jinn*...."[79]

Mehdi lingered, scrutinizing the ruins warily, eyeing the book splayed on the sand, its pages rustling, torn away one-by-one on the wind. He shrugged and turned his back on the place, hastening to rejoin his companion.

"What's the matter with you?" said Saleh, looking askance at him. "You look like you really *have* seen a ghost."

Mehdi shuddered and drew his *kufeya* round his face and neck. "All the more reason for us to be on our way."

*The End*

---

[78] Arabic and Hebrew term for "valley."

[79] The Bedouins relate many tales of *afriit* (pl. *afariit*): mischievous demons or spirits who taunt men, sometimes haunting particular locales. Alternatively, *jinn* (genies) are said to exclusively take on human form. See Joseph J. Hobbs, B*edouin Life in the Egyptian Wilderness*, (Austin: University of Texas Press, 1989), 60.

# GLOSSARY

**Consequence Research Project (CRP):** A trans-coalitional, trans-galactic research project funded by HDT licensing and certification fees, tolls, fuel taxes, government grants, commercial development authorization fees and research stipends. Interested parties include, within the Fourth Galactic Quadrant, for example, the PMC, T.E., Time Guard, the GTA and myriad commercial and private entities. The mission of the CRP is that of a non-governmental watchdog intent upon ascertaining, via the application of rigorous scientific standards, the impact of HDT activity upon the Cosmic Time Architecture.

**Cosmic Clock Project (CCP):** An engineering scheme initiated by the Molemen to gain omnipotent control of the CTA by way of cubing the sphere – originally a metaphorical concept referring in ancient times to the squaring of the circle, but in the hands of the Molemen a hyper-dimensionally expanded technological reality. Earth is to be established as the first of eight planetary lattice points that comprise the major cosmological components – the so-called clockwork pieces – of the CCP.

**Cosmic Lexicon Project (CLP):** The CLP aims to compile and define into a single, searchable, cross-translational database all words in all languages across the universe, continually monitoring for usage both written and verbal so as segregate contemporary, archaic and obsolete usages and iterations. Funding is both public and private.

**Cosmic Time Architecture (CTA):** Reality as such, in hyper-dimensional terms, incorporating both n-space and n-time. See *Hyper-dimension.*

**Emergency Immolation Beacon (EIB):** A hyper-dimensional SOS. Namely, an unrestricted, trans-hyper-dimensional signal burst that necessitates a self-destruct command on behalf of a TDC-issued transponder. It is the only remote command that will override the security buffers, physiological fail safes and genetic identity links that bind a transponder to exclusive use by its end user. As such, an EIB command requires chain-of-command series of authorizations.

**Galactic Intelligence Administration (GIA):** A venerable, cosmos-wide, labyrinthine, pan-governmental intelligence network consisting of field agents, operatives and an enormous, far-reaching infrastructure of overt and covert programs, policies, committees and attendant political oversight. Controversial from its beginnings, the funding for the GIA is allocated by way of semi-annual, usually bitterly contested sub-galactic hearings whereby current programs are subjected to public scrutiny. Its mission is to safeguard the so-called Free World and it inevitably struggles against a lack of political unity.

**Galactic Law (GL):** The substance and legitimacy of Galactic Law draws upon so-called Normative Jurisprudence (as opposed to Analytic Jurisprudence, legal positivism and legal realism which reject origins and definitions of law as anything beyond that which Man establishes in a subjective manner) and therefore acknowledges the existence of objective, psychological and therefore biological archetypal origins. GL, in other words, is understood as inherent within and a natural expression of the behavior of free individuals in their compassionate state, and expresses an intuitive, pancultural, pan-temporal, arguably objective realization of $n$-manity (where $n$ = any cognizant race or individual, e.g. *hu*manity) and ethics. It is officially established within the Fourth Galactic Quadrant legislature. It may be appealed to by any resident entity demonstrating a pursuit of life, liberty and happiness.

**Galactic Transparency Alliance (GTA):** An organization of nations pledged to abide by the oversight and inspection authority of the Time Guard, Pangalactic Mythology Coalition (PMC) and the protection and stability of the Cosmic Time Architecture (CTA). The GTA contributes annually to the funding for Consequence Research.

**Ghost Impression Database (GID):** HDT events leave behind traceable forms of space-time evidence – transport residue, wakes, ghost impressions, etc. - that diminish in intensity following the event. Ghost impressions are unique examples of such evidence because they do not propagate or disperse from an epicenter or generation point but rather remain as subtle, impermanent impressions in the "fabric" of space-time. The GID is a log of such impressions and therefore plays its part in the history and analysis of HDT traffic. It has been continually compiled and reviewed for centuries, from the very first attempts at hyper-dimensional travel, as a tool in the responsible, ethical oversight of and attention to the integrity of the CTA against threats known and unknown (not yet recognized or understood as such).

**Great Conflict:** A general term describing any of the interminable series of pan-galactic wars (or world wars) that have inevitably if not cyclically strained Mankind's ability to transcend its arguably innate biological requirement for organized violence and conflict.

**Hyper-Dimension:** Also Hyper-Dimensionality. Of or relating to a space-time manifold of more than four dimensions (normally perceived as three dimensions in Euclidean space and one dimension in time) and incorporating the mathematical concept of n-space. As an example, a 0-sphere is a pair of points; a 1-sphere is a circle; a 2-sphere is a sphere in three dimensions and a 3-sphere is a 3-dimensional sphere in four spatial dimensions, otherwise known as a hypersphere. Stereographic projection may be used to visualize the hypersphere's parallels, meridians and hyper-meridians. Alternatively, a 2-square is a cube in three dimensions and a

3-square is a tesseract. Time, normally perceived within three dimensions - past, present and future – may also be expressed, akin to $n$-space, in terms of the hyper-dimensionality of $n$-time.

**Hyper-Dimensional Obfuscation Fold (HDOF):** The fold flattens space-time, the engineering mechanism of which requires vast quantities of fuel – energy – which can, for example, be supplied via the consumption of a white dwarf, of which several hundred are located within range of the latest SnoGlobeCon coordinates. See the chapter entitled, "The Agony of the Moth."

**Hyper-Dimensional Travel (HDT):** Also referred to as Hyper-Dimensional Transport (referring typically to cargo) and Hyper-Dimensional Transporter (the machine or instrument that enables it). HDT is an otherwise generic term for any device that allows for hyper-dimensional (time and space) travel. There is no universally standardized design and myriad examples exist throughout the cosmos although only several reliable, Time Guard sanctioned, tested and approved manufacturers exist in any particular space-time coordinate.

**Pangalactic Mythology Coalition (PMC):** An ancient (established late Golden Age), perpetually paradoxical (ostensibly by design) assemblage of otherwise intellectually and spiritually intrepid, preternaturally open-minded thinkers of all biological configurations and vocations. The group, although galactically vast, has remained intentionally leaderless and theoretically anti-institutional throughout its history, electing by true majority a Viceroy tasked with directing the activities of each sub-contingent.

**Mythological Revitalization Initiative (MRI):** Theoretical nomenclature to describe the process of intentional, formalized cultural mythological rebirth. Preceded by cultural mythological schism, disorientation, disintegration or collapse.

**Origin Analysis**: A technically sophisticated examination of the provenance, source or point-of-generation of an inanimate object. The science hinges upon the influence of space-time upon the sub-atomic and subtle body nature of an object — otherwise identical versions manufactured in different space-time coordinates, for example, will present different OA evidence as will any otherwise identical objects with different space-time residence profiles. Take a thing from here to there, in other words, and its OA nature may or may not be traceable depending upon the sophistication of the analysis and the influence of obfuscation technology.

**Pan-Galactic Archive (PGA)**: A venerable institution, one aspiring to integrate the lending, archiving and research functions of a typical academic library with the archaeological, anthropological, ethnographical, scientific and mythologically exploratory fieldwork and scholarship of the galaxy's most elite, well-funded and rigorous museum research programs.

**Tetrahectatricontakaidigon Enclave (T.E.)**: A peripatetic, quasi-governmental body with embassy qualities that physically relocates whenever security threats come to diminish its functionality. It represents the core 432 cultural components (thus the polygon descriptor portion of its name) present within the known universe. The institution resembles both the American Pentagon in its guise as a powerful yet bureaucratically hindered department of defense, and the United Nations (established in the twentieth century in New York City) in its role as a life-affirming and otherwise benevolent peacemaker in line with Galactic Law.

**Time Detective Contingent (TDC)**: A cantankerously autonomous division of the Time Guard that recruits, trains and employs a renowned, some may say notorious cache of Time Detectives in both exclusive and freelance capacity to prevent and investigate crimes against Time - so-called time crime - otherwise defined as an unwarranted appropriation, transgression, stoppage, deflection, hindrance, warpage, overlapping, obfuscation, abuse or tyranny of or related to the Cosmic Time Architecture (CTA).

**Time Guard**: A perpetually autonomous organization with unpublicized ties to the T.E., it has comprised, throughout its obscure history, an essentially elite group of specialists, including Time Detectives, Time Lords, et al. The study of the origin and history of the Time Guard is ancient and obscure enough to have developed into its own field of official academic scholarship.

# NOTES

a    From Joseph Campbell's *The Hero with a Thousand Faces* (Novato: New World Library, 2008, p.124) Copyright © Joseph Campbell Foundation (jcf.org) 2008. Used with permission.

b    Joseph Conrad, "Youth: A Narrative" (1898).

c    Richard Wilhelm, *The I Ching or Book of Changes,* 3rd ed., trans. Cary F. Baynes, Bollingen Series XIX, (Princeton: Princeton University Press, 1990 [1967]), pp.723-24. Republished with permission of Princeton University Press; permission conveyed through Copyright Clearance Center, Inc.

d    Gerardus Van der Leeuw, "Primordial Time and Final Time," *Man and Time: Papers from the Eranos Yearbooks,* Bollingen Series XXX, Vol. 3, ed. Joseph Campbell, (Princeton: Princeton University Press, 1957), p.325. Republished with permission of Princeton University Press; permission conveyed through Copyright Clearance Center, Inc.

e    Ibid.

f    Joseph Campbell, *Myths of Light: Eastern Metaphors of the Eternal,* (Novato: New World Library, 2003), 74.

g    With minor paraphrasing by the author, citation: Saint Augustine, *The Confessions of Augustine,* Book XI, Chapter XIV. Paragraph 17, ed. William G.T. Shedd, (New York: John Wiley, 1860), 313-14.

h    Excerpt from CREATIVE MYTHOLOGY: THE MASKS OF GOD, VOLUME IV by Joseph Campbell, (New York: The Viking Press, 1968, pp.122-23), copyright © 1968 by Joseph Campbell. Used by permission of Viking Books, an imprint of Penguin Publishing Group, a division of Penguin Random House LLC. All rights reserved.

i    Hellmut Wilhelm, "The Concept of Time in the Book of Changes," *Man and Time: Papers from the Eranos Yearbooks,* Bollingen Series XXX, Vol. 3, ed. Joseph Campbell, (Princeton: Princeton University Press, 1957), pp.229-30. Republished with permission of Princeton University Press; permission conveyed through Copyright Clearance Center, Inc.

j    Hellmut Wilhelm; Richard Wilhelm, *Understanding the I Ching: The Wilhelm lectures on The Book of Changes,* trans. Cary F. Baynes & Irene Eber, (Princeton: Princeton University Press, 1995 [1960]), p.134. Republished with permission of Princeton University Press; permission conveyed through Copyright Clearance Center, Inc.

k    Hellmut Wilhelm, "The Concept of Time...," 231-32. Republished with permission of Princeton University Press; permission conveyed through Copyright Clearance Center, Inc.

l    Ibid., 224. Republished with permission of Princeton University Press; permission conveyed through Copyright Clearance Center, Inc.

m    Joseph Campbell, *The Hero with a Thousand Faces,* 3rd ed., (Novato: New World Library, 2008 [1949]), 168.

n    Jean Clottes, *What is Paleolithic Art?: Cave Paintings and the Dawn of Human Creativity*, (Chicago: University of Chicago Press, 2016), 144.

o    James Guetti, *The Limits of Metaphor: A Study of Melville, Conrad, and Faulkner*, (Ithaca: Cornell University Press, 1967), 187.

p    Carl Jung, *The Portable Jung,* ed. Joseph Campbell, (New York: Penguin Books, 1976 [Viking Press, 1971]), pp.350-51. Republished with permission of Princeton University Press; permission conveyed through Copyright Clearance Center, Inc..

q    Hellmut Wilhelm, *Understanding...*, 15. Republished with permission of Princeton University Press; permission conveyed through Copyright Clearance Center, Inc.

r    Ibid., 84. Republished with permission of Princeton University Press; permission conveyed through Copyright Clearance Center, Inc.

s    Joseph Campbell, *Historical Atlas of World Mythology, Vol.1: The Way of the Animal Powers*, (London: Summerfield Press, 1983), 8-9.

t    For territory held by PRH: Excerpt from THE MASKS OF GOD: ORIENTAL MYTHOLOGY, VOLUME 2 (p.29) by Joseph Campbell, copyright © 1962 by Joseph Campbell, renewed copyright © 1990 by Jean Erdman Campbell. Used by permission of Viking Books, an imprint of Penguin Publishing Group, a division of Penguin Random House LLC. All rights reserved. For UK & Commonwealth (excl. Canada): From Joseph Campbell's *The Masks of God Vol.2: Oriental Mythology* (Arkana, 1991, p.29) © 1991, Digital Edition, Copyright © 2014 © Joseph Campbell Foundation (jcf.org). Used with permission.

u    *Mahabharata, Book XII.* Heinrich Zimmer, *Philosophies of India*, ed. Joseph Campbell, Bollingen Series XXVI, (Princeton: Princeton University Press, 1989 [1951]), 123, 125. Republished with permission of Princeton University Press; permission conveyed through Copyright Clearance Center, Inc.

v    Joseph Campbell, *The Hero...*, 59.

w    Ibid., 11.

x    Tilo Schabert, "An Introduction," eranos.org, retrieved 10.30.2019.

y    Ibid.

z    Ibid.

aa    William Makepeace Thackeray, *The History of Henry Esmond, Esq.*, (Chicago: Scott, Foresman and Co., 1902 [1852]), 50-51.

ab  Dante Alighieri, *Vita Nuova*, trans. Mark Musa, (Bloomington: Indiana University Press, 1973), 4.

ac  Joseph Campbell, *Pathways to Bliss*, (Novato: New World Library, 2004), 99.

ad  From Joseph Campbell's *Myths of Light* (Novato: New World Library, 2003, p.72) Copyright © Joseph Campbell Foundation (jcf.org) 2003. Used with permission.

ae  Joseph Campbell, *The Collected Lectures of Joseph Campbell*, Lecture I.1.1 (audio) – "The Celebration of Life."

af  *Heinrich Zimmer, The King and the Corpse: Tales of the Soul's Conquest of Evil*, ed. Joseph Campbell, (Princeton: Princeton University Press, 1975 [Bollingen 1948]), 26. Republished with permission of Princeton University Press; permission conveyed through Copyright Clearance Center, Inc.

ag  From Joseph Campbell's *The Hero with a Thousand Faces* (Novato: New World Library, 2008, p.337) Copyright © Joseph Campbell Foundation (jcf.org) 2008. Used with permission.

ah  Richard Wilhelm, *The I Ching*..., 321. Republished with permission of Princeton University Press; permission conveyed through Copyright Clearance Center, Inc.

ai  Ovid, *Metamorphoses*, trans. Frank Justus Miller; G P Goold, (Loeb Classical Library, 42), 82-83. Public domain.

aj  Joseph Campbell, *The Hero*..., 196.

ak  Ibid., 18.

al  Joseph J. Hobbs, *Bedouin Life in the Egyptian Wilderness*, (Austin: University of Texas Press, 1989), 60.

Made in the USA
Monee, IL
27 March 2021

9f50d5dd-625e-4590-bbc9-59e8297d2603R01